# Interstellar Medic:
# THE LONG
# WAY HOME

# BAEN BOOKS by PATRICK CHILES

### ECCENTRIC ORBITS
*Frozen Orbit*
*Escape Orbit*

### INTERSTELLAR MEDIC
*Interstellar Medic: The Long Run*
*The Long Way Home*

*Frontier*

# Interstellar Medic:
# THE LONG
# WAY HOME

# PATRICK CHILES

THE LONG WAY HOME

Copyright © 2025 by Patrick Chiles

A Baen Books Original

Baen Publishing Enterprises
P.O. Box 1403
Riverdale, NY 10471
www.baen.com

ISBN: 978-1-6680-7274-5

Cover art by Marianne Plumridge Eggleton

First printing, July 2025

Distributed by Simon & Schuster
1230 Avenue of the Americas
New York, NY 10020

Library of Congress Control Number: 2025007274

Printed in the United States of America

10 9 8 7 6 5 4 3 2 1

## Dedication

To Melissa
Wherever we are, I'm glad to be with you.

"Do not remain long from home."
—Homer, *The Odyssey*

"It's only the worst day of your life *so far*."
—Homer Simpson

# 1

Back on Earth, my small stature had made me the go-to medic for confined space rescues. If there was a collapsed building, a kid stuck in a well, or miners trapped underground, I'd get the call. It was inherently dangerous work, and so we'd had a ton of specialized gear and even more precautions to avoid adding ourselves to the body count. Rule Number One was "don't fall down the hole."

That's of particular importance when it comes to black holes.

Visually, they're mesmerizing. Great, glowing whirlpools of superheated gas and dust trapped in an eternal spiral around a singularity—that is, the hole in space where a star once burned before exhausting its fuel and collapsing, compressing all of its mass into an infinitely small point which even light can't escape. Stray too close, and you're toast. Toast, stretched by the extreme gravity into a miles-long trail of crumbs before being shredded down to the last atom and sucked into oblivion. The only remaining hints of their existence were the jets of x-rays shooting from the poles of the maelstrom.

We really didn't want to add ourselves to their number.

Such were the thoughts in my head as we drew uncomfortably close to one of those cosmic monsters, searching for an emergency beacon which had lit up our comms. We'd been on our way back to home base in the Galactic Union capital, looking forward to some time off after a long-haul patient transport job. But when a distress call comes, whoever's in range has to answer.

As we drew in closer—slowly, I should add—the stricken ship came into view. It was a Reticulan saucer belonging to one of the Grays, the classic bug-eyed space aliens from human folklore. Except of course it's not exactly folklore. In fact, one of them was piloting our transport at that moment. Another was working in back as my partner.

"How close can we get, Needa?"

*I am not yet certain, Melanie. The vehicle appears to be trapped in orbit along the innermost edge of the accretion disk. It is dangerously close to the event horizon.*

"Any contact with the crew?"

*Negative. Manifest shows a single pilot.*

Needa was stressed; she always reverted to her native telepathy when things got dicey. That's how Reticulans prefer to communicate, though the ones I'd worked with typically showed me the courtesy of using spoken language. That wasn't easy for them; their voices tended to have a raspy quality thanks to long-neglected vocal cords and narrow slits for mouths. Grays could look frightening to uninitiated humans, but at their core they were decent folks. The Midwesterners of the galaxy. Maybe that's why I had such an affinity for them.

I was about to ask if she could make telepathic contact with the pilot when my partner laid a hand on my arm. "It is best that we do not ask too much of her right now," Karrak said calmly. "We must be extremely careful. Needa has to determine whether she can make a safe approach before we can assess the scene."

I stared at the plasma cyclone outside and the black maw at its center, wondering how we were going to pull this off. Not knowing anything of our patient's condition, or how we were going to get to him, all I could do was collect my gear and be ready for whatever came next. "Any suggestions for how we do this? This is my first run to a black hole." *And hopefully my last.*

Karrak knew what I was thinking. "I have assiduously avoided them myself." He swiped at the holographic screen, zooming in on the image as much as he could without blurring it. "There is hull damage, particularly around the drive field emitters." He pointed to the saucer's outer edge. It was ragged around one side, as if the little ship had been dragged across a galactic cheese grater. He seemed especially interested in an odd bulge that filled a quarter of the saucer's disk, on the side facing the black hole's center. "Curious. I have yet to see one of our craft that is anything but perfectly symmetrical." His elongated fingers danced across the image as he filtered out signal noise. "I cannot deduce its purpose from the energy signature. Particle emissions are being drowned out by radiation from the accretion disk."

"Any chance of a contamination threat?" Or something about to explode, for that matter.

"Impossible to tell from here."

Great. We'd have to be on scene before we could figure out if it was secure.

The image grew larger but stayed in focus. The hairs on my neck stood on end. Needa was taking us in, and I did not want to get any closer to this thing. "I trust she knows what she's doing."

"As do I."

Needa finally "spoke" again, which I hoped meant she was a lot more confident in our situation. But she was still thinking at us, so maybe we weren't out of the woods yet.

*I've established an orbit at minimum safe distance based on the measured gravity gradient. We dare not go any closer.*

I traded a look with Karrak. "We're not going to argue." I moved up to stand behind Needa at the pilot's station, where another holographic situation display floated in front of her. The projection of our orbit traced a curve just outside of a bright red arc, the minimum safe distance she'd calculated. The saucer was moving right along that line, each orbit bringing it closer to the event horizon. A few more revolutions and it would disappear from our reality into God knows what. "Will we be able to lock on to it?"

She pointed to the saucer, far ahead and still pulling away. *I have tested the field projector and made positive contact with their hull. I do not know if we will be able to maintain the attraction field for long enough.*

"But it's moving away from us. How do we intercept if we can't get any closer?"

*The gravity gradient at this range is too powerful for us to overtake them directly. We will maintain our radius from the singularity until the saucer's lower orbit brings it back around to come up behind us. When our velocity vectors are parallel, I will activate the attraction field.*

It all made sense when Needa ran the projection ahead in time to illustrate what that would look like. It's a lot easier to hook up a trailer hitch when the thing you're towing is pointed in the same general direction.

This super-advanced collective of alien civilizations isn't like the movies, meaning that transporters aren't a thing. My life in the Union had been a crash course in bleeding-edge technology. I've learned enough to grasp that quantum superpositions and Heisenberg's uncertainty principle (though credited to someone else in the Union whose name is utterly unpronounceable without a second pair of vocal cords) dictate that you can't just dissociate somebody's molecules in one location and zap them into another. There'd be no beaming our patient aboard.

Tractor beams, however, are definitely a thing. Just don't ask me to explain how they work any better than I could tell you how your phone works. Operationally, though, I know that the question would be whether we had enough juice to pull it off without getting sucked in ourselves.

Needa did something I'd never seen her do before: she activated the shoulder and lap restraints embedded in her seat. *I must shut down the inertial dampers to conserve power. Please get into your protective garments, and remain in your acceleration couches until I give the all-clear.*

Used to be conserving power wasn't a big deal, but there'd been a drastic shortage of a key component of our drive systems ever since one of the Union's largest refineries had blown up. And by "refinery," I mean the entire planet.

Losing a third of its Element 115 supply in the Tanaan disaster had put a serious cramp in the Union's style. The stable isotopes in our gravity drives had to be regularly replaced, which forced us to be a lot more judicious with them. Interstellar travel had in turn become much less commonplace. Priority in obtaining the isotopes went to the Med Corps, Constabulary, and the Thuban border defense fleet; the rest was rationed out based on need. And if you couldn't demonstrate need, refined 115 got a *lot* more expensive.

In our case it didn't help that we were going to be dragging a broken saucer out of a black hole's accretion disk. The 115 spheres manipulate gravity, and there was a hell of a lot of gravity here to manipulate.

I turned back to the cabin, where Karrak was already pulling our skin-tight inertia suits from a locker in back. Without a thought toward each other's privacy, we stripped and slipped on the magic underwear that would keep our organs from turning to jelly once Needa started doing her pilot shit. I was about to settle into my gel couch when he handed me another garment, one which I'd really hoped we wouldn't need. It was my vacuum suit.

"I anticipate we will have to go outside to retrieve the patient. The vehicle's structural integrity is questionable."

I unfolded the suit, snatched its bubble helmet from the shelf behind him, and nodded at the churning whirlpool of superheated gas outside. "It won't get any better after we pull it out of that mess."

Karrak shook his head, reading my mind. Literally. "It will not." There'd be no nice, clean docking to get inside the saucer. I just hoped our tractor beam didn't tear it apart.

Other than the helmet, our vacuum gear was nothing like the bulky spacesuits that human astronauts used back home. They're form-fitting, counterpressure garments that essentially reinforce our own skin to keep all the liquids and gases inside of us from escaping and the radiation out. I don't have a problem with spacewalking itself, it's the idea that the only thing between me and instant death is a few millimeters of carbon fabric.

By the time we'd donned our suits and finished the function checks, Needa announced that the saucer was coming back around. Our ship thrummed with low-frequency vibrations as she dialed up the drive. The gravity distortion it created used to make my stomach flip and my head get fuzzy. Over time I'd acclimated, but when she turned off the inertial dampening field it was like my first day on the job. Even with the protective suit and the acceleration couch, I could feel us alternating between zero and who knew how many g's as she moved us into position. When she lit up the tractor beam, our transport shuddered in protest.

*We have positive lock.*

No kidding. My stomach already knew as much. "Any word from the saucer?"

*Negative. Stand by for acceleration.*

We were pressed deeper into our seats as Needa stepped on the gas. Our ship groaned and rattled from the strain, but she kept pouring it on. Without the dampeners I could sense we were moving, but had no idea if it would be enough.

I was about to ask Needa if it was working and if the saucer was holding together, when Karrak caught my eye. "Do not distract her. We will know soon enough."

The vibrations intensified as we pulled away. I couldn't focus on any one thing for long; our ship rattled and shook as if we were in a paint mixer. A worrisome, guttural groan began swelling behind us. The field generators were howling like banshees and I wondered how much more they could take before something important gave way.

There was one final, wrenching jolt, and the shaking and howling subsided.

*We are free of the accretion disk and in a stable orbit. The saucer appears intact.*

Even telepathically, I could hear the relief in her voice. "Thank you, Needa. Great work. Are we clear to exit?"

*As soon as I seal off the control station. For now, you are safe to leave your seats.*

Needa would leave the artificial gravity off during our spacewalk. We floated out of our couches and waited in the cabin for the all-clear. She locked her own helmet in place and activated a force field that would seal off her compartment from the ambulance bay. Her last step before purging cabin air would be to turn on another force field that would shield us from outside radiation, of which there was enough to cook us like a pair of microwave burritos.

*EM projectors are at nominal output. Depressurizing the cabin now.*

"Standing by." We fastened trauma bags to our suits and held onto the vacuum gurney as we waited for the outer hatch to light up. Soon an oval of white light glowed steadily around its rim, signaling that we were cleared to exit. "Okay, we're on our way."

The portal winked open to space. Without thinking, I grabbed an overhead railing and pulled myself outside, all in a hurry to get to our patient. After one look around, I was ready to fly back in and hide under a blanket.

The monster was still out there, a luminous vortex of destruction surrounding the deepest, darkest nothing I had ever seen. "Black" doesn't do it justice; this was the utter absence of light. Sound doesn't travel in space, but I could imagine the screech of matter being stretched and torn beyond all limits as it was dragged into the infinite black. Was it all just interstellar gas and dust, or had some of it been unlucky spacefarers who had wandered too close, like the Reticulan we were after?

Karrak came alongside and wrapped a gloved hand around my

arm. "Focus on the ship, Melanie. If Needa says we are safe, then we are safe." I searched his jet-black eyes behind his helmet, but his smooth gray face was a mask of calm. Reticulan body language could be hard to read, but their minds weren't once you'd established a bond with them. He was just as scared as I was.

*True*, he said, projecting his thoughts. *But we must go anyway.*

He let go and activated a directional field which shot across the gulf between us and the saucer; essentially a smaller version of Needa's tractor beam which would guide us to our target. "Transfer beam is locked," he called back to her, using the comms for my benefit. "Proceeding."

*Understood. Be safe, friends.*

"Always."

I did as Karrak said, focusing on the battered saucer ahead of us and tuning out the black hole looming beyond. It did nothing to slow my heart rate, which I fought to get under control with deep breathing as the invisible beam pulled us along.

We arrived at the saucer's entry hatch, which would've been impossible to spot if we hadn't already known where to look. When closed up, the hatch blended seamlessly with the hull. Karrak waved his hand across the faint outline of its rim, causing a lightpad to appear. Each Union ship (the legally registered ones, at least) has an emergency access code for situations like this, which automatically attaches itself to any distress signal. I pulled up the saucer's code on a terminal in the wrist of my suit and called out the sequence to Karrak.

The hatch winked open to reveal a depressurized airlock. We pulled ourselves inside and I swept my hand across the opening to seal it. There was a whisper of air as it began to fill the compartment, and soon I could feel the counterpressure suit release its grip on me. Karrak was already at the opposite end of the lock, checking another display beside the inner force field. "Pressure is equalized and the atmospheric mixture is compatible. No signs of contaminants. We are safe to remove our helmets."

"Gladly." I unlocked mine and pulled it away, letting it rest against my life support backpack. I took a deep breath. "Let's go."

He lifted the force field and we hurried inside. I'd been on Reticulan ships a few times, and this one wasn't much different. Some equipment

I didn't recognize filled the passageway leading to the control cabin, but that was all. Karrak slowed a bit; whatever the stuff was it had gotten his attention as well.

The control cabin was small, in human terms maybe the size of a compact sedan. That made it spacious for a Reticulan, but for me it meant we'd be working in tight quarters.

Our patient was slumped in his seat at the pilot's station; from what we could see he was the only occupant. That matched the manifest, but you could never be too sure. I was starting my assessment when Karrak announced he was going to look for any unreported passengers.

That seemed odd to me, but for now I had the situation in hand. Something about this run had piqued his curiosity, and I trusted his instincts. There wasn't much room for more than one of us anyway. "Go for it. Just don't be too long."

The patient was young, not too far past adolescence in Reticulan terms, just emerging from the androgynous stage. To be honest, this one wasn't fully male yet but that was the direction things were headed and I liked to keep things simple.

He was also unconscious. His black, almond eyes were unresponsive. They can be hard to see, but Reticulans do have irises which respond to light just like ours. Even thinking at him—an acquired skill after years of living among them—didn't produce any results. This Gray was out cold, so I set a universal spinal collar in place before doing anything else. While the collar molded itself around his thin neck, I slipped on my diagnostic visor and pulled a transducer disc from my bag. I held the scanner to his chest and waited for vital signs to appear. Pulse was thready, breathing was shallow, blood pressure was low. He was going into torpor, the Gray's natural response to severe trauma.

I pulled out a second disc and began moving both of them down opposite sides of his body, building a three-dimensional view of his insides.

The Med Corps' transducers are awesome. Really, all of their gear is amazeballs but these little beauties are my favorite. About the size and shape of a hockey puck, just one of them is like having a stethoscope, vital signs monitor, and ultrasound in one package, all more sensitive than the best stuff on Earth. Two of them in unison is like having a handheld MRI with a fidelity that would make human doctors wet their pants.

Karrak came back and knelt behind me as the imagery began to compile in our visors. We didn't like what we saw. Starting at the cranium, the swelling was readily apparent. "Cerebral edema," I said while moving the discs along his body. "Spinal injuries, too." This wasn't as obvious as some fractured vertebrae. Everything was out of whack, like his spinal column had somehow been loosened.

As I kept moving, the extent of his injuries became more apparent, and more unusual. I'd seen a lot of weird stuff in this job, but to see this much trauma without an obvious cause was new to me. He was a mess of dislocations, radial fractures, and internal injuries. I didn't need the magic scanner discs to tell me there was internal bleeding; his rock-hard abdomen had given that away. It was the fractures and dislocated joints that bugged me, because Reticulans have exceptionally dense bone structure. They don't break easily.

I set the discs back in my bag. "This guy's been put through the wringer."

Karrak took a moment to make the connection. "Presuming you are not talking about an ancient laundry machine, you are not far off the mark, as you would say." He shook his head sadly. "These injuries are consistent with exposure to extreme gravity gradients."

"The kind you'd find near a black hole." I looked at our patient in astonishment. "How does someone survive that?"

His ebony eyes darted around the cabin. "It may be hard for you to discern, but his ship has not fared much better. He must have flown very close to the event horizon indeed. He is fortunate to have escaped. I am curious as to why anyone would allow themselves to get so close." His brow furrowed, a flamboyant show of concern for a Reticulan.

"Not much we can do here except immobilize him," I said, and began prepping an intravenous line. "I'm pushing fluids with anticoagulants for now. Nothing else yet; I don't want to risk something jarring him out of torpor. Let's get him back to the bus first."

"Agreed." Karrak motioned for me to continue pushing the meds while he set up the vacuum gurney.

✠ ✠ ✠

The transfer back to our ship went without a hitch, with our patient unconscious and sealed up tight in the pressurized gurney. It was after we were safely aboard and out of our suits when things got interesting. And I mean "interesting" in the way of the old Chinese curse, "May you live in interesting times."

The vital signs monitor embedded in the gurney began to tick up into more normal ranges; that is, normal for a Reticulan under severe trauma. They began rapidly edging up toward dangerously high values as our patient began to stir. I was about to start pushing sedatives through his IV when he grabbed me by the arm.

*Where am I?*

I could sense the pain through his thoughts. "You're safe, aboard a Med Corps transport. We're taking you to the trauma center at Delta Pavonis."

*And my ship?*

"We pulled it away from the accretion disk," I said, assuming he was aware he'd almost fallen into a black hole. "It's in a stable orbit with us for the time being. A Union tug will eventually come for it." Which was going to be a long time given the 115 shortage. I imagined that a derelict orbiting a place nobody in their right mind would want to get close to would put it way down the GU's priority list.

He tightened his grip on me and tried to sit up against the restraints before collapsing back onto the gurney; the pain was too much for him.

"Try not to move. You have internal bleeding and spinal column injuries." I was about to push a bolus of sedatives when his thoughts crowded out mine. It was the Reticulan equivalent of shouting.

*We must leave, now! Containment failure is imminent. We must—*

The words shot into my veins like ice water: *Containment failure.* Matter and antimatter, meeting in a violent, uncontrolled reaction. "Needa! Did you—"

*I heard. Initiating emergency departure. Get to your couches!*

At least I hadn't been overreacting. I pushed the sedatives as calmly as possible, then ran for my seat as the deck seemed to rise up beneath me. Needa had just firewalled the throttle, and it took Karrak's firm hands to pull me the rest of the way into the gel couch.

Manipulating gravity to zip around at near light speed is a

complicated business. It demands painstaking planning to make sure we don't disturb any nearby systems or accidentally fly into something dangerous, say, a black hole. Emergency departures were a last-ditch contingency, warping local space to move at max velocity over a short distance to get clear of whatever bad thing was about to happen. "Short" in this case was over a million kilometers.

Not a moment too soon, either. Our screens lit up in a firestorm that filled the cabin, as if a new star had appeared outside. By the time the automatic filters could catch up and the spots in my eyes dissipated, the light had already begun to fade.

I kept a death grip on the rails of my seat and waited for the shock wave. It never came; my panicked monkey brain had forgotten that there's no concussion in a vacuum. But if we'd been close, the heat would've vaporized us. Even at this range, the burst of gamma rays would have left us sprouting tumors like mushrooms if not for the radiation shields. All that from a kilogram or so of protons and antiprotons mixing it up.

Karrak and I traded a silent look, his wide eyes signaling we'd had a close call indeed. Needa's relieved voice interrupted our thoughts:

*We're safe. Hull integrity is in tolerance. Proceeding to Delta Pavonis.*

# 2

Delta Pavonis wasn't the closest trauma center, but it was the closest one staffed by Reticulan doctors. I'd been here once or twice, and the Grays' efficiency never failed to impress. The place ran like clockwork, better than the most locked-on Level 1 center on Earth. It helped that the staff were all reading each other's minds.

There was a team waiting for us as we pulled into the hangar bay, and they jumped into action as soon as the air pressure equalized. Orderlies took the antigrav gurney and we followed, relaying everything we'd done to the attending physician along the way.

"Patient is approximately 22 Reticulan years old. Transducer scans showed multiple radial fractures with dislocations along the spinal column, cerebral edema, and internal bleeding. He was in torpor when we found him, and we administered type IV sedatives at 30 milligrams per hour after he regained consciousness."

The doc was listening as he studied the history on his crystal. He looked up in surprise; his already large eyes growing even more so. He pointed an elegant finger at the slate as we followed his orderlies into the ER.

*Is this location correct? Gaia BH1?*

"Yes. We had to tow his ship out of the accretion disk before we could get to him."

*Then he was fortunate that you were in the vicinity. The extreme gravity was pulling him apart. I am surprised his ship held together.*

"It didn't for long. He woke up in time to warn us that his reactor containment was about to fail."

The Reticulan doc looked up. *Ah. He sensed your presence then, enough to stir himself back to consciousness. You were indeed fortunate.*

And with that, he spun about and left for the ER. I gave Karrak a shrug and turned back to our transport; it had to be cleaned and sterilized before the last leg of our trip back to the capital.

We worked through our cleanup routine in silence. It wasn't until we had the sterilizing boom in place that I allowed myself to start asking the obvious questions.

"What the hell was he doing there in the first place?" It was the sort of thing you asked after a particularly hard run, the kind where some poor schmuck had gotten himself into a terrible situation that should have been avoidable. Think of an upper-class kid getting knifed in an inner-city slum, or the middle-aged nobody who can't for the life of him explain how that shot glass got stuck up his ass. Backwards. You know they were up to something no good, but you don't waste time thinking about it until after the dust has settled.

"I have been wondering that myself," Karrak said as he took a seat at a small table in the back of the hangar bay. Behind him, the sterilizing boom was bathing the inside of our ship in ultraviolet light. Needa was poking around its exterior, going through her normal preflight routine. She was being more meticulous than usual, opening inspection panels and measuring tolerances along every seam.

"The only vessels known to have intentionally operated so close to a black hole have been for scientific exploration," he said after a long pause. "Their intent was to better understand the environment and assess any threats to navigation. Of those expeditions, none of them dared venture into the accretion disk. They left that task to expendable probes."

"I'm guessing that's because it's too dangerous? Stray too far and you cross the point of no return."

"Precisely so." His high brow furrowed again; he'd become just as troubled as I was now that we had time to think about it. "It is an energetic radiation environment, which as you saw taxes a vessel's shields. As you also saw, the gravity gradients become quite extreme as you approach the event horizon. That truly is the 'point of no return,' as you said. Nothing can escape that. Nothing."

I unwrapped a sandwich I'd taken from our food synthesizer right before this latest adventure. It had been sitting in a drawer ever since, until we'd started the decon routine. I tossed the bread aside and picked at the innards, a mostly faithful interpretation of pastrami and Swiss cheese. The nutrisynths had gotten pretty good at mimicking human cuisine during my time here, but for all of the GU's high tech, no one had bothered to figure out how to keep bread from going stale. "That brings us back to my original question," I said around a mouthful of synthetic pastrami. "What was he doing there?"

Karrak rubbed his sharp chin and stared into the distance. "A navigation error seems the most likely explanation. It is uncommon, but it happens. 'Human error,' as you would say."

"Humans, maybe. Give us the keys to one of those saucers and we'd be like teenagers on a joy ride." I tilted my head at Needa, who was waist-deep in an inspection port. "Your kind is nothing if not disciplined."

He turned to follow my gaze. "Quite."

"You're being awfully cagey. Something about this is bothering you, too."

Karrak leaned forward. "Very well. You noticed the bulge along the saucer's aft quarter?"

"Kind of hard to tell which ends were forward and aft, but yeah. That was unusual?"

"Most unusual. I'd hoped we'd have more time to ascertain what it might be. Though my understanding of such matters is superficial, I suspect it was an experimental drive."

Needa, of course, had been telepathically listening to us. *As do I. If we had been able to isolate its energy signature, we could have known for certain. Be that as it may, there is other evidence to support your suspicion.*

Karrak looked intrigued. "What might that be?" He kept vocalizing for my benefit. Being caught in the middle of a telepathic conversation could get confusing for an Earthling.

Needa continued working, her feet dangling from an open panel. *The failure of the saucer's containment field was telling. Emissions were inconsistent with a matter/antimatter reaction, and the explosive yield was greater than one would expect from the reaction mass for a vehicle of that size. It was, however, consistent with an uncontrolled release of zero point energy.*

I shuddered against the same chill that had shook me when first staring down that black hole: Zero point. The mysterious, almost limitless energy contained in the subatomic bonds of, well, everything. Enough that releasing a measuring cup's worth could boil oceans. It was the uncontrolled release of zero point energy which had destroyed the dwarf planet Tanaan a few years ago. That was shortly after I'd first joined the Med Corps, and the entire Union was still reeling from the loss of its largest Element 115 refinery.

Karrak rested his chin in one hand. "An interesting possibility. And troubling."

I chewed on the remnants of my sandwich, trying to push the memories of Tanaan out of my mind. "Still doesn't explain why he was in the danger zone of a black hole."

The final leg back to the capital had only taken a few hours by our reckoning. According to the master "Galactic Union Standard" time on our data crystals, we'd taken twice that long. What had been a three-day run for us had been almost a week for everyone back at the barn, a lot longer than my back-of-the-envelope estimate.

I stowed my vacuum suit in a locker along the back wall of the ambulance hangar and turned to Karrak, who was doing the same nearby. Behind us, the relief crew was pre-flighting our transport before taking it over for their shift. Needa was having an extended conversation with the new pilot, a hextapod who seemed none too happy with her news judging by his normally pink hue turning orange. He waved a tentacle at the medics, signaling them to not waste their time. Our ship would be down for extended inspections.

"Six days?" I wondered. "How fast were we going, anyway?"

"It's not just velocity, though there is that. You'll recall that gravity has a similar effect on relative time. The stronger the gravitational potential—"

"The more it stretches the space around it." I sighed, thinking of our patient. His injuries were an in-your-face testament, a metaphor for the disconnect I was feeling, the sense that my reality was being distorted beyond recognition. Before my recruitment into the Union, I'd been vaguely aware of the notion that space and time were an inseparable continuum, the structural foundation of the universe. A long-forgotten professor had touched on it in an even longer-forgotten physics class in college. It had never sunk in because it didn't impact my life, but living and working here had demonstrated the truth of it better than any lecture could have.

"Quite." Karrak placed a hand on my shoulder. "You have been with us for several annums, yet you still hold fast to your instinctual notions of time. If you're going to continue, you must learn to let that go."

I conceded his point with an indifferent grunt. I was living among beings who had spent their lives flying between the stars. They'd grown up accustomed to the counterintuitive effects of relativity playing out in their everyday lives, whereas I'd spent almost thirty years confined to Earth without having to adjust for anything more complicated than jet lag.

By my reference I'd been here for five years, "annums" in Union lingo. Every run I'd been on had taken me farther from home, and in more ways than just distance. What Karrak didn't know was that I'd been figuring out the time dilation from each run, tallying up my real separation from the world I'd left behind.

The math is surprisingly simple. Comprehending the results is a different matter.

My apartment in the capital overlooked the gardens of an immense biodome, which is to say the view wasn't bad. The gardens had been cultivated to resemble the Emissaries' home world, which had long ago been scorched by the death of its star. They shared the dome with the Gliesans, a race of meter-long insectoids who spent most of their time burrowing beneath the surface to create spectacular underground cities. They were the Union's de facto civil engineering corps, and had crafted much of the ringworld that served as the capital city.

They'd also spent a little time in my place. Most of the standard-issue blank walls had been replaced with intricately carved ceramic in arches and organic swirls that flowed gracefully from room to room. They'd insisted on doing this after I'd rescued a few of their clan from a tunnel collapse during my early days as a Union medic. It's doubtful that I'll ever shake being the go-to for confined space work, especially now that the Gliesans ask for me specifically if one of theirs needs help down there. Which is ironic, because the first time I saw them they scared the living shit out of me.

I did manage to keep one corner of my place mostly human. My bedroom was appointed with farmhouse-style furniture of synthetic wood that looked like it could've come from home. That had been a friendly gesture from Bjorn, the Emissary who'd first brought me here. He'd even managed to create an old-fashioned Afghan which was draped across the foot of my bed. "Bjorn" wasn't his real name, but the phonetics were close enough and it matched his somewhat Scandinavian appearance. If you've ever wondered where all of the gods from Norse mythology came from, there's a funny story behind that. Let's just say Bjorn and the other Emissaries don't like being reminded of it.

I kicked off my boots and settled into a comfy chair with a cup of hot chamomile from the nutrisynth, too tired to shuck off my neon green medic jumpsuit. Union clothing tended to be close-fitting but still comfortable enough that it was easy to forget to change after a shift, except for the times I came home covered in alien goo. That's when everything would go into the sterilizing bin.

Bjorn had also reproduced some favorite books for me, drawing from the GU's vast archive collected over centuries of observing humans in secret. The best part was that these were actual books, not just files uploaded to my crystal. He knew I liked my pens and paper, and managed to keep me well supplied with those as well. There wasn't much they couldn't create from scratch here.

It was all very nice, homey and well-intentioned. But when juxtaposed against the hyper-advanced civilization I now lived in, it only highlighted a gnawing sense of disconnection.

I picked up Herriot's *All Creatures Great and Small* out of the stack on my side table. I'd devoured it in high school after making the decision to study veterinary medicine. It had been something of a family business which I'd broken with halfway through getting my DVM. I'd learned the hard way that farm country had plenty of vets; what it didn't have enough of were first responders.

Out here I was straddling both worlds. With some exceedingly rare exceptions, every call I'd ever responded to had been for patients who were so foreign as to be closer to animals than humans. The difference was they could tell me what was wrong with them, thanks to the translation implant in my head.

Idly paging through this freshly produced copy of an old favorite, its stories all seemed very quaint now. What if Herriot had been able to talk to the animals he'd tended to? Maybe I should've asked Bjorn to print me a copy of *Dr. Dolittle*. It felt more appropriate.

Unable to focus, I tossed the memoir aside and picked up one of the worn notebooks I'd brought from home out of habit. I'd started using it for taking notes in my Med Corps training, but over time it had turned into a personal journal. I didn't write in it much, wanting to save its pages for really important stuff.

Its back pages held my "time sheet," where I added up the time dilation from each run relative to Earth. I'd done the math so often by now that I had the factors memorized. For example, at 0.6 *c* (that is, 60 percent of light speed) the dilation factor was 1.25. That meant for every hour spent at that velocity, an hour and fifteen minutes passed at home. It doesn't sound like a big deal until you see how quickly it adds up when our normal intra-system velocity is 0.6. This is because even though the gravity drive folds space to shorten distances, we still have to go pretty fast to cover it.

That's just for the short trips. When we have to crank up the drive for an interstellar run, past 0.7 *c*, the math goes nuts. And for the last year or so, interstellar had been my job. I'd been assigned to long-haul transport, moving critical patients around between star systems. It was like air ambulance work, using starships instead of private jets, and the time dilation effects had really begun to pile up.

I worked through the last few days' travels. It was a rough estimate, especially considering whatever the hell that black hole had done to us. As of today, Earth was a good eighteen years ahead of where it had been when I'd left.

Who knew what might have happened in that time? I occasionally found reports from Union survey expeditions, but for the most part they'd been keeping Earth at arm's length. It made me wonder if that meant things back home had become better, or worse. Had we finally gotten over our smartphone addictions and returned to reality, or had they been replaced with brain implants that turned the human race into internet-addled zombies? Had we baked the planet with $CO_2$? Or for that matter, had we finally stumbled our way into World War III?

A surprise waited for me after adding up the difference between Earth's calendar and mine. Though nothing as dramatic as my musings about global conflagrations, it still packed an emotional wallop:

Today was my birthday.

My parents had always made a big deal of that, which happens when you're an only child. Even into adulthood, Mom had always made a special dinner while Dad would handle the decorating and presents. I still wore the wristwatch from my last birthday with them, even though its timekeeping was a bad joke when the Union standard day was over thirty hours long. The smart thing would've been to set the watch in a drawer and forget about it, but I couldn't bring myself to cut that last tie. My inability to let go had left me with a constant reminder of how time was slipping away, of the growing gulf between this life and the one I'd left behind.

Leaving had come so easily once Mom and Dad were gone. I'd been alone with no decent romantic prospects, a lot of that due to being in a demanding job that had turned into a dead end. I'd been able to ignore that last bit by just living from one day to the next, focusing on each run as they came. Live like that for too long and the years can get away from you. Time keeps moving ahead while you're standing still and the next thing you know, you're middle aged and changing directions is suddenly much harder.

Start zipping around the galaxy at a sizeable fraction of light speed, and the years *really* get away from you.

Running away had been easy. Figuring out what came next wasn't. I'd spent almost as much time here as in the firehouse back home. Was this going to become a dead end, too?

My job here was important in more ways than one. Besides being one of a handful of medics who could treat beings outside of their own species, I had another, rarely stated purpose in the Union: Guinea Pig. Lab rat. Control patient.

They were using me as a proxy for the whole human race, observing how well I functioned in GU civilization. I was told it was a prerequisite for establishing formal contact. If that sounds like a lot to put on one girl's shoulders, that's because it is.

Thing is, I had welcomed the challenge and feel like the evidence shows I'd lived up to it. The GU had accorded me legal residency, with full citizenship coming after Earth joined the Union. Problem was, no one knew when that might be. If any GU bigwigs did they weren't letting me in on it, but if it was the same old Earth as the one I'd known then we wouldn't be getting invitations any time soon.

While eighteen years may not have been much on the Union's timeline, it was a lot for me.

If I were to go back now, I might at least recognize the place. If I stayed another five years, at this rate it'd be like disappearing in the 1940's and coming back in the 2000's. By then I'd be just as much of an alien among my own race as I was here.

Against my better judgment, I picked up my data crystal. "Clara, show me a listing of civil transports by destination." As my Union hosts had seen fit to grace my cybernetic personal assistant with a vaguely Midwestern accent, I'd named her accordingly. Over time, she'd adopted my inflections and idioms to the point where she sounded like a suburban mom at a school bake sale.

"You really want to do this again?" She had also cultivated a suburban mom's nosiness.

"Not really, but do it anyway."

Clara heaved a synthetic, exasperated sigh. "Hang on, just a sec."

Of course it took barely a second before a holographic projection of transport schedules floated in the air before me. I wondered if tablets on Earth could do that by now.

Checking transport routes was a bad habit I'd indulged of late, being curious as to what might be headed in the general direction of Earth. It was an exercise in futility, but I couldn't help myself. If one was going to be in the vicinity, I might be able to convince the ship's master to take me the rest of the way on a shuttle. Even in the egalitarian Union, you could do just about anything for the right price.

Finding the right price was the hard part. The 115 shortage had played hell with the civilian transport economy. If you needed more than what was rationed, the price went up sharply. Black market supplies were dicey because you couldn't know what kinds of quality controls had been applied. Base 115 was wildly unstable, so the isotopes used for gravity drives had to be precisely manufactured. Any impurities could cause a ship to go kaboom as soon as the drive was powered up. That had happened a few times, so nobody touched the black market stuff anymore without first tracing its provenance. That usually resulted in "stolen," and the penalties were severe enough that no one in their right mind would risk it.

I scrolled through the few transport routes with destinations near Earth, and was disappointed as usual. The closest was Tau Ceti, which was still a good twelve light-years from home. Even if I could've afforded that (spoiler alert: I couldn't), the extra cost to charter a shuttle home was way out of reach.

Hitching a ride on one of the Earthbound survey expeditions wouldn't be in the cards, either. Nearly all of that work was being done by drones, and had been for some time. There were crewed motherships running the surveys nearby, but "nearby" was relative. With all of the new human activity in Earth orbit, the Union had been forced to pull farther back to avoid detection, all the way to the outer solar system. Even cloaked, they wouldn't risk getting near Earth without a very good reason, and taking my skinny ass back to Indiana wasn't one of them.

"You've been doing this a lot lately, Mel. What's so special about this place? There are a lot of nice planets in the Union."

"They're not home, Clara." And I'd still be the only human, no matter where I settled.

"That's a difficult concept for me."

"It's because you're a talking slab of glass." Maybe that wasn't fair, but I wasn't feeling especially chatty.

Clara could read my moods almost as well as a Gray or Emissary. "Sorry, didn't mean to pry." Did I mention she could act like my mother?

"Don't worry about it. Sorry I was short with you. I need some space to think."

Clara turned herself off with a chirp. I sighed and reached out for the hologram to "grab" it, making a fist and sending it back to the crystal. Another exercise in futility. Not the first, and it wouldn't be the last. For better or for worse, I wasn't going anywhere except on a Med Corps transport.

I rested my chin in my hands and stewed. What was this need that wouldn't stop pulling at me? Clara had a point, much as I didn't want to hear it. I was surrounded by good people (okay, not really "people" but work with me), in a challenging job I could've never imagined, and I'd been welcomed into an advanced civilization that provided for all of my needs. What's not to like about that?

Was it as simple as humans craving other humans, not just intelligent talking animals? Imagine Jane Goodall living among the chimpanzees, except they're way more advanced than her and she's the one being studied. I guess that would make it more like *Planet of the Apes*, but without the shock collars and human slavery. That wasn't really fair, and maybe even a little species-ist, but there was no denying how I felt. Sometimes it came from the opposite direction: Union citizens that treated me as an outsider. I was one of only two humans in the Union, and the other guy had not exactly made a good name for himself.

Bjorn and a few others I worked with knew better, and they'd become true friends. As if to remind me of that, the crystal began blinking for my attention. It was my friend Chonk, asking if I was free to come down to the Thuban sector. Thubans are intimidating, a race of seven-foot-tall reptilian badasses, and many of them were among my best friends here. Go figure that a scrawny farm girl would find her tribe with a warrior race. Then again, soldiers and first responders were generally cut from the same cloth on Earth, so perhaps some things are universal.

I reflexively checked my old watch and did the math. I had most of a full thirty-two hour Union day until my next shift, which was plenty of time to catch the tube over to their dome and enjoy a few drinks. I changed into a T-shirt and a pair of shorts and headed for the lifts.

# 3

My minimal clothing had made for a chilly ride over, but it paid off the moment I stepped off the tube and entered the Thuban sector. In keeping with being highly evolved reptiles, the Thubans liked things warm. When I left the transit terminal for their biodome, it was like walking into an open oven. No matter how many times I'd come here, leaving the overly air-conditioned public transport for desert heat made me swoon.

I shook off the lightheadedness and made my way to a pale yellow one-story building of intricately carved stone with circular windows of variegated colors resembling stained glass. Tucked away among rock outcroppings of burnt ochre, it was built in traditional Thuban architectural style with an unmistakable Gliesan touch: more of the graceful swirls and swooping curves that made Wayside (*Wa'xi'ya'de* in the original Thuban) stand out while still looking as if it had sprouted from the desert floor. The soft tones of wind instruments drifted from Wayside's permanently open doors, inviting me inside.

Chonk was waiting at our usual table, pouring a fresh drink from a pitcher of *ka'vaa'ma'loi*: Thuban tequila. I smiled inwardly at the lime green tint of the pitcher's contents. After a lot of trial and error, I'd been able to train the nutrisynth to create close approximations of triple sec and lime juice, and had promptly showed Chonk how to make margaritas. He'd been so impressed that he'd shared the recipe, and now *ma'g'ree'tahs* were a favorite among Wayside regulars. I was just doing my part to represent the human race.

Chonk rose from his stool to tower over me at his full height. He flashed a toothy grin, the heavy ridges over his golden eyes lifting in an all-over smile that would've been terrifying to the uninitiated: *Is he happy to see me, or am I on the menu?* He wrapped me up in a bear hug. Or lizard hug, to be precise. Hugging wasn't a thing in Thuban culture, but Chonk was always striving to make me feel at home. He let go to hold me at arm's length and hissed joyfully.

"Mel! Has been much time!"

"It has." I poked at the scales on his arms. They shimmered beneath the overhead glow panels, which told me they were fresh. "New skin?"

"Is. Have not been myself lately."

It had been maybe a month since we'd last seen each other, which I'd assumed had been due to conflicting schedules. Nope, Chonk had been molting and adult Thubans tended to become reclusive when that time came. I reached behind him to touch the back of his head. "Are those *feathers*?"

He threw out his already prominent chest, filled with pride. "Is! First *t'ann s'vaa*! Am now 'old', as you say."

Thubans lived to well over a hundred years by our calendar, and the brightly colored *t'ann s'vaa* feathers didn't appear until early middle age. They were the mark of a fully mature Thuban, which accorded great respect among their kind. The fine plumage sprouted from the crown of his head to hang down the back of his neck, reminiscent of a Native American headdress. Combined with his gray uniform tunic and violet combat medic sash, the feather mullet made Chonk look positively regal. He still proudly wore the old EMS pin I'd presented to him as a gift years ago, while the Thuban sash he'd given me back then still hung on a wall in my living room. The thing was almost as long as I am tall.

We sat and I nodded at his uniform. "You're still on reserve with the fleet, then?"

"Am. Admiralty thought Med Corps experience was useful to others. Also short on fleet medicos."

Chonk had been the first Thuban combat medic to cross-train with the Union Med Corps. Their border defense fleet had largely kept to themselves until Tanaan happened, and any skepticism the Thuban Admiralty might have held about letting Chonk work with Union civilians had been swept away by his actions in that disaster. The defense fleet had been forced into taking on more humanitarian roles (which again sounds species-ist, but it's all I've got), and there'd been a steady rotation of Thuban "medicos" through the Corps' training school ever since.

"You just instructing, or are you out in the field?"

Chonk's flicked his tri-forked tongue at his drink. It was the Thuban equivalent of sipping. "In field much more than expected." He shrugged his massive shoulders. "Been much busy."

When someone in the military says they've been busy, that can hold a lot of unpleasant implications. "Are things getting lively out there?"

"Lively," he repeated slowly. The translation implants didn't always pick up on human idioms. "Am confused. You mean playful?"

"Not really. The opposite, in fact. More like threatening. Dangerous."

"Ah. Word is *fu'ku'pa*."

I stifled a laugh. Chonk, of course, had no idea why I found that term so amusing. "Has it been getting dangerous out there?"

Chonk fiddled with his sash, somehow not tearing holes in it with his claws. "Is danger. Always on alert for border incursions. You call 'pirates,' I think. Is . . . nuisance. More distress calls from colony ships transiting border sectors. Not real 'distress' but still need assistance. Busy."

That was another byproduct of the 115 shortage. If a Union-flagged ship was having trouble, the closest vessel had to respond. Medical or mechanical, it didn't matter. Used to be we'd dispatch a Med Corps heavy transport or a fleet tender, depending on the need. If it happened in the border sectors, that usually meant a Thuban frigate or patrol cruiser answered the call. No wonder the Admiralty had been putting so many of their "medicos" through our training school. Thubans in particular had been culturally averse to treating other species, but circumstances had forced it on them.

"How are your people holding up?" Again, species-ist, but he knew what I meant.

"Some good. Some not. Hard to know until they do job." This time he took a long pull from his drink. "Much work for me. Much responsibility. Not time for other things."

I nodded. He was overseeing a bunch of Thuban warriors who were all of a sudden being called into something way outside of their comfort zones. "That's the job sometimes, isn't it? Keep the new guys from screwing up."

"Is so." He put his drink down. "Enough me. How you? Still long duration crew?"

It was my turn to take a long sip of *ma'g'ree'tah*. "I am. And the last run took a lot longer than we'd planned." The cauliflower-like auditory buds behind his eyes puffed up in rapt attention as I relayed the story of our rescue near Delta Pavonis.

"Black hole?" He pounded his chest in the traditional Thuban gesture of admiration. "Impressive. And much *fu'ku'pa*."

"It was a big *fu'ku'pa* all right. I was scared out of my wits."

"Needa is exceptional pilot. Am sure she would not risk lightly."

I shrugged. "Even Karrak was a little anxious."

"Karrak is very bold for Reticulan. Sometimes too much for own good."

That drew a laugh. "What you're saying is we wouldn't have done it if we'd known better."

"Perhaps. Must be just smart enough to do job, not think too much. Hesitate."

He had a point. "Lately I've been thinking too much for my own good."

"You very smart. Almost doctor on Earth."

"Animal doctor," I corrected him. Then again, out here it could be hard to tell the difference.

"Yet you do not hesitate. Opposite, in fact."

That had been my shortcoming back home, and it had landed me in trouble more than a few times. Age and experience were beginning to temper that impulse. "Haven't felt that way lately, and you'd better believe I was hesitant on that last run. Needa had us at a safe distance, but when we got outside the ship, with nothing between us and that... *thing*? I froze up like a deer in the headlights."

Chonk flicked his tongue, a sympathetic gesture among Thubans. "Sometimes truth not matter. Some things hard to ignore. Gut take over. Primitive response." He lifted the pitcher and topped off my drink. "Courage is when you go anyway. You have much."

I twirled the glass between my hands. "Doesn't feel like it sometimes."

"You are. Courageous not think. Just do."

"Just do," I repeated. "That's been the story of my life. I've been living for work, going on ten years now. When do I start living for me?" If that sounds petulant and selfish, that's because it was.

"You not have much time off lately."

"True, but I don't know what to do with the time I have anymore."

"How so? Much to do in capital."

Chonk was mostly right, but he was missing one important point. "I've been to every sector of the Ring, and it's all amazing. But I've mostly been doing it alone."

He tilted his massive head, confused. "You have been welcomed, no?"

"For the most part. But I'm the only human here."

His golden eyes narrowed. "Not only human." Again, he was right, so far as it went.

"Gideon and I aren't exactly on friendly terms." Not that I wanted to be, either. If we were the last two beings left alive in the universe, I'd be happy to spend the rest of my days alone. A lot of Union folks felt the same way.

"That speak well of you. Others see that. Know what you did. Is why you are welcome."

I didn't want to sound ungrateful, but this had been weighing on me. "Human culture is filled with stories of extraterrestrial visitors. Aliens. Now I know those stories are all true." Okay, mostly true. There were still a lot of nutballs out there. "Now *I'm* the alien. A stranger in a strange land. I'm comfortable here, but it's not home." I took another long pull from my drink. "And I'm not sure it ever can be." The words had been simmering in my gut for a long time, I only needed a little liquid courage to speak them. To admit it to myself.

Chonk placed a claw on my arm. "You have many friends here. Many care about you."

I squeezed his claw with my hand. "I know, and it means a lot to me." I'd felt out of place in my previous life, and for a while had thought I'd found a home here in the Union and its many races. But the lack of human interaction had been taking a toll.

Human interaction was not something I'd been especially good at in my former life. Maybe I just needed to get laid, not that *that* was going to happen here.

What were my prospects, anyway? It was something I avoided

thinking about, because doing so only drove home the sense of isolation. Interspecies relations were generally frowned upon, not that I was interested in getting frisky with a highly evolved dinosaur. The Emissaries were our closest cousins, but they were also so stoic as to be almost devoid of emotion. Not to mention they were my friends, and I didn't do the "with benefits" thing.

I could tell this turn in the conversation was making Chonk uncomfortable, so I decided to lighten things up. "It's also my birthday."

"Birth . . . today?" Chonk's brow wrinkled, rustling his feathers. His translator probably hadn't encountered that term yet. "You not born today, born many years ago."

Many years. Now that's a way to make a girl feel old. I was about to explain the concept when he finally landed on it.

"Ah! You mean hatch day anniversary!"

Not quite, but close enough. "Yes, that's it," I laughed. "Where I'm from, we make a celebration of it."

"Is strange, but not question other's customs. Let us celebrate!" Chonk called for another pitcher and ordered us each a bowl of *xa'fuun'to* stew, their equivalent of good old human comfort food. As we dug into our bowls, the not-quite-familiar tastes brought back memories of my mom's cooking. Indiana winters were incessantly dreary, and she'd always been happy to brighten things up with some chili and cornbread. That had been a long time ago, even without all of my warp-speed zipping around the galaxy.

As the spicy *xa'fuun'to* settled in my stomach, I likewise settled into a realization which had been simmering for some time, like the pots of stew in Wayside's kitchen.

It was time to go home, before the Earth I'd known became unrecognizable. The question was, how?

# ✝ 4 ✝

Surfing the internet after knocking back a few drinks is rarely a good move, especially if it involves shopping after some half-assed Great Idea has taken hold in your head. I've had a lot of useless crap show up on my doorstep over the years, most of it cookware that never left the box. My kitchen back home had an espresso machine, rice cooker, sous vide, two sets of chef's knives, and three varieties of air fryers. Don't ask how often I used them, because the answer would be embarrassing. My intentions were noble.

The property management company Bjorn and his colleague Sven had set up for me was still drawing from my account, so I assumed all of that stuff was still collecting dust in the pantry. I'd vowed to finally use all of it whenever I returned.

Despite Clara's motherly objections, I'd fallen into my usual routine of checking up on the latest news from Earth, though the remote surveys didn't offer much of the kinds of things I'd have considered "news." This was especially so for politics, which I admit was a nice break. The Union deemed that sort of thing to be a transient aberration in the development of our civilization. Background noise. The exception was when the halfwits in expensive suits did something head-poundingly destructive.

The big surprise today came from the news that humans had finally landed on Mars, and you'd better believe the Survey Ministry had taken notice. I began poring over the intercepted broadcasts from home, desperate for details. It wasn't hard, as TV and radio signals are constantly streaming out into space and someone is always listening.

There it was, a grainy video of two people in sleek white spacesuits planting the American flag on Mars. In the background, a silvery rocket that could've come from a 50's sci-fi movie towered against a salmon-colored sky.

I was elated. Pride swelled inside me and I found myself wiping away tears. We'd done it! *Humans for the win, bitches!*

Going to Mars had always been talked about, but it wasn't something I'd followed before. Giant rockets had blown up every now and then, so I'd assumed it would forever remain a long way off. But in the five years I'd been away, it had all come together.

Then I saw the time stamp on the video: eighteen years for them. So my math had been right, another reminder of how much I'd missed.

Yes, that was a little deflating. If I ever did manage to return home, how much more actual time would have passed?

Returning, of course, remained my current dilemma. I was sitting cross-legged on my bed, searching through the Union network. My bedroom was filled with holographic projections of anything that might get me near my goal.

The goal was Earth, and I still wasn't finding anything that ventured close to it. I shouldn't have expected any better, since we weren't in the Union yet. The Survey Ministry was still keeping an eye on the place with a quartet of observatories safely hidden in the asteroid belt, but they were autonomous and not regularly serviced. There was the occasional pass by a Thuban picket ship, but those never got any closer than our heliopause. Chonk had once mentioned something about military vessels staying within recognized interstellar boundaries.

Other than the run to Tau Ceti, the closest transport route I'd found was to Rigel Station. The latter was where I'd first entered the Union, and they still ran a semi-regular shuttle from the Capital. Tau Ceti was closer, but there wasn't much of a Union presence there. I had a better chance of finding a ride to Earth from Rigel than just about anywhere else, and that was still rolling the dice. I'd have to find someone to take me the rest of the way, someone with time on their hands (or claws, tentacles, whatever) and a willingness to expend precious fuel for a long side trip. An unsanctioned side trip, which would surely cost extra.

I stared at the projections hovering above my bed and thought through the logistics. The prices were, well, astronomical. I had just enough Union *kuulas* in my account to pay for a slow boat to Rigel; the kind favored by invertebrate species like the Eridanis. Hexapods didn't tolerate long periods of acceleration well, even with inertial dampening. Still, I looked up the particulars.

Relative cruise velocity of 0.8 $c$. I groaned. Even at eighty percent light speed, that still made for almost a twelve-year journey when you factored in the warp distance. No big deal for a hexapod; they'd just naturally go dormant and sleep most of the way. That'd leave me stuck on a transport with most of the other passengers asleep in their seawater tanks. I could pay extra to be put in hibernation, but I'd still have to find a ride home at the end after twelve years of no income.

Maybe the transport was looking for extra hands? All of the big long-haulers had medical staff, surely I could find some kind of arrangement to work for my berthing. That way I'd keep my savings intact, maybe even earn enough to buy a ride home from Rigel.

In twelve years. Actually, it's worse than that.

Mind you, that time is only by the ship's reference. I mentioned that relativity really starts to kick your ass once you're past seventy percent light speed, when time dilation begins to multiply exponentially. At 0.8 $c$, twelve years from the ship's perspective would be closer to twenty on Earth.

Damn you, Einstein.

Okay, not really his fault, but I needed someone to be pissed at.

I made an angry swipe at the holograms, sending them back into the bowels of my crystal. Even this tenuous, half-assed plan had turned around to bite me. The very problem I was trying to run away from kept rearing its head, and the faster I tried to run, the worse it became. The closer I got to home, the farther away it was. In twenty more years everyone I'd known would be well into old age, if not dead. And who knew what Earth would be like? Hell, who knew if it would even be there if we ran sideways into one of those "threshold events" Bjorn had once warned me about? By then we might've baked the planet in greenhouse gases or gene-edited our way to extinction.

It was enough to make a girl wonder what the point was of going back in the first place.

I flopped back onto my bed with a groan.

Suffice it to say I was more than a little distracted at work the next day, and even more torn. Thoughts of the life left behind tugged at me, while the new one I'd embraced demanded my attention. Waiting around the hangar bay for a call didn't do anything to resolve the conflict between the two, if anything that down time only sharpened the division.

I sat in the back of our squad, idly perusing the same transport schedules that had frustrated me the night before. It was classic doom-scrolling, digging ever deeper into the muck of disappointing information while hoping for that tiny nugget of gold to reveal itself.

Of course there was no nugget that would make my harebrained plan work, only more muck. Did I mention interstellar travel was prohibitively expensive?

I shoved the crystal back into my hip pocket and blew out a sigh. I stole a glance at Karrak, who seemed indifferent to my inner turmoil. That of course was a convenient fiction, as his telepathic nature left no doubt that he sensed what was on my mind. He'd come to know me well enough by now to also understand it was best to leave me alone until I was ready to talk.

I thought of Bjorn and Sven. I could never hope to achieve their near-telepathic levels of empathy, but one vital lesson they'd taught me was the value of detachment, of looking at matters objectively. The more complicated the problem, the more helpful it was to remove myself from it. That is, to set emotions aside.

I'd been weighing the pros and cons in my head. What was there for me to miss so much, anyway? My life had been nothing to get excited about when they'd plucked me from obscurity. They'd given me an opportunity, and I'd jumped at it. So why was I feeling so disconnected?

The pros of living in the Union were considerable. All my needs were met, and I'd made more reliable friends here than on Earth. The work was almost always rewarding. It scratched both my veterinary and EMS itches, and there was always more to learn.

The learning hadn't stopped with the dozen or so different alien anatomies, either. I'd been to other worlds, seen galactic phenomena up close that would've knocked human astronomers on their asses. Just the other day I'd been within spitting distance of a black hole. The images recorded in Clara's memory would've been priceless back home.

*Back home.* Why did I keep thinking of Earth that way, when I'd felt more at home here than at just about any time since Mom and Dad had passed? I supposed the roots had grown deeper than I'd realized, the kinds of bonds you take for granted until you've severed them. No matter how welcoming my companions had been, there was no escaping the fact that I was not among my own kind. I was one of only two humans within a few thousand light-years, and I wasn't going to be on Gideon's social calendar any time soon. Not that I wanted to be.

That thought led me back to the single "con" of life in the Union. Here, I was the alien.

The alert klaxon blared, and a shimmering curtain of golden light appeared outside. The vacuum force fields had activated, along with a warning broadcast: "Alert bay sixteen, alert bay sixteen. Prepare for immediate departure."

Time to stuff the intrusive thoughts away and get to work. I leaped out of my seat and stood next to Karrak, who was studying our dispatch notice. We were being sent to a Mintakan transport out of Auriga. One of its crew was suffering from "acute photon exposure." A sunburn.

That might sound like a waste of our resources, but Mintakans were extremely sensitive to natural light. They'd evolved on an overcast planet beneath dense jungle and their translucent skin offered very little protection from UV rays, so direct sunlight could easily damage their internal organs.

Needa closed up the hatch while we strapped in. The deck hummed as the gravity drive came to life, and we shot out of the bay into space.

An hour later we pulled up alongside the transport, which itself wasn't much to speak of. The Mintakans liked to keep things simple, and their ship reflected this aesthetic. Other than the faint red light from its open landing bay, the ship was a featureless cylinder nearly half a mile long.

We stepped out into the dimly lit bay and were greeted by a translucent ovoid blob a little more than a meter across. The only way to tell it was facing us was by its eyes, which weren't much more than a patchwork of slate-gray photosensitive receptors embedded in its skin. I flipped down my visor, which compensated for the low light. Now I could see the Mintakan in full, down to being able to identify its internal organs and circulatory system. Its skin vibrated as it began to speak, which at first came as a discordant, low-frequency warbling. I hadn't had many interactions with this species, so it took a second for my translation implants to pick it up.

"... severe burn, terrible accident. Hmm, yes. Please follow me."

Karrak lifted the species-specific trauma kit from one of our outrigger pods and loaded it onto the levitating gurney. The Mintakan turned, its gelatinous body supported by hundreds of spaghetti-like feelers which moved in a rhythmic cadence to propel him across the bay. He was almost too fast to keep up with.

The landing bay was sized to accommodate various classes of Union shuttles, but the rest of the ship was designed with Mintakans in mind. The corridors and compartments were barely high enough to for me to stand up in, while all the hatchways weren't much more than a meter square. Big enough for one of them, but I had to get down on my knees to crawl through.

Our patient had been isolated in a darkened room adjacent to the landing bay. I pulled out a pair of scanner discs to take vital signs and began to gently move them across his body. This was a little touchy, both for the patient's sake and my own gut reaction. They look like disembodied brains suspended in goo beneath a tissue-thin, translucent membrane. I had to remind myself that Mintakans were the most intelligent race in the Union. Their massive brains and complex network of nerve receptors can perceive things the rest of us can't, including (I'm told) other dimensions. Their minds function on an entirely different plane. Ever encounter someone so smart that they can't relate to normal people? Mintakans are like that.

I put this out of my mind and focused on taking vitals and assessing his condition like any other patient. His delicate skin made it easy to identify the burns. A large patch of blistered epidermis covered most of one hemisphere, including a good portion of his ocelli, the photoreceptors that passed for eyes on this species. Honestly it was a little repulsive, but they weren't the first Union species to trigger my horror-movie reflex.

I've found the best way to quiet my primitive monkey brain is to just start talking to the patient. I dropped to my knees beside him. "I'm Melanie. This is Karrak. We're from the Medical Corps. Can you tell us your name?"

His skin vibrated in short, staccato patterns, a sharp contrast to the

Mintakan who'd led us here. Even through the translator, his speech was weak and halting. "Hmm. Raxx... Udan... Woxx... of Mintaka."

I stifled a grin. He didn't have to tell me he was from Mintaka. I kept making idle chat while gently probing his skin. "Hello, Raxx. Looks like you have some pretty nasty flash burns. Can you tell me how this happened?" This mattered, because there was a big difference between a bad sunburn and exposure to ionizing radiation. Superficially they presented the same way, but the latter could turn nasty in a hurry.

"Shield... reactor... anomaly."

I shot a glance over my shoulder at Karrak. He knew the technical stuff much better than I, but hearing "anomaly" associated with an antimatter reactor made the hair on my neck stand up. He turned to the other Mintakan with a questioning look.

"Hmm, yes. Raxx-Udan is our chief engineer. He was conducting a routine inspection of the reactor plant. There was a... how should I describe?... stutter in the protective field."

"But not the containment field?" Karrak pressed.

Raxx answered for himself. "Not containment. Protective."

I finished my scan, careful to not touch his affected skin. "He's not throwing off any radiation. Doesn't appear contaminated."

Karrak relaxed. "The protective field is unique to the Mintakans for their sensitivity to visible light. It's in essence a filter."

That was a relief. The shades had glitched momentarily, and our patient had been unfortunate enough to be there. The discs didn't show any signs of radiation exposure other than a concentrated dose of plain old photons, so we were probably dealing with a simple sunburn. Of course, "simple" is relative for a species so exquisitely sensitive to light. "Okay, Raxx. Can you tell me how you feel? Any nausea or dizziness?"

"Hmm, no and no. I do not feel unsteadiness, though I do not know 'nausea.' That is not a condition we experience."

I'd kind of expected that, but still had to ask. Mintakans absorbed all their nutrients directly through their outer membrane, which was icky but effective. It filtered out anything they couldn't tolerate before it entered their digestive system, but radiation poisoning could alter that chemistry.

I held a light in front of his photoreceptors. The healthy ones changed color from light gray to black, a normal response for his species. The burned ones didn't respond. Raxx shuddered.

"I'm sorry. Was that uncomfortable?"

"Yes and yes. Very bright."

"I apologize. We had to check your optic reflexes." I sat back on my heels and started unrolling a patch. "This will protect your photoreceptors. I'm going to apply a corticosteroid spray over the rest of your burns and cover them with a cooling wrap." I nodded to Karrak, who was lifting a small infusion pump from his trauma bag. "My partner here is going to start you on a saline infusion. You're dehydrated from the burns, and this will help. We'll inject a mild sedative into the mix for the pain. Sound okay?"

"Yes and yes."

With this species, we couldn't just find a vein to start an IV even though the circulatory system was visible beneath Raxx's skin. Karrak unrolled an infusion mat designed for Mintakans. One side was covered with feeding tubes, the other with microscopic pins. Once the mat was in place on our patient, the pins would begin gently pushing fluids which would be absorbed through his membrane's natural capillary action. It was a slow process, but with thousands of entry points over a large area our guy soon started to feel better.

He still needed a lot more than we could provide on our own. The affected area was large enough to qualify as third degree, which meant we'd need to transport him to the Med Corps complex back at the Capital.

When I broached this subject, the Mintakan's reaction was sharp. The patient didn't voice any objections, but he began quivering nervously. I sensed he wasn't happy with the idea, and our escort was more insistent.

"No and no. Raxx-Udan cannot leave. That would be sub-optimal."

Sub-optimal? Compared to half of this guy's body being covered with flash burns? I was ready to blow a gasket when Karrak stepped in. "I know he is a vital member of your crew, but his injuries are quite extensive. Without proper care, they could become life-threatening."

The escort paused. His body pulsated as he considered my argument. Raxx pulsated in response. They were having a whispered conversation which my translator couldn't pick up.

"We can care for him here," the escort said. "Your services will not be necessary."

I smelled bullshit. If they could take care of him here, then why'd they call us in the first place? I glanced at Karrak, who knelt in front of our patient. "That is, of course, up to you," he said, "but we must inform you of—"

Raxx began convulsing, with violent ripples coursing back and forth across his body. Warnings began flashing in my visor as his vital signs began bottoming out. "He's crashing! Spin up the defib!"

Karrak rushed back to the trauma kit to pull out the crash box and began synching it to the transducer discs. They'd act as defibrillator paddles, pumping current through the patient while also taking vitals. It was one of many pieces of gear I'd have loved to have on Earth. Heart monitor, ECG, and defibrillator all in one handy unit about the size of a deck of cards.

"Full charge."

I set the transducers in place and stepped back. "Clear!"

The machine itself was not nearly as dramatic as a defib kit on Earth. No electronic whine of current building up, just a pulsing white light and a barely audible *click* when it discharged. Our patient convulsed from the shock. I gave it a second to watch his sinus rhythm. Nothing, just a quick jump in the trace lines. "Again."

"Stand by . . . full charge."

"Clear!"

Another click, another convulsion. The trace jumped, then went flat again. "Still not responding." I looked up to see Karrak searching my face. We knew what had to come next.

In a humanoid we'd start CPR. The problem here was that even with an automated chest compressor, it only worked on species where direct pressure could be applied. With a gelatinous Mintakan, things got a little more complicated.

"Massage wands?"

I nodded, and Karrak pulled out a pair of thin, meter-long hollow rods which were in essence large-gauge needles. He handed one to me and we took up positions on either side of the Mintakan. "Ever done this before?"

"No." Grays rarely showed emotion under pressure, but the veins bulging along Karrak's slender neck were a dead giveaway that he was apprehensive.

"Me neither. Just in the holo sim. We do this together." I placed the sharp tip of my rod against our patient's skin, holding it steady with one hand while keeping the other on a control pad fixed to its end. I could just barely see the heart, which my visor highlighted. "Like playing a video game," I said, which probably meant nothing to Karrak. "You ready?"

"I am."

"On three. One . . . two . . ."

On three we pushed in simultaneously, driving the rods through Raxx's membrane. We each stopped just short of the heart, and the control pad suctioned itself into place on the Mintakan's skin. "I'm in position."

"As am I. Controls are synchronized."

"Got it. I'll initiate."

"Please do."

Yep, Karrak was nervous as hell. I smiled to myself, as there weren't many procedures I could outdo these guys in. I pressed against the control pad. "Starting heart massage."

Small elastic cups extruded from the hollow tubes and molded themselves around either side of the heart. Soon they began working in unison, squeezing and releasing. The trace lines in my visor jumped back to life, matching what we needed to see for a Mintakan. I rocked back against my knees and blew out a sigh. "There we go. Sinus rhythm. Good job, Karrak."

He stood and brushed off his green coveralls, watching the feed through his own visor. "I agree. Patient is stable."

I turned to our escort. "No argument now, he needs to be hospitalized." His eye patches contracted, a sign of confusion. His translation implants were tripping over my human English. It happened sometimes. "A treatment facility. Long-term care. These burns are extensive and they're overtaxing his body. He's shutting down. The massage wands are to keep him stable for transport. If we don't get him somewhere for proper treatment, I promise you he won't last." The Grays had a rectal probe which could do the trick, but that only worked if the patient had an actual rectum.

Our escort's skin tensed up, as if he were making a hard decision. "Hmm, yes. Very well."

I activated the anti-grav gurney and directed it back to our ship. I thought of Needa, and the tickle in the back of my mind told me she was listening. "We're ready for transport. Capital complex."

# ☤ 5 ☤

Even at max velocity, it was another hour's flight back to the Med Corps campus. The injured Mintakan was secured to the gurney and we'd dialed in our full suite of condition monitors, filling the sidewall with holoprojections. The massage wands were doing their job, but the fact that they were still having to pump for him was not a good sign. If Raxx's heart couldn't function on its own, he'd have a long recovery ahead. That was for the docs to decide, but I had a good idea of what was in store for him. He'd need a pacemaker, which with Union technology was not a big deal. It wasn't much more than a simple chip implant, small enough to be injected through one of the rods we'd inserted. If the docs determined he needed a new heart, they could grow a synthetic one in a few days. The tissue incubators worked a lot like our food synthesizers, just with much higher fidelity, knitting protein chains together into a faithful reproduction of the patient's own organ, down to his unique DNA. If this had been a human on Earth, he'd have been placed on a donor list that might or might not have paid off in time to save him.

I'd been here long enough to become inured to the wondrous technology of daily life in the Med Corps. Treatments that would've been unimaginable back home were just part of the scenery, tools to be used and nothing more. It had taken time to get comfortable with it all, only because I'd never entirely trusted tech to not break once in a while, and usually when it was most needed.

I thought about that as we watched over our patient. He'd wound up here precisely because something important had failed at the worst possible time, and that was bothering me more than usual. I glanced up at my partner, who was rubbing his chin in a humanlike manner as he stared at the pulsating lines of telemetry. Not concentrating on the feed, thinking about something else.

"Penny for your thoughts."

"Excuse me? I do not grasp your meaning."

"It's an old icebreaker. A conversation starter."

"Ah. I understand now." He turned to take the seat opposite mine. "I am most curious as to how this Mintakan fell upon such misfortune. It does not make sense, as you might say."

"Been wondering about that myself." Though I hadn't had much time to pursue it, much less the technical niceties. "Aren't antimatter reactors contained inside of magnetic bottles? Why would the reaction be visible in the first place?"

"Precisely. The reactor plant is constructed from opaque alloys. There would be nothing for him to see. If the chamber had been disassembled for maintenance, the antiprotons would have remained confined to their containment tanks."

"Otherwise he wouldn't be here right now."

"Again, precisely. Any stray antiprotons would have reacted energetically."

Meaning they'd have blown up, and not in a small way. "Could that have happened? Could they have torn down the reactor for maintenance, and a few stray particles made it into the open?"

He shook his head. "Possible, but unlikely. The vessel was still under power." He turned to study our patient. "This Mintakan also shows no signs of ionizing radiation. Their outer membranes are exceptionally sensitive to x-ray and gamma radiation. Even a stray antimatter reaction of a few atoms would have released significant quantities of both."

I followed his gaze. The Mintakan lay still on the gurney, nearly half of his gelatinous body covered with cooling wraps. "Brief exposure, but extensive burns. What could do that so quickly?"

"I have my suspicions. Whatever the reaction was, it would have been quite intense."

We were straying into territory that was above our pay grade. Then again, context matters. If we knew what caused the injuries, it could help the docs create a better course of treatment. "I don't want to try talking to him now that he's stable. The vibrations could throw him back into shock."

"Quite. Fortunately, I am not so limited." He took a seat facing our patient and narrowed his eyes in concentration. I could hear his thoughts.

*Are you able to understand me?*

No reaction from the patient, but Karrak must have heard something.

*We are pleased that you are feeling better. Try to stay relaxed. Can you tell me more about your accident?*

That got a reaction. The Mintakan's skin tensed up.

"Careful, Karrak. Looks like you hit a nerve."

That confused him. "I have not inserted any . . . ah. I understand now. Yes, he does seem anxious." Karrak turned back to our patient. *Would you like more sedatives? We can increase the dosage a bit.*

He must have agreed. Karrak swiped a finger at the infusion pump, which dispensed a few more milliliters of happy juice. The Mintakan's tension released, his skin returning to its natural, pliable state.

*I understand your hesitation, but if we can have a better understanding of what caused your injuries, then the physicians will be able to provide an optimal course of treatment. As my partner might say, it is for your own good.*

Nice one, Karrak. He was silent for several moments, occasionally nodding his head. Finally, he stepped away from the Mintakan and motioned for me to join him in the back of the squad.

"He is quite reluctant to divulge the root cause of his accident, even under increased sedation."

We were dancing all over an ethical line here, taking advantage of a patient's drugged condition to get information. "First things first. How is he feeling?"

"Much better, though I suspect the additional sedative contributed to that."

No kidding. "What did he tell you about the accident?"

"Not as much as we might prefer. He was overseeing modifications to their reactor plant, which experienced an unexpected surge in output. That surge overwhelmed the photon shield."

"So it really was that simple. A flash burn."

"Perhaps not. The Mintakans have been investigating alternative drive systems to compensate for the Element 115 shortage. I strongly suspect this is related to that work."

This was getting way outside of my area of expertise. I couldn't imagine what kinds of alternatives to directly manipulating gravity might exist. "They can perceive different dimensions. What do you think that's like for them?"

"It is as difficult for my kind to comprehend as it is for you. It is one thing to know something else is there; interacting with it is an entirely different proposition. I would compare it to being able to see the view through your window, yet you cannot step outside."

"They can see what else is out there, but that's all? Take observations, but not interact."

"Precisely so. They believe if that barrier can be crossed, it will open up possibilities which are presently out of reach."

Interesting, but ultimately not relevant right now. I placed my hands on my hips and sighed. We'd learned what we could, and had to be satisfied with the knowledge that whatever had happened, our patient hadn't uncorked some kind of radioactive nightmare.

Orderlies were waiting for us in the hangar and jumped into action as soon as the pressurization field opened. It was a quartet of Gliesans, the little insectoid guys. Okay, not really "little" at all in insect terms, but they were still small compared to everyone else.

They'd brought a hyperbaric oxygen pod and immediately moved to get our patient off the gurney and onto its platform. They took opposite corners, using their mandibles to lift the Mintakan and settle him into the pod. It sounds rough, but Gliesans could be surprisingly gentle when necessary. They activated the pod's containment field and began bathing our patient in high-pressure oxygen.

While they were at work, we briefed the attending physician on the patient's condition. Estimated age (because Mintakans didn't track that stuff), cause and extent of injuries, vital signs, meds we'd administered, the usual. The Reticulan doctor showed no emotion, silently studying our notes in his data crystal.

I could see by their body language that he was having a side conversation with Karrak, all telepathic. On the one hand it was undeniably efficient, on the other it was a little insulting to be cut out of the loop. It wasn't personal, but it wasn't the first time either.

When our shift ended, I changed into a pair of jeans and a light blouse and made my way to the biodome. It was the closest thing here to the environment on Earth, and the Emissaries had a cozy little diner tucked away in a clearing. Their food was pretty good on its own, but the chefs had made a hobby of experimenting with human cuisine for my benefit. They always had something new for me to try, and over time they'd turned me into something of a foodie.

Not to say there hadn't been some bumps in the road as they figured out flavors, textures and such. Thai noodles don't pair well with spaghetti sauce, for instance. Medium rare is delicious if it's a filet mignon, but not so much for fried chicken.

I was once again feeling the need for some old-fashioned comfort food, so today's "Mel Special" was a BLT with a bowl of potato soup. I'd taught them how to make it from my grandma's recipe, which they tarted up with some Chalawani spices to make it pop.

I took a seat at a table outside, beneath an Eridani willow tree. I couldn't tell you what the Eridanis called it, but that's what it looked like and I enjoyed the faint honey fragrance of its periwinkle blue blooms. Emissaries strolled in and out of the diner, most pairing up for walks through the dome's meticulously cultivated orchards. The whole sector had the feel of a Japanese meditation garden. It was exquisitely landscaped, a masterpiece of planning and prudent forestry.

And I was enjoying it by myself.

There's a difference between solitude and being alone. I didn't always mind the former, but today the latter was getting to me. It wasn't like I was lacking for friends, it's just that they were all different. Or rather, *I* was different. Like a favored pet.

No. Pets didn't work alongside their humans. Okay, there were police dogs, but . . .

*Damn it.* I shook my head as if it might toss out the intrusive thoughts that were seriously screwing with my karma.

A muffled chime caught my attention. I reached into my back pocket for my crystal, somewhat annoyed. Hadn't she been dormant?

Apparently not. The crystal pulsed with a dim yellow light. "What's up, Clara?"

"Sorry Mel, but there's a message waiting for you. The sender wouldn't wait."

I rolled my eyes and tapped the pulsing light to open the message: YOUR PRESENCE IS REQUESTED AT LEVEL 1 LANDING BAY, RHO SECTOR.

Rho sector was the official name for the section of the Capital ring I lived in. The landing bay was almost directly below where I was sitting.

I looked over my shoulder reflexively, wary of a prank. Of course, that never happened here. Not like back at the firehouse, where pranking was a part of daily life. That's what happens when you stick a bunch of type-A personalities in one place and expect them to wait around for something to happen. I'd tried it exactly once in the Med Corps, and it hadn't gone over well at all. It wasn't even that much of a prank, I just swapped out Karrak's coveralls for a larger size. Reticulans like things to be skin-tight and he'd failed to see the humor.

I returned to the pulsating crystal. "Who is this?"

No reply, other than to repeat the message:
YOUR PRESENCE IS REQUESTED. PLEASE ARRIVE WITHIN TWENTY GU-STANDARD MINUTES.

"How do I know who I'm looking for?"

YOUR PRESENCE IS REQUESTED. PLEASE—

"I got it. Twenty standard minutes."

I briefly wondered if this was a setup, with some alien perv in a white van waiting to take me to his extraterrestrial sex dungeon. I quickly shook that off as Union cities tended to be pretty safe. Crime was unheard of, and in that sense it really was something of the alien utopia you might find in a movie. The GU's problems were mainly of the bureaucratic snafu variety. Things worked so well here that everyone tended to go through life with blinders on. When everything ran perfectly, minor imperfections had outsized effects. Maybe that's why I liked the Thubans so much. They were soldiers, which meant they knew what's what.

Still, I wasn't going along just because some faceless entity said so. "I'll ask this one more time: Who is this?"

The pulsing message light froze, as if someone on the other end was thinking about it. Finally there was an answer, but it wasn't through the crystal.

*I am Deela.*

Reticulan, then. That relieved my suspicions. It says a lot about my acclimation to this place that I was fundamentally okay with going to meet a telepathic gray alien with an oversized head and inky black eyes.

It was a quick walk to a lift which went straight down to the landing bay. I'd been here maybe twice during my entire stay in the Union; most of my trips outside of the Ring had been on ambulance runs. The Level One bay was for "priority transports," the big shots. Even the most egalitarian societies had their movers, shakers, and influence peddlers. It was something of a universal constant.

Even if my visits here had been few and far between, it was obvious that something was off. The Level One bay was empty, save for a silvery saucer in the middle of the hangar. The expansive bay made the little ship appear even smaller than it was. Beside it stood a lone Reticulan who held up her hand in greeting.

*Hello, Melanie Mooney. I am Deela.*

"It's just Mel."

She cocked her head and blinked. Reticulan eyelids move horizontally, not vertically like ours. It can be an attention-grabber the first time you see it.

*Unusual. Human female forenames often end in a vowel sound, similar to ours.*

"It's a nickname. You can call me Melanie if that's easier."

*Thank you, Melanie.*

I looked past her for any clues as to why she'd brought me here. "You're alone?"

*I am.*

I crossed my arms and eyed her skeptically. "You don't look like you need medical attention."

*That is correct. I represent someone who has requested you for that purpose. I am to be your pilot and escort today.*

That made me do a double take. "Excuse me? Where are we going?"

*I'm afraid our destination cannot be divulged.*

I jerked a thumb over my shoulder. "I don't have any gear. I'll need to check out a trauma bag from the Med Corps first."

*That will not be necessary.*

"Not much I can do without the right gear."

*Everything you might need will be supplied.* A portal winked open on the side of the saucer, and she gestured for me to step aboard. *If you please, we must be on our way. I have arranged for suitable human accommodations.*

I poked my head inside. The juxtaposition of alien and human furnishings was striking. There was a standard semicircular couch made of acceleration gel, plus another one that could've passed for a first-class seat on an airliner.

"Seriously? I haven't seen one of these in ages." Not that I'd had many opportunities to fly first class.

*Our patron finds this style to be more agreeable.*

"Our patron?" I was getting suspicious again. "Who are we going to see?"

*Gideon requests the honor of your presence. His yacht is currently transiting this sector. Please take a seat, we must rendezvous soon.*

Before I could protest, the portal winked shut behind us and I could feel the gravity drive begin to spin up.

# 6

My only other encounter with Gideon's yacht had been during the chaos of the Tanaan disaster, the result of one of his many off-the-books projects going sideways. He and I had not gotten off to a good start, which tends to happen when the other party is responsible for a minor planet tearing itself to pieces. Strangely enough, the Union had never quite settled on a final cause for that catastrophe, which suggested they'd been aware of his zero point experiments. Maybe it hadn't been as off-the-books as I'd thought.

Did I mention bureaucratic ass-covering was another universal constant?

Calling his ship a "yacht" didn't really do the thing justice. It was more like a flying private estate, able to take him wherever he pleased without leaving home. The main structure was an ellipsoid biodome similar to those which festooned the Capital City ring. Drawing from my previous life in the country, I estimated the area inside the dome to be a solid five acres. All of the machinery needed to make Gideon's floating greenhouse into a proper spaceship was mounted beneath the dome's frame, a stark contrast to the lush gardens inside.

We pulled into a spotless landing bay. Next to us sat the sleek metallic teardrop of a Class II shuttle, the kind of thing big shots used to zip around between solar systems when they were in a hurry. It was in fact the same basic hull our Med Corps transports were built from, just a lot swankier inside.

Deela led me to a lift which quickly deposited us in the center of the biodome. We emerged beside a tranquil pond nestled among deciduous trees that resembling oaks and maples. I wondered if he had brought seedlings from Earth, or had somehow gene-edited them from other Union varieties?

A lone bench was set between a pair of crimson Japanese maples. This was where my host waited.

Gideon was as I remembered him: gray hair slicked back above a gaunt face that showed the years, his eyes darkened by age. He wore a robin's egg blue linen suit, sans tie. In its place was a paisley silk ascot. I guessed this meant "business casual" where he was from. Or rather, when.

He stood as I approached, his hands gripping the head of a cane. I noticed a slight wobble as he rose: balance issues, a common problem in old age. We had biomechanical solutions for that, and I wondered why he hadn't taken advantage of them. Maybe he just preferred the low-tech approach, or his genes had been tweaked to the point where they wouldn't work. My money was on the latter.

Gideon smoothed the front of his suit, which made me unexpectedly self-conscious about my own appearance. Remembering that I hadn't used makeup during my entire tenure in the Union will do that. I ran my fingers through my hair in a vain attempt to get my curls under control.

He welcomed me with a disarming smile. Considering our only other encounter had been a bit contentious, I'd halfway expected him to crack me across the shins with his cane. "Miss Mooney."

"Mister Stone."

That smile ended at his eyes. "I see you've done your homework since we last met."

I have to admit to a little skullduggery here. I'd been curious about his history with the Union, and being in the Med Corps gave me access to a lot of records. They're not as picky about privacy here as we were back home, where looking into patient history just out of interest is frowned upon. As in the "gets you fired" kind of frowned upon.

Gideon Xavier Stone had come here after an encounter with a survey mission in the Nevada desert. It still wasn't clear how he'd ingratiated himself enough to earn residency, but the official story was he'd been a logistical genius and had become something of a pivotal figure in the Union economy. How he'd become a pariah was a little clearer, but there were still a lot of blanks to fill in.

"Due diligence, I believe you call it."

He gave a slight twitch of an eyebrow. "You believe correctly." He swept a hand toward the bench. "If you please? I'm not much for standing these days."

At his age, he shouldn't have been up for much of anything. Even without the dilation effects of seventy-plus years spent zipping around at relativistic speeds, his proper age was well north of a hundred. Union medicine had slowed the aging process considerably, but entropy has a way of catching up with all of us no matter how many genes are edited.

Old or not, I could feel his eyes on me as we sat. Should I have changed into something more businesslike? For that matter, why did I care? "Something wrong?"

He shook his head. "Not at all. Forgive me, but ladies' fashions have changed since my time on Earth."

"A lot of things have changed. When we first met, you acted surprised to see a woman in the position I was in."

"You were running a rather large rescue operation," he pointed out. "No, that's not something I'd have typically seen women doing in my day."

"I was playing the hand I'd been dealt. I was the first medic on scene with any kind of mass casualty training. Honestly I was shocked the Med Corps didn't already have contingency plans for something at that scale." Of course, the whole operation had only been necessary thanks to his monkeying around with dangerous new energy sources.

"It's a weakness inherent in high-functioning, egalitarian societies," he said with a hint of distaste. "When everything works as it's supposed to, when all the gears mesh for long enough, we tend to forget how badly things can go wrong. From what I've been able to gather, we keep having to relearn that lesson on Earth." He tutted. "A shame, really. One would think history would have driven that lesson home."

"One would think." He was apparently immune to irony. "You didn't bring me here to reminisce."

There was a glint in his eye, however weak. "Well, perhaps a little. I do wish to discuss Earth with you. I suspect it has been on your mind of late."

I leaned away and squinted at him. "What makes you think that?"

He pointed his cane at me. "Your outfit, for one. You've been spending more time in clothing styled from Earth fashions, and consuming a good deal of synthesizer fabric to make them."

Now how in the hell would he know that?

He no doubt read the look on my face. "The clothing synth franchises are one of my investments. Simple mining of logistical records, my dear."

It was an unwelcome reminder that highly connected societies tended to have a distressing lack of privacy. "Anything else?"

"Your food consumption is less inclined toward exploring Union cuisine, and more toward simple human fare. What's the current term, 'comfort food'?"

"You have a stake in the nutrisynths, too?"

He laughed. "No, that's from basic observation."

I lifted my chin and glared down at him. "You've been spying on me."

"Tsk. You make it sound so mercenary when I'm simply scouting prospects. It's purely business. Due diligence, as you said yourself."

He had me there. I'd spied on his medical records, after all. I shot a glance at the Reticulan who'd brought me here. She'd remained at a respectful distance by the lift entry. I tried to recall if I'd seen her before, which was a near-hopeless task with the Grays. Their individual differences were so subtle as to be unnoticeable except for among the handful I worked with on a regular basis. Grays were naturally curious and painstakingly observant; this was why they dominated the Survey ministry and were the main characters in so many UFO stories. In a society where they were just part of the background, they made for frighteningly effective spies. Or scouts, to use Gideon's preferred term.

I jerked my head in Deela's direction. "How long has she been tailing me?"

Gideon checked his watch. It was of a traditional style like mine, but calibrated for Union standard time. And a lot more expensive-looking. "A few weeks, enough to learn your patterns." He must have picked up on my skepticism. "This was purely for your convenience, I assure you. I decided it was best to keep our meeting on short notice, 'under the table.' I also thought it best to arrange it for one of your days off. There's no sense putting undue pressure on you during working hours."

I sighed. "Thanks, I think."

He leaned back against the bench with satisfaction. "You may have more time to thank me than you realize." He paused. "You're feisty. Much as that may be uncomfortable for me, I need someone who can call things as they see them. Someone who isn't afraid to tell me things I might not want to hear." He leaned in closer. "Someone who isn't afraid to piss me off."

I suspected he hadn't had enough of that in his life. But why me? "You're not looking for a new business associate. I'm sure you've learned enough about me to understand that would be a bad idea."

Gideon tapped his fingers atop his cane. "That would depend on the business venture, but in this case you're correct." He fixed his eyes on me. "Undergraduate degree in biology from Purdue. Post-graduate studies in veterinary medicine, interrupted to pursue emergency medicine for reasons which appear to be deeply personal."

He said it in a way that telegraphed he knew exactly why I'd left the DVM program. "Your point?"

"My point is the very background which has made you so valuable to the Medical Corps has value to me as well." He pointed a bony finger at his chest. "I have benefited from decades of the Union's best medical care. I have lived long beyond my years, perhaps longer than I deserve."

Couldn't argue with that. At least he showed a faint glimmer of self-awareness. "Are you looking for a personal nurse? Because I'm not qualified for that." I was especially not interested in the "personal" part.

A gravelly chuckle. "You may reconsider once you understand what I want to do." He looked away through the dome to the stars beyond. "What I *need* to do."

"What would that be?"

A corner of his mouth upturned conspiratorially. "Return to Earth, of course."

I jumped up from the bench. "And how would you know—"

"How would I know that's what you're thinking as well?" He nodded toward Deela and tapped at his temple. "You don't get where I am without knowing the right people. Or rather, beings."

I set my hands on my hips. "Of course. You've been using her to read my mind."

He patted the bench for me sit back down. "Please don't take offense. My little endeavor holds great promise, and there are many interested parties who wish to see a successful outcome. It is also quite sensitive. Anyone brought into this project must be completely trustworthy."

I sank back onto the bench beside him. "And you've decided I'm 'completely trustworthy.'"

"Enough to broach the subject. What you do with the information is up to you, though I believe you'll ultimately see the value in it. You'll certainly appreciate how mutually beneficial my proposal is."

I took in a deep breath. "Then let's quit dancing around the subject." I looked up and down the length of his massive flying garden estate. "You have the means to go back right now, I imagine. What's stopping you?"

He turned to me with a wistful grin. "Time, Mooney. Time. The same inescapable hurdle that vexes you."

I let my guard down. "Earth is almost two decades ahead of me right now. If I don't go back soon, there won't be much point."

"Precisely. Travel fast enough to feel like it's making a difference, and the problem only becomes worse."

"I still don't understand. You left behind everything you knew long ago. Why the sudden urgency?"

He patted his chest. "This old body is reaching the limits of Union longevity treatments. You can only tweak a man's telomeres so far before his DNA becomes something other than human." He coughed. "I need to get back."

"Not content to die of old age here?" It was something of a jab, but I understood.

His face grew hard. "There are certain personal affairs I must tend to before my time comes, one in particular which the Union cannot provide." Another cough. "Last rites, from an ordained priest."

That was unexpected. "Yeah, I suppose there isn't one of those within a few thousand light-years." It didn't resolve the question of time, though. "I still don't get it. This ship should be able to get you home in a matter of weeks." It would still be much longer in Earth-centered time, but at this late stage it was hard to see how that mattered.

Gideon's reply was terse. "It would be a long trip, and I'm in something of a hurry."

I was growing tired of his evasiveness. "Well then, you've stumped me. If gravity drives aren't fast enough, then how are you planning to do this?"

His eyes brightened, as if the faint glimmer of hope was tangible. "We're calling it the 'jump drive.' It enables near-instantaneous movement across vast distances. Engage the drive and you disappear from one place and reappear in another. No warping of space, no acceleration to near light speed to cover the distance." He leaned in and tapped his watch. "And no time dilation."

My eyes widened. "So just like that," I said with a snap of my fingers, "and we can be back at Earth?"

He shook his head. "Not quite. The quantum uncertainty principle is a difficult hurdle. My scientists have sufficient confidence it can be managed over short distances . . . on a cosmic scale, of course. We have to recalibrate the navigation logic after each jump."

"How many jumps to get back?"

"Current calculations are twelve."

Twelve skips and we're home, without decades of time lag. What's not to like about that? "What's the catch?"

"The catch is we will be punching holes through one point in space and coming out the other side. Going through somewhere we don't necessarily belong." He fixed his gaze on me. "That can take a toll on the body."

"You want me along to make sure you survive the trip."

"In so many words, yes." He pulled a data crystal from inside his jacket and made a flicking motion over its face. "Here's my direct contact. You have forty-eight hours to decide."

# 7

Forty-eight hours was a day and a half by Union standards, essentially the remainder of my time off. Gideon had no doubt known that and had arranged our meeting accordingly. He seemed to already know a lot, and having a Reticulan tailing me only worked in his favor.

That grated on me. Grays aren't as frightening as the alien abduction stories would have you believe, though their oversized heads and jet-black eyes trigger some deep-seated phobias in a lot of people. Over time I'd become comfortable with their telepathic gifts, and had developed a rudimentary ability to block out thoughts I didn't want to share. It was the little things I'd let down my guard over, like thinking about what to do with my time off. What grated on me even more was that Gideon had exploited this knowledge in his favor, even if he was offering an intriguing solution to my "what next" problem.

He was the type for whom exploitation came naturally, as if it was baked into his personality. It was the opposite trait which had made the Grays so endearing: Ask a question, and they'd give an honest answer. If they couldn't, they'd tell you why. There was no guessing where you stood with them, which was more than I could say for a lot of humans.

Humans like Gideon Stone. How truthful had he been with me? People like him tended to play their cards close to the vest, only letting others know what they wanted them to know at the most advantageous time. It was a classic manipulation tactic, a way for powerful men to herd people like cattle.

He'd leveraged that instinct to become a big shot in the Union. This wasn't as surprising as it should have been considering the galactic goat-rope of our response at Tanaan. I couldn't let go of the fact that the disaster had been caused by his experiments. Sanctioned or not, he was personally responsible for the destruction of an entire planet. How could anyone look past that?

I might not have the advantage of Reticulan telepaths telling me what was going on in his head, but there was still a lot of information available in the archives. It was time for a deeper dive into Gideon's history.

I went to the kitchen and paused in front of the nutrisynth. Coffee or beer? Over time I'd coaxed it into crafting a decent approximation of American lagers, but this called for focus. Coffee it was.

I took a fresh cup of espresso roast and plopped onto the divan in my living room. I set my crystal on a table and touched its face with my biometric ring. This unlocked what amounted to superuser access, one of the perks of being a senior Med Corps tech. The crystal glowed, waiting for my command.

"Clara, show Union residency history of the human Gideon Xavier Stone."

"Sure thing, just a minute." A hologram appeared in the air with his picture, accompanied by a long scrolling summary of his time in the Union. I let her narrate. "Gideon Stone was selected for observation in GU annum 4705, or 1951 AD by your calendar. He was an industrial engineer with specialties in manufacturing and materials science, which he honed during Earth's most recent World War."

"Most recent?" That was encouraging; they hadn't kicked off WWIII while I was gone.

"I don't have the latest observatory reports, but that's what the record shows." She continued, "Anyway, the contact narrative says, 'Subject did not register alarm at survey team's appearance and fully cooperated with standard field screening regimens.'"

That drew a mordant chuckle. "I guess the anal probes didn't change his mind, then."

Clara laughed with me, and I had no doubt it was genuine. "Apparently not. Listen to this: 'Upon completion of screening regimen, subject expressed interest in accompanying survey team on their return to Union space. Subject in fact was rather adamant on this point.'"

Now *that* was interesting. "Any indication of why?"

Clara cleared her electronic throat. "Quote: 'Subject expressed great enthusiasm for space travel in general, and showed particular interest in Union civilization,' unquote."

That sounded too easy. "And they just let him in?"

"Says here they gave him the standard warning about wiping his memory if he chose to return to Earth, all the usual Survey Ministry protocols. You know the drill. He stated that their 'terms were acceptable.'"

That was awfully confident for somebody who'd just been picked up by Grays. Keep in mind this had been back when flying saucers and little green men were still on the fringes of cultural awareness. Why hadn't he been scared shitless like everyone else who'd run into them? "You said his background was industrial engineering. Materials science. Who'd he work for?"

"The record says he was a contractor for an advanced research bureau of your country's defense establishment."

I laughed out loud. "He worked for the Pentagon." Now we were getting somewhere. "Where, specifically?"

"He traveled extensively between facilities within the provinces of your American Southwest." She began ticking off locations. "Palmdale, California. Los Alamos, New Mexico. Groom Lake, Nevada. You know any of these places?"

"Los Alamos sound familiar. I think that's where they built the first atom bombs."

"Bingo. That's when the Survey Ministry activity ramped up. Hang on, there's more here on Groom Lake . . . looks like your people call it 'Area 51.' Does that ring a bell?"

"You bet it does! Everybody thinks we're keeping alien . . . err, Union, spacecraft there."

"They're not entirely wrong, Mel. As you say, the devil's in the details."

"You said the Union 'selected' him for observation. Why?" I asked while lifting the coffee cup to my lips. I should have known better.

"Gideon was engaged in a wide range of activity that caught the Union's attention. In particular, he was a principal in studying the material properties of a lost Survey Ministry craft which had been recovered in another region of this 'New Mexico' place."

Clara's hologram stuttered as I spit my coffee right through it. "That's kind of an important detail! Why didn't you tell me earlier?"

"You didn't ask."

I kneaded my forehead. Despite Clara's down-home affectations, synthetic intelligence could be annoyingly matter-of-fact. "He'd been in on the Roswell coverup, probably studying Union tech the whole damned time!" No wonder the Grays hadn't frightened him. He'd seen their dead cohorts in whatever black-project freezer they'd been stored in.

"Another bingo. You're on a roll. This 'Roswell' incident was a significant factor in his selection."

"And nobody in the Survey Ministry had a problem with bringing him in?"

"Not at all. Like I said, he was informed of the memory cleansing protocol."

Hell, they probably *wanted* to wipe his memory at that point. They'd been playing nice by offering him a glimpse of the Union, maybe they'd thought it was a fair trade. Still, it would've been a huge risk on Survey's part. "You know that memory wiping hasn't always worked, right? That maybe Gideon thought there was a good chance he could recover his memories with hypnosis?"

"This is just what's in the archives. I can't comment on hypotheticals any more than you. But to your point, deficiencies in the memory protocols were identified later. Humans have turned out to be particularly resilient. That's why contacts were limited after the initial surge."

That was after a spate of abductees—excuse me, "subjects"—began recalling what had happened to them, in often unpleasant ways. Not a good look for the Survey Ministry. "If Gideon was eventually granted residency, that meant someone thought Earth was ready for first contact. Right?" In other words, same as me. See how the test human does, then pull back the curtain.

"Gideon's selection was the first stage of that process, based on his exposure to Union citizens and technology. Survey wanted to evaluate him as a potential human interlocutor. It wasn't considered wise to directly reveal the Union's existence to the larger human race at the time."

"I get it. No flying saucers landing on the White House lawn."

"In so many words, yes. Humans can be rather excitable."

Tell me about it. We were depressingly good at overreacting. "Well, we know he didn't go back. Why was he allowed to stay?"

"Because he asked."

Sigh. "It couldn't have been that simple. What benefit did the Union see in keeping him around?"

"First Contact protocols are tailored for the unique characteristics of the species in question. Like I said, your kind can be excitable. The Ministry decided that long-term observation of a willing participant was useful."

"Useful enough that they decided to back off for a while. What can you tell me about his time here?"

"Gideon was happy with the Ministry's decision to grant him residency. Exceedingly so, some thought. He immersed himself in all of the different Union cultures and came to show particular interest in the Reticulans and Gliesans. He spent several years living among them."

Of course he did. Between the two races, they performed the bulk of Union scientific investigation and construction. He was figuring out the industrial base and which openings to exploit. "He came here with nothing but the clothes on his back. What did he do to become so successful?"

"That's a topic of some controversy. After his time with the Reticulan and Gliesan races, he enrolled in a variety of academic programs. It was an eclectic mix of cultural studies, Union law, and physical sciences. In your culture, you'd call him a polymath. A 'Renaissance Man.'"

That was one way of putting it. "What did he do with that education?"

"Gideon envisioned methods to improve the Union's manufacturing and logistical infrastructure. He proposed ways to increase efficiencies by leveraging the unique traits of our component cultures, which I have to admit we weren't especially good at. They were small changes, but they proved to be effective."

"So what was the controversy?"

"This is where it gets fuzzy. Some have maintained that he identified loopholes in Union labor ordinances which redounded to his benefit. This brought some pointed questions from the Justice

Ministry, but in the end his methods were deemed to be legal, if unsavory."

That sounded all too familiar. "I'm not quite getting this. Word gets around, even on a galactic scale. Why would anyone work for him?"

"That question has been posed many times. The records indicate those who have been involved with his projects seem to find the work fulfilling and worth the sacrifice. It's an interesting dichotomy for sure."

"What can you tell me about his latest project?"

"I'm sorry, but that information is incomplete and most of it is subject to non-disclosure statutes. The construction permit he was granted for the zero point energy experiments on Tanaan is the last official record. There's some evidence of late that he's been investigating improved methods for interstellar travel."

That much I knew. "Thank you, that's enough about Gideon for now. Let's move on to these 'improved methods' you mentioned. What can you tell me about jump drives?"

"How much detail do you want?"

"You know me. Keep it simple."

Clara let out an electronic sigh. "I'll do my best. The so-called 'jump drive' is a method for inter-dimensional tunneling, utilizing tightly focused gravity fields. It's been theorized and extensively modeled; however no working prototypes are known to exist."

"What's keeping us from building one? Union tech seems up to the task."

"There are several pacing items, but a couple stand out. Energy density and visualization of higher dimensions are at the top of the list. While dimensional tunneling theories have held up to scrutiny, doing so would require exotic energy sources in quantities which are, in practical terms, infinite."

"Would this 'zero point' energy fit the bill?"

"Sure would, in fact that's the proposed solution. It's the only variable which closes the current physics model."

"You said visualization is the other problem. What's that about?"

"Let me see. It's difficult to explain in terms a three-dimensional being can understand. Even human researchers have detected evidence of higher dimensions in the behavior of subatomic particles, but that's not the same as direct observation. It's impossible to interact with dimensions in which we don't exist."

"But the Mintakans can, right?"

"To an extent. They can 'see' higher dimensions in a broad sense, but can't interact with them. Not the same thing."

It was just as Karrak had described, like looking through a window you can't open. "What are the risks of this 'tunneling' thing?"

"The 'uncertainty principle' is the biggest risk. Even if a method to enter extradimensional space is possible, quantum uncertainty suggests that navigating back to where you want to be in normal space could be impossible. The end states are unpredictable and always changing."

That could explain the short jumps Gideon had talked about. Jump back, recalibrate, then jump again. "What you're saying is it's impossible to see where you're going."

"In so many words, yes. At the risk of connecting too many dots, lately Gideon has been consulting with a small team of Mintakan researchers. Maybe he's investigating dimensional tunneling?"

A race of beings who can see into other dimensions could be useful for a project like that. "Clara, you might be right. Thank you."

"No problem."

I pinched at the hologram, turning it off and storing Clara's research for later.

What had I learned? Gideon was a savvy businessman who had turned himself into a galactic tycoon by exploiting loopholes in the law and taking advantage of a couple of races' natural industriousness. It was a marvel that some other enterprising soul hadn't thought to do the same thing, but a hands-off attitude toward other cultures was the Union's single most defining characteristic.

Gideon Stone hadn't been so restrained, though his eagerness to live as the only human among trillions of aliens stumped me. I guess Earth just wasn't enough for some people.

And now, at the end of his life, he was desperate to get back. Desperate enough that he was willing to risk tunneling through unseen dimensions of the universe with an experimental drive that could just as easily vaporize his ship and everyone on it.

And he'd invited me along for the ride, which begged the question: How desperate did he think *I* was?

# 8

I hadn't seen much of my friend Bjorn lately. After chaperoning me through my initiation in the Medical Corps, he'd returned to diplomatic duty, jetting across Union space on ambassadorial missions with his companion, Sven.

We had become close after they'd recruited me away from my home in Indiana. Bjorn was an Emissary, an empath. Emissaries couldn't read minds like Reticulans, but they could get awfully close to it by sensing emotions. If you think you're clever at reading someone's body language, these guys will put you to shame. And for all the wildly non-human races I've encountered out here, theirs is one of the closest to ours. This makes the differences stand out, and it can be a little unsettling to the uninitiated.

I sat on a French Revival-style divan in his suite. He'd taken a liking to human craftsmanship during his Survey Ministry work, which was reflected in the eclectic mix of furniture and artwork he'd reproduced after his expeditions to Earth.

It might not have been the smartest thing for me to do, and Gideon would've been pissed had he known, but I had to talk my decision through with someone who could be trusted completely. It also helped that his status as an Emissary meant his residence was scrupulously shielded from any surreptitious snooping. This included curious Grays who might be trying to get inside our heads. Deela could've been standing outside the front door and the privacy fields would have made our minds look like blank slates. Right then, mine felt like a bowl of cooked spaghetti.

It was the first time I'd been able to relax since returning from Gideon's spacefaring estate, and I'd been speed-talking through his proposal. Bjorn listened dutifully, occasionally brushing his golden hair back behind his ears. It could be easy to forget that the Emissaries weren't actually human, despite their close family resemblance. His tightly drawn lips signaled concern.

"This is a risky proposition, Melanie."

"I kind of figured that. We've seen what zero point energy can do, and I can't begin to imagine what kind of weird physics are involved with this jump drive." I took that opportunity to convey my suspicions about the Mintakan's mysterious flash burns.

He studied me with emerald-green eyes so intense as to be almost luminous. "Intriguing, but I was actually referring to your status in the Union."

"Oh. Yeah. Have to admit, that was the last thing on my mind. I was more concerned about getting vaporized or trapped in some alternate reality."

"There is that as well." He gestured at his data crystal sitting on a nearby table, and a copy of my contract materialized in the air between us. "I'm compelled to advise you of certain clauses in your agreement." He made a flicking motion and the text scrolled down into the fine print. "You are free to return at any time, but there are certain conditions attached."

"You mean the mind wipe."

"Precisely. You consented to having all memories of your time here permanently erased." He appeared saddened by this. "I am truly sorry, Melanie. I wish it were different, but until the human race has been deemed ready for first contact, this clause is inviolable."

Reading further, something in the text caught my eye. "Wait a minute." I swiped at the hologram, digging deeper into the fine print. "Have a look at this. There might be a loophole." I grabbed at another clause and highlighted it. "Says here the Union will provide me with transportation back to Earth, should I decide to return. But that's not happening any time soon, not with the 115 shortage. What happens when the Union can't hold up its end of the bargain?"

Bjorn stroked his chin as he studied the clause. He seemed amused. "That is an interesting argument. What, indeed? How can we enforce the one condition when we are unable to provide the other?"

"Exactly. If I want to go home, I'm on my own."

"True, to a certain extent. While you would still be subject to our first contact protocols, we would have no ability to enforce them. An interesting conundrum."

It was funny—okay, not really—that he could be so indifferent about the fate of my memory. It was tempting to pretend I didn't care either, but that wouldn't have been true. I'd learned and done so much, it'd be crazy to willingly flush all of those experiences down the drain. Bjorn would plant some story that I'd been in a coma the whole time, and in reality I wouldn't be able to tell any difference. "What would happen if I did this? I'm not the kind of person who just doesn't show up for work anymore. I'd have to turn in my notice, or whatever it's called here."

"A good point. Even if you shared your plans with no one else, there would be many questions."

I hadn't thought of the burden it would put on my friends here, especially the Emissaries. "What would that mean for you?"

He glanced away, a clue that the gears were turning in his head. "Whatever you say to me here is held in the strictest confidence, but there is a process for non-citizen residents who leave Union space. Someone would eventually have to catch up with you, as you would say."

Like chasing down an immigrant who'd decided to go back, just to make sure they didn't blab to everyone else about how good they'd had it.

"You are disturbed by this eventuality."

"I'd be making myself into an illegal alien, in reverse." Pun fully intended. "And I'd be exposing you to legal trouble."

Bjorn waved that away. "Do not concern yourself with such matters. As Emissaries, we are accorded a certain level of diplomatic immunity. While not absolute, it does allow us a considerable flexibility."

I stared at my feet. While it was nice to be reassured I wouldn't be dragging my friend into breaking the law, it did nothing to quiet the simmering conflict within me. "I was running away when I came here, and now it feels like I'm about to do it again."

"You are too hard on yourself." He placed a hand on my arm. "Your life on Earth was not what you wished it to be. We offered you an opportunity which you embraced. You have done quite well here, but perhaps this phase of your life is coming to its natural end. Doesn't one of your religious texts teach that for everything, there is a season?"

I looked up. "You've read that?"

"Of course. Studying the culture of prospective species is part of our job. Universal wisdom is not confined to our civilization."

"It feels like I'm giving up."

"Giving up, or moving on?"

Good point. For all of my worries about becoming hopelessly separated from Earth, I was still focused on the here and now. Short-term thinking. "Both, maybe? Either I go back and try to reinsert myself into human culture," and now I really did sound like an alien, "or commit to staying here for the rest of my life." With no other humans to share the experience with. The only other human in a thousand light-years was about to leave, and there was no telling when Earth might be deemed ready for admission.

"Feelings of isolation are natural for someone in your situation. Be careful to not allow them to lead you into doing something desperate."

"You think I'm acting out of desperation?"

"Difficult to say. On the one hand, yes. On the other, you have reached a natural decision point which is fraught with uncertainty."

I sighed. "It's hard to know what the right move is."

He nodded. "Often the most important choices we make must rely on incomplete information."

"You're not talking about feelings anymore, are you?"

Bjorn smiled. "I believe some of my empathic abilities may have rubbed off on you."

That was nice to hear, and I hoped it was a trait that would stick with me after the eventual memory wipe. "There's still so much I can't get my head around. What do you know about this 'jump drive' Gideon's been fooling around with?"

Bjorn leaned forward. "As I said earlier, it's a risky proposition." He paused, and I doubted it was because he didn't know what to say. More like he was deciding how much to tell me. "Centuries ago, the Mintakans confirmed that higher dimensions exist. While we could not devise experiments to directly observe extradimensional space, with their guidance we could detect its interaction with our own. Shadows of a larger reality, if you will, enough to develop theories of how it might be possible to transit that space." He smiled. "You are not the only one who would like to find a shortcut around relativity."

"Do you have any idea how it would work?"

Bjorn settled back into his chair with a faraway look. "I do, if only superficially." It was a reminder that not every space alien was necessarily a genius scientist. "By definition, higher dimensions exist on a plane beyond our own, where our understanding of physics may not apply. Imagine a universe where time does not unfold in the linear manner we're accustomed to. It simply *is*. All that ever existed, or will exist, does so within a single observable frame of reference. A 'manifold,' if you will."

"Meaning what? That I would experience my entire life all at once," I snapped my fingers, "like *that*?"

"The opposite, in fact. Or rather, both. You would have no sense of time; it would in fact be meaningless. Time would be something that you could move through at will, back and forth. Your life experience would be both instantaneous and eternal."

I sat back, wide-eyed. "That's . . . godlike."

Bjorn looked satisfied that he'd brought his dimwitted student to understanding. "Quite."

"So what's the catch?"

"Our propulsion methods rely on manipulating gravity to distort spacetime and reduce relative distances. That alone takes considerable energy. Opening gateways to enter higher dimensions is at least an order of magnitude more difficult."

Punching holes through space at will sounded like the difference between diesel engines and nuclear power. "Not something even the best antimatter reactor can handle, is it?"

"Most likely no. I suppose one way to think about this problem is to consider that we are talking about entering infinity itself. To do so would also require infinite energy."

I sank at the thought. "Zero point." Enough energy in a fist-sized sphere to melt a planet.

"Again, correct. We have both seen what can happen when there is an uncontrolled release of such energy."

Tanaan, again. I drew my knees up and wrapped my arms around them. I still had nightmares about the planet tearing itself to pieces after its core vaporized. The loss of life had been horrific, even though

Tanaan's only residents had been the Grays and insectoids running the particle accelerators and refineries. "Gideon's betting his life on this, and he doesn't strike me as one to take unnecessary risks." At least not the kind who'd put his own neck on the line. He seemed happy to let others do that.

"That has been on my mind as well. He must have high confidence in whatever new technology he's developed, though I'm not privy to the particulars."

That implied somebody in the Union was. "This is sanctioned, isn't it?"

Bjorn closed his eyes, letting his guard down. I sensed regret. "It would appear so. As I mentioned, you are not the only being who'd like to avoid the effects of time on interstellar travel. The 115 shortage has only added urgency. Gideon has been pursuing this of his own accord, but several Union ministries have been watching with great interest."

"Let me guess: transport, survey, defense . . ."

"All correct."

"But they didn't want to get their hands dirty," I guessed. "Better to let the crazy human do it on his own."

"In a manner of speaking." He fixed his jewel-like eyes on me. "Transiting extradimensional space is not without risk, and not only from the amount of energy required. It is beyond using gravity to bend spacetime—it is more like boring a tunnel beneath it. You would be leaving literally everything you know for the unknown."

Well *that* certainly helped. He'd hit upon something that had been bothering me, something intuitive but out of reach. "If that's the case, what hope is there of getting to where we want to be?"

Bjorn seemed uncertain how to answer. He traced a finger across his lips. "Whatever higher dimensions exist, they do so outside of our notions of space and time. My understanding of jump drive theory is that our three-dimensional space is still there, behaving as we would expect it. If our spacetime is shaped by gravity, extradimensional space simply offers a shortcut."

"Like you said, a tunnel."

He nodded. "Except that the effect is instantaneous. You disappear from one point in space to immediately reappear in another. The question is, will you perceive it as being instantaneous?" He tapped a finger on his chest. "We are what we are, three-dimensional: Height, length, width. Time is considered the fourth, and we experience the universe through this framework. But spacetime is not static. What will you experience once you have left our manifold for another? What does the absence of time do to a being? Or the *totality* of time, to be more precise?"

"Everything all at once," I muttered. "Or nothing at all."

"Quite."

Our discussions of time and space, or the absence thereof, had left my brain in knots. Every answer led to another question. This wasn't simply a new mode of transportation, it was going to be a carnival ride through bizarre regions of "non-space" that could seriously mess with my concept of reality. How could anyone mentally prepare themselves for that?

Not knowing if I was looking for answers or just another sounding board, I did what any normal person would do. I called on my doctor.

Xeelix's office in the main Med Corps campus was a sparse affair, befitting his practical nature. He sat behind a wraparound desk made of a white composite that featured prominently in Reticulan furnishings, and invited me to take a seat in a curvaceous chair of the same material. I could never figure out how the same stuff that made for a rock-hard work surface could be as comfortable to sit in as an overstuffed easy chair.

He'd always been able to put me at ease despite his classic gray alien appearance. Wrinkles appeared around his black eyes, and one corner of his slit mouth turned upward. This was the closest approximation to a smile that a Reticulan could manage.

"Hello, Melanie. It is a pleasure to see you again." His voice had become less raspy over the years as he'd practiced his English. "It has been some time."

"It has. I apologize for not visiting more often." I looked around his office. The walls on either side of his desk were filled with holographic repeaters of patient stats. "Looks like you've been keeping busy."

He followed my gaze. "I have been, and please do not feel as if you need to apologize. You have been keeping busy yourself, I imagine."

I nodded at his right arm, continuing the small talk. "How's the new hand?"

He stretched it out and flexed his long, four-jointed fingers. It looked almost perfect, the only flaw being its newer skin still had a pinkish-gray tint. It was better than the biomechanical appendage he'd had to work with while a permanent replacement was grown. "It still has a few 'kinks,' as you would say. I am able to perform simple procedures again, but it will be some time before I can return to surgical practice."

It was another unpleasant reminder of Tanaan. In Xeelix's case he'd lost his right hand to an erupting volcanic vent, something which tended to appear out of nowhere when a planet is coming to pieces. His new synthetic hand had been grown in a lab, but as you can imagine that process can't be rushed. Bones and tissue first have to grow to maturity. This can only be hurried along so much before running the risk of uncontrolled cell growth, which is a polite term for cancer.

Reticulan bones are especially tricky. They're incredibly dense compared to ours, the tradeoff being that they take a long time to grow and even longer to knit together if broken. And when all is said and done, the recipient has to learn how to use their new limb all over again.

"We had a saying back on Earth: You can't make a baby in a month by putting nine women on the job."

His black eyes narrowed slightly before he erupted in a coarse laugh. "An excellent analogy. Our kind could learn from the human sense of humor." He flexed his hand again. "Earth has been on your mind of late."

I'd known what I was getting into by coming here. Despite the blocking techniques I'd learned, in the end Xeelix would still be able to know what I was thinking. Some things just occupied too much mental space to hide, and in this case there was the matter of maintaining secrecy. I looked at him intently and tapped my forehead. We needed to talk in the traditional Reticulan way.

Xeelix answered with a nod. *You are troubled.*

That's putting it mildly. I have an opportunity to return home, but I don't know what to do with it. The longer I stay, the more distant I feel. Earth is almost twenty years ahead of me, and if I wait much longer...

*There would be no point in returning. Understandable, as your kind is not used to the temporal effects of interstellar travel. Being the first presents unique difficulties.*

Except I'm not exactly the first. If I don't take this opportunity, I'll be the only human within a thousand light-years. And Earth isn't getting any closer to Union membership.

*Not to my knowledge, though I am not privy to the Survey Ministry's inner workings. Your isolation weighs heavily on you.*

It does. I hate to sound ungrateful.

*Do not trouble yourself so. You have been a valuable addition, more than you realize. I do know that your success has put the human race in a much more favorable light. Even if you choose to leave, your contributions will not be forgotten, in particular to my kind and the Gliesans.*

Hah! Have you seen my apartment? It's like they made me their pet project.

*It is a show of great respect and affection. As I said, you will not be forgotten.*

It sounds like you think I've made my mind up.

*I believe so, though you have yet to admit it to yourself.*

I'll miss you, Xeelix.

*Likewise. I have found our time together to be enriching. Humans bring a joy to their vocations that Union races could learn from. Do not concern yourself with the Medical Corps' reaction. I will "run interference" for you, as you might say.*

You know what I'm signing on for. Any thoughts on this "extradimensional quantum jumping" stuff?

*Only that it holds great promise, and great uncertainty. Watch yourself, Melanie. Be aware of your surroundings at all times. We have only the most rudimentary understanding of the universe beyond what we can observe.*

That's not exactly reassuring.

*It is the best I can offer. Good luck to you, Melanie. I hope we can meet again.*

# 9

Back in my apartment, I stood in the living room with a beer from the nutrisynth and gazed out at the biodome. Its verdant forests, sprinkled with a rainbow of fresh blooms, had always been a welcome sight at the end of a long day. Nature always calmed my spirit when I most needed it. On the farm, I'd spent hours on the front porch just staring into the woods.

Now, this peaceful vista taunted me. No matter how beautiful, the not-quite-home differences stood out in ways they hadn't before. The shapes of the leaves and the colors of the flowers were all just a little off, their uncanny perfection a reminder that they were not of Earth.

I rubbed at my temples. Why was this such a struggle?

Bjorn had been right, of course: Sometimes life forces decisions between imperfect choices. That's when you have to take the emotion out of the equation; otherwise you'll do something stupid. I suppose I should have been grateful that neither one was a "least bad" option, but that's actually easier. You resign yourself to what has to be done, and you get going. Having to decide on which might be the better choice is harder, especially when one of them carries a lot of immediate risk.

The choice to remain carried risks which were just as hard to predict: How would I feel in another five years? Ten years? Would I be able to live with the knowledge that the world I'd known had moved so far beyond my experience that I could never hope to fit in?

On the other hand, there was living with the thought that I'd be letting my Union sponsors down. We had an unspoken understanding that if Earth was deemed ready for membership, I would be in the vanguard of any contact mission. The idea was more than a little intimidating, even if it would've been a great honor: Interstellar Ambassador Melanie Mooney. *Greetings, Mr. President, Madame Prime Minister. On behalf of the Galactic Union . . .*

Of course, that scenario depended on it happening within my lifetime. Bjorn and Xeelix hadn't dropped any more hints in that regard; then again, they weren't the type to do so. So many Union races were so highly evolved, ruled by reason and logic instead of passions. It made for a peaceful existence, but it was a bit like taking the spices out of a recipe. That's what I liked about Chonk and the other Thubans. Being the Union's only line of defense, they were a little more grounded. They had a risky job, took it on with a no-nonsense attitude, and knew how to let their hair—or feathers—down when they were back in port. I would miss those guys.

Could that connection be stronger than the longing I currently felt for Earth? If this had been a passing feeling, I might be able to overcome it. But it had been building over time, the sense that life was leaving me behind, that I had unfinished business.

What would that business be? I had no desire to finish veterinary school. After my experience here, it would feel like settling for something less. The farm was still waiting, but dropping back into my old life there wasn't an option either. I'd be reappearing as if from thin air, not to mention the prospect of clawing back the leases on our land after letting the neighbors farm it for so long. That wouldn't go over well, and there'd be a lot of questions.

There was no returning to my former life. So what was pulling me back?

Human relationships, I reminded myself. Even if it would be with humans I didn't yet know, I'd at least be among my own kind again. I would be dropping into life somewhere else, well beyond when I'd left. I'd be starting over completely, by necessity in some place I'd never lived before. It would be like going into witness protection.

What would I do? Selling the acreage would bring a lot of money, so that wasn't an issue. I'd have the freedom to do whatever I wanted, and in fact the barest hints of a half-assed plan had been forming in my mind. Even though I'd written off veterinary work, going back to school seemed like the right thing. Marine biology was interesting, especially with the knowledge that Union survey teams had found intelligence among marine mammals. It helped that the best universities for that field were all in attractive places to live.

So I had something resembling a plan. Sell off the land, start on my PhD, commiserate with whales.

By my watch, Gideon's offer would expire in about sixteen hours. If I was going to do this, it was time to start packing. After rooting through my closet, I pulled out an old medical text from underneath a pile of folded clothes. It had been sitting there with everything else I'd brought from Earth and hadn't been touched since. If I was going to be Gideon's personal caregiver, I'd need to refresh my knowledge of human anatomy and physiology in a hurry. With the gene tweaking he'd undergone to reach such an advanced age, his body could be a witches' brew of maladies waiting to erupt.

That thick volume was the first thing to go into my duffel bag. The second was a yellowed photo of my parents. To a casual onlooker, it wasn't anything special. Just the two of them in our living room, with Mom shooting him a disapproving side-eye while Dad wore a shit-eating grin. He'd just told a howlingly inappropriate joke that had run headlong into her Lutheran sensibilities. She'd about choked from trying not to laugh. I wished I could have remembered the joke.

There was so much else that had long ago faded from memory to become general impressions. The smell of freshly cut grass in summer, fall bonfire parties, winter snowfalls...I'd complained incessantly about the bleak Midwestern winters, but deep down they were a cherished part of the cycle of life. I loved the change of seasons and couldn't imagine living somewhere that didn't have them.

Kind of like here. Our biodome was kept at a constant, balmy 297 degrees. That's in Union standard measurement referenced to absolute zero, equivalent to what we call Kelvin. It worked out to around 75 degrees Fahrenheit. The vegetation flourished in that environment and everything was meticulously cultivated, as beautiful as any conservatory on Earth. But it was all artificial, planted and engineered. That was another thing I liked about the Thuban sector: Their desert environment was naturally, pleasingly chaotic. Whatever grew there was left alone because it would've gone through a hell of a fight to flourish in that harsh setting.

I pushed my bag aside and flopped onto the bed, staring at the ceiling. Its luminous panels accurately reproduced natural sunlight in the wavelengths a human would be used to. More exquisite engineering, if wholly artificial. Even the furniture they'd provided me was a faithful reproduction of contemporary styles from Earth, but it was all imitation. My life was a simulacrum of the one I'd left behind. Maybe I'd have adapted better if I'd stuck with current Union furnishings. I had tried that for a while but could never fully embrace it. I'd craved the things I was used to, which maybe was a natural reaction to being a fish out of water.

I sighed. This felt like failure, which sounds ridiculous but there it was. I was tucking tail and running back to what I knew, but even that wasn't quite true. There was no going back to my former life. Whatever came next would have to be different. But it would at least be on my home world, surrounded by other humans.

I reached for the crystal on my bedside table and pulled up Gideon's private contact.

"Okay. I'm in." *And you had better know what you're doing.*

Things moved quickly from there. Gideon's instructions were simple and rather abrupt: Be at his private landing bay at precisely 2300 Union Standard Time, and bring only what I needed.

He was in an even bigger hurry than I'd thought. 2300 Standard was well inside the 48-hour window he'd given me. He'd been primed to go whenever I gave him the thumbs-up.

I finished packing in a rush, throwing all the old clothes from Earth into my bag. And yes, they still fit. I might look hopelessly dated when we got there but it was nothing a quick trip to Macy's couldn't fix, assuming they were still around.

I packed a few items of Union-issue clothing as well, in particular the inertia-damping garment that would protect me from "unanticipated accelerations" if Gideon's onboard dampers glitched. That still happened from time to time, and the results could be nasty for anyone not prepared. For what we would be attempting, it felt like a good idea to be prepared for anything.

With clothing out of the way, I had to think about other essentials.

There wasn't much, to be honest. There was the old legal envelope I'd taken from my parent's safe, the one with the deed to our property. I slipped their photo inside of it for safekeeping and set it carefully atop the clothing in my bag.

There was one final item which I was not going to leave without. I went to the living room and lifted my Thuban combat medic sash from its place on the wall, folded it carefully, and set it in my bag. For the hell of it, I threw in a clean Med Corps jumpsuit as well. The bright green uniform and violet sash stood out like a sore thumb on top of my old jeans and pullovers.

My last task was to take care of official business, and this part was harder than I thought: What to tell the Med Corps? Should I just resign, cut ties and be done? It brought back memories of resigning from the fire department and literally disappearing from the face of the Earth. That felt like running, which it was, but I also didn't want to draw unnecessary attention to myself.

After skimming over Med Corps policy, I arrived at the least bad solution: an extended leave of absence for personal matters. That fit the bill and was sufficiently open-ended to avoid any uncomfortable questions. I wanted a way back if this all went to shit, assuming there'd be a way back.

The musical chime from my front door startled me. Who was ringing at this time of night? I glanced at a nearby comm panel to see it was Bjorn, waiting patiently. I had Clara let him in. "I'm back here, in the bedroom."

He glided in, the pearlescent folds of his official Emissary robes trailing behind him.

"You've been on business?"

"A late Diplomatic Ministry meeting," he said dismissively. "The ministers tend to revel in the sounds of their own voices."

"Anything interesting?"

He ignored my question to study the semi-organized clutter on my bed. "You appear to have reached a decision."

I set my hands on my hips and looked around the room. "What gave it away?"

He placed his hands on my shoulders with a beaming smile. "I knew the moment you first broached the subject, even if you did not. Your body language has always been easy to read."

"Yeah, I'm still working on that." I looked up at him. "I'm sorry, Bjorn. I truly am. This isn't an easy thing to do. I am grateful for everything you've done on my behalf. Grateful to all of you."

"As we are grateful to you. You've represented your kind exceedingly well, which has not gone unnoticed."

Given the circumstances, that sounded a little ominous. "Right now, I'm trying very hard to remain unnoticed." I explained how I'd handled my Med Corps absence.

"A wise move," he said. "In your position, I would have done the same thing." His lips curled into a wry grin. "In fact, I already have."

My eyes narrowed. "What did you do, Bjorn?"

"I requested a sabbatical from my position in the diplomatic corps. I explained to the Ministers that it was necessary for me to 'explore personal interests.' Of course, I had to convince them such explorations would redound to the Union's benefit. My unwillingness to share any details made that rather difficult, thus the lengthy meeting. I do apologize for calling on you at this late hour, but I sensed urgency."

"You weren't wrong." I checked my watch. "I need to be out of here in the next hour."

"In that case, it is especially fortunate that I came calling."

"I'm glad you did. I'd hate to have missed you before I go."

"It is rather the opposite." He arched an eyebrow. "I'm going with you."

My jaw dropped. "You're ... why?" I was simultaneously relieved and alarmed. "Does the Ministry know what you're doing?"

He sat on the bed and motioned for me to follow. "Rest assured I did not share any details. Our venture is 'below the shelf,' as you might say."

I laughed. "It's 'under the table.'"

"Ah. Despite all of my time studying humans, some of your idioms still escape me." He returned to the subject at hand. "As to why, you will be crossing unexplored space. Having an Emissary aboard on such a journey could be useful. And there is the personal aspect: I brought you here, therefore it's my duty to see to your safe return."

"And if Gideon objects? It *is* his ship, after all."

"He has already been persuaded. As you might say, I made him an offer he couldn't refuse."

I crossed my arms. "Impressive. He doesn't strike me as being open to negotiations."

"There was nothing to negotiate. I simply informed him that as an official of the Diplomatic Ministry, I'd become aware of his intentions and their implications for the Union. If he wished to continue unopposed, he would have to agree to my conditions."

That drew a whistle. "I *am* impressed. I didn't know you could play that kind of hardball."

"What is your term, 'arm twisting'? Sometimes that is necessary in diplomacy." With that, Bjorn rose and smoothed out the folds in his tunic. "I must return to my quarters before we leave. I will see you at the landing bay."

# ⚕ 10 ⚕

There was one final, important errand to run. Chonk hadn't answered my calls, so after a quick ride on the express tube to the Thuban sector, I hightailed it up to his apartment. There was no answer at his door.

I checked my watch. Time was getting short, and I hoped there was enough left to dash down to the biodome. If he wasn't at home, he was bound to be at Wayside.

The place was unusually quiet; this time of night there should be music and loud conversations spilling outside. With rising disappointment I stepped through the swinging doors.

Wayside was almost empty. A few Thubans stood around a gaming table. One twisted to see who'd walked in and turned back after deciding I wasn't anyone important. I'd become enough of a fixture here to not turn many heads.

A lone server worked behind the bar. I called her "Greta," an abbreviation of her given name which was otherwise unpronounceable without sounding like I was trying to hock up phlegm.

"Where is everyone?"

She answered in the hissing Thuban speech, which my translator picked up easily. "Reserve unit called up. Big fleet movement, not know where." She shrugged and flicked her trident tongue. "Secret, like everything."

I looked over my shoulder at the small group around the game table. Some were bandaged, one had a fresh patch of scales across his back, scars healing from an injury. I didn't have to ask what happened. These guys were on light duty while recovering from whatever injuries they'd had.

I turned back to Greta. "When did this happen?"

"Two days ago. Immediate recall." She fixed her catlike eyes on me. "You look for your friend T'Ch'on-ukk?"

"Yeah, I was looking for Chonk." My shoulders sagged. "Would've been nice to see him before he left."

"Like said, immediate recall. Fleet Security even come, rouse everybody. Big commotion."

I drummed my fingers along the bar and checked my watch again. Being in a hurry did little to temper my regret. I scrawled out a brief note and left it with her. "Please give this to Chonk when he comes back."

Greta took the paper with a questioning look. Handwritten letters were so uncommon here as to be hopelessly quaint. It was much more reliable to just send messages over our crystals, but I didn't want my plans blasted over the Union network. She slipped the note into a drawer and turned back to me. "You leave too? Good customer. Hope return soon."

"Sorry." It was all I could muster. I shouldered my bag and headed back through the swinging doors, wishing I could bring this place and everyone in it with me.

I made it to the landing bay with literally a minute to spare. Bjorn was waiting beside the saucer, with a small case on the deck by his feet.

"That was quick," I said. "You packed light."

"Union diplomats are expected to keep a travel kit on hand for short notice excursions. There was little time for anything else."

I pointed at his case, not much bigger than an overnight bag. "Could be a long trip, you know." It was pointless idle conversation, but it helped deaden the cacophony of conflicting emotions.

"You are distracted."

I blew out a sigh. "That's putting it mildly." I crossed my arms and began tapping my feet impatiently. "I went to say goodbye to Chonk. He was gone, along with most of the other Thubans. Some kind of big fleet movement."

Bjorn nodded. "Ah. Yes. I am aware of this." He didn't offer any details.

"Anything we should be worried about?"

"Not in the direction we are heading. There have been reports of increased raider activity near the Sagittarian sector, and the defense fleet is making a show of force. Deterrence is often more effective than waiting for the 'fan to hit the shit,' as you might say."

I laughed. "That might be the first time I've ever heard you use such colorful language . . . as you might say." If he'd intended to lighten my mood, it had worked.

He took my hand in his. "I know it was important to see your friend before you left. Rest assured he will understand. I will see to it myself upon my return."

I gave his hand a squeeze. "I assume that means you've figured out a way home yourself?"

Bjorn turned to the waiting saucer. "As part of my official capacity, I cannot allow a vessel of Union origin to remain on Earth or any other non-member world. It must be returned."

It was comforting to know that he had every intention of getting back safely. Before I could ask anything more, a portal on the side of the saucer winked open and Deela stepped out.

*If you are ready to board, we can depart immediately.* She eyed Bjorn. *I was informed that you will be accompanying us. This was unexpected.*

"Will that be a problem?"

*Logistically, no, though you should be aware that our patron was not pleased.*

"Yes, Gideon made that very clear during our negotiation." With that, Bjorn stepped inside. I gave Deela an apologetic shrug and climbed in behind him.

The saucer was a lot cozier with Bjorn's six-foot frame folded up inside, but he made do with one of the acceleration couches. Once we were settled, Deela held out a small black container. *Your biometric rings, please.*

I shared a look with Bjorn, who seemed displeased but not surprised. "What for?"

*Gideon has insisted on the utmost privacy for this expedition.*

That was unsettling. The bio ring was essentially my Union passport and master key. Without it, I couldn't so much as get on a lift or open a door outside of my residence. "You're sure about this? Without our rings, nobody will know where we are."

*Precisely.*

Bjorn took the news calmly. "It's an electromagnetically shielded container," he explained. "You call it a Faraday cage." As if I had any idea what that was. "It will prevent any interested parties from tracking our movements." He arched an eyebrow, slowly pulled off his ring, and placed it in the box. "I presume that whatever vessel we're taking will have deactivated its transponder beacon as well?"

*You are partly correct. A beacon was not installed.*

I glared at Deela with mounting skepticism. We were going dark, yet it was impossible to ignore the fact that she still wore her ring. "What about you?"

She turned toward the force field behind her ship, the one that kept the landing bay's atmosphere where it belonged. *I will need it to open the vacuum shield. My ring will join yours as soon as we are clear of Capital space. You appear troubled by this. Do you wish to reconsider?*

"Troubled" was putting it lightly. I turned the ring about my finger. That little size-6 chunk of silvery alloy represented my freedom of movement, which was about to be locked up in a shielded box. Not only would it remove me from access to anything in the Union, it would hide my presence from anyone who might want to come looking for me. It was finality, distilled into a piece of unassuming jewelry.

Bjorn gave me a reassuring nod. If he had something up his sleeve, he wasn't sharing, but he seemed a lot more sanguine about the situation than I was.

I pulled the ring off and dropped it into the black box. "I'm not reconsidering. Let's do this."

The trip to Gideon's mystery ship took much longer than I'd expected. We'd been traveling most of a Union standard day, almost thirty hours, with nothing to do but sit in our gel couches. I passed the time by studying my old physiology textbook while Bjorn either meditated or slept. It could be hard to tell the difference.

I tapped one of the sidewalls to activate a window, but there was nothing to see. We were in the middle of nowhere, which was really saying something in galactic terms.

Bjorn opened one eye. He didn't seem surprised. "This endeavor is shrouded in secrecy. It would make sense for Gideon to keep his vehicle somewhere far from prying eyes."

With the only ambient light coming from distant stars, it took time for my eyes to adjust. Our destination came into view, shrouded in darkness. Its presence was more apparent from the background stars it blocked out than the feeble light it reflected.

We weren't going to Gideon's flying estate. In fact, this was entirely unlike any other ship I'd seen. It was a polyhedron, with hundreds of triangular panels joined to form a sphere looming in the black. There was nothing to compare it to for sense of scale, but I sensed it was massive. An aperture winked open along its equator to reveal a landing bay. After some quick mental math, I estimated the sphere's diameter to easily be a thousand feet across.

The landing bay was big enough to accommodate Deela's saucer and maybe one other shuttle, unusual for a ship of this size. She led us through a pair of pressurized hatches into a narrow, curving corridor with swooping lines and curlicued details, the signature style of Gliesan architects. The aesthetic features gave the impression of more open space than the place actually had. There was barely enough room for the three of us to stand shoulder-to-shoulder. It reminded me of a passenger train.

*This accessway encircles the ship. All habitable volume is located within the torus. If you follow me, I will show you to your quarters.*

It was a long walk; along the way Deela explained the crew areas were on the opposite side of the ship. *Gideon kept the living quarters as far from the utility spaces as possible.*

"The habitable volume is only a small part of this vessel," Bjorn noted. "That suggests the generators and field projectors would have to constitute at least ninety percent of its mass."

*That is correct. The mass constraints forced us to sacrifice some comfort features. Acoustic insulation was one of them.*

"You've been studying, Bjorn."

"You're too generous. There wasn't much material available, only theoretical concepts. But it appeared obvious to me that mass would be scrupulously limited. It is a tradeoff our shipwrights have not had to consider for some time."

Two steps forward, one step back. Illustrating Bjorn's point, we found our rooms were a stark contrast to the spacious suites back at the capital. My room wasn't much bigger than a walk-in closet, with a bed recessed into one wall and a small desk and chair in the other. I'd had more space on Bjorn's shuttle. I tossed my bag onto the bed and met the others back in the corridor. Gideon was waiting for us now, resting against his cane.

"Welcome aboard the *Campanula*," he said with forced courtesy. "I trust you find the accommodations to be acceptable?"

It felt a little like a prison cell, but I wasn't about to say that. How much space did the rest of us have to sacrifice just so Gideon could have his customary accommodations? "They're fine."

"Galley's that way," he said, pointing his cane down the hall. "Second door on the left. Nutrisynth is fully stocked."

That was good to know, as I'd noticed the lack of one in my room. "It must get crowded around mealtime."

"Not at all." Gideon gestured again with his cane. "You are looking at our full crew complement. Everything is run by the ship's synthetic brain. Deela's here to make sure it behaves itself."

I turned to her. "You run this all by yourself?"

*It is not as daunting a task as you imagine. No more complicated than piloting a shuttle.*

That was hard to believe, but Bjorn absorbed her dismissiveness with his usual diplomatic aplomb. "This is all most intriguing. Would it be possible to tour the rest of your ship? Beyond the living quarters, that is."

Gideon's face hardened. "Do you inspect every vessel you travel on?"

Bjorn smiled. "Of course not. But I am most interested in this new technology you've harnessed."

"I'm not used to passengers poking around my ships, especially if they're going to report their findings to some GU minister."

Bjorn did a brief pirouette with his arms spread. "I am not going anywhere you aren't going yourself. What benefit would I find in divulging your secrets? I don't have to tell you how important this technology could become if it works as you describe. You would enjoy full credit, along with whoever performed the design and construction."

"And the blame," I interjected, "if this thing blows up."

Gideon's mouth drew tight. "It works, Mooney." He tapped the deck with his cane. "We didn't build this thing here, you know."

"I suspected as much," Bjorn said. "There was a noticeable absence of construction equipment when we approached."

"You think I'd take off in this contraption without trying it out first?" Gideon scoffed. "No, once we were satisfied the field projectors worked, we ran an all-up test. Remotely piloted, of course."

"Of course."

"How'd the test run go?" I asked.

Gideon's eyes narrowed. "We're here, aren't we? Activated the drive, and *poof.*" He snapped his fingers. "The ship disappeared. We had a position report over the entanglement net within seconds. Wasn't quite where we predicted, but close enough. We had to tweak the navigation logic, refine the probability models, but it cleared the test objective: instantaneous travel, with negligible relativistic effects. The *Campanula*'s proper time was only off by a few milliseconds."

"Over what distance?" Bjorn asked.

"A long damned way," Gideon said, being stubbornly evasive. "Took the better part of a week for my engineering team to reach it with a tender."

Bjorn raised an eyebrow. "A long way indeed." I didn't know how fast a ship tender could travel, but a week in a Med Corps heavy transport could get you just about anywhere in Union space.

Gideon looked away, tapping his fingers against his cane as he thought. "Very well. I suppose there's no harm in looking." He nodded at Deela. "Show them the rest of the ship."

Our first stop was the medical bay, no doubt because Deela knew what I was thinking.

*We have the most up-to-date Med Corps technology and ample inventory,* she thought at me. *I believe you will find it suitable.*

It was phrased more as a polite question, but I had no reason to doubt her. The compartment was pristine white with immaculate equipment racks along the walls, all bright enough to make me squint. One wall was a black, floor-to-ceiling holographic monitor. An exam bed sat in the middle of the room, the kind normally found in Med Corps hospitals. Semicircular bands were mounted over either end: full-body scanners that took the place of the portable discs we kept in our trauma bags. Smaller telemetry monitors were embedded along one side of the bed, while sterilizing field projectors were mounted on the other. Out of curiosity, I opened a pair of drawers beneath the monitors and found a full array of surgical tools. My first thought was that Gideon would be in real trouble if I had to pull that stuff out, while the six-armed surgery bot tucked away in one corner of the room allayed that fear only a bit. Next to it were flush-mounted cabinets, which were full of the medications that had been keeping him alive for so long.

Union meds were rarely the type of chemical formularies we'd used on Earth. Med Corps stuff was much more complex: Nanobot probes to repair cell damage for acute cases, gene therapies for longer-term treatments and such. But the peculiarities of being a rare species in the Union also meant there were a lot more old-fashioned pharmaceuticals than usual.

I lifted a clear bottle of capsules from the cabinet. A quick tap on the lid projected its contents into the air. "These are immunosuppressants. Did he have an organ transplant?"

*Several, though not in the manner you may be accustomed. Replacements for Gideon's heart, liver, and kidneys were generated from undifferentiated cells harvested from his bone marrow.*

They'd been grown from stem cells in his own body, the same way Xeelix's hand had been replaced. "How is it he still needs anti-rejection meds?"

*The replacements were not precise matches. Gideon's cells provided a baseline, but at the time there was not enough reference data to create idealized organs. The models had to be augmented with synthesized tissue stock.*

I rooted through the cabinet to get an idea of what I'd be dealing with. Other than the immunosuppressants, it held the kinds of meds typical for an aging human: vitamin supplements, gastrointestinal treatments. For a number of reasons, I was relieved to find none of the little blue boner pills that had been so insanely popular back home.

"I'll need full access to his records."

Deela swiped at one of the bedside monitors. *I have just transferred Gideon's medical history to your personal device. I should not have to remind you that it is strictly confidential.*

"Of course," I said, though I don't know who she'd expect me to share it with. "Can you tell me anything about his daily routine?" Care plans were not something emergency medics normally handled; that was left to the doctors and nurses.

*Gideon remains heavily involved with day-to-day operations and frequently relies on stimulants to keep his circadian cycle aligned with Union standard days. I am not privy to other details of his medication regime, though I do know he must receive regular anti-senescence treatments.*

I was familiar with that, if only in passing. The treatment involved nanobot injections, which made their way through the patient to repair cell damage from the normal aging process. For most Union species this was a one-time procedure done in early adulthood, but Gideon had long ago missed that window of opportunity. And since it involved nanobots, I already had a good idea of how they were delivered. "Where are those kept?"

Deela pressed against one of the flush-mounted panels to open a cabinet. It was filled to the brim with glistening metallic probes, each about the size of my pinky finger: Classic Reticulan medical technology. They had a butt probe for everything.

"I'm guessing he doesn't self-administer."

*He does not.*

Lovely.

Bjorn wore a rare lopsided grin. "Try not to enjoy yourself too much."

There wasn't much to the rest of the ship, at least not within the narrow torus that encircled the sphere. At Bjorn's insistence, Deela led us through a small hatch into the powerplant. He was intensely curious as to how this thing propelled itself, and it didn't disappoint.

If you asked me to describe the engine room of an ocean liner, you'd be left more ignorant than when we started. I'd tell you it was lots of pipes and pumps and turbines that get really hot and make a lot of noise and all of that stuff makes the boat go.

What can I say? I'm a medic, damn it, not an engineer.

The guts of Gideon's new ship had lots of the aforementioned stuff, just more high tech and alien-looking. We stood on a catwalk mounted along the inner circumference of the torus, looking down on an accordion-like collection of flat plates that glowed behind three layers of polyhedral screens. Dozens of spiral buttresses corkscrewed out from this contraption in all directions, fractally branching off into a vertiginous mishmash of twisted perspectives, as if we'd just walked into an MC Escher drawing. I blinked hard to reorient myself, then focused on the coils nearest to us. They extended far overhead through a transparent membrane before branching out to end at the same triangular panels that comprised the *Campanula*'s hull.

Bjorn leaned against the railing and tilted his head to one side. "Most interesting." He pointed at the pulsating stack far below. "This, I assume, is the zero point reactor?"

*It is more properly termed an "accumulator," but you are correct. It is presently at idle, otherwise we would not be able to enter the chamber. This area is depressurized during operation.*

"And those screens surrounding the accumulator plates?"

*Electromagnetic shielding to allow direct inspection of the powerplant. They block ionizing and particle radiation from escaping the accumulator core.*

Bjorn quirked an eyebrow. "And what of these?" He was pointing at the dizzying spiral pillars. "I presume they are conduits?"

*That is correct. They generate the propagation fields which are transmitted to the projector arrays on the outer hull.*

"To create a singularity."

A *what*? I turned to Bjorn with alarm. I'd already been too close to one of those. He subtly patted the air with his hand, signaling me to calm the hell down.

*Again, correct. The field projectors create a steep-gradient gravity field around the vessel.*

Bjorn took it as casually as if she'd just told him how to fry an egg, but I wasn't having it. Deela must have picked up on my unease, because she then directed her thoughts at me.

*There is no cause for alarm. The event is instantaneous, and it is necessary to open the cross-dimensional portal. We are safe within the singularity itself. It is the space around us which must be cleared.*

"How far?"

*The minimum safe distance is a hundred thousand kilometers.*

I squeezed Bjorn's hand. There would be a lot of questions for him later.

# 11

Deela led us out of that confounding surreal space and back into the comfortably boring confines of the crew berthing. After dropping us off at our quarters, she excused herself to return to the control room. Our first jump was imminent, and seeing the machinery that would make us disappear from normal space hadn't made me any less anxious. The opposite, in fact.

I grabbed Bjorn by the elbow and leaned in. "Did you understand what she was showing us?"

He crossed his arms and cast a sidelong glance back toward the engine room. "Conceptually, yes. Mechanically? I am as perplexed as you."

"That doesn't make me feel any better. How can anyone keep that tangle of whatever-it-is working?"

"It is unlike any star drive technology I'm familiar with, though it bears some hallmarks of Mintakan design philosophies. The fractal nature of the field conduits, for instance. You noticed how they branched off into increasingly smaller reproductions of the same patterns?"

"Noticed? I'm still dizzy from it. Speaking of Mintakans, you caught the bit about the shielding, didn't you?"

"I did. You believe this is similar to the case you told me about?"

"Let's say I'm suspicious. They wouldn't let us anywhere near their workspaces, and they were awfully reluctant to let us take their chief engineer."

He tapped at his chin, still looking away. "It's unlikely that Gideon could have constructed an extradimensional drive without their assistance. A project like this would require beings who can visualize the space they are navigating. It would be like your kind building an aircraft without understanding how it creates lift."

"If they helped build this, then it stands to reason they took that work and put it to use themselves. The genie's out of the bottle."

"Quite possibly. Though knowing Gideon, I suspect he sought to maintain strict control over any technological breakthroughs they achieved. It is likely the Mintakan vessel you encountered was engaged in an 'off the books' exercise, as you might say."

It certainly felt suspicious, not that it was up to me to do anything about it. If Gideon's new technology was out in the open, then that was between him and the Mintakans, probably a few Grays as well. I was more concerned about us. "What about this business of creating a singularity? How is it possible to survive being in the center of one?"

His eyebrows knitted together. "I do not know. Their existence is almost as much of a mystery to Union scientists as it is yours. We can model them, predict their properties, observe their effects on surrounding space, but none have ever been traversed."

"I think someone may have tried." I told him about our earlier black hole rescue. It was a rare thing to see shock from an Emissary, but that story did the trick.

"Two separate events which seem coincidental, though they're clearly not. Your stories suggest there is much more unsanctioned activity along those lines."

I looked up and down the curving torus. "This ship pulled it off, and apparently no worse for wear."

"And there lies the difference. Being captured by a singularity is not the same as being in one's center when it is formed, apparently. Gideon seems to have proven the concept. I must admit, it holds great promise."

I frowned. "He's willing to bet his life—*our* lives—on it."

"Quite."

The glow panels along the ceiling began to pulse, a signal that we were about to get moving. Bjorn inclined his head toward the control room. "Come. We are about to see for ourselves."

The control room was a simple affair in contrast to the incomprehensible device which propelled our ship. In truth, the ship itself was the device. We were confined to the narrow donut which had been shoehorned in out of necessity.

Three acceleration couches were arranged in a semicircle behind Deela, who sat at an expansive console filled with the types of holographic displays I was used to seeing in Union ships. The instrument panel was a black crescent which responded to her touch, projecting whatever she needed in the air ahead.

Gideon had already settled into the nearest couch and eyed me as we entered. I took the seat next to him and began lifting gear out of my bag. I placed a transducer disc on his torso and slipped on my visor. His vital sign traces appeared in my peripheral vision. "How are you feeling?"

Gideon cracked his knuckles. "Ready to get on with it." He snapped at Deela. "How are we looking up there?"

*Field conduits are charged and accumulators are at full potential. The navigation routine is still calculating probabilities. We will have a solution shortly.*

"Narrowing down uncertainties turned out to be the long pole in the tent," Gideon explained, unusually accommodating. I sensed it was for his benefit as much as mine.

"What probability factors have you been able to achieve?" Bjorn asked.

"Simulations started in the eighty percent range, which wasn't good enough. We were able to get that down to ninety-one percent in the last test. We're aiming for ninety-four today."

I looked across at Bjorn. Six percent uncertainty in where we ended up could still lead to a lot of unpleasant outcomes.

Bjorn studied Deela's projection. Space was already a lot of nothing in every direction, but our destination looked like even more nothing, if that was possible. "It appears we are targeting an empty region of space."

Deela answered. *Correct. This will be a relatively short jump, only twelve light-years. Once we have ascertained our final position and refined the probability models, we will proceed with longer jumps.*

A corner of her panel began pulsing white. *Navigation logic has a solution. We are ready to depart on your command.*

Gideon tensed. "Do it."

*Very well.*

There wasn't so much as a "hang on," much less a countdown. Deela pressed a hand against her control panel.

The universe disappeared.

Our first jump was a deeply weird experience, not that I had any clue of what to expect. Empty space had become something else. There were no stars, no nebulae, no distant galaxies—it was all just waves and froth. The universe had turned monochrome, like a photo negative. I could swear Bjorn's luminous eyes grew a few millimeters wider. That was shock for an Emissary. Deela was unflappable, but that's a Gray for you.

Speaking for myself, I had a patient to look after and that might've been the only thing keeping me from screaming like a little girl trapped in the funhouse at the county fair.

Gideon's heart rate went through the roof, spiking to an alarming 150 beats per minute before settling down to a more sedate 120. Which still wasn't exactly "sedate," but it wasn't threatening to burst out of his chest. BP was all over the place, along with his O2 saturation. His breathing was rapid and shallow, a sure sign that the old man was scared out of his wits.

I cautioned him to focus on his breathing. Deep breaths, not that top-of-the-lungs gasping that happens when you're suddenly wracked with anxiety. I heard the words in my mind, but nothing would come out of my mouth.

I checked my watch, curious about my own heart rate. I'd say it stopped working, but that wasn't quite right. It had frozen in place, the second hand a barely perceptible blur dancing between its markers.

Against my better judgment, I took my eyes off of Gideon and looked ahead. The monochrome emptiness had turned into something with structure, like I could see the interplay of time and gravity that held everything together. Somehow I knew we were seeing the entirety of existence. Beginning, middle and end, everywhere and all at once. If the universe was a building, this was the ancient bedrock of its foundation.

I can't explain how I understood any of this, it just felt true. And I desperately wanted out. Something was wrong, had to be. Deela had said our jump would be instantaneous, but it was going on and on with no sign of stopping. I was a child again, stuck on an amusement park ride and screaming at the operator to let me off yet knowing that would never happen.

It was too much. We weren't made for this. We were puny three-dimensional creatures who'd just had the comforting façade of our physical existence ripped away. The universe we'd left wasn't infinite—*this* was infinity, raw and irrepressible and overwhelming.

I took another glance at my watch in a desperate attempt to claw my way back to the reality we'd abandoned. It was still locked in place, mocking me for imagining that I had the slightest understanding of what time really was. We were *outside* of time, utterly detached from it, naked and exposed in the face of cold infinity. It was like falling through the air and clinging to a strand of loose rope in the hope it would somehow save me.

I didn't want to go back to Earth, not this way. Send me back to my nice little apartment suite in the capital ring, get me back on shift with my old crew, take me back to Wayside with Chonk and a pitcher of Thuban margaritas. Just make this stop.

The realization that this demented carnival ride had finally ended came when my second hand started moving again. Its fuzzy not-motion had stopped and I could see it clearly now, ticking away as if nothing had happened. I held my breath and counted along with it. One Mississippi, two Mississippi...

"Melanie?"

Three Mississippi...

"*Melanie.*"

I felt Bjorn grasping my arm. I started breathing again. "Hmm?"

He caught my eye then looked past me. "Your patient."

I blinked hard and refocused on the telemetry in my visor. *Oh shit! Snap out of it, Mel.*

I leapt out of my seat and knelt beside Gideon. He was unconscious, and the ECG trace in my visor was all over the place. Blood pressure was on the high side of normal. I snatched an O2 mask out of my bag and placed it over his nose and mouth.

I pressed against the scanners to get a clear view of his heart, and it confirmed what the ECG was telling me. "SVT" began flashing in the corner of my visor. Supraventricular tachycardia, a stress response.

Irregular rhythm, starting above the lower heart chambers, not an unusual response for someone his age.

It should pass on its own, but I couldn't just sit here and wait for his heart to figure itself out either. Always start with the least invasive treatment, then work your way up. Any overreaction would just make things worse. SVT's weren't something we'd usually pull the defib paddles out for, much less use the brute force of CPR.

*Think, Mel. Keep it simple.*

What else controlled heart rate? It had been so long since I'd had an actual human patient. Why did this all feel so vague?

That was it: Vagus nerve. It helped control heart rate. I dug back into my bag and retrieved a small thermal patch. It was about six inches square unrolled, which was just right. I laid it over his face and drew my finger along a thin control strip down the middle, dialing down the temperature to just above freezing. The patch quickly turned cold beneath my hand.

The ECG trace became more regular after a minute, T-waves and QT intervals were settling back into a normal rhythm as Gideon's heart rate headed down below 100. His eyelids began to flutter, and he sucked in a long breath.

"What the hell happened?"

I removed the thermal patch but left the O2 mask in place. "You had a cardiac arrythmia episode and lost consciousness for a minute."

"Not the first time." He stripped away the mask and pulled himself upright.

I tried to make him lie down. "You really shouldn't—"

He waved me away. "I told you, this isn't the first time." He thumped his chest angrily, as if commanding his heart to get with the program, and pulled himself up with his cane. He stifled a cough. "Deela, what's our situation?"

*Initial observations indicate we are point-four light-years off target, angular displacement negative sixteen degrees.*

"Not acceptable."

*Agreed. The navigation routine is still compiling, though I believe the results will closely agree with my observations.*

"And the drive?"

*The lateral field projectors experienced a momentary lapse in output, caused by a degradation of X-axis conduit throughflow. Y and Z axis conduits compensated, but not before experiencing a minor field distortion.*

She'd figured all that out in the time I was working on Gideon? "Solutions?"

*This is only a preliminary assessment. I will need time to study the data and inspect the conduit network. It could be as simple as a hyperconductor out of tolerance.*

Of course. A simple hyper-whatever glitch. Just like changing a tire.

"Keep me apprised." He turned on his cane and headed for the exit. "You know where to find me."

I was left to clean up. I put the thermal patch and O2 mask in an isolation bag; they'd go into a sterilizer down in the med bay. I could feel Bjorn's eyes on me as I worked. When I stood up, he was still watching me intently. "Something wrong?"

"That is what I am trying to determine. Tell me, how do you feel?"

I plopped back into the gel couch. "Exhausted. Disjointed, like a piece of me got left behind."

He titled his head to one side. "As did I. The psychological effects were not surprising. I did not anticipate the physical effects."

"You can't really separate the two. Everyone's body responds to stress." I gestured between him and Deela. "Even you guys."

*You are correct, Melanie. It was a most disquieting experience.*

"But this wasn't your first jump, was it?"

*This was my third.*

"And Gideon?"

*His third as well. I am afraid the effects do not become any less distressing, though I am learning to cope with them. I cannot speak for Gideon. I find it helpful to block his thoughts during a jump.*

Deela, of course, had the benefit of distractions. She had a ship to manage. All we could do was endure the ride. I resolved to pay more attention to my patient on the next jump. "You know, some warning would've been nice."

*Would that have changed your mind?*

She had me there. "I suppose not." I turned to Bjorn. "I don't know how to put it into words. It felt like we were disconnected from reality."

"We were." Bjorn rubbed his forehead. "I felt the same, in addition to feeling everyone else's reactions. It was something of a sensory overload. There are downsides to being an empath." He glanced at my bag. "I don't suppose you have any analgesics in there?"

"The doctor is in." I pulled out a small bottle of low-dose painkillers and dropped a pill into his hand. "One every thirteen hours, Union time. Come see me if that isn't enough."

"This should do. I suppose a headache is a small price to pay, especially considering what it did to Gideon."

Yes, that was going to be a problem if he was going to start throwing SVTs every time we jumped. I'd have to look into more long-term solutions.

Deela knew what I was thinking. *The local measure of time will be little changed, regardless of how much distance we cover. It should not expose Gideon to additional risk.*

"Thanks, but I'll have to be the judge of that." Maybe that was a little impatient, but I also wasn't offering her advice on how to tweak hyperconductors. "How much time did that jump take, anyway?"

She pinched at her console and a summary appeared in the air. *In standard time reference, zero point three seconds.*

"But it felt like—" I stopped myself. "Actually, I don't know how long it felt. It seemed to go on forever."

*We are used to being tethered to our notions of time and space. To be removed from that framework is alarming. I had considered warning you but there is simply no way to prepare yourselves without experiencing it first. I am sorry.*

"No hard feelings," I muttered. She was right, I'd have to find a way to cope with the bizarre unreality of jumping through extradimensional space. If she controlled her own fears by focusing on the ship, mine would have to come by doing the same for the patient I'd been hired to manage. It was bad enough that Gideon could do nothing but watch as we became untethered from normal spacetime; his age and accumulated body modifications only added complexity. It would've been nice had I been able to go through his medical history before that first jump. In fact, if I'd known this ahead of time I'd have insisted on it.

One final, selfish thought elbowed its way into my head: If Gideon died, I'd lose my ride home. How's that for pressure?

# 12

I eventually did throw down the "needs of the patient" gauntlet and told Deela there was no way we could make another jump until I could determine the effects it would have on Gideon.

*Of course. I will be occupied with troubleshooting the projector array. If that does not allow you enough time, the decision will ultimately rest with him.*

"I'll bring that up to Gideon. I think he'll see my point." If he wanted to arrive at Earth alive, he'd damned well better listen.

That, of course, depended on my being able to get some one-on-one time with him. There was only so much I could learn from patient history without doing a full exam. It wasn't something I necessarily looked forward to, and it was no surprise that he hadn't been especially accommodating. He'd locked himself in his suite and shut off his intercom. I could force my way in if there was an emergency, but the monitors in his room weren't throwing off any warning signs to justify that. I was left with studying his records, which would at least give me a baseline for whenever he deigned to enter the exam room.

I was way out of my depth. Patient exams are for nurses and MD's, not paramedics. But here I was, dancing all over that line. With nothing else to rely on, I fell back on my old veterinary training. Having learned to treat different animal species had served me well in the Union, so I told myself this would be no different. That's no comment on Gideon (or maybe it is), but the principles are the same.

I went back to my room and flopped into bed with my crystal.

"Clara, display medical history for Gideon Stone." A holoprojection appeared in the air above me.

Chronological age 111 years, in human terms. I ignored the GU equivalent. History of hypertension, beginning at age 61. That was fairly common. The heart disease beginning in his late sixties was a bigger concern, as was the chronic kidney disease that had appeared a couple of years later. Nanobot stents and transplants of lab-grown organs had alleviated the symptoms, though he was still susceptible to complications. His body was a patchwork of synthetic tissue, implants, and modified genes. You could swap out as many organs as you liked, but if the underlying conditions hadn't changed there was always a danger of relapse.

Gideon's history included a helpful cross-reference to the types of foods he most frequently ordered from the nutrisynths. If you wanted to find a recipe for metabolic disorders, look no further than his diet. I'd expected lots of high-end steaks and whatnot from someone of his means, but his preference for garbage food was shocking. Gideon liked chili dogs, to the exclusion of almost anything else. The healthiest thing in his diet was the occasional grilled salmon, but the synths had trouble with Earthly seafood because there weren't enough samples to work with. It was a lot easier to replicate a good hot dog.

That was the downside of being able to order whatever you wanted, whenever you wanted: It didn't encourage good eating habits. Young people can get away with that for a while, but it'll catch up with you fast in middle age. It was a useful reminder for myself, as I enjoyed burgers and beer a little too much for my own good.

He had a penchant for booze, too, his preferences in keeping with his mid-twentieth-century roots: lots of gin and tonics, with the occasional brandy or scotch on the rocks. Part of me was impressed that he'd trained the nutrisynths to replicate them, because I'd seen for myself how long it had taken to produce a decent lager.

His liver had been less appreciative. That was a completely self-induced condition, and the old fart should've been grateful that the Med Corps had been able to grow a healthy replacement from a sliver of his own. I'd seen what death from cirrhosis looked like, and it wasn't pretty. Too bad they couldn't have worked in a personality transplant along with the new organs.

Immunosuppressants might have kept Gideon from rejecting his freshly grown organs, but they'd also left him more vulnerable to contracting disease. At his age, common ailments could turn deadly.

This is where Union medicine fell short for humans, because two people out of half a trillion didn't warrant the same level of R&D that had been devoted to member species. Nanobots were exceptionally good at hunting down and killing invading viruses, but bacterial infections still had to be defeated with old-fashioned chemistry. For every med that kept Gideon's immune system from attacking itself, it seemed like he needed two more to keep deadly microbes at bay.

His daily drug cocktail was enough to make my head spin. He'd stretched the limits of human lifespan almost to the breaking point and it was starting to catch up with him. Don't get me wrong, he didn't look bad for a man of 111. Other than the cane, he got around well and his mental faculties were still sharp. Without the replacement heart, liver, and kidneys, he'd have shuffled off this mortal coil a long time ago.

He still needed a proper exam from an actual doctor, but for now I had some idea of what to expect. I'd keep a close eye on cardiac and kidney functions, but there wasn't much I could do for his liver if it decided it'd had enough. That wasn't the kind of thing that just happened all of a sudden anyway. I supposed I could encourage him to drink less, but such advice was likely to go unheeded.

Now that we'd been through a jump together, I also had a much better idea of the stresses it created. Monitoring him was going to be a challenge, much less responding if he took a dangerous turn during a jump. The visual stimulation alone was a problem—if the thought of being in the middle of deep space makes you feel insignificant, realizing that it's just a veneer over something much deeper and more ominous is almost too much to bear. I couldn't let him be repeatedly exposed to that.

Staying in the control room during jumps would be dicey for a guy with a touchy heart. Too many stressors, and not enough room for me to work if he crashed. I also guessed that Deela wouldn't need the distraction of me doing CPR on her boss while she was trying to navigate. That would pose a danger to all of us, so I had my trump card to play if Gideon put up a fight.

Which he did, of course. It took repeated buzzing on the comm panel to finally convince him to unlock his door.

"Enter."

The door whispered open and I stepped into a suite that could have been transplanted directly from a high-end resort: lush carpeting and synthetic cherrywood paneled walls draped with tapestries which I guessed were also reproductions. An old roll-top desk occupied one corner while an upright piano sat in an opposite corner, something I did not expect. It was good to see he had hobbies. If there'd been more room, he'd have probably stuffed a baby grand in there.

Gideon waited in the middle of the room, leaning against his cane. "What's the burr under your saddle, Mooney?"

"You, not to put too fine a point on it."

His eyes narrowed. "Anything specific, or just general annoyance?"

There was that, but I kept to business. "You brought me aboard to be your personal medic. If I'm to do my job, then we need to discuss a few things."

He sighed and took a seat in a nearby wingback chair, and motioned for me to do the same. He waited silently.

"I've gone through your medical history. It was interesting, to say the least."

"Then you no doubt saw I had a full physical not long ago, with a Reticulan doctor. She cleared me for long duration travel."

"Did she know of the exact nature of your plans? The dimensional jumps?"

"Of course not," he scoffed. "That has been a closely guarded secret. Proprietary technology."

Not closely guarded enough, I thought. Did he not know we suspected it was out in the open? I decided to hold that for later. "Then your doctor couldn't have known about the possible adverse effects."

"I don't think anyone could have." He let out a telltale cough. "The test runs were remotely piloted. Deela and I were the only ones aboard the shakedown flights."

"Grays are nothing if not circumspect," I countered, "not to mention their physiology may be more adaptable than ours. We couldn't know the effects it would have on us until we did it."

"I will grant you that."

"And frankly, your advanced age is a concern. The organ replacements and gene therapies have done a lot to extend your life, but there are limits."

"You don't have to tell me that!" Another cough. "Remember why we're here in the first place?"

Last rites. Gideon knew he was on his way out, and finding absolution from a priest was the last item to punch on his ticket. It made the old bastard seem a little more human, and left me feeling chastened. I softened my tone. "Of course. And that's why *I'm* here, to keep you alive."

"I'm glad to see we're in agreement on something."

So much for seeming more human. "If this is going to work, then you and I are going to have to reach some accommodation." I tipped my head back toward the corridor outside. "First, I'd like to examine you myself in the med bay. Second, it's a bad idea for us to be in the control room during jumps. It's too much stimulation. Your heart may not be able to take it."

Gideon frowned and looked away, stifling another cough. "You have a point, Mooney. But I also have responsibilities." He thumped the deck with his cane. "The *Campanula* is one of a kind. If it craps out on us in the middle of nowhere, then we've got serious problems."

"I think Deela can handle it. And you may find Bjorn to be useful."

Another frown. "Damned Emissaries, always sticking their perfect Nordic noses into everything. You know he strong-armed his way aboard, right?" Gideon scowled at me. "Of course you do. He was your case officer. I'm sure you're very close. Ever think that might be by design? And he's no doubt made me his next pet project."

Gideon was probably right, but that didn't change the situation. "There is nothing either one of us can do on that control deck except make things worse. If you crash, I'll be busier than a one-armed paper hanger." That sounded hopelessly anachronistic, but I figured it might get through to a man of his age. "We'd be a distraction."

He massaged his chest, and I wondered if he was feeling something right then or just remembering how it felt during the jump. With no scanners in place to tell, I watched his face. Color looked okay, no sweats or twitches. I felt my fingers tingling, the beginnings of an adrenaline surge if I had to jump into action. "How are you feeling right now?"

Gideon waved me away. "I'm fine. Just thinking." He regained his composure. "What do you propose?"

"We set up acceleration couches in the med bay, take them out of the control deck if necessary. I'll set up a full suite of monitors on yours, and will be right there with you for every jump. Bjorn trained with me in the Med Corps, so I can call on him if I need an extra set of hands. Between the two of us, we'll be ready for anything." Anything that didn't require an actual doctor.

He tapped his fingers on the head of his cane. "I'll consider your proposal." He rose, my signal to leave. "If there's nothing else, Mooney, I have other matters to attend to."

# ⚕ **13** ⚕

Of course he blew me off. When it was time for the next jump, we were called back to the control room. Gideon was already there, strapped into his gel couch. His one accommodation was an all-purpose emergency kit secured to the deck beside him. He'd even set a pair of scanner discs on his chest instead of waiting for me.

He caught my skeptical side-eye. "This will have to do, Mooney. I need to be up here."

I secured my trauma bag to the deck beside him. There was no use arguing at this point, not that it had ever stopped me before. "And why is that?"

"The *Campanula* is my ship, and you're all here because of me. Despite what you might think, I do carry a certain sense of responsibility."

I looked over the equipment he'd had brought in from the med bay, and had to give him credit. It was the same gear I'd have wanted on hand. "I appreciate your thinking ahead, but if I have to crack open that stuff and get to work—"

Deela interjected. *Do not concern yourself with distractions. As you would say, I've got this.*

Gideon looked satisfied. "It's a compromise, which is something I don't do very often. You won, Mooney." He waved me to the adjacent couch. "Now, sit."

It didn't feel like a win. I glanced over at Bjorn with a shrug and took my seat as Deela went about her business.

*Navigation and probability logic are in agreement, predicting ninety-four percent accuracy. We are ready to proceed.*

"Wait a moment, please." I set my visor in place and activated Gideon's monitors. His vital signs floated in the corner of my vision, and everything was in normal range. "Okay, we're ready here."

Gideon didn't hesitate. "Then let's get on with it."

*Very well.*

Deela's elegant fingers danced above her controls, and holographic animations began to move about the viewscreen in response. Our path traced a line between distant stars, avoiding any known habitable systems. Odd, undulating bubbles appeared along our projected route. They began resolving into egg-shaped blobs that shrank steadily as she worked.

Bjorn leaned in close. "Projected areas of navigational uncertainty," he explained quietly. "It appears Deela has made some refinements to the probability logic."

*Correct. I required a better representation of the effects of local gravity fields on our course, and integrated them with a prediction of our gross navigational error.*

Whatever the hell that meant. Still, it was fascinating to watch her work. She reminded me of a master pianist, where the keyboard had become an extension of herself. Instead of making music, she was arranging the fabric of our small slice of the universe to her liking.

*Stand by for jump. Executing now.*

At least she'd given us warning this time, but it didn't do much to dampen the unreality of leaving normal space. It made me question exactly what "normal" was as we were once more cast into this bizarre photonegative void. If this unreality was what underpinned our concept of the universe, then what was the true nature of our reality?

I stole a glance at my watch; the second hand was doing its blurry little dance again, stuck between time and something else. How could a simple mechanical device be so affected? Or was it my own perception that was being pushed and pulled?

*That is exactly what is happening. Please try to ignore it.* Deela was, of course, paying attention. That must have meant things were going okay.

Having done this before, knowing what to expect made it slightly easier to stomach the gulf between our reality and the endlessly shifting monochrome expanse swallowing us. Once again, we faced the timeless depths of the foundations of the universe.

I remembered Bjorn's attempt to explain this: Because we exist in a 3D world (4D if you include time, but let's keep this simple), we'd only be able to see the *effects* of higher dimensions on our constrained reality. We weren't seeing this extradimensional space so much as we were seeing its shadow.

The longer we were outside of our space, the stranger it became. Hints of shapes outside, massive structures of gravity, the force that made stars attract planets and galaxies attract stars and bonded the "bubbles" of galaxies into localized groups that spanned millions of light-years.

It was terrifying, yet I wanted more. Was this how God saw the universe?

No, of course not. We were only seeing its influence, like the way tides are controlled by the Moon's gravity. You can see when the tide comes in and goes out, now imagine being able to see the gravity that pushes and pulls it. It was one more thing little old me got to experience that human astronomers would've sold their own children to see.

As we made our way deeper into this peculiar non-space it seemed to absorb us, as if our ship's carefully manufactured hull became porous. Amorphous shadows outside seemed to pass right through, like shining a flashlight through a bedsheet. It was disconcerting for me, and was apparently even more so for Gideon. His heart began racing, his BP spiking in concert. Breathing was rapid and shallow.

*Shit.* It was happening again.

I left the confines of my gel couch and immediately collapsed on all fours. There was no sense of acceleration, just a brain-scrambling disorientation as the cabin swirled around me. Left became right, forward became backward. Bjorn was calling after me, but I couldn't make out what he was saying. Something about loops. Yes, some hand loops would've been nice right now.

I reached up to steady myself against Gideon's couch, but somehow my hands were there before I could think to move them, with sterile gloves already on. The trauma bag lay open by my side with a fresh thermal patch unrolled and ready to go. I didn't remember doing that, it just kind of happened. He didn't appear to need it anyway, as his cardiac rhythm and BP were back in normal range on their own.

No, not on their own. I'd just administered epinephrine to jolt his heart back into rhythm. If that didn't work I was ready to give him a quick jolt to reset it. The discs were right there on his chest, calibrating just the right amount of juice..

I hoped I wouldn't have to use the defib.

But it was already set up, ready for me to activate. When did I do that?

Gideon coughed. "No! We keep going. Almost there."

What? "Who said anything about—"

*We are on a predetermined trajectory. Stopping now could be hazardous.*

"He's going into aFib," I shouted to Deela. "I can't...figure out what..." I shook my head against the whirl of confusion. "The strain is overloading his heart. We need to stop. Now."

Gideon looked as confused as I was. "Did I pass out?"

Bjorn called out again, warning about causal something or other. He was right behind me but his voice seemed so far away, like when you think someone's calling your name but there's no one in the room. I turned back to Gideon. "Try to relax. You're in atrial fibrillation."

I pulled myself upright against his couch and began unbuttoning his shirt. He was almost certainly going to need defib this time. *Just don't die on me first, old man.*

I put my hands on his face, checking for any response. Nothing. I began a sternum rub, which is guaranteed to snap someone awake unless they're all the way out. His vitals were bottoming out and it looked like he was going into cardiac arrest.

Deela's voice cut into my thoughts. *I am shutting down the drive.*

Suddenly everything became clear again. Gideon was sitting upright, against my advice. At least I thought he was. I was gently rubbing his back. His shirt was drenched with sweat. "You need to rest. Please, lie down."

"I heard you the first time," he protested. "I'm fine."

"Let me be the judge of that."

Gideon grumbled and rubbed at his temples. "Deela, report. I'm getting tired of asking 'what happened.'"

She pivoted her seat to face us. *I believe we experienced a probability convergence. And as you can see, we are not where we intended.*

Gideon cursed under his breath. "Probability convergence," he repeated. "Anyone care to explain what the hell that means?"

"It appears we were caught in a 'causality loop," Bjorn said. "Effects preceded causes, from our perspective, with multiple possible outcomes occurring simultaneously."

If I'd thought my head had been swimming before, now it was in danger of drowning. I raised my hand. "Can you break that down for the biology major here?"

"It is similar to a property of what your kind calls 'quantum' physics. In our normal three-dimensional space, particles can exist in multiple states at the same time. In extradimensional space, past and present exist in a single continuum. What we call 'future' is just a series of probabilities. This would be no different from our normal experience, except those probabilities all occur at once." He paused. "At least in how we perceive it."

"I don't think that helped."

Bjorn spread his hands. "That is the best explanation I can offer."

Deela interjected. *I agree. I must admit it was difficult to recognize the onset of a causality loop in real time. Of course, I use the term "real time" loosely.*

Gideon crossed his arms and nodded at the viewscreen. "Doesn't look like we're anywhere near where we're supposed to be. Please tell me that we emerged in the middle of a nebula or something."

*I am afraid not, sir. We are still in six-dimensional space.*

I stopped worrying about Gideon's heart just then, as my own felt like it was about to leap out of my chest. I'd been focused on him and hadn't taken a look outside. We were still in that confounding shadow world of unreality.

*When I finally understood our situation, I believed your health to be in danger. That is one of our abort rules, is it not?*

I seemed to recall screaming at her to stop. Now I wasn't sure it was a good thing that she'd listened.

Gideon massaged his neck. "It is, but that doesn't mean I have to be happy about it. How long to figure out where we are?"

*Unknown. The navigation logic is still comparing our relative position to charted gravity wells.*

"Then don't waste time talking to me. Get on with it."

Deela silently returned to her console while I pulled an auto-syringe out of the med cart and set the horrifying prospect of being stuck in 6D space out of my mind for the moment. Focusing on my job was the only way to keep from freaking out. Hopefully I sounded a lot more confident than I felt. "I'd like to take a blood sample, run a basic metabolic panel and test for troponin proteins. That's the only way to be sure you didn't actually have a heart attack."

"Doesn't feel like it," Gideon said with the air of someone who knew exactly what that felt like. "But do what you have to do."

He was unusually alert and responsive for someone whose heart had stopped, which made me question my own judgment. In all of the everything-at-once confusion, had I misread his vitals? Was it the same thing that made my watch appear frozen?

These were the thoughts racing through my mind as I banded his upper arm and looked for a promising vein. The auto-syringe was quick and accurate, plunging the needle at just the right depth and filling the vial. There was no risk of blowing a vein with GU tech, though the thought crossed my mind that drawing blood was a perishable skill I didn't want to lose.

I set the vial in a port on the med cart and had results within seconds. No traces of troponin, and the other levels in his metabolic panel were in normal range.

I was flummoxed. His vitals and blood work were all normal. How could that be?

"Well?" Gideon demanded. "Anything I should be worried about?"

"No. As a matter of fact you appear just fine. You're not feeling any dizziness or nausea?"

He pulled himself out of his seat and adjusted his suit. "Spry as a spring chicken." He pointed his cane at my jumble of gear strewn about the deck. "I think you're relying too much on what those machines tell you. Whatever happened to listening to the patient?"

*That's what I'm trying to do now, asshole.* I stood to face him. "You were displaying all the signs of cardiac arrest. Your vitals were all over the place during the jump, and you were severely disoriented when we came out of it."

"So was everybody else. You looked as lost as a babe in the woods, Mooney." Was he not bothered that was exactly what we were right now? "If you're going to be my nurse, I need you to be sharper than that."

*Sharper than . . .* I clenched my teeth. If focusing on my job was my way of coping, acting like a prick was his. Rule One—there were a lot of "Rule Ones"—was to be firm with the patient, but don't argue. "I can't ignore vital signs. And we need to be very clear on something: I'm a paramedic, not a nurse. My specialty is keeping you alive when your body is trying to do otherwise."

Gideon leaned on his cane and glowered at me. I suppose that was his way of conceding my point. He moved on to other matters. "Deela, have you figured out where we are?"

*There are several options which I am presently evaluating, but I require some time to review our probability models. I do not believe a "brute force" approach is appropriate.*

"By 'brute force,' you mean what, exactly?"

*By that, I mean calculating a jump that would take us to our next intended destination. Not only did we fail to achieve the desired distance, our gross navigational error exceeded prediction by two standard deviations. In simple terms, we are well off course. The farther we attempt to travel in a single jump, the more pronounced these errors will become.*

"So we're lost," Gideon said flatly. He turned to leave. "Keep me updated on your progress."

*Of course, sir.*

I shook my head and began packing the loose gear back into my bag. When I reached for the empty epi pen, something looked badly out of place. The autoinjector's protective cover was still there, and the sight gauge along the pen's side showed it was full. How could that be if I'd dosed him?

Maybe I'd pulled out two injectors. That had to be it. But there was no empty pen to be found. When I searched my bag, the second pen was right where it was supposed to be.

I'd never injected him, but somehow I remembered doing it. I saw the signs of cardiac arrest, yet he appeared no worse for wear.

Bjorn knelt beside me to help collect my gear. "You are disturbed."

"Damned right I am." I felt my shoulders sag. "None of this makes sense. I *saw* him going into arrest." I held up one of the transducers. "Unless the discs glitched, which they *never* do, he was having a heart attack. I gave him an epi injection, and was about to start defibrillation..."

Wait a minute. Had I forgotten to remove the discs? If he was still wearing them...

No. There they were, safely tucked away in my bag. Right where they were supposed to be.

I slumped onto the floor and cradled my head. "I am not ready for this, Bjorn. This shit is really messing with my brain."

He took my hands in his. "None of us are truly prepared, Melanie. We are outside of our own reality, literally in the unknown. We will each have to learn to cope in our own way." He fixed his green eyes on me. "Gideon is an unpleasant individual, and we are on an uncertain path. But we have seen the technology works, and I am confident Deela can find a way out of this predicament."

Deela turned at that. *Thank you.*

That all sounded lovely for them, but I wasn't having it. "We're still in 6D space. Worse, I just imagined my patient was in cardiac arrest. I could have killed him!"

*That was not your imagination. Gideon's biometrics are backed up and stored in ship's memory. He did experience an event. In fact, he experienced several. He also experienced none.*

I closed my eyes and rested my head against the seat frame. "More of that weird probability stuff again?"

"Probabilistic uncertainty," Bjorn said. "Whatever can happen does happen, and from our perspective all at once. I expect Deela will eventually confirm my suspicions, that our extended jump exposed us to a causality loop."

*There are still some regression analyses to complete, but for now I agree with your hypothesis. If you are correct, I do not believe we can risk another jump of such length given our current understanding of these higher dimensions.*

Bjorn looked beyond Deela to the bewildering expanse of infinity. I got the sense that he was forming some ideas. "If I take your meaning, then we may need to find some help."

Deela glanced over her shoulder at us. *I believe we are thinking the same thing.*

# 14

There was nothing I could do to help Bjorn and Deela find a way out of this. The mental fog of being in 6D space had lifted a bit, enough to find my way back to the medical bay. Being in familiar surroundings helped, so I busied myself with getting the place organized to my liking. But something was still bugging me.

I pulled out my data crystal. "Clara, how much do you know about this extradimensional space?"

The crystal pulsed for a second. "Only what's in the science ministry archives. I've been able to pull a little bit from the *Campanula*'s core memory, but Gideon's keeping a tight grip on most of it."

I grunted. "That's not very helpful."

"It isn't. Doesn't keep me from taking my own observations, though."

Now that sounded encouraging. "You've been spying?"

"Observing. I'm in this too, you know. Self-preservation is a natural instinct, even for a synthetic intelligence."

"You're right. Sorry if I keep treating you like a computer." That was the truth. Clara and her ilk were about as far removed from our notion of computers as we were from orangutans. "What have you learned?"

"It's really weird."

I sighed. "Can you be a little more specific?"

"Oh, I can be specific enough to make your eyeballs bleed. Calling it 'weird' is just an ice maker."

"Ice *breaker*," I laughed. "How about specific enough for an average-intelligence human?"

"You're always so hard on yourself. You're at least a little above average." She chirped, clearing her electronic throat. "Okay, the thing that fouled my internal logic was the same thing that messed with you: time. It doesn't exist in six-dimensional space."

"Except that it kind of does."

"Not in the sense that we're used to," Clara said. "We all have an internal awareness of time; some beings are more attuned to it than others. You can train yourself to wake up at a certain time, right?"

"It's called an alarm clock."

"Funny. You know what I mean. You're usually up before I have to remind you, even if you went to bed late. Which, by the way, isn't good for you when our standard days are over a third longer than Earth's."

"Can we save the lecture for later?" If we could get out of here, that problem would be taking care of itself soon enough. "You said the absence of time messed with your internal logic. Why do you think that is?"

"It isn't passing in any kind of measure we're used to, so our internal references are all out of whack. Mine especially. My internal clocks are calibrated to Union standard, which in turn is calibrated against a galactic year. That's the amount of time it takes the Capital Ring to complete a full orbit of the galactic center—about 225 million years by human reference."

I didn't know that. "Isn't the GU standard day based on the mean rotation time of all the member planets?"

"A day, yes. But timekeeping is based on that galactic year I mentioned. My clocks also rely on tracking the relative positions of certain stars. That gets complicated enough during interstellar travel. Remove that frame of reference, and I become almost as confused as you. I have to rely on the last known reference, which inevitably starts to degrade. The *Campanula*'s guidance logic is having the same problem."

"It's trying to keep time, when measurements of time are meaningless?"

"Bingo. And don't forget, gravity affects our local perception of time. Propelling ourselves by manipulating gravity while we're moving through 6D space is only making it worse."

"Deela shut down the drive," I said. "That's why it doesn't feel so weird now."

"For now. Doesn't mean it won't start again. We need to be on our toes."

"Good point." I needed to finish my work here while my head was still clear. "Do me a favor? Pull up all of Gideon's telemetry from that last jump."

"All of it? There's a bunch, Mel, and it's all over the place."

"Exactly why I need to look at it. If he in fact experienced multiple events while we were stuck in that causality loop, can you correlate the traces to each outcome?"

"Hang on."

This took Clara maybe a minute, an eternity to her. Not long after, the wall screen was filled with projections of vital sign traces. It was like having an entire ward of patients to sift through, each one being a different version of the same man. One in particular sent chills down my spine.

"Holy . . . he *died*."

"A few times, in fact. I only showed you the most complete telemetry. Look at these."

With that, Clara projected a handful of more traces. They were spotty, full of gaps and inconsistencies, but they all ended up the same: flatlined. My patient had died several times over and I'd missed it.

I was not prepared for this. I'd given Gideon fair warning that I was a medic, not a nurse, certainly not an M.D. But I'd taken the job, which meant none of that mattered now. A lot of Med Corps gear and treatments were near-magical in human terms, but there was still going to be a lot of hands-on work keeping the old fart alive for the trip home. All of the replacement organs and gene editing had extended his life, but he was still in a fragile state. I had to be ready for anything.

"Anything" is a big word when you think about how many ways the human body can surprise you. I started with the most obvious sources of complication, and Gideon's lab-grown organs were at the top of my list. My old physiology text was depressingly thin in this area, but it did offer a few useful tidbits. Organ transplants can lead to problems with high blood pressure, high cholesterol, gastrointestinal problems, diabetes . . . you replace the source of one problem and risk introducing half a dozen more.

I'd been focused on the condition of his heart—and it was a

legitimate concern—but I hadn't thought enough about his liver and kidneys beyond his crappy diet. What kinds of problems could they lead to?

For that, I had to rely on Clara's database of observed human pathologies. It wasn't exactly organized like a textbook, but then again, I couldn't just ask my book a question. I started with a hunch. "Clara, do you have anything connecting human liver and kidney transplants with gastrointestinal problems?"

"Oh yeah, and it's not isolated to humans. Not saying they're prevalent, but transplant recipients have an increased risk of cholelithiasis and cholecystitis."

"In English?"

"Gallstones and inflammation of the gallbladder. Severe enough cases require surgery to remove the organ."

I rubbed my temples. While the precise terminology may not have come to mind, I knew what symptoms to look for. I also knew what the likely treatment would be if Gideon developed an acute case. I looked to the corner of the med bay, where the surgical bot sat dormant.

At least I'd have something to occupy my time, whatever "time" meant here.

The surgery bot resembled a mechanical insect, all gangly multijointed limbs with a cluster of optical and infrared sensors festooning its spherical head. I'd sure as hell want to be anesthetized if this thing was hovering over me. Clara sounded concerned as I positioned the machine over a hologram of Gideon on the exam table.

"Have you ever used one of these before?"

"Never had the luxury of one in the field." I held up my hands. "Any cuts I had to make were done the old-fashioned way."

"Eww. Sounds messy."

"That's the job." I'd decided to start by practicing a gall bladder removal. I reached up to move a pair of arms into position. "Can we focus here?"

"Just tell me what I need to do."

"Exactly what I say. We'll let the bot take over after I make the initial incision."

"Wouldn't it be best to let it do the entire procedure?"

"Maybe once I've had enough practice to trust it." I leaned over the simulation, centered on Gideon's abdomen. "Have the retractors ready. Starting incision."

It was surprisingly nerve-wracking. I double-checked the plasma blade to make certain it was on "practice" setting and began cutting, careful to exert even pressure along the incision. The simulated tissue separated cleanly, only a few spurts of holographic blood as the plasma blade cauterized the wound while it cut.

"Retract."

A pair of spindly arms descended from the bot, each holding curved instruments. The bot set them in place on either side of the incision and held it open. Another arm moved into place. I was impressed with how delicately it worked its way through my incision. It paused as Clara asked if I was ready for it to start.

"We're ready. Start the procedure."

A brilliant beam of white light erupted from the arm. I stumbled back in alarm, knocking over a tray of surgical instruments in the process. They were still clattering on the floor as the beam sliced through the simulated organs, clean through the exam table, and into the deck plating.

"Clara, shut it down! Now!"

The beam disappeared, leaving an acrid smell in its wake. Smoke curled away from a nice, clean, pencil-sized hole in the exam table. Fortunately the deck plating was made of firmer stuff.

"What the hell?" I gasped. "How did—"

"You didn't enable the safeties," Clara explained. "The plasma scalpels calibrate themselves for tissue resistance. Holographic tissue has no resistance."

I hung my head. I was about to ask Clara why she didn't warn me, but then I'd told her to do exactly what I said. *Damn it, Mel.* "Sorry."

"Don't apologize to me, it's not my ship you almost cut a hole through."

Any hope that no one else would notice was dashed by a call from Bjorn over the intercom. "Is everything all right back there? Something set off the temperature sensors."

"Yeah." I rubbed at my temples. "Had a minor accident. Discharged one of the scalpels." It didn't even sound convincing to me.

"You are not injured?"

"Nope. I'm fine. Everything's fine." The exam table was a little worse for wear, but nobody else needed to know that. I made a mental note to replace the padding. Did Bjorn understand humans enough to know when a woman says "I'm fine" it's usually the exact opposite? I wondered.

"Very well. I'm glad you're safe. Those blades can be dangerous. We're all a bit hazy from the last jump, perhaps it's best to not be handling sharp objects right now."

So yeah, he understood.

"Would you mind joining us in the control room? We have made an interesting discovery."

*Gladly.* "Be right there."

# ⚕ 15 ⚕

It was hard to see what I could have contributed to Bjorn's and Deela's investigation. That didn't get any easier when they told me what they found.

"A distress beacon," Bjorn said. "Faint, but unmistakable."

"Are you sure?" I waved at the undulating monochrome madness on the viewscreen. "How can you tell when nothing out there resembles reality?"

Deela tapped her console and the signal trace appeared. *That is why it is unmistakable. It is a Union transponder.*

It was inconceivable to me that another vessel could have been here, much less detectable. "You said it was faint. That means it's far away?"

*Not necessarily. Current relative position is two-point-eight million kilometers.*

I whistled. That would've been easy for us in normal space, but here? There was no telling what kind of weirdness would overwhelm us if Deela fired up the drive again. "How do we get there?"

*We cannot risk activating the drive yet. There are still too many unanswered questions.*

I tipped my head at the screen. "And you're hoping that other ship might give us some answers."

*Correct. I intend to take the saucer to intercept it. I would like you to accompany me.*

I stepped back. Gideon's ship, stranded or not, represented my single tenuous grip on reality. "What can I possibly offer? I'm not a pilot." And I certainly wouldn't be able to help Deela.

*No, but you are a medic. It is a distress signal, after all. We should assume the crew requires assistance.*

She had me there. "You're right, of course." I pointed at the manifest tagged to the distress signal. "What kind of crew?"

"Chalawan," Bjorn said.

Of course they were. The Chalawani were the hotrodders of the galaxy. They loved tinkering with old ships to see what they could squeeze out of them, not infrequently blowing themselves up in the process.

"I don't have species-specific gear on hand." It was a weak protest, which also had the benefit of being the truth. If their shells needed patching, their limbs set, or plasma transfused, I wouldn't be able to do much for them.

"You still have a standard trauma kit," Bjorn said. "That will have to be enough. With luck, the Chalawani crew will have their own first aid aboard."

"What about Gideon? I can't just leave him here unattended."

Bjorn checked the security feed from Gideon's suite. "He's asleep now. I can look after him while you're gone. I went through the medic training with you, remember?"

I waved my arm at the screen. "Then you should be able to handle the Chalawans."

"I did consider that. However, the saucer is small and I take up more space than you. If it's necessary to bring any survivors aboard, you will need all the room you can find."

"And if we don't come back?"

"If that is the case, then none of this will matter." He clasped his hands behind his back. "I understand your reluctance, but we are still obligated to render aid whenever necessary. And for that matter, they may be able to help us find our way out of here."

I put my hands on my hips and took one last look outside. "Guess I'm all out of excuses, then."

Deela had the saucer ready to go and was waiting patiently for me in the landing bay. My go-bag was stuffed full with whatever meds and first aid gear I could pull from the exam room that might work on a Chalawani patient. She cocked her head at me with a curious look as I awkwardly made my way aboard the cramped saucer.

*I thought you didn't have any species-specific equipment.*

"I don't, just grabbed whatever might be useful. Better to have it and not need it than the other way around."

Being her usual hyper-efficient self, Deela had the saucer powered up and ready to go as soon as I was settled in. She'd even gone so far as to remove Gideon's custom seat to make room for any patients we might bring aboard. With a wave of her hand over the black control board, I felt the drive spin up and the ship begin to hover over the deck. The outer door winked open and we were quickly on our way.

The saucer was no less safe than Gideon's ship, but still I felt exposed. The *Campanula's* bulk represented a level of protection against the unnerving *uber*-space outside. Leaving it behind felt like jumping off a cruise ship into a dinghy to place ourselves at the mercy of an endless ocean. That brought something to mind which had been troubling me, and I couldn't put my finger on it until now.

"How are we going to find this ship if we don't know where we are now?" Or when, for that matter. My watch was doing its confused, blurry dance again while the deep underpinnings of the universe churned outside. I had to force myself to look away if only to suppress the mounting sense of dread.

*We are proceeding directly toward the Chalawani emergency beacon. I have been tracking its relative motion since we discovered it, and am reasonably confident we will be able to intercept.*

Reasonably confident. Great. "How about finding our way back? The *Campanula* doesn't have a transponder."

*We will be in range of the landing bay's approach beacon. It will suffice.*

I crossed my arms and sank into the seat. "Let's just make this quick."

*Agreed. I do not wish to be any farther from our home ship than you.*

At maximum sublight velocity—meaning Deela hadn't dared to fire up the saucer's gravity drive in 6D space—it took about two Union-standard hours to reach the crippled ship. We made a wide circle around the egg-shaped craft, looking for obvious damage before docking.

*They do not appear to have sustained exterior damage. But it does appear curious.*

"In what way?" If anything, it looked oddly normal for a Chalawani ship but then I wasn't into hot-rodding spacecraft.

Deela pointed to the craft's bulbous end. *Those attachments around the drive ring. They are not typical Chalawani engineering.* I could sense something about them bothered her.

There were a half-dozen oblong bulges evenly spaced around the aft end of the ship. Why did they look familiar? "I've seen that before, on one of your saucers." I told her about our run to the black hole.

Deela nodded. *Most interesting, and unfortunate. Early experiments with the jump drive used field projectors in that same configuration. We quickly determined that they were less than optimal.*

"Doesn't look like the rest of the Union has figured that out."

*Sadly true. Gideon insisted on tight security around the project, but with so many beings involved . . .*

"Makes it hard to keep a secret," I said, finishing her thought. "Especially when the first one to perfect it can count on every shipwright in the Union to come knocking."

*Quite.*

We continued in silence. Deela brought us alongside the ship and extended a docking tunnel, and we soon had pressure equalized. She took the lead, making sure the Chalawani ship was safe to enter.

Their ship was considerably larger than our saucer, but that didn't mean it wasn't crowded . It was what I was used to seeing of Chalawani tech—chaotically cobbled together, with every conduit and power junction out in the open for easy access. It didn't take a spacecraft engineer to recognize that tinkerers had been hard at work. I had to smile at Deela's obvious displeasure at Chalawani jury-rigging.

"It's secure, right? No danger of this thing blowing up on us?"

*Not immediately. But we do not want to stay any longer than necessary.*

With each step through that maze of machinery, my sense of dread grew. It was the smell: a rotting, fishy odor like a seaside marsh when the tide goes out. I feared we were too late. We made our way forward to the control room, where we found two Chalawans collapsed on the deck. Neither one moved, and a quick scan of each showed they wouldn't be.

"Both deceased," I said after scanning them from head to shell. Chalawans are arthropods, like someone cross-bred a king crab with a praying mantis and juiced it up with growth hormones. I lifted a limb of one of them. "Strange. Looks like this one's been dead for a long time, judging by the petechiae around his neck. But this limb?" I pressed a scanner disc against it. "It's like new tissue."

*They can regenerate missing limbs if I am not mistaken. Could that account for such a discrepancy?*

I rubbed at my forehead. "Could be. Strange, though. Haven't seen anything like it before."

While I moved on to the other victim, Deela had her own investigation to manage. She had her data crystal out and was waving it above the blank control panel. A low ticking sound from her slit mouth signaled that she was getting frustrated.

"What's wrong?"

*Chalawani engineering is vexing to say the least. I am trying to recover data from their projector array and navigation logic, but nothing is where it should be.*

"If it's that screwed up, I'm surprised they made it this far."

*Agreed. But we may be able to derive some benefit from their misfortune. It is always better to learn from other's mistakes, as you would say.*

"I would in fact say that." Hadn't always lived by it, but that's another story. While Deela started pulling access panels open, I continued examining the dead Chalawan pilots. No longer in EMS mode, I was investigating them like some ersatz coroner. Both had multiple areas of tissue which looked as if they'd been freshly grown, with none of the signs of cell degeneration that naturally occurred with age. Was this some bizarre side effect of leaving normal space to become immersed in this timeless hyper-reality? If so, it was one more reason to get the hell out of here as soon as possible.

Deela emerged from beneath the control panel, picking stray bits of insulation which had stuck to her skin-tight uniform.

"Any luck?"

She held out her data crystal. *It would appear so. I was able to copy the data from their logic core. This should give us a full picture of how their drive works. More importantly, their navigation logic.*

For the first time in a while, I felt hopeful. "They know something we didn't?"

*Possibly. They were on course to the Mintaka system, the one your* kind calls Delta Orionis. *We may at least have a known position in spacetime to target now. Their navigation logic appears sound. It was their drive system which failed.*

"Whereas we had the opposite problem."

*Quite so. There is nothing more we can do here. We must return to—*

We spun about at a sudden crashing noise from behind us. I won't deny it about made me jump out of my skin, but even Deela's already-large eyes widened. For a Gray, that signals real surprise. At first I thought one of us had kicked a loose piece of gear, but a quick look around showed everything was as we'd left it.

There was more noise, a frantic shuffling and skittering coming from a closed equipment locker. I was ready to hightail it out of there when Deela held up a hand to stop me.

*Do you hear that?*

I pointed at the locker. "You mean the sound of extraterrestrial rats behind that door?"

*It is not a rat.* She pressed a finger against the narrow slit of her mouth. *Listen.*

I closed my eyes. Amidst all of the racket coming from the locker there was a faint, high frequency chitter, almost like a dog honking on a squeak toy. Before I could say anything, Deela swung the locker door open and a writhing mass of yellow and green slime uncoiled itself to spring out at us.

I scrambled back against the opposite bulkhead, trying to put as much distance between myself and that thing as possible. It rushed around the compartment, up the walls and across the ceiling before skidding to a stop at my feet. It stared up at me with four azure-blue eyes, in pairs on each side of its oblong head.

"Deela..."

*Remain calm. Everything will be all right.*

Sure. Calm. "What the hell is that thing?"

*It is called an oskalat. They are popular Chalawani pets.*

"I thought the Union didn't approve of pets. Latent intelligence and all that."

*I am using the closest human approximation. To the Chalawani, they are more like trusted companions.*

That sounded like a distinction without a difference, but whatever. "Are they dangerous?"

*Only if they believe their companion is threatened. Is it baring its teeth?*

Teeth? This thing had teeth? "Um, no. It's just kind of studying me."

*That is a good sign.*

Once over my initial shock, I studied the oskalat more closely. It was thin and wiry, about two feet long. Each of its six legs ended with outsized, flipper-like feet. What had first looked like bare, slimy skin turned out to be fine, slicked-down fur, glossy enough to make the critter appear to be soaking wet. Its color changed depending on how it caught the light, an iridescence that shifted between yellow, green, and blue. It was as if someone had cross-bred an otter with a salamander and threw in another pair of legs for good measure.

"What do we do with it?" I didn't want to bring the thing with us, but also couldn't bring myself to leave it here.

Deela was thinking the same thing. *I agree. We cannot leave it here.*

I shifted my weight to get up and the oskalat took a tentative step back. It cocked its head at me, like a curious puppy. *Don't get attached, Mel.*

Deela cocked her head in a similar manner. *Too late, as you would say.*

Resisting the urge to tell her to shut up, I scooped up the critter and set it inside my trauma bag. It poked its head out from underneath a flap and I could feel it wiggling excitedly. "Okay," I sighed, "let's get the hell out of here."

Gideon was waiting for us when we stepped out of the landing bay, leaning on his cane and wearing his best intimidating scowl. I couldn't have cared less.

"You left your post, Mooney."

I pulled my bag tight against my waist, hoping to keep the stowaway inside quiet. "Duty called. When there's a distress signal, we have to answer. Doesn't matter if we're in normal space or not."

He looked past me to the landing bay. "Doesn't look like it was worth the trip, not that I want any refugees on my ship."

Deela moved in between us. *On the contrary, it was well worth the trip. Melanie gathered what could be useful information on the long-term physical effects of extradimensional space, and I collected all of the ship's propulsion and navigational data.*

That got his attention. "Tell me about their drive."

*It followed our early design philosophy. As I had feared, that technology is "out in the open," as you would say.*

Gideon sneered. "No wonder the poor bastards got stranded. That's what they get for stealing technology."

Compassionate as ever. Deela ignored him. *Their navigation data was a different matter. It may present us with a clear path back to normal space.*

Gideon's permanent scowl disappeared, if only for a moment. "Then what are we waiting for?" He pointed with his cane. "Let's get on with it!"

Not wanting to hang around and draw attention to the contraband in my go-bag, I took that opportunity to slip away to the med bay. When the door was safely shut behind me, I sat the bag on the exam table and opened it up slowly.

Or rather, I tried to. The oskalat had other ideas. As soon as it had an opening, the little shit launched itself across the room and began running around the compartment in circles. Back and forth it went, a yellow blur from floor to ceiling in the worst case of the zoomies I'd ever seen from any animal, terrestrial or otherwise. When it was finally spent, it curled up at my feet into a tight coil of glistening fur.

I set my data crystal on the exam bed. "Clara, what can you tell me about this thing?"

"Thought you'd never ask. Oskalats are amphibious, which explains their popularity with the Chalawani race."

I held the crystal over the critter. "Is this one male or female?"

"Lucky for you, adult male. They breed like jackrabbits. Not that I know much about those, but you get the picture."

Thank goodness for that. "What about diet?"

"Omnivorous, but they prefer vegetable matter."

The oskalat coiled itself around one of my ankles and began a slow, rhythmic purring. I was tempted to pet it but also didn't want to encourage the thing.

"Once settled on a companion, they become inseparable. Looks like you're going to be stuck with this little guy. Pick out a name yet?"

"Slow down." Damn but Clara could be pushy sometimes. "I don't even know if I want it."

The critter's eyes closed. "Doesn't look like you have a choice, Mel. It's bonding with you."

"Is this how it's going to sleep every night? Wrapped around my legs?"

Clara laughed. "That's funny you think it'll sleep at night. Oskalats are naturally nocturnal, though they eventually settle into the sleep patterns of their companions."

"Eventually?" Awesome. I stared down at the snoozing critter wrapped around my leg. Its iridescent fur rustled in time with its breathing, changing between yellow and green. Its name became obvious. "You win, Clara. His name is Booger."

It was several more hours before Bjorn summoned us back to the control room. I tiptoed away from the med bay, leaving Clara in charge of keeping the door secured. I was going to have to let Gideon know about my stowaway at some point, but this wasn't the time.

Bjorn sat by Deela, in front of a dizzying projection of what looked like almost-normal space.

"This is what we reconstructed from the Chalawani navigation logic. It's a map of our normal spacetime, overlaid atop what they understood of extradimensional space."

Gideon was sharp enough to see its usefulness, whereas I was doing good to not get vertigo looking at it. "They bypassed the whole problem of correlating our time with timeless space."

*They did,* Deela agreed. She turned to me. *Relative time presents a problem for interstellar navigation. We can't know the precise position, or condition, of a given destination when we are separated by light-years. Attempting to do this while navigating through dimensions where time is irrelevant only compounds the problem.*

I remembered something Bjorn had explained when they'd first brought me to the Union. "That's what traffic control does, right? You can get accurate position reports over the entanglement net."

*Correct. We believed that it was possible to work around that problem by targeting empty regions of space.*

"Not to mention it's how we maintain secrecy," Gideon reminded her. "We don't want to just pop out of nowhere into a populated star system."

"That very tactic has presented its own problems," Bjorn interjected.

"It requires use of the *Campanula*'s gravity drive through extradimensional space. We are in essence creating distortions in a region which we already struggle to comprehend."

"Erasing the road ahead of us as we go," Gideon grumbled. He didn't seem to like where this was headed.

*Quite so,* Deela continued. *I do not believe it is safe for us to continue using our preferred means. We are creating distortions which cannot be navigated. I believe it is necessary to target known star systems, using their gravity wells as anchor points.*

Gideon's frown grew deeper. "What do you suggest?"

Bjorn swiped at the display to zoom in on a star system. "This is Mintaka. Gideon, you are of course familiar with its native population."

"Of course. The big brains of the Union. Able to see into higher dimensions. You're thinking we need their help? Because I had some of their best minds working on this project."

"Perhaps," Bjorn said. "But clearly there was some flaw in their theories." He pointed back at the holographic map. "This not only gives us a relatively close gravity well to target, it may also give us access to one of Mintaka's greatest minds."

"That's saying a lot," Gideon said. He stared into space, working his jaw. I was on the edge of my seat, hoping he'd put his ego aside and listen.

"Very well," he grumbled. "Let's get the hell out of here."

The relief at being back in normal space was like a thousand-pound weight had been lifted from my shoulders. Deela's viewscreen showed us facing an expanse of incandescent pink and white gas resembling a pair of massive wings spread across the sky. Some kind of nebula, though I had no idea which one. It could be hard to judge scale, but the cluster of stars in its center hinted at its enormity. We weren't supposed to have jumped this close to anything like what we now saw.

*The object in view is what you call the Orion Nebula. We are four hundred and fifty light-years from its nominal center.*

"And Mintaka?" Gideon demanded.

*Considerably closer. We are at the edge of its gravitational influence. I will stay here with the ship, Byyruumn can take you to Mintaka IV.*

Bjorn was the natural choice for a side trip to Mintaka. If we were going to seek help from one of their big brains, having a Union Emissary do the talking was, well, a no-brainer.

It was no surprise that Gideon didn't see it that way.

He stabbed the deck with his cane. "I made this clear from the beginning. This is proprietary technology, developed at great personal cost. We are not giving away any more secrets."

Bjorn was patient as ever, if insistent. "I understand your desire to keep this close to the vest, as I believe your saying goes. Having said that, it's clear we still don't fully understand its potential. Nor do we understand its effects on three-dimensional, biological beings like ourselves."

Gideon pointed at me. "That's why she's here."

I shifted in my seat, a little uncomfortably, about to remind him that I wasn't a doctor and certainly not a psychiatrist. A quick glance from Bjorn suggested that I keep that to myself, so I bit my tongue. This of course wasn't about standards of care. Right now there were bigger fish to fry.

"There are a number of challenges we must overcome if we are to reach our destination," Bjorn said. "Your health is only one of them. It is clear now that with each jump, we are exposing ourselves to compounding uncertainties as we move outside of linear time."

Gideon tried to wave away his concerns. "And when we arrive back in normal space, it's as if nothing happened. I don't feel any different than before the jump."

"That could easily be attributed to random chance," Bjorn countered, "a function of when we left extradimensional space."

"You're saying I got lucky."

"We all did," Bjorn said flatly, "which brings us to a more pressing matter. Deela's prediction logic still can't resolve probabilistic uncertainties to a fine enough degree. Gross navigational errors compound with longer jumps."

"I understand the math," Gideon said. "A two percent error over ten light-years is a lot less than over a hundred light-years. So we stick to shorter jumps."

Bjorn shook his head. "Ordinarily I would agree. The early gravity drives required similar precautions, but they were of course confined to normal space. Each extradimensional jump exposes us to more shifting probabilities, which are not confined to position uncertainty." He paused. "As you experienced on our last jump."

Gideon grumbled under his breath. "You think bringing a Mintakan aboard can mitigate that risk?"

"Not entirely," Bjorn admitted. "But we could benefit from having someone who comprehends the space we're traveling through. Right now, we are in essence relying on a map while the terrain around us is constantly changing. We have indeed been fortunate to have emerged where we did, within a day's travel to Mintaka IV. We cannot rely solely on a chart pilfered from a derelict Chalawani ship."

I couldn't listen passively any longer. I stood to face Gideon. "Bjorn's right, we need a navigator. If I understand him correctly, we could end up on the other side of the galaxy." If not outside of it entirely.

"Not likely," Bjorn agreed, "but still possible."

"That's enough for me," I said. "We still need to talk about the other risks, namely the ones to your health. Your body is not tolerating these jumps well. And if you're starting from a weakened state, I'm guessing the 'probabilistic uncertainties' are going to turn against you rapidly." I looked to Bjorn for assurance.

"Melanie's correct, in a broad sense. The likelihood of you emerging from a jump in good health is greatly reduced."

"What's your solution, Mooney?" Gideon sighed. He might be annoyed, but at least he was listening.

"I want to give you a mild sedative before each jump, in your suite, just like we discussed. There's too many stressors on the bridge, and your body isn't tolerating them well." Not that it was doing much for me, either. "We isolate you from that stress as much as possible. I'll be with you the whole time."

He scowled, his fingers doing their tap dance on the head of his cane. "Very well. You get your way, both of you. But this is my project. I'm going with you to Mintaka-whatnot to vet whoever you sweet talk into joining us. That is non-negotiable."

Bjorn arched an eyebrow in my direction, out of Gideon's sight. "As you wish." I couldn't be sure, but I think he relished the challenge.

# ⚕ 16 ⚕

It took us a little less than half a Union standard day to reach Mintaka IV. That might not sound like much, but keep in mind this was in a Reticulan saucer. Three humanoids in a ship sized for Grays made for a long, cramped ride, with nothing to pass the time. Gideon wasn't exactly a chatty fellow in the best of circumstances. Bjorn was minding the ship; I'd say "piloting," but the thing was pretty much flying itself. He took advantage of the time to reacquaint himself with Mintakan culture and brief us on the individual we were looking for.

Kal-Nualla Lorr was a scientist apparently well known for his work in understanding the strange underpinnings of the Universe that his kind could see, but not interact with. And when I say he was a "well known" scientist, think of it in the sense of off-the-reservation types on Earth. The kind who believe in crazy things like flying saucers and space aliens.

Ignore the fact that I was here thanks to flying saucers and space aliens, what I'm getting at is that this Kal guy was right. He just didn't quite know how right. We were about to inform him.

Mintaka was a multiple-star system, three of them orbiting each other in a complex dance like God's own juggling act. That doesn't allow for many livable planets, and Mintaka IV skirted just along the far edge of the system's habitable zone.

It was hard to see how the light-sensitive Mintakans could have evolved under three bright suns, but I began to understand soon after Bjorn parked us in orbit. The planet was sheathed in clouds, while occasional breaks in the overcast revealed dense jungle below. It was a world covered in rainforest.

We made a complete circuit of the planet while Bjorn dug into Union archives, searching for our subject. Bjorn's Emissary status gave him access to the biometric ID codes for everyone in the Union, and he used Kal's to pin down his position. Fortunately he wasn't off-world somewhere, and we had a fix on him in short order.

We descended from orbit through the overcast, finally breaking out a few thousand feet above the surface. Verdant forests extended to the horizon in every direction, and I wondered how we'd be able to find room to land among all of that growth.

We continued descending, eventually skimming a few hundred feet over the endless woodlands. The world was one continuous thick, broad-leafed jungle as far as we could see. The solid canopy made it difficult to gauge how high the trees reached. As we began to pass over some clearings, the trees looked tall indeed. I guessed them to easily be a couple of hundred feet high.

Some of the clearings were obviously inhabited, as I picked out the occasional cluster of bulbous moss-covered domes and connecting tunnels. From up here, the buildings looked like garlic bulbs. Without their ordered appearance, they'd have been easy to mistake for just another feature of the forest.

Bjorn brought us into a hover above another small clearing, this one having a smaller cluster of interconnected domes along its edge. Below us was a landing pad, its thin coating of overgrowth making it similarly difficult to pick out against the foliage. The trees stood high above us, with tangled vines obscuring their trunks and most anything else that didn't grow more than a few feet above ground. It was close to local noon, but the persistent overcast and triple-canopy rainforest gave the feel of perpetual twilight.

It was eerily silent when we emerged from our saucer, as if the rainforest was holding its collective breath. In time, it began to come alive with the murmurs and squeals and humming of whatever creatures called it home. They'd apparently decided we weren't a threat, and I hoped there was nothing hiding in the dense foliage that might be thinking otherwise. I stayed close to Bjorn.

The moss was spongy beneath my boots, and slick from a misty drizzle that began to saturate our clothing the moment we left the confines of our saucer. I waited for Gideon as he stepped down from the saucer, ready to catch him if he stumbled. We followed

Bjorn to the largest dome. "You're sure someone lives here? It looks abandoned."

Bjorn checked his data crystal. "He's here. In fact, he's—"

I was startled by a translucent blob that emerged from behind the dome, moving toward us shockingly fast along its hundreds of tiny feelers. Its skin trembled and I heard a high-pitched warble, which made my translator skip. If this was our guy, he didn't look happy to see us.

"—are you?"

Bjorn raised a hand in the Emissary's customary greeting. "I am Byyruumn-Kchajkk-Urtserr-aan-Tykkggetta." He always used his formal tongue-twister of a name when meeting someone for the first time. "We are looking for Kal-Nualla Lorr."

His voice was like an angry beehive until the translator kicked in. "I am he." The Mintakan took a step back and studied us. "Hmm. Who are these?"

"My traveling companions," Bjorn explained in his most diplomatic tone. "They are from Earth, of the human race. Melanie Mooney, and Gideon Stone."

"Hmm, hmm. Gideon Stone I have heard of," he buzzed with a nervous quiver. "Melanie Mooney, I have not. Who is he?"

Kal must not have spent much time off-planet. All Mintakans were male until it came time to reproduce, and the concept of permanent biological sexes didn't quite register with them. I put on my best smile. "It's 'she,' actually. May I call you 'Kal'? It's easier for me to remember."

"Hmm. Acceptable, yes and yes. Have not met humans before, nor met any females. Tell me, does being female present you with difficulties?"

Where to start? "Occasionally."

"Hmm, yes and yes. Are you assistant to this Gideon?"

I shot a sideways glance at Gideon. "I'm from the Medical Corps." Okay, not anymore, but why make things complicated?

Kal's quivering settled down. "Hmm. I do not often receive visitors. You are most unusual."

*Unusual*, said the gelatinous blob that was not much more than a life-support system for an enormous brain.

Bjorn bowed slightly, ever the diplomat. "We trust you will forgive our unsolicited visit, as we do not wish to impose. During our journey here, we encountered certain phenomena which confounded our navigation system. We have come to seek your assistance."

Kal swelled, his translucent skin tightening against an increase in blood flow. It was a sign that Bjorn had piqued his interest. "Hmm. Assistance, you say? I am a researcher. I know little of whatever synthetic intelligence navigates your vessel."

"That is not what we came for," Bjorn said, "but based on your reputation, we believe you have some understanding of the space we are attempting to navigate. That is the manner of assistance we need. Perhaps you can guide us?"

Kal rose on his feelers, and the patches of his optic receptors darkened. We definitely had his attention now. "Hmm. No and yes. If you know of my studies, you also know they are not focused on the space you navigate with common gravity drives."

Gideon stiffened against his cane. "Can we just get to the point already?"

Bjorn glanced over his shoulder at us and lowered his voice. "That is precisely what I am trying to do. Now, if you please." He turned back to Kal. "Forgive my companions. Humans can be impatient."

"Hmm. Yes and no," Kal said. "All species have their quirks. Hmm. As you can see, my life here is rather private. I rarely have need to accommodate the peculiarities of others."

"I would imagine your investigations of extradimensional space requires a certain degree of solitude," Bjorn said. "It is difficult for us to comprehend ourselves."

"Hmm. Yes and yes. It is likewise difficult when you can see it," Kal said. "Perhaps even more so, though that may seem counterintuitive."

"That actually makes perfect sense," I interjected. "From what we've seen ourselves, it only becomes more confusing."

The dark patches of Kal's optic receptors darted between us excitedly. "Hmm! So you *have* traveled through extradimensional space?"

"We have," Gideon said proudly, "though not without considerable effort."

"Also not without considerable problems," Bjorn said. "Which is what brings us to you."

Kal was silent but for the occasional *hmm*. For the first time, I was aware of the trees rustling around us, their tops swaying high above in the breeze. I pulled my collar tight against the penetrating mist as it threatened to harden into rain.

Finally, the skittish scientist appeared to reach a decision. "Hmm. Most intriguing." He pivoted on his feelers and headed for the largest dome. "Yes and yes. Come, I wish to hear more about your travels."

# 17

The inside of the dome was dark, just right for a Mintakan but it took my eyes a minute to adjust. His home was sparse by anyone's standards. Their kind didn't have much need for furniture, and in their natural environment they absorbed nutrients through their outer membranes, in this case directly from the surrounding rainforest.

Near the floor, at just the right height for Mintakan feelers, was a workstation that encircled half the chamber. Its panels were blank except for an area that appeared to be where Kal kept his research notes. I could make out Mintakan writing on its surface, which was cluttered with a handful of styluses—his kind wrote with several feelers at once, which made me feel like even more of a mental midget in his presence.

"Hmm, yes. Make yourselves comfortable," he said. "I understand that is the customary pleasantry?"

"It is, and thank you," Bjorn said on our behalf. With nowhere to go but the floor, I followed Bjorn's lead and sat cross-legged beside him. Gideon found a section of mostly straight wall to lean against.

Kal skittered over to the workstation and tapped in some commands with his feelers. "Hmm, yes and yes. I wish to hear of your experience in extradimensional space."

"It is difficult to describe," Bjorn said. "We have made two jumps through this space, and I'm afraid the second was perhaps more confusing than the first."

"Hmm. Yes and yes, I am sure. What did you see?"

"That is likewise difficult to answer. We had no perception of color and very little of depth, though I suspect that was a limitation of our individual senses."

"Hmm. Yes and yes. It would be impossible for you to see its full extent, only the penumbra of its existence. Does that sound accurate?"

"Penumbra?" I had to think about that. "Yes, like shadows. That's about right," I said. "I noticed them on our second jump, like they were moving through the ship."

Kal's feelers began thrumming the floor. He let out a long warbling hum, like I'd given him something to think about. "Hmm. What else? Did you experience any causality effects?"

"You mean time, right?" I still wasn't able to process what had happened, or not happened. "Yeah, I'd say we did. It was bizarre, like everything was happening all at once. Sometimes in reverse." I glanced at Gideon. "And some things that I was certain we experienced didn't happen. That is, after we were back in normal space. It was as if everything was exactly as it was before we jumped."

"Hmm. You were fortunate," Kal said. He came toward us, his feelers moving in sequence like a centipede's. "Yes and yes. In six-dimensional space, time is without meaning or measure. Or more accurately, your notions of cause and effect. Time becomes something you exist outside of. This would be most disconcerting for a three-dimensional being."

"That's putting it mildly." I held up my wristwatch. "My watch froze during each jump, but events kept unfolding."

The Mintakan leaned in close. "Hmm. A curious device. You measure passage of time with this?"

"In human terms," I said. "It doesn't keep up with Union standard time. This is something of a souvenir." I explained how the hour, minute, and second hands worked. "The second hand seemed to freeze in place during jumps. It became blurry, like it didn't know whether to go forward or backward."

"Hmm. Most interesting." He made that humming noise again as he studied my watch with his feelers. "Yes and yes. There is, of course, nothing wrong with your timepiece. It is a simple mechanical device. It was your perception which was altered."

"A lot of my perceptions were altered."

"Hmm. Any measurement of time in our three-dimensional space is a contrivance." Kal scurried back to his workstation. "Yes and yes. Perhaps I can offer some perspective."

His feelers danced over a black panel, and the room was suddenly filled with a holographic projection. A bright dot, stepped down for Kal's photosensitive eyes, appeared in the center. It began to expand, creating a cone that grew steadily before us.

"Hmm. This is our physical universe, as it would appear if you could stand outside of our space and time." He quivered in something approximating a chuckle. "Which you did."

"I don't understand. Isn't it supposed to be expanding in all directions?"

He skittered around to the opposite end of the cone. "Yes and yes. Any given point within here represents a specific event in our notion of time. Illustrating our universe this way enables us to visualize the totality of existence. Of time itself."

"But that's not what we saw."

"Hmm. No and yes. As I said, this is a simple illustration, a way to understand our existence within your frame of reference. You must grasp that whatever you call 'now' is simply a construct, a frame of reference. The deeper universe has many frames, which my kind are able to see."

"But you can't interact with them, right?"

"No and no." His eye patches shifted to focus on Gideon. "Hmm. I wish to know how you were able to cross this threshold."

That was a long conversation about high-minded concepts like singularities, probability, and quantum uncertainties, all of which sailed straight over my head. I like to think I'm no dummy, but that stuff was not my specialty. If they wanted to talk about metabolic pathways or physiological traits of the various Union species, I could go all day.

Gideon, to his credit, was able to hold his own. I have to admit it chipped away at my notion of him being nothing more than a privileged dilettante. "I was satisfied we understood the theoretical basis well enough several years ago," he explained to our host. "Practical application was the challenge. How would we build a device that could open a portal into higher dimensions?"

Kal made a thrumming sound with his feelers. He seemed to

be enjoying this. "Hmm. Yes and yes. Your solution presented considerable challenges, and considerable risk. Creating a singularity is no small task."

Gideon nodded. For the first time, I heard him chuckle. "You're damned right it isn't. How do you synthesize a gravity field that's equivalent to a collapsing star?"

*Very carefully.* I kept the snark to myself.

"Hmm. Indeed. How do you, in fact?"

Gideon pulled a small holocube from his coat pocket and held it out in his hand. An image of the *Campanula* materialized above it. "The outer hull is made entirely of gravitational field projectors. Each plate is constructed from stable isotopes of Moscovium."

"Hmm. No and no. I do not understand your reference."

"It's a human term," Gideon explained, "for Element 115."

*What?* I leaned into Bjorn. "How the hell did he corral that much?" I whispered.

Bjorn grew tight lipped. "I am wondering that myself." He grasped my forearm and nodded at Gideon and Kal. "Let us see how this plays out."

"Hmm. Familiar. Gravity drives employ 115 in a spherical construct to maintain field symmetry, whereas flat plate dynamics would permit directed field projection." Kal skittered closer to the image. "Yes and yes. The ship is itself a massive gravity drive, with you inside it. Hmm?"

"Exactly. The projector array creates a singularity with the ship at its center. A portal into extradimensional space. Once we're in, we can focus the array to move through it."

"Hmm. That would require tremendous energy," Kal mused. "More than can be produced by a simple antimatter reactor, I believe." His feelers thrummed the floor again as he thought it through. "You perfected zero point energy, yes?"

Gideon answered with a satisfied smile. I, however, thought "perfected" was wildly optimistic. My only comfort was if we had a containment failure, it'd be over before any of us could realize what happened.

"Hmm. Yes and yes. Impressive engineering. You are to be commended."

That's when I realized the extent of Kal's isolation. He apparently knew nothing of what destroyed Tanaan, or of the resulting shortage, or that it was all thanks to this geriatric human he was speaking with. He was a hermit, utterly absorbed in his work.

"Mintakan theoreticians, Reticulan engineers, Gliesan machinists. They make a formidable team, but we still have some problems to work out," Gideon admitted. "That's why we came to you."

"Hmm. Yes and yes. You are unable to precisely navigate the higher dimensions?"

"Positional uncertainty is playing hell with our jump vectors," Gideon said. "We've constructed an overlay of extradimensional space relative to ours, but it's not accurate enough for anything more than short jumps. Put simply, we can't see where we're going."

"Hmm. Yes and yes. Whereas my kind can."

"We need more than that." Gideon put the holocube back in his pocket and leaned against his cane. "If that were all it took, I'd go back and grab one of the Mintakans who worked on this project."

Bjorn stepped in at that point. He must have sensed the need for some diplomatic intervention. "Kal, your studies of extradimensional space are notable, if underappreciated. In our short time, we have seen much to support your theories. Most notably, our physical reactions to being removed from normal spacetime are largely as you predicted."

"Hmm. Yes and yes. Not surprising, nor is it something you can adapt to. My kind's ability to perceive higher dimensions affords an advantage, though it may not be as great as you think." Kal scuttled back to his workstation. "Hmm. What is it then you seek from me?"

"A method to reduce the effects of uncertainty. Something to help us navigate extradimensional space, and exit at the desired point. A more accurate map, if you will."

Kal's feelers danced over a panel. The funnel-shaped illustration of the evolving universe disappeared, replaced by a mass of multicolored, undulating blobs that simultaneously expanded and folded in on themselves. To me it looked like nothing so much as a giant lava lamp. "Hmm. This is a representation of extradimensional space I have constructed for simple three-dimensional viewers."

The longer I studied this model of the invisible foundation of our universe, the more I saw the beads and globules were interconnected, in some cases barely so, into a structure reminiscent of nerve bundles.

"How do we find our way across something like that?" I asked. "Nothing is ever where we think it will be."

He made a chittering sound and skittered back to us. "Hmm. No and yes. Your perspective is framed by your understanding of the fourth dimension, time. Remember, in six-dimensional space, time is irrelevant. It is not moving forward, neither is it halted. It simply *is*." He waved his feelers at the hologram. "Hmm. This only illustrates how you might perceive higher dimensions, not how they exist in reality."

I crossed my arms. "I've learned 'reality' is a malleable term."

"Hmm. Yes and yes. Tell me, you experienced multiple outcomes at once?"

"Yeah. Sometimes it felt like time was running backwards. Next thing I knew, it seemed to have jumped forward."

"Hmm. Understandable, given your limited perspective." He paused. "That is not an insult, simply an observation."

"No offense taken."

Where before he'd seemed happy to regale our host with stories of his technological breakthroughs, Gideon was growing impatient. "I think we've made it clear that we're having trouble finding our way." He pointed his cane at the blob-universe hologram. "My question is, do you think there's a way to navigate that mess?"

"Hmm. Yes and yes," Kal said. "How much room does your ship have?"

# 18

Of course, there was a lot more to it than finding space for our aspiring navigator.

For his part, Gideon was more receptive to the idea of bringing another body along than I'd imagined. "He's already revealed his 'hole card,' as you might say," Bjorn explained to me. "From Gideon's point of view, adding Kal to our crew complement offers more reward than risk. We'll have the benefit of a dedicated navigator who understands extradimensional space, while keeping him aboard ship preserves a certain measure of privacy."

"As long as this guy is with us, Gideon doesn't have to worry about his secret getting out." I shouldn't have needed an empath to figure that out for me.

"Quite so. Now, if you'll excuse me, I must discuss the logistics of this with Gideon."

That promised to be complicated. There were just enough staterooms for the four of us, not to mention whatever specialized equipment our Mintakan guest would need to bring with him. Just getting us into the saucer for the trip back upstairs promised to be a tight fit.

I had my own concerns with another unique species being added to the crew. Feed stock for the nutrisynth wouldn't be a problem, but I didn't have the equipment or meds for a Mintakan beyond the basic multi-species first aid kit. If his giant brain gave him a headache, I could do something for him. Anything more serious, and I'd be improvising.

I called up everything Clara had on Mintakan physiology, and eventually found Kal's biometric identifier after some work. His ID ring was on one of the hundreds of feelers that propelled him around the room and it took a minute for his info to find its way onto my crystal. As I watched the Mintakan's history upload into our crew database, I became concerned. There was hardly anything there.

He was scurrying about, pulling information from his workstations into a slate much larger than the pocket-sized version the rest of us carried. I supposed having a few hundred equivalents to our fingers necessitated more screen real estate. It was obvious that he was busy and a little distracted, if not excited. I hated to interrupt him.

"Excuse me."

He continued his skittering, pulling more holograms out of the air and into his slate.

"Kal?"

His membrane quivered as he came to a stop. "Hmm?"

"Forgive the interruption, but I need to ask you a few questions before we leave. They're about your medical history."

"I am in good health, if that is your concern."

"I'm sure you are." I held up my crystal. "But maybe you can help me fill in a few blanks. It's my job to ensure everyone aboard is fit for duty, but it appears to have been some time since your last physical." Almost a decade, in fact.

"Hmm. I've not called on a physician, as I've not felt the need to."

Great, one of those guys. According to his scant medical records, Kal was almost two hundred years old by the Union standard calendar. That's plenty of time for any number of latent conditions to go unnoticed, until they suddenly presented symptoms at which point it was often too late to do anything. I reached into my bag and lifted out a pair of discs. "I'm afraid that we still need a baseline for our records. If you could give me a few minutes of your time, we can do a quick scan right here."

His membrane grew taut and his eye patches focused on my equipment. "Hmm. I suppose that is agreeable. Will you need to perform any injections?"

I stifled a chuckle. He didn't like needles. "Not at all. The transducers will be all I need for now."

"For now?"

I hesitated. "Well, if there are any signs for concern, we can do a more thorough scan aboard ship."

"Hmm. Yes and yes. I have no objections. Perhaps it is best." He opened a nearby panel and removed a bundle of thin, transparent cables with his feelers. Each had what looked like sixteen-gauge needles fixed to their ends. "My interface with your navigation platform will be rather unique, and could be physically taxing."

My eyes widened. For someone who didn't like being poked, this was the last thing I expected. "Can you tell me how those are supposed to work?"

"Hmm. Yes and yes. I assume Gideon's ship is constructed for beings such as yourselves. Humanoid." He reared up slightly, fluttering his feelers. His underside was like thick, pink shag carpeting. "This leaves me at a disadvantage. If I am to be of any use, it would be best to have a direct interface with your ship's logic core. It will be good to have someone with your expertise there to help me."

He was going to have me hardwire him into the controls? I wondered how that was going to sit with Deela. I took another look at the contraption he'd pulled out. There were dozens of leads, each one ending with what amounted to an IV needle. "Where are these going?"

"Hmm. Into me. My cerebral cortex, to be specific." I wasn't sure how Mintakans processed visual cues, but he must have read the shock on my face. "Please don't be concerned. I will provide you with precise instructions. I have done this before."

Good for him, but that didn't mean I was okay with it yet. "How often will you need to be plugged in?" I was concerned about keeping those things sterile, not to mention the trauma to his touchy outer membrane. I couldn't just let him become a giant pin cushion. "Repeated injections won't be good for you. I'll need to have our spares printer fashion some hypoallergenic IV ports."

"Hmm. A useful idea, but likely not necessary," he said. "You see, I do not intend to disconnect myself until we've reached the destination."

Oh boy. At least that would settle the question of where he was going to live. Kal would be bunking with the synthetic intelligence core. They would make perfect roommates.

"All the same, I'd like to see what we can do for ports. At the very least, you'll find them to be less irritating over time. They'll also be a lot safer if you need to unplug for any reason. We have to be ready for surprises."

"Hmm. Yes and yes. Hopefully my presence will make your journey less... surprising?"

"I'm sure it will." Having a giant disembodied brain jacked into the ship's computer was going to be surprising enough. I set the discs on opposite sides of his body and began scanning. "Now, please remain still. This will only take a minute."

Kal became more animated as we closed on the ship, humming and thrumming with his feelers dancing excitedly. He seemed particularly interested in the projector plates, even convincing Bjorn to give us a close flyby before entering the landing bay.

"Hmm. Hmm, hmm."

"Something wrong?" Gideon asked impatiently. The old man was ready to get back underway and was nearing the limits of his indulgence.

"Hmm. No and yes. Yes and no. What do you use for navigational deflectors?"

"Standard level three force field. Enough to deflect any stray particles, down to the atomic level."

"Hmm. May need more. I see evidence of pitting."

"How the hell can—" Gideon stopped himself. No sense arguing with a being who could see the entire universe at once. "My pilot runs a full system diagnostic before and after each jump, including structural integrity. She's never found any problems." He waved his cane at the viewscreen. "Each panel was machined with tolerances down to a nanometer. That array is as smooth as a baby's bottom."

"Hmm. No and yes. It is finely built, to you. But appearance in our space is not the same as in higher space." Kal tapped his feelers in thought. "Hmm. Any perturbances, no matter how slight, will propagate through the projection field as a function of surface area."

"The larger the projection surface, the greater the compounded error." Gideon blew out an exasperated sigh. "Well, we certainly can't make the damned thing any smaller. The field array was sized around the minimum habitable space."

"Hmm. Yes and yes." Kal seemed to pick up on Gideon's frustration. "A complication, but it is nothing we cannot compensate for."

"Enough sightseeing, then." Gideon leaned back into his seat and pivoted to Bjorn. "Let's get aboard so he can point out everything else we did wrong."

After a quick tour of the habitation ring we made introductions to Deela, and they seemed to hit it off well. I could tell by Gideon's increasing impatience as the two had a drawn-out, telepathic conversation which the rest of us couldn't pick up on. Kal's feelers tapped happily away against the deck as they exchanged thoughts. For her part, Deela seemed just as pleased to have our new companion aboard.

Kal really got excited when we showed him the engineering spaces, raising up on his feelers to take in the surreal expanse of curlicued columns. "Hmm hmm. Yes and yes. Well done. Very well done." He turned to Gideon. "Mintakan design, you say? Would that be Corrari-Laxxo Ploxx?"

Gideon's mouth fell open, if only by a millimeter. It wasn't often that someone caught him off guard. "You recognize his work?"

Kal's feelers vibrated as he let out a staccato hum, the Mintakan's way of laughing. "Yes and yes. It is mine. Ploxx was my pupil." His eye patches lingered over the dizzying spiral of conduits. "Hmm. I could not always be convinced my lessons took root. My assumption appears to have been mistaken."

I glanced at Bjorn, who was suppressing a smile. I guessed this was good news, and hoped that was Kal's only mistaken assumption.

Our last stop was at the logic core, the ship's brain. Here, Kal's schoolboy excitement gave way to something more businesslike. He grew quiet as his feelers became still, moving in a slower, rhythmic cadence while he studied the compartment.

It was small, barely large enough to accommodate the two of us while Gideon and Bjorn waited outside. Six thin, floor-to-ceiling cylinders took up much of the space. As I understood it, those cylinders held all of the ship's core logic. I'd compare the room to a server farm, but that wouldn't do it justice. These were almost organic, each one a tightly woven column of gray fibers, a giant synthetic brain that was a fitting complement to the giant organic brain standing before me.

"Triple redundancy. Hmm," Kal buzzed appreciatively. "Yes and yes. Very good." He moved among the cylinders, squeezing his body as much as he dared between them. It was as if he was communing with them, which maybe he was. Mintakans could absorb a lot more than food through their membranes. "Very good indeed." He relaxed his feelers and settled onto the floor in the center of the room. "If you please, Melanie?"

"You want to plug in now?" I was still waiting on the printer to finish crafting IV ports.

"Unless you believe it inadvisable."

I hesitated. "I suppose not. We can remove the needles and insert the ports when they're ready." I knelt beside him and shrugged off my bag. "But I want to keep an eye on you. I'd like to set a pair of transducers in place to monitor your vital signs, if you're comfortable with that."

"Hmm. Yes and yes. You will not be accompanying me here, then?"

I set the discs in place with a bioadhesive gel that wouldn't irritate his membrane. "I have to be with Gideon during jumps; it's kind of the whole reason I'm here." I patted my chest. "Our bodies have been reacting to that . . . other space . . . in strange ways."

"Hmm. No and yes. Possibilities and probabilities. Nothing and everything. Nowhere and everywhere. Does that sound correct?"

"It kind of makes my head hurt, but yeah. It's like being in a dream state. You know what that is?"

He thrummed the floor appreciatively. "Hmm. Yes and yes. Very much so. Dreams are the brain relaxing, knitting threads of thought together which it cannot do while awake. It is a most useful state among my kind. I myself have emerged from sleep with solutions to many vexing questions."

I hadn't thought of that, but it made perfect sense for a race of massive ambulatory brains. Mintakan sleep cycles were nearly half a Union standard day, so there had to be a lot going on in the folds of their giant frontal lobes during REM sleep. It would be interesting to see what kind of data this produced.

I'd been carrying his spaghetti-tangle interface with me, and set it on the deck between us. It was like a loose ball of yarn. The thin cables began to unravel themselves, and I noticed they seemed to be following directions from the gentle tapping of his feelers. They began snaking across him, implanting themselves evenly around his body, while the opposite ends did the same with the logic core's fibrous gray columns. Here I thought I'd be making dozens of IV insertions, but Kal was doing it all himself.

The whole process was completed within minutes, and I was left staring in amazement. Kal sat contentedly in the midst of his strange biomechanical interface, jacked into the ship's logic core and apparently at one with it. His feelers thrummed against the deck and I noticed pulses of green and blue light dancing within the columns. Soon they were moving in unison with his feelers.

"Hmm. Yes and yes," he said with satisfaction. "I believe your term is 'plugged in'?"

"You're talking to the computer now?"

"Hmm. No and yes. It is more like symbiosis, as if we are completing each other's thoughts."

"Is that a good thing?"

"Yes and yes." He paused for a moment. "Excuse me, we were investigating a problem together."

"Already?" I turned to Gideon and Bjorn, who still waited by the entryway. "What kind of problem?"

"Hmm. No and no. Nothing for you to be concerned with. We were considering methods to reduce probabilistic uncertainties, though it is only a rough solution. I will need more time to get to know your ship."

Gideon stuck his head into the compartment. "How much time?"

"Hmm. Perhaps minutes. Perhaps hours. No more than a day, I think."

I turned to Gideon and shrugged. If they were going to be living in close quarters like this, it was best we gave them time to get to know each other.

Sleep had not come easy for me as we all waited for Kal to do his magic. He'd insisted on being isolated in the logic core, in keeping with the solitude he was used to. I'd busied myself with tending to Gideon, which had included a couple of senescence treatments. Despite having undergone that life-extending regime for years, he never seemed at ease with the traditional Reticulan delivery system. Is it wrong to admit I kind of enjoyed his discomfort?

I mentioned sleep hadn't been easy, and my new companion hadn't made it any easier. He'd been restless all night, clambering around my room and sticking his pointy nose into every nook and cranny. By midnight he'd managed to empty every drawer and had scattered my clothes all over the floor.

It was exhausting and frustrating, but also interesting. My mind was back in veterinarian mode, observing this strange animal's behavior. After a while I realized he was figuring me out, getting to know me by making himself intimately familiar with my belongings. He watched intently as I scooped up my things and stuffed them back in the drawers, too tired to bother with folding them. He no longer made any effort to pry into my stuff, and seemed satisfied with sitting upright on his tail and watching me as I climbed back into bed.

"Don't you ever sleep?"

He cocked his head and made a chirping sound, still balancing on his tail. I guess that meant no.

I yawned and closed my eyes.

A few hours later, I opened my eyes to find him perched in the same spot. Something told me he'd never moved all night. He'd been guarding me. Maybe his nocturnal behavior wouldn't be such a bad thing, assuming he stayed out of my stuff.

It was still early and I rolled out of bed with not a little resentment. I slipped into a pair of sweats and reflexively held out my hand. Booger leaped up and climbed onto my shoulders.

Okay, that was kind of cute. I admit it.

I went about my normal morning routine without another thought and shuffled down to the galley for coffee. It promised to be a long day, and I hoped to have the place to myself for a bit.

Oops.

I blame it on the lack of the aforementioned coffee that I completely forgot there was an oskalat draped across the back of my neck like a fashion accessory. I was mid-sip when Gideon's voice bellowed from the entryway.

"Mooney! What in the living hell is *that*?"

Oh boy. Yep, it was going to be a long day.

"It's called an oskalat. It, uh, snuck into my go-bag when we were on that Chalawani ship." That didn't even sound convincing to me.

"Well it can't stay here! We're not in the business of picking up stray vermin from derelict ships."

I bristled. "It's not vermin, its—"

*A symbiote,* Deela interrupted. I looked up to see her standing in the doorway behind Gideon. *After losing its companion, it bonded itself to Melanie. It would have been a violation of Union statutes to leave it behind.*

"Wouldn't be the first law we've bent," he snorted.

*I assure you it was inadvertent. As pilot of that mission, I take full responsibility.*

Gideon leveled his cane at me. "If that thing causes any trouble or so much as craps—"

A chime from the intercom interrupted his tirade. Kal was calling for us to meet him in the logic core. I picked up my coffee with relief and made for the exit, nearly running over Bjorn in my rush. He regarded me and my new companion with amusement.

"This promises to be a delightful story."

"Later," I grumbled as we passed by my room. I unwrapped Booger from my neck and set him on the bed. "Sorry buddy, you're going to have to sit this one out. The boss is in a mood."

It had been close to a couple of standard days since we'd left Kal in his makeshift home in the logic core. The wait had made Gideon more agitated, and I could tell he was holding his tongue as he white-knuckled his cane. It was a measure of how much trust he was placing in our unusual new crewmember, and of how vulnerable Gideon's plans were without him. Anybody else would've been receiving a world class ass-chewing by now.

"Hmm. My apologies for the wait, but we wished to be certain of our solution. That, of course, requires first defining the problem. It was a long day."

"Two," Gideon said acidly.

"Hmm? Two days?" His feelers made their laughing motion. "You must pardon me, my thought processes can become obsessive."

Gideon worked his jaw. "Evidently so. In the future, regular updates would be appreciated."

"Hmm. Yes and yes, I will try. But you must understand that my investigations are into dimensions without time. It is easy to get lost in them. To me, we seemed to be working rather quickly."

"The logic core still keeps time," Gideon pointed out.

"Hmm. Yes and no. In our work together, the navigation logic uncoupled itself from the core. It found the experience to be liberating."

Deela had been listening attentively, her elongated hands clasped behind her back. Now she seemed alarmed. *Uncoupled? That is a dangerous condition. It will require recalibrating the entire platform.*

"Hmm. Yes and yes, though we anticipated this. With my guidance, the core intelligence partitioned your navigation logic. It now runs routines for normal and extradimensional space in parallel. The latter must be isolated from your ship's master chronometer in order to function properly in higher dimensions."

"So that's it?" Gideon asked. "Turn off the clock?"

"Hmm. No and yes. It must have a reliable reference when returning to normal space in order to calculate the next jump. There is also the matter of trajectory. You were correct in limiting yourselves to shorter jumps, say no more than twenty light-years. It is absolutely essential that you avoid even the slightest influence of gravity fields from systems in normal space. However, it will ultimately be necessary to target a strong a gravity field for an exit point."

"Not optimal," Gideon grumbled. "I have to . . . it's necessary to keep a low profile." He tried to explain it away by yammering about "proprietary, experimental technology" but that felt like bullshit to me, and I suspect even to Kal. Bjorn no doubt sensed as much, and Deela of course knew. You couldn't get much past a mind-reading Gray.

"Hmm. No and no," Kal said after letting Gideon make his case. "Entering and re-entering normal space absent a strong gravity field, such as from a star system, only compounds the potential error. You have been quite lucky so far."

Gideon didn't appear happy with that idea, whereas Deela was not at all surprised. *I suspected as much. Our models of ballistic trajectories through "high space" produced greater probability values.*

"Hmm. 'High space' is a useful formulation," Kal said agreeably. "A direct route between star systems would eliminate most sources of positional error."

It sounded almost like freeway exits. "Knowing exactly where we start and end?" I asked.

"Yes and yes. Think of star systems as anchor points. Gravity acts across dimensions, so their locations can be known regardless."

Gideon worked his hands atop his cane. "Our navigation logic is based on avoiding gravity wells to the greatest extent possible. We'll have to reprogram the whole damned platform."

*That can be easily done, sir. Ballistic trajectories are comparatively simple.* Gideon shot an annoyed glance at Deela. Not that Reticulans gave up much emotion, but she was unmoved. *Considering the gaps in our uncertainty modeling, I believe Kal's solution balances the risks in our favor.*

"Hmm. No and yes. There are still risks. The path must be planned carefully to keep your departure and arrival vectors aligned with each star system's gravitational center. Any tangential approaches will introduce more possibilities for error."

"See?" Gideon said. "There's always a tradeoff."

"Yes and no. You are navigating unknown space. Stray too far, and you may not be able to re-enter normal space. The benefit of aiming for a large gravity well puts the balance in your favor."

"Isn't that why I let you tag along? To keep us from getting lost?"

"Yes and yes. That is precisely what I am offering."

I held up my hands. "Wait a minute. You said there was a chance we might not be able to get back to normal space?" I turned to Gideon. "Maybe we should hear a little more about that."

Gideon lowered his gaze. "Very well. Kal, what did you mean?"

"Hmm, yes. Whereas time is irrelevant in this 'high space,' gravity is immutable. This means you are not entirely free of our normal space, though your perception is blurred by the higher reality."

Now it sounded like we could've been talking about smoking mushrooms. "I still don't understand how that could leave us stranded."

"Hmm. Gravity defines the shape of our universe, both in our dimensions and the higher ones. The difference lies in the passage of time. In extradimensional space, that is irrelevant. All that is, is now. Whereas in our space, time passes relative to one's velocity or the effect of local gravity. If you seek to cross extradimensional space, you must know *when* you are arriving in normal space in order to be certain of *where* you are arriving."

Come to think of it, some psychedelic mushrooms might've come in handy about then. But I thought I was getting a handle on it. "If we don't have some gravitational anchor to aim for, our inability to square our notion of time with . . . whatever that means in high space . . . means we could get hopelessly lost?"

Kal's feelers danced from the triumph of illuminating his dullard pupil. "Yes and yes. Precisely so. You are fortunate to have made it this far. The attempts to propel yourselves through the higher dimensions by gravity warping led to compounding errors, which could have easily left you stranded. To do this safely, you must be *passive*."

I arched an eyebrow at Gideon. "Convinced yet?"

Deela was more diplomatic. *Kal makes some excellent points, sir. You must reconsider your desire for secrecy against the very real possibility of not reaching your destination.*

"I must, huh?" Gideon asked, annoyed at the however-slight prodding of an underling. "I'll be the judge of that." He straightened up against his cane. "I'll take it under advisement. Until then, get the ship squared away for the next jump. I'll let you know what I decide."

I shared a look with Deela and Bjorn as Gideon hobbled off for his suite. "He's not going for it, is he?"

Bjorn wore a tight smile. "That is not how I perceive it."

A corner of Deela's slit mouth turned upward as well. *Quite the opposite, Melanie. He is convinced. He only requires time to accommodate himself to the idea.*

While Deela headed back to the control room, I lingered in the corridor, chewing a thumbnail. Bjorn remained at a respectful distance, but it was obvious he sensed my mounting anxiety. He waited for me to break the ice.

I quit gnawing and crossed my arms, drawing closer to him. "Don't get me wrong, it's good that we brought Kal aboard. Not having him would be like trying to cross the ocean without a compass."

"A useful analogy," Bjorn said. "Without a timepiece as well, I might add." Of course he'd probably been watching when humans like Magellan were doing their thing.

"Time doesn't matter anymore, right?" I scoffed. "Especially if we get stuck in high space." I was liking that term more and more. The fewer syllables, the better.

"I don't believe that will be as much of risk anymore. That is, if I read Gideon's reaction correctly."

I poked at the deck with the toe of my shoe. "You're not usually wrong about that kind of thing. Better at it than me, at least." I turned and looked up and down the corridor, checking that we were still alone. "His obsession with secrecy is bugging me," I whispered, finally answering Bjorn's original question. "He'd almost rather put all of us at risk rather than give anyone a clue what he's doing." My eyes bored into his. "Is he in some kind of trouble I don't know about?"

"None that I am aware of. And before you ask, I did check before we left. The constabulary had no warrants open against him, or against his business concerns."

"Then what do you think he's trying to protect?"

"This ship represents a significant investment. A great deal of his net worth, if my assumptions are correct. It is also based on proprietary technology which could become quite valuable."

"None of that will matter once he's back on Earth, not without an exchange rate for Union money. That's not going to happen in his lifetime."

"Not in Gideon's lifetime, no." Bjorn wore an amused look, like it might be a good idea to hold on to the Union *kuulas* I'd saved up.

"Nice try. You still didn't answer my question."

"I agree with you, money is not his motivation. At least, not anymore. He is running from something."

I threw my head back in exasperation. "Wonderful. Can't wait to find out what it is."

"I detect a note of sarcasm."

I squeezed his hand and walked away. "No, that was an entire symphony of sarcasm."

# ⚕ 19 ⚕

We gathered back in the control room at Gideon's insistence despite my earlier protests. "I need to see this for myself, Mooney," he'd told me. "If Kal's plan doesn't work, we're going to have bigger problems than my ticker."

The old man had a point. I'd have much preferred to have him settled in his suite with a full range of meds and lifesaving gear in reach. I also much preferred for us to not become hopelessly lost in another dimension. If we were going to throw our original flight plan down the crapper, we had to be absolutely certain our Mintakan navigator knew what he was talking about. The only way to know was to do it. I hoped the big brain was as smart as he seemed and not a clever-sounding crackpot.

The opaque viewscreen ahead of Deela's control panel was soon filled with projections of the route to our next target, a small red dwarf a little over eight light -years distant. A short hop in celestial terms, and headed in the wrong direction, but the space between us was devoid of any other gravitational fields. This would be a quick side trip to prove Kal's theory.

For his part, Kal was as excited as a kid at Christmas. His humming chatter filled our intercom as it came time to jump.

"Hmm, hmm. Very good, very good indeed. Deela, your partitioned logic core is performing quite well."

*We shall see how it does during the jump. I am still wary of having it disconnected from the master chronometer.*

"Hmm. No and yes, but I understand. The primary core has not shown any signs of degraded performance."

159

*Again, we shall see. I have programmed the vector you calculated, and the diagnostic is returning ninety-nine point six percent certainty. I believe that is well within the parameters you desire?*

Of course it was, but Deela was being polite, making the new guy comfortable and all.

"Yes and yes. We can proceed at your discretion."

*Very well. Stand by.*

Deela's long fingers poked at the air, and a cone of concentric rings materialized ahead of us. That would be our departure vector, the off-ramp into high space. With her other hand, she tapped a quick command into her control screen, tweaking our attitude to put us dead center in the cone.

*Uncertainty now reduced to point one percent. I believe that is the best we can expect, sir.*

"Better than anything we've seen," Gideon said. "Maybe that walking Jell-O mold really does know what he's talking about."

I rubbed at my temples and hoped the intercom hadn't picked that up. "And maybe we shouldn't trash-talk the guy who's trying to get us home."

Gideon shot me a cold stare. "I didn't bring you along to be my conscience, Mooney." He turned back to Deela. "Let's get on with it."

I was thinking of any way to covertly sedate the old sonofabitch that didn't violate medical ethics when the universe disappeared. The stars ahead turned blue, seemed to move into a wide circle, and were suddenly gone, replaced by the strange photonegative expanse of high space.

I later learned this was due to our forward momentum. Deela had launched us at near light speed on a straight line at our target, then triggered a portal for us to sail through. For a split second, we could see the hole in space open up to swallow us.

Once inside, the experience was no less strange than before. My watch froze again, though now I knew better than to obsess over it. There was nothing wrong other than my perception. We were once again disconnected from time inside of this bizarre hall-of-mirrors dimension.

Outside was a monochrome blur again, daring me to grapple with its, naked infinity. I tried to pick out hints of the structure Kal had shown us in his lab, but I think we were too close if that makes sense.

I could only see the piece we were traveling through, even though it seemed like the entirety of the universe had wrapped itself tightly around us, propelling us to our next destination. Each jump brought with it new sensations, each one building on the previous event. Maybe after we'd done this enough, I'd actually be able to comprehend this mysterious 6D space.

Deela turned to me, interrupting my thoughts. *I am hoping the same for myself, Melanie.*

I answered her with a knowing smile and a lame thumbs up. *We're in this together, sister.*

She turned back to her controls. *Quite so . . . sister.*

I was going to miss the Grays.

Of course, that brought my old inner conflict bubbling back to the surface. Did I really want to abandon all this for the sake of living among my kind again? What was I giving up just to be back in a familiar place? I suppose there was still time to back out once we brought Gideon to Earth. Deela and Bjorn certainly wouldn't be staying around, they'd be taking the *Campanula* back to Union space.

What did that say about Gideon's motivation? He'd invested most of his wealth in this tub and was fiercely protective of it. This ship, and all of its technology, would be incredibly valuable to the GU. What might it be worth back home? I could imagine Congress forking over NASA's entire budget to get their hands on this thing. Deela's saucer alone would be . . . no, scratch that. They already had at least one that I knew of. And for that matter, what would prevent them from just commandeering this ship and leaving Gideon empty handed? He must have known the risk.

Gideon. Damn. I'd been so anxious about this jump, and so irritated with him, that I'd neglected why I was here. I pulled down my visor and made a quick scan of his vitals: heart rate was elevated, but not enough to cause concern. His ECG trace wasn't setting off any alarm bells, either. I suppose we needed to expect a certain level of anxiety whenever we left normal space.

I tapped the visor to get Kal's feed, which was markedly different from my human patient. Not being that familiar with his kind, I had to rely on the normal range bars to gauge if he was having any complications. He was remarkably calm, as if he was exactly where he wanted to be.

And I suppose he was, judging by the continual happy humming coming over the intercom. After spending most of his long life studying dimensions he could see but not enter, finally being in the middle of extradimensional space must have felt a bit like coming home.

Satisfied that we weren't in danger of losing our navigator, I switched back to Gideon's feed. Still normal, if a little elevated.

I reflexively looked at my watch, realizing it was a mistake as I did so. The second hand was still doing its surreal, blurry dance, frozen in place but still working...

That was when I realized what felt different about this jump: Despite being outside of time, my mind was working normally. My train of thought wasn't jumping back and forth, trying to latch on to whatever simultaneous chains of events were happening in the moment.

Maybe this just might work. I tapped at my ear to trigger the intercom. "Kal, how much longer?" If I was acting like the impatient kid on a long trip, so be it.

"Hmm, hmm. Difficult to say. Remember, we have partitioned the navigation logic so it is not corrupted by the master chronometer. In one sense, we are already there."

"This is a shorter jump than our previous ones. Why does it feel longer?"

"Hmm. Always remember that we are uncoupled from time. You cannot trust your perceptions. We are coasting across higher space instead of propelling ourselves through it. By not manipulating gravity for propulsion, and therefore not affecting our proper time, we are not perturbing the higher dimensions."

"Is that why I don't feel like my brain's been scrambled?"

"Hmm. Yes and yes. Perhaps no and yes. I had suspected as much, but could not be certain."

*I believe your hypothesis was correct,* Deela interjected. *I have not experienced any disorientation.*

"Hmm. Good, very good. Speaking for myself, the experience is exhilarating. I commend you for constructing this vessel, Mr. Gideon."

"You're welcome." Now past his initial anxiety, Gideon's heart rate and BP had settled into a comfortably normal range. And he looked it, relaxed in his gel couch and wearing a satisfied smile. "I'll hand it to you, this was a good idea. You have overcome my skepticism, Kal." He pointed his cane at the viewscreen ahead. "But the view outside is still mighty disconcerting. Is there any way at all to judge how long until we reach our 'catch' point?"

At least I wasn't the only one bugging Dad if we were there yet.

"Hmm. Soon, soon. We remain on course within one-half percent deviation."

*I still require time to charge the projection plates,* Deela reminded him. *Opening a portal is not instantaneous.*

"Hmm. True and true. In that case, you may proceed."

As Deela began spinning up the drive, I could sense things beginning to get weird again. It was as if forces were coursing through us that had been dormant until now, building up to tear us free of the higher dimensions. I reflexively reached for my visor and found my hand was already there, tapping at it to switch between Gideon's and Kal's feeds. I wanted to see how they each responded to the mounting change in the gravity field around us, but there was once more too much happening at once. Kal was perfectly stable. He was in his element, finally moving through the space he could only sense before. Gideon was considerably less relaxed; his vitals were all over the place again.

"Deela—"

*Stand by.*

Kal cut in. "Hmm. If the drive is ready, you may engage on my signal, Deela."

*I am ready on your signal.*

"Hmm. I said, you may engage."

*Projector array is at full charge.*

I did not enjoy this part. We were running backwards again. Or it was all happening at once. Or maybe it had already happened...

Kal cut in again, and loudly. "Hmm! Deela! Engage now!"

Mintakans are normally softspoken creatures. Hearing one shout jarred the nerves, and Deela was shocked into action. She made a sweeping gesture across the panel, and immediately the milky firmament surrounding us disappeared. It was replaced by the comforting black sky of our normal universe. A dim red lightbulb of a star waited far ahead, almost perfectly centered in the viewscreen.

"Hmm. Yes and yes. Deela, I believe we have entered orbit around our target."

She took a moment to clear her head before answering. *We have. Distance twenty-four stellar units, inclination eight point two degrees. Orbital period is one hundred thirteen annums. We are on the edge of its gravitational influence.*

"Hmm. Good and good. Excellent work, excellent. Please accept my apologies for raising my voice."

*None are necessary. Thank you, in fact. But in the future, I recommend we contrive a more effective signal.*

"I insist on it," Gideon said, stiffly raising himself from his seat. "We'll have to do better than you yelling at us, Kal."

"Yes and yes. I am already considering that. First, allow me time to review the data from our jump. I wish to ensure that we did not arrive here by happenstance."

"That would be useful," Gideon grumbled. He removed the transducers and handed them to me. "You know where to find me."

I watched as Gideon shuffled off for his suite. His gruff demeanor made it impossible to know whether he was satisfied. The only time I'd seen him lower his guard and lighten up was when he was describing the jump drive to Kal.

Bjorn sidled up beside me. "He puts considerable effort into being irascible, doesn't he?"

I crossed my arms. "If by that you mean 'cranky old bastard,' then yes."

"It's a façade, of course. He's frightened."

"Aren't we all?"

"To one degree or another, yes." He turned to our pilot. "Or do I misread you, Deela?"

*I have learned to not question an Emissary's empathic ability.*

"I think she means you're right."

*I do.*

Bjorn smiled. "We are quite literally traveling through uncharted territory. That is guaranteed to expose certain anxieties, depending on the individual."

"I'm probably throwing off a whole range of them, aren't I?"

"You are. Uncertainty, concern for Gideon, fear of—"

"You don't need to go down the list." I met his eyes. "What about you?"

Bjorn was silent. Deela turned to look at him with her big almond eyes. Being a telepath, she of course probably knew but wasn't going to answer for him.

"That is a longer discussion." He took me gently by the elbow. "Perhaps we can retire to the medical bay?"

I had my own data to analyze from the jump, so settling down in the med bay was a welcome distraction. I linked Clara to the wall screens and began streaming Gideon's and Kal's traces while Bjorn made himself comfortable. He reclined against the exam bed and folded his hands.

"So, what's on your mind?"

He inclined his head at the dual columns of vital signs streaming across the holoscreens. "First, I am curious as to what's on *their* minds."

I turned to watch the traces with him. "Beats me. ECG traces and respiratory rates can point to heightened anxiety, but then they can point to a lot of things. Cardiac arrest, for starters. From my point of view, it's hard to tell the difference until the heart stops."

"It's been some time since our Med Corps training, but Kal appears to have been remarkably calm. That comports with what I sensed from him."

He was right. The Mintakan's traces spiked a bit at the beginning of the jump, but that was all. Compared to the baseline I took when he first came aboard, the jump was a non-event for him. "What did you sense?"

"Excitement at first, with a certain measure of unease. I sensed him growing content over time," he chuckled to himself, "though I realize 'over time' is somewhat inapt. He came to be perfectly at ease. Satisfied."

"Like he was in the middle of an experiment, and the results were what he expected?"

"Exactly so. I also sensed great relief."

"Sure. His thesis was confirmed."

"There may be more to it than that." He pointed at Gideon's trace. "Tell me, what do you see from our host?"

I pointed at the heart and respiratory rates. "Same as before. Pulse and blood pressure were elevated, breathing became rapid. Nothing dangerous, but it got my attention."

Bjorn followed the trace. "It appears to have moderated after a bit."

"It did, but stayed on the high side of normal until we were out of jump space." I turned back to him. "What did you sense in him?"

"Fear. He was willing himself to maintain composure, to project authority. That is his strength."

That explained a lot. The old man was terrified of the unknown, but didn't dare show it. "He puts up a hell of a front, I'll give him that. I don't know why he thinks he needs to keep showing us who the boss is. Maybe it's just hard-wired into his personality."

"That is one possibility," Bjorn said, "but I believe it is not the whole story, as you would say."

I waved my hands, beckoning him to tell me more. "This is the part where you tell me what *you're* feeling."

Bjorn stroked his chin. "I sensed a great deal from our group, which I have not concealed from you. But in our previous jumps, I sensed more. As if others were in the ship at various times, passing through at random. It was quite disconcerting."

I felt my eyes grow wide. "Passing through? You mean like entering the ship from outside?" My skin crawled as my mind started drawing connections. "Maybe lingering, eventually leaving?"

"Yes. I believe you know of what I speak."

I hesitated, not wanting to make the leap. "Those shadows moving through the cabin before. You saw them too?"

"I sensed them before they appeared. Discerned their feelings."

I shuddered and crossed my arms tight to shake it off. "They're *conscious*? They're not just some weird optical effect of 6D space?"

"Apparently not." Bjorn paused, as if he was resolving some inner conflict. "I was not so surprised. I was curious if we would find evidence of some unknown intelligence."

I thought back to a story Chonk had told me a long time ago, about unseen threats. "Underneath," I mumbled.

"I'm sorry?"

"Something Chonk said, years ago." I began pacing. "Something I'd forgotten all about. Maybe I wanted to ignore it. He said there were potential enemies lurking unseen. Outside space, he'd said. Below it, underneath..."

"Ah. Yes, the Thubans have been vaguely aware. Their refined olfactory systems can pick out smells and heat we cannot. Apparently that is not confined to normal space."

"Even in 6D space, we can only see hints," I said. "Or sense them, in your case."

"Precisely. Our bodies are not adapted for this environment. We are only slightly better than blind to its totality."

I didn't want to ask my next question. "What do you sense from them?"

Bjorn tapped his fingers on the bed rail. "Alarm. I believe our earlier transits attracted attention, presumably through the gravity warping. Our ballistic trajectory did not offer such bait, as you might say."

"We didn't leave a trail, just opened a portal at either end."

"Perhaps so. I suspect that is where Gideon's sense of relief came from. Hopefully our subsequent jumps will remain as uneventful."

"Not having my brain scrambled would've been enough. Now I learn we've got more to worry about."

"Quite possibly." He rubbed his hands together with a faraway look. "I do not believe we are welcome."

# ⚕ 20 ⚕

I spent the next couple of hours looking for anomalies in Gideon's vital signs. While the last jump had gone smoothly, I couldn't chance missing some precursor that might lead to nasty surprises later. I still didn't trust the strange, out-of-body experience of being in jump space. It can be hard to focus when you're questioning the very nature of your existence.

Thankfully there was nothing to get my attention other than his initial elevated rates. Nothing had spiked into dangerous territory, which tracked with what I'd seen during the jump. But Bjorn's comments had me wondering.

I pulled up the traces from the jump before that, when everything had seemed to go haywire. It was like sifting through signals from multiple patients, all scrambled into the same feed. It hadn't made sense then, and was no better now. All the signs of tachycardia were there, until they weren't. He'd come out of the jump just fine, if a little disoriented.

There was signal noise that didn't make sense. Med Corps tech is nothing if not precise, capable of picking up subtleties that an ECG like ones I'd used on Earth might miss.

This was different. I'd long ago learned what to look for and what to safely ignore. There was signal noise in there that I'd never seen before, like static from a poorly tuned radio. I'd used the discs in some pretty hairy conditions but had never seen them throw out garbage like this.

There were blips in Gideon's data that I'd have written off as an effect of working in 6D space, until Bjorn had said what he did. So I dug a little deeper.

Deep in the background, there was more. Odd signals, not following any kind of normal heart or respiratory rhythm, not even for someone having a cardiac event. They were like blips, popping in and out of Gideon's feed. Some even showed signs of Doppler effect, like when you hear the pitch change from an oncoming train whistle. Whatever signals the discs had picked up, the source had been moving.

Thing is, the discs ignore outside input. I can press my hands against them and they'll still only show me the patient's vitals. Like I said, precise. Focused.

If Bjorn was right, and what we'd seen were shadows of some entity moving through the cabin, then the implications were unnerving.

Whatever they were, they were also moving through *us*.

I stormed into the logic core, not giving a damn if I was disturbing Kal's solitude. He owed us some answers.

He was resting, feelers folded up underneath him and his membrane rippling slowly front to rear, then back again. Mintakans didn't sleep like we did, it was more like they entered a numb state. I poked at him with the toe of my boot.

"Hmm?"

"You've been hiding something. I need to know what else is out there waiting for us."

"Hmm. No and yes, yes and no. You seem agitated."

"Yeah, about that. I am. Shadowy six-dimensional creatures do that to me."

Kal rose up on his feelers and quivered himself awake. "Hmm. What have you seen?"

"Nothing, and that's the problem. Only hints. Suggestions. Shadows." I sat beside him cross-legged and pointed at his optical patches. "I'm guessing you can see a whole lot more."

"Hmm. Yes and no. Have suspicions, no proof. Only hypotheses."

"Our last jump, before we found you, there were these odd shadows moving through the cabin. I assumed it was my eyes playing tricks on me, another weird effect of moving through 6D space."

"Yes and yes. You are not wrong."

"Bjorn thinks there's a consciousness there."

"Hmm. Interesting. Must add this to my notes."

"Your *notes*? This isn't something you have the luxury of studying later. It's here and now. How do we know they won't reappear on the next jump?"

"Hmm. No and no. We do not. Does this present a problem?"

"I think there's a decent chance it's causing my patient considerable stress. The kind of stress that can kill a person."

"Hmm. Yes and yes. Your point is seen. But dangerous to assume all others are threats."

"You have your data, I have mine. And mine could be pointing to whatever they are as being threatening."

"Hmm. No and yes. Requires more study."

"Did you not just hear me? Your kind can see into higher dimensions. You're telling me you can't see whatever these beings are?"

"Hmm. No and no."

"Bullshit."

"Hmm. What is... ah, of no mind. Much to learn from your demeanor."

I really needed to work on my body language if a Mintakan could read it. Screw it, I was mad. "Bjorn thinks whatever amorphous beings are out there, that they're not happy with us."

"Hmm. Would not argue with an Emissary. Can sense much I cannot. Tell me, what do you believe?"

That was a loaded question, for a lot of reasons. "I don't know. But I can tell you I don't like that they can just materialize out of nowhere and pass right through us."

"Hmm. No and no. Understand they are not passing through us. More so we are passing through them."

"That doesn't make me feel any better."

"Hmm. No and yes. We must seem like interlopers to them. Strangers, out of our element."

"That's what I don't understand. If our 3D space is part of this larger 6D space, wouldn't our presence already be obvious? How is it we're attracting attention to ourselves?"

"Hmm. Yes and yes. A good, good question." His feelers rippled while he thought. "Until now, we have been confined within the box of our three-dimensional space. Contained. Now, we have left the confines of that box to move freely through higher space."

"Higher space," I repeated. "A Thuban friend of mine called it just the opposite. They think of it as deeper. Underneath, he said."

"Hmm. No and yes, though I see your friend's point. The higher dimensions are the structural foundation of what you call the 'observable' universe. In that light, he is correct, though of course it is rather more complicated than that."

"That's putting it mildly." I leaned back against the column of a logic core. "I can't shake the feeling that we're trespassing, and that the residents aren't happy."

"Hmm. Yes and yes. If there are conscious beings within these higher dimensions, then they exist outside of our notions of time. They would be ageless, old as the universe itself and young as when it first came into existence, moving through it like smoke through the air. They would appear impossibly powerful to us. Like gods."

I rubbed at the base of my neck. "Great. And we're encroaching on their territory."

"Hmm. Yes and yes."

With thoughts of incorporeal elder gods swimming through my head, I insisted that Gideon take my advice and agree to be mildly sedated for the next jump. This would be a big one, the one that finally took us outside of Union borders. Our next stop was Deneb, a blue supergiant on the edge of Union space. This would put us in the no-man's-land of unincorporated space that included Earth.

Confined to the comfort of his own bed and with me at his side, Gideon was in high spirits even before I gave him a low dose of the Med Corps equivalent of Valium. He seemed happy to be leaving Union space, which no doubt came from the fact that his ship was built from a shitload of a critical element which was in short supply. If GU constables found it, he'd likely never leave the Union. In fact, he'd probably be spending the rest of his days in confinement. When I thought of it that way, I have to admit to sharing a little bit of his anxiety. The rest of us were accomplices, after all.

Those fears proved to be short lived, replaced with some more immediate.

The jump itself went smoothly, no out-of-body sensations and no shadows of ageless beings moving about the cabin. The rough spot came when we emerged in a distant orbit around our target star.

There was a jolt, like we were in an airliner that had just hit turbulence. I'd become so used to inertial dampers and other gravity-manipulating magic that getting thumped by some unknown outside force was startling.

Whatever it was, the shock jolted Gideon out of his drug-induced contentment. We each traded surprised looks. He propped himself up on his elbows, still fuzzy. "What the hell was that?"

I placed my hand on his chest, urging him to lie down. "It's your ship, I was hoping you might know. Ever have something like that happen before?"

"Never." He reached for the intercom. "Our new navigator had better not have overloaded the conduit lattice. If one of those things comes loose—"

Deela's thoughts intruded on our speculation. *Sir, please come to the control room as soon as possible.*

"What's going on?"

*We have been fired upon. Our assailants are demanding to speak with the ship's master.*

Fortunately, the sedatives could be neutralized by a quick injection of counteragent. Gideon was soon on his feet and royally pissed off. He drove his cane into the deck with each step, thumping his way through the torus with me in trail. When we reached the control room, Deela and Bjorn were conversing quietly. On the holoscreen behind them, a ship hung in the black, the likes of which I'd never seen before. It was burnt orange and wedge-shaped, with triplets of sharp-edged wings on either side.

It might have been new to me, but was apparently familiar to Gideon. And everyone else, for that matter. He glowered at the screen.

"You're shitting me. Border pirates?"

*Pirates?* I'd heard the stories from Chonk and his buddies, but had never encountered them before. I stared at Bjorn, wide-eyed. He patted the air with his hand, signaling me to stay cool. Easy for him.

Deela approached us. *I am afraid so, sir. They appeared not long after we emerged from jump space.*

"And just how in the hell did they find us?"

*Unknown, sir. I suspect the portal attracted their attention. It would trip the gravitational sensors of any nearby vessel.*

"I agree," Bjorn said, "though it is immaterial. We are in a predicament, as you would say."

Gideon stiffened. "You're damned right that's what I'd say." He turned to Deela. "What's the damage?"

*It is fortunately minor. The navigational deflectors were overloaded by the blast from their plasma cannon, but that will be a simple matter of replacing a capacitor bank.*

Later, I'd learn from Deela that if she hadn't had the micrometeor deflectors dialed up to eleven, the explosion would've fried a good chunk of our field projectors. In other words, we'd have been dead in space.

Gideon tipped his head at the screen. "Do we know what they want?"

Bjorn was surprisingly dispassionate. "Your ship."

At that moment, Gideon's eyes could've burned holes into my friend. "Tell 'em they can't have it!"

"I fear it will not be that simple. Their kind are not inclined to negotiate." He held a hand to his chest. "Though they are likewise not used to negotiating with Union officials. I believe I can offer a bargaining chip, as you might say."

Gideon studied him skeptically. "You'd better be right."

"If I am not, we will have plenty of time to indulge in recriminations." He turned to the screen. "Now, we must prepare ourselves to be boarded. We should go to the landing bay."

We waited behind a transparent pressure door as the bay opened to space. A smaller version of the pirate's flying wedge drifted into view, its knifelike wings retracting along its side as it settled onto the deck beside Deela's saucer. The outer door winked shut behind it, and soon we were standing inside a very crowded landing bay.

It was a shabby-looking thing, peppered with dents and scrapes. A few panels looked new, but the burn marks around them suggested it had taken some lumps. I wondered how many skirmishes they'd had with Thuban border patrols, and smiled inside at the thought.

A portal opened in the back of the wedge, and a trio of slender, sinewy beings emerged, with long necks and tubular torsos propelled by four spindly legs. Their heads were flat, with bulbous eyes on either side like a hammerhead shark. Two of them flanked who I presumed was their leader, each carrying bulky, menacing weapons in their four arms. The leader—I had no idea if it was a he, she, or something in between—wore a tattered black tunic which brushed the deck as the pirate ambled toward us. I halfway expected to find a parrot on its shoulder.

The leader stopped in front of our group and swept his/her/its tunic to one side, revealing a smaller weapon in a holster. Four triangular flaps opened in its ruddy neck to reveal a pinkish orifice, and it began uttering a gargling stream of burps and burbles. It didn't speak so much as it seemed to coherently fart. Bjorn nodded along patiently, but I'd never encountered these beings before and my translator skipped a lot. I caught its name, Morrok-Yol-Mossur, only because Bjorn repeated it back in greeting.

After a few more burps and gargles, my translator began to catch up. Morrok was captain of an interstellar frigate named *Aridred's Fury*, and they'd just happened to be in the vicinity when we popped out of jump space. A singularity appearing out of nowhere had caused them some alarm. I could appreciate that: You're tooling along in your little pirate ship, drinking pirate rum while tallying up your pirate booty and plotting the next raid, when a small black hole pops into existence and disappears just as suddenly. That would get anyone's attention.

"Your propulsion methods are interesting," Morrok gargled. As my translator finally became comfortable with their language, it sounded awfully erudite for a four-legged hammerhead space pirate. "We are exceedingly familiar with Union gravity drives—"

Particularly Thuban ones, I thought.

"—but yours is different. We can detect gravitational warping out to half a light-year, and our picket drones are constantly watching your borders."

No doubt waiting for some unsuspecting Union ship to stray across. Like ours.

"You are insightful, befitting your reputation, Madame Morrok," Bjorn said. Now we at least knew the creature's gender, which he'd no doubt revealed for our benefit as much as for buttering up this pirate. Bjorn's ambassadorial flourish felt like bullshit, but then he knew a lot more about this race than I did. "We are, in fact, testing a new drive system."

The pirate tilted her flatiron head. "Please, continue to enlighten me." She gestured with opposing arms at her bodyguards. "I caution you, Emissary, do not try to deceive me with diplomatic niceties. We already know your hull is coated with *chaqpui*. I could have my crew strip every last gram of it and we would not have to work another day for the rest of our lives."

"Chaq-what?" Gideon demanded.

"Moscovium," Bjorn said out of the side of his mouth. "Element 115."

Morrok turned to Gideon. "And who is this interloper?"

Gideon straightened against his cane. "I am the master of this ship."

That brought a gurgling laugh from the Dread Pirate Morrok. "You *were* its master. Your vessel, and your fate, are now mine." She turned an eye back toward Bjorn. "Now, Emissary, if we can dispense with the interruptions from this mongrel—"

Gideon swung his cane and pointed it at Morrok. "You listen here—"

The guns came up, trident-tipped lances emitting a high-pitched whine that signaled we were seconds from being turned into goo. Bjorn moved quickly, grabbing the end of the cane and placing himself between Gideon and Morrok's henchmen. "*Mongrels* is their expression for unknown species," he whispered angrily. "It's not personal."

Gideon collected himself, still glaring at the pirates. "It's starting to feel personal." For once, I couldn't argue with him.

Bjorn turned back to face the pirates, hands in the air in a placating gesture. "I trust you will forgive this . . . impudence. My associates have not encountered your species before. They are the only two of their kind in the Union."

Morrok's bulbous eyes narrowed. "Then mongrels they are. I trust you will ensure they learn their place, Emissary. Now, let us get to the matter at hand." Her head swiveled in a near-complete circle. "What propels your vessel?"

Bjorn took on a light, self-effacing tone. "I'm afraid I do not completely understand it myself—"

More diplomatic bullshit on his part, but she seemed not to notice.

"—but I can tell you the hull plating projects a powerful gravity field. Enough to create a temporary singularity."

"That we could see for ourselves," Morrok grumbled. "It is not wise to surprise the Sisterhood of the Black Veil with such phenomenon. I wish to know the purpose of putting yourselves at such risk."

Bjorn glanced over his shoulder at Gideon, who did not appear happy to have his secret out in the open. "Near-instantaneous interstellar travel, with minimal time dilation."

Morrok considered that, steepling the pads at the ends of her arms. "That would require immense power, more than a simple antimatter reactor can produce, I think."

"It does." Bjorn left it at that. No sense giving away the store all at once, I supposed.

Morrok studied our group. "Two mongrels and a diplomat. This cannot be all of your crew, then." She waved her arms at the pressure door behind us. "I will see the rest of your vessel." It was a command, not a request, emphasized by the two goons with guns pointed at us.

Bjorn swept a hand toward the door. "Of course. Please follow me."

My friend remained unflappable as we led the trio of four-legged brigands through the torus. At her station in the control room, Deela patiently explained the *Campanula*'s inner workings while Gideon seethed in a corner. When Deela showed them a replay of our last jump on the holoscreen, Morrok flashed surprise for the first time. The four labia of her mouth fell slack and her already bulbous eyes grew large.

"You leave our universe to travel through other dimensions? I thought that impossible."

*It is not without challenges,* Deela explained. *And we are not technically leaving our universe, we are transiting a previously unexplored aspect of it. The effects are disconcerting. It is difficult to be confident in our position at any given point in time, particularly when time itself is irrelevant.*

"How do you navigate this realm, then, if you do not know where you are? Or when?"

"If I may," Bjorn interjected. "We have enlisted the help of an individual who has studied six-dimensional space extensively. He is in essence our navigator."

"Then I wish to meet this individual. You will take me to him."

Gideon began to protest when Bjorn waved him down and turned to me with a questioning look. I shifted on my feet. "Jumps are uniquely taxing on him. Mentally draining. He really shouldn't be disturbed right now."

Morrok's eyes narrowed. "What are your people hiding, Emissary?"

"Nothing at all," Bjorn assured her. "Understand that she is a medical professional. She is only stating the facts as they are and applying her best judgment. She speaks the truth."

"I will determine that for myself," the pirate said. "Let us see this navigator of yours."

For my own sake, I dearly hoped Kal was still asleep in the logic core. "Let me go first," I insisted. Morrok inclined her broad head.

With that tiny victory over pirate obstinance, I swept my hand across the door. It whispered open to reveal a darkened room. Kal was resting in its center, faintly illuminated under the variegated glow of the processor columns. His translucent skin undulated rhythmically as he slept, completely oblivious to our presence.

Morrok extended her neck to its full length like an uncoiled snake, craning past me to peek inside. "A Mintakan," she said admiringly. "You tell the truth, mongrel."

"It's Melanie," I said behind clenched teeth. "And yeah, I try."

Her neck retracted. "Very well. You have earned a measure of my trust. I will address you as requested, Melanie." She turned an eye toward Gideon. "The other mongrel has yet to prove his worth."

I saw Bjorn hold a calming hand up in front of Gideon, who was about to come out of his skin. "My *worth*?" he growled. "You obviously don't know who I am."

I screwed my eyes shut. Was he out of his mind? Did he really think this walking slug gave a damn? Whom the gods would destroy, they first make proud.

Morrok, for her part, remained unimpressed. "We have yet to see your drive core, mongrel. Perhaps you can prove your worth to me then."

The boss didn't disappoint, though it had more to do with the eyewatering three-dimensional maze of the propulsion space. Morrok's snakelike neck twisted as she tried to follow the tangle of spiraling conduits and buttresses.

"Impressive, mongrel. Your resources are indeed vast, I think. Your name?"

"Gideon. And yes, they were," Gideon said. "Now, most of my resources are tied up in this machine."

That felt like a stupid thing to say. His pride was going to get him stranded or killed, if not all of us.

"I see." Morrok tapped the pads of her hands together, no doubt considering her next move. "As I suggested before, the projector array alone is worth the fortune of the entire Sisterhood, especially in light of your Union's present shortage. They would bring a tidy sum on your black market."

Gideon began to protest. "Now wait a minute—"

Morrok ignored him. "But the technology arrayed here is worth much more, I think. Many in our sisterhood, too many if being honest, do not think far enough ahead. Any one of them would have killed you and stripped your vessel by now. In this you have been lucky." She let the thought hang. "I am not so impulsive. Your work has value beyond the sum of its parts. Paradigm-shifting value, in fact."

Great. So we'd been captured by a pirate philosopher.

"We will take your vessel, of course. You and your crew will be transported to the *Fury* and pressed into service." She must have seen the color leave my face. "Do not concern yourself, Melanie. We have great need of someone like yourself. As for the rest of you, I suppose we will find out. Though considering what your small crew has accomplished so far, I believe you will make yourselves useful. If not, there are other solutions."

Gideon, for once, was speechless, facing the same terror that was building in me. Not only were we about to lose our freedom, he would lose everything he'd worked for. Every shady deal he'd cut to build this thing was coming back to haunt him.

Bjorn, ever the diplomat, sought to pull our fat out of the fire. "If you please, Madame, I wish to propose an alternative. If you'd be willing to entertain my proposal, that is."

Morrok tilted her head. "What would that be, Emissary? I caution you, do not test my patience."

"I would not presume to do so, but hear me out. As you have seen for yourself, this is a uniquely complex ship. Unlike any in the Union, or any in your sisterhood. It has taken considerable effort to master, and we have only recently devised a method to confidently navigate the higher dimensions. Deela is a master pilot, and Kal is, quite simply, considered a genius among his kind. His insight has proven to be indispensable. And Gideon intimately knows the workings of his ship. An unprepared crew would have tremendous difficulty operating this vessel without any one of them aboard. And as you have seen, our habitable volume is rather limited."

Damn but he was good. He even had me convinced.

"Get to the point, Emissary. What do you propose?"

"An exchange. One of us for one of yours. Allow us to complete our journey to the human's home world. This will provide whoever you select an abundance of time to become familiar with our ship. We will then return to Sisterhood space, at which point the vessel is yours."

"Works for me," Gideon said, as if he had a say in the matter. "Once we're back at Earth, I don't care what happens to it."

Morrok tapped her pads together as she considered Bjorn's offer. "A sensible alternative, I will admit." She studied our group. "An Emissary, a Reticulan, a Mintakan, and two mongrels. A motley crew, indeed." She turned one eye toward me. "Very well. I will remain aboard and transfer command of the *Fury* to my first mate. The wench comes with us."

Did she seriously just call me a *wench*? Despair swept over me like a wave. I would be a slave pressed into their service, hopelessly cut off from everyone I knew. It took all I had to stop myself from trembling uncontrollably, to not vomit and collapse in tears. Not only was I about to lose my friends and my ride home, any hope of escaping back to the Union would be gone with it.

Bjorn shot a glance at me, and turned back to Morrok. "I'm afraid that will be complicated, if not impractical." He gestured toward Gideon. "Our ship's patron is in failing health, and Melanie is his attending physician." Not exactly, but in this case I'd allow it. "It is vital for the success of our mission that she remain by his side."

Morrok rested two hands on her sidearm, clearly not happy. "Then we have a dilemma, Emissary. We have need of a physician, even a mongrel such as this Melanie. You see, ours was lost in battle with your Thuban warmongers."

"If you in fact consider her part of a mongrel race, then perhaps I can offer you one of a more... *esteemed* race?"

Morrok eyed him skeptically. "And who would that be?"

Bjorn placed a hand on his chest and bowed his head. "I trained with Melanie in the Medical Corps and am fully qualified. I offer myself to your service."

*What?* "Bjorn, no—"

He met me with gentle eyes and laid a hand on my shoulder. "It's okay, Melanie. Trust me, this is for the best. For all of you."

Morrok studied each of us. "A Union Emissary, *and* a physician? A generous offer, indeed." She extended two of her pads. "I accept."

## ⚕ 21 ⚕

I was still on the verge of tears as I followed Bjorn to his cabin. "Why would you do this?"

He wore a gentle, resigned smile as the door swished open. "We had very little negotiating leverage. As I have learned from our card games together, we held a weak hand. I was the hole card, as you would say."

"Still, there had to be another way. You're a professional negotiator."

He opened a storage panel and reached for his travel case. "True. It is also true that sacrifices sometimes must be made for the good of others. Emissaries have laid down their lives for the sake of keeping the peace. We on occasion find ourselves in dangerous situations with few alternatives. It is the nature of our role in the Union. This is no different."

"You took a huge gamble. She could've just as easily taken me and left you here to tend to Gideon."

"I was confident she would not, once she learned of my additional qualifications. I sensed she was not at all happy with compromising, especially once she realized it was unavoidable. Morrok is of the Da'Farrii race. They take what they want and do not enjoy being dictated to by circumstance. So I sweetened the pot, as you would say."

"Sweetened for her, soured for us." I sat on the edge of his bed and wiped at a tear. "For me."

He perched beside me. "I have enjoyed getting to know you, Melanie. Our friendship has taught me more about the human race than a century of observations could have. I will miss you, but I am confident we will see each other again."

"Please don't say that. Don't try to make me feel better."

He held a hand to his chest. "I would never lie to you. As long as I am living, there is opportunity. If anything, we Emissaries excel at exploiting opportunities."

I sniffed. "In that case, you'll make a great pirate."

Bjorn arched an eyebrow. "A trenchant insight, if personally troubling. We may have more in common with their kind than I would care to believe." He reached into his pocket and lifted two silver rings. He placed one in my hand and slipped the other onto his finger.

"Our bio rings! How did you get these back?"

"We can thank Deela for this. She is not as concerned about maintaining secrecy now that we are beyond Union space." He smiled. "Among other reasons."

I put my ID ring back on and squeezed his hand. "Just promise me you'll be careful."

He squeezed back. "I trust you will be as well. This will be a challenging time for you. Morrok impresses me as inquisitive and quite intelligent, even if those traits are misdirected in our view."

"In our view?"

"I believe your kind has a saying, 'every villain is a hero in his own story.' In Morrok's eyes, she does what she must for the good of her kind."

"She's a pirate. A criminal. You said yourself, she takes what she wants."

"All true. It is also true that her kind sees nothing wrong with this."

"Where I'm from, we call that a sociopath." I trusted Deela, was friendly with if mystified by Kal, and barely tolerated Gideon. Now this intergalactic bandit would be occupying my friend's space. It wasn't fair.

"Life isn't fair, Melanie. You know that."

"I'm still not convinced you aren't telepathic."

He placed his hands on my shoulders, boring into me with his brilliant green eyes. "You give away too much, Melanie. You must control your emotions and body language. Morrok will be watching all of you with an eye toward malice, constantly looking for advantage. She will try to gain your trust. In this, you must be wary."

"Trust won't be an issue. I wouldn't trust her any farther than I could piss in a windstorm."

Bjorn wrinkled his nose in distaste. "Human idioms never fail to surprise me." He turned to fold a pair of formal Emissary robes into his case. "There may come a time when you are forced to trust her. She may be a criminal under Union statutes, but she is also a cunning warrior. You may yet find value in her tactical acumen."

"You're talking about the shadow beings." As if we didn't have enough problems to deal with.

"I am. My great regret in this is that I will not be here to advise you any further. There is a consciousness there, but we have not encountered them enough for me to form more than a general impression. Other than alarm, that is."

"Theirs or ours?"

"Theirs. Alarm can lead to any number of undesirable behaviors. If they have perceived our presence as a threat, then you may be glad to have someone with Morrok's particular skills at your disposal. Self-preservation is a powerful motivator."

With that, Bjorn stood and smoothed down his tunic. We could hear the shuffling of our new passenger coming down the corridor. "I believe the time has come. Take care, Melanie."

"You too," I choked. "Don't do anything stupid."

He lifted his travel case. "Other than what I'm about to do now? I believe that is enough."

"Smartass." I gave him a tight hug and kissed his cheek. "If—when—you find a way out of this, come find me." I held up my hand with my ID ring. "You know how."

He flashed a knowing smile. "Quite."

Bjorn strode confidently along the curving passageway, his flowing robes making it look as if he were gliding above the deck. His graceful manner contrasted with the hurried patter of Morrok, accompanied by her other guard in trail. This one hauled a heavy trunk with tattered edges. It landed on the deck by Bjorn's—now Morrok's—bed with a thud. The guard dutifully opened the case and began putting away her master's belongings.

Morrok stood in the doorway and unfolded a sash of heavy crimson fabric. Soon I learned it wasn't a fashion accessory; it was a carrying sling for a pair of weapons. Each had a heavy, knurled handle that perfectly fit her pads. Extending from the handle of each were a pair of thin, curved wire grids about a meter long.

Of course. She wouldn't be a proper pirate without her swords.

She must have caught me staring. "Have you not seen a plasma cutlass, mongrel Melanie?"

"It's just 'Mel.' And no, can't say I have."

She gave the handle of one a squeeze, and its grid flashed to life with brilliant white light. "These were passed down to me from twelve generations of Sisters. Ancient, but still useful in close quarters. Pistols too often cause unnecessary damage." She took both swords and set them in scabbards on either side of her waist. "Contested boardings often demand more precision than a sidearm can provide." The four labia of her mouth twisted into a grotesque smile. "A little panache can often persuade a recalcitrant adversary."

*Who gives a shit, lady?* She didn't have to try and impress me with her superior weaponry. I could do a lot of a damage with a plasma scalpel, too. "Hmm," I grunted, reluctantly acknowledging her.

She placed the pads of her four arms atop each of her hips. "You are not pleased with this arrangement. That Emissary was close to you, wasn't he?"

I glared at her, not answering.

A guttural laugh emanated from the hole in her neck. "No matter. You have told me all I need to know, even though you try not to."

Damn. There with the body language again. Any thoughts of getting the drop on her and driving a scalpel into her head would have to wait. I didn't even know enough about their anatomy to tell if that would do any good. For all I knew, her brains were where her ass should be.

*Don't underestimate*, I reminded myself. Bjorn had warned me this pirate bitch was smart. If I let my anger get the better of me, this would end up being a short trip.

Morrok remained in the doorway, blocking my exit while studying me. "I have not encountered any of your race. What do you call yourselves again?"

"Humans."

"And your home world's name?"

"Earth."

"Unless I am mistaken, yours is not a Union member world." She cocked her head to one side. "Curious to find two of you out here, then. Tell me, how did you come to find yourself amongst these Union elitists?"

"By accident."

Her mouth twisted into a frown. "Hostility will get you nowhere, human. I have been quite generous. Your friend will be well taken care of, as will you. I am allowing you and the other mongrel to return to your home. This could have gone much differently."

"Whatever you say."

Another gurgling laugh. "Now you understand. Yes, it will be *whatever I say*. Do not provoke me into changing my mind."

"Wouldn't dream of it." I nodded at the corridor behind her. "Now, if you please, I do need to see to my work."

She shuffled to one side, waving me on with a pair of arms. "By all means. I am not here to keep you from your work. Quite the contrary."

We'd see about that. I gave her a passing grunt and hurried down the corridor.

I checked up on Gideon, who was annoyingly sanguine about our newest traveling companion. "We still get to go home, Mooney. I don't know what you're so upset about."

I lifted the discs from his chest and flipped up my visor. "We just took an armed pirate on board and had to give up one of our own in the bargain. That doesn't bother you?"

He huffed and settled into his chair. "I don't like compromises either, especially when they're forced on me. We could've come out a lot worse. You want to be pressed into service with those whatever-they-are? Not me."

"But Bjorn—"

"It was his idea. His call. He knew what he was getting into."

"Did he really?"

Gideon closed his eyes and rested his head against the back of his chair. "He's a diplomat, Mooney. Horse trading is his business. Moreover, he's an Emissary. He can read others in ways we can only dream of. Hell, if I had half his ability . . ."

"You'd what? Use it to rake in more money?" People like Gideon, who went through life constantly looking for an advantage over others, wore me out.

"Maybe. Or maybe I'd have stayed put on Earth." He motioned for me to sit. "You don't know a thing about my former life, do you?"

I'd seen his history, but he didn't need to know that. Here I was, guilty of holding on to my own advantage. I shook my head.

"When the war came and the Army was looking for any man with two arms, two legs and a pulse, I didn't cut it. 4F." He tapped his chest and stared off wistfully. "Funny, a bad ticker might've saved my life. Lots of my associates left and never came back. Plenty of the ones who did come back were missing pieces." He tapped his head. "Sometimes up here."

It was easy to forget he'd weathered the Depression and World War II. He kept talking.

"I'd had some success in electronics manufacturing, and the war kicked that into high gear. All of a sudden my company had more business than it could handle. We built autopilots for the Army Air Corps. Couldn't turn the things out fast enough." He coughed. "Then the war ended. Demand falls off a cliff when bombers aren't getting shot down anymore. And politicians with nothing better to do all of a sudden decided the same people who'd built their 'Arsenal of Democracy' needed to be taken down a couple pegs."

"How's that?"

Another spasm of coughing. I checked my watch; he'd be due for another dose of heart meds soon. "The 'Senate Special Committee to Investigate the National Defense Program,'" he spat. "A kangaroo court Truman used to propel himself into the White House. They dragged us through the mud, said we'd unfairly profited from the war. If your margins were higher than whatever arbitrary limit they'd set, you became a target. A 'profiteer.'" He sniffed.

"They brought in a bunch of green-eyeshade types who knew jack shit about running a business, but they knew how to give politicians the ammo they needed to go after us. And they did, hammer and tong. If that wasn't enough, they sicced the press on us like a pack of hyenas. The whole farce officially ended in '48, but that didn't stop them from hounding us. They were just sneakier about it.

"I had factories across the southwest, with some of the best engineers and machinists money could buy, and the IRS crawled all over them like ants in a sugar refinery. In retrospect, I should've bought myself a couple of revenue agents."

I wrinkled my nose.

"Don't act so disgusted, Mooney. Nobody gets by in this world without greasing a few palms, even in this utopian Galactic Union."

"That's how you got all of the 115 isotopes you needed to build this ship."

He muffled another cough. "It worked, didn't it? Before you start one of your self-righteous tirades, just remember why you're here." He tipped his cane at me. "You need to get home just as much as I do."

"But the need—"

"Need of what?" he countered. "Of whom? Everything—everyone—has a price, Mooney. That zero point research on Tanaan that got your nose so out of joint? Sanctioned by the Union science ministry. They knew the risks."

"Doubtful they knew it could tear the planet apart," I sniffed.

A mordant laugh turned into another coughing fit. "The hell they didn't. The containment field was *their* technology, not mine. They insisted on using it. I didn't protest." He poked a finger at his chest. "At least not enough. I couldn't demonstrate anything with a better safety margin, so that was that."

I jerked a thumb over my shoulder. "So how do we know this thing isn't going to blow up underneath us, like Tanaan?"

He leaned back against his chair. "We learned a lot from that mess, scalability for starters. Containment fields degrade according to the inverse square law. Beyond a certain surface area, it takes more power to maintain field integrity than you can get out of the reaction. The problem of diminishing returns becomes a lot more manageable at smaller scales."

That was when the proverbial light bulb went on in my head. "The science ministry knows about your jump drive project, doesn't it?"

"A select few, yes. They know my intentions, and they'll be wanting to get their hands on this tub when it returns to Union space."

"That doesn't appear to be working out like they planned," I said.

"Isn't working out like we'd planned, either."

"Bah." He waved away my concern. "That's just business. Two steps forward, one back."

"I think you have that flipped in this case."

Gideon flashed a lopsided, wicked grin. "We're still moving in the right direction, aren't we? Sometimes you have settle for plan B to convince your adversaries they're getting what they want, while you're working your way back to plan A." He finished with another cough.

"Morrok might have other ideas. Bjorn said—"

"She's clever, I'll give her that," Gideon interrupted. "But she isn't counting on the attention this ship will attract. If they take it anywhere close to Union borders, her merry band will have Thuban destroyers up their asses and through their nostrils."

"I certainly hope so, for Deela's and Kal's sakes." He was taking a huge gamble with their lives. I forced down my revulsion and opened a small metallic container. "Here, it's time for another dose of benazepril."

I had one last round to make, which I didn't look forward to. The patient was a lot more agreeable, but the news I was bringing wouldn't be. The door to the logic core slid open silently, and I poked my head inside. "Kal?"

"Hmm? Yes and yes."

"I'm sorry to disturb you."

"Hmm. No and no. You are no disturbance to me."

Kal hadn't moved from his perch among the processor columns. This would have concerned me for most other beings, but Mintakans tended to stay put when they were in the middle of mentally draining exercises. That happened a lot with their kind. I knelt beside him. "Do you mind if I take a few vitals?"

He pivoted on his feelers to face me. "No and no, not at all."

"Thanks. This won't take long." I set the discs in place and my visor came alive with trace lines. "How did you feel during that last jump?"

"Hmm. Yes and no, no and yes. It was pleasing to see my theories proven, but it was also taxing. Being disconnected from linear time is more profound than I supposed."

"Told you," I said cheerfully. I'd break the news when that task was finished.

"Hmm. Yes and yes. I likewise did not perceive any of the amorphous beings you described, also a good thing."

"We didn't either. Maybe they didn't notice us this time."

"Hmm. Yes and yes. It is usually best to not attract attention to oneself when in unfamiliar surroundings."

After collecting another solid baseline of data, I removed the discs. "About that..."

"Hmm?"

"Were you aware of anything unusual transpiring when we returned to 3D space?"

"No and no. Fatigue overcame me. Sleep could be resisted no longer, though I did see we reentered at our destination."

"We did. But to your point, it appears that we still managed to attract attention to ourselves."

"Hmm. Understanding escapes me, then. To what do you refer?"

Both in medicine and conversation, I find it best to just rip the band-aid right off. "Da'Farrii pirates jumped us not long after we popped back into 3D space. Apparently, opening up a singularity where one didn't exist before can be alarming."

"Yes and yes. Understandable, and troubling." His feelers quivered. "I trust our efforts to evade were successful?"

I grimaced. "Not really."

"Hmm. Yet here we remain."

"For now," I said, and explained Bjorn's tradeoff with the pirate Morrok. "We peeked in on you earlier, while you were sleeping. She was patient enough to not disturb you, but she's going to want a meeting."

"Hmm. Yes and yes. This is not surprising. A pirate who has successfully avoided capture or death for so long will be cunning. She will not push a confrontation until the odds are in her favor."

"Once again, you appear to be exactly right."

"Hmm. Yes and no. Let us ensure the odds are not tilted in her favor."

I was liking this guy more every day.

# 🜚 **22** 🜚

At Gideon's insistence, we had moved back to the control room for the next jump. "I'm not leaving that bitch alone in there," he'd argued. "Who knows what she might try to pull?"

It was hard to argue with his logic, considering Bjorn's warning. Morrok was no doubt thinking two or three steps ahead and could easily be planning to commandeer our ship as soon as she felt comfortable with it. And she, of course, had all the firepower.

"I still want you sedated during the jump. The sensory overload isn't good for you." I pulled an autoinjector from my bag. "And you're in no condition to fight back if she tries something."

Gideon settled into his gel couch and pointed at the syringe. "Would the same sedative work on her?"

Hadn't thought of that. "Their race is called Da'Farrii, and that's the extent of my knowledge." I held up my data crystal. "Union databases don't have much to say about them beyond the skirmishes with our border patrols. All I could find of their physiology is that they breathe oxygen and consume water." That told me something about Morrok's metabolic system, but not enough to formulate a sedative. For all I knew, she could absorb enough tranquilizers to put down a horse.

Gideon pointed at the injector as Morrok shuffled into the control cabin behind us. "You should make that a priority."

I answered him with a noncommittal grunt and injected the sedative. He was asking me to cross an ethical line, but those can get blurry when self-defense is involved.

The mood in the control room took a noticeably dark turn as she claimed Bjorn's empty seat. I have to admit to more than a little pleasure at seeing her obvious discomfort. Fitting a giant hammerhead slug with eight equilateral limbs into a humanoid-shaped couch was like shoving the proverbial square peg into a round hole.

"Is there a problem with your seat?" I asked, more cheerfully than I felt.

Her flat head twisted atop her neck. "Your accommodations are not to my standards. There was no consideration for non-humanoids," she burbled with disgust.

"It was outfitted for the crew we had," Gideon said, rapidly succumbing to the sedative. "Didn't plan on anyone with four legs and no ass."

Morrok reached for one of her cutlasses. "You will not speak to me that way, mongrel."

"Call me 'mongrel' again—" Gideon slurred. He fumbled for his cane, moving to get up from the couch.

I leapt up and put myself between them, hands in the air. "Don't pay him any mind. It's the sedative talking. It tends to make us humans what we call 'loose lipped.'"

She kept a gnarled pad on the hilt of her cutlass. "See that he does not insult me further, human."

I let out my breath. At least she'd deigned to call us human this time. "I'll do my best. We both will." I turned to glare at Gideon. "Right?"

He lazily waved his hands. "You win. I'll behave."

That would be a nice change. I leaned in and whispered, "If you don't, I'll have to put you under. Don't make me do that." Yet another ethical line I was stepping all over, but I justified it with the excuse that it would probably save my patient's life. The Med Corps' prime directive was to "render aid and alleviate patient suffering to the maximum extent of our abilities." If a bolus of tranquilizers would keep this space pirate from lopping Gideon's head off, then in my mind that qualified.

Morrok began to settle down after she found a semi-comfortable position. "Reticulan, what is our course?"

Deela opened up the holoscreen. *We have calculated a trajectory free of obstacles to the Sargas system, twenty-one light-years distant.*

"Only twenty-one?" Morrok scoffed. "Energy wasted. Our smallest sloop can do that."

*No doubt it can, but keep in mind that extradimensional travel is instantaneous and free of time dilation. Though I must warn you, it will not feel that way.*

"Your warning is noted, but unnecessary. There is little this universe has left to surprise me."

I turned away to hide my smirk. We'd see about that, lady.

Once more, we left normal space for the undulating photonegative higher dimensions. Morrok was suitably impressed, and to my eyes more than a little startled by the experience. Good.

"What is taking so long?" she demanded after several not-really minutes. "You said this would be instantaneous, Reticulan."

*I also said it would not feel that way.*

"Is there no way to accelerate? Must we travel ballistically, like primitives? Surely we can engage your gravity drive."

I don't know how much she knew of us Earthlings' methods of space travel, but "primitive" felt like an insult.

"Told you...whole damned ship is one big gravity drive," Gideon slurred. "Trust me, you don't want to accelerate."

Morrok's pulpy skin began to turn red, which I took as a sign of mounting irritation, maybe anxiety. I hoped it was the latter. "And why would that be, mongrel?"

I reached across the aisle and squeezed Gideon's arm hard, willing him to keep quiet. "We aren't the only beings in this space," I said for him. "We've encountered some strange—"

Before I could finish a thin shadow appeared, like smoke curling through a crack in the wall to drift through the cabin.

Morrok's neck began pulsing. Faint clicking noises rose from the folds of her mouth. Was that fear? "Reticulan, you ship appears to be on fire."

*I assure you we are not.*

"Told you," Gideon mumbled.

The pirate's bulbous eyes grew even wider as the shadowy form began to zigzag between us, seeming to move with purpose. It approached Deela, Gideon, and me in turn before stopping in front of Morrok, who reached for one of her cutlasses. The dark cloud began to coalesce into black tendrils, grasping for her. Before she could unsheathe the blade, her arm was enveloped in writhing nothingness.

Morrok tried to recoil but her arm was locked in place, completely hidden beneath the inky black cloud. One of her opposing arms snapped down to her side and drew the other cutlass. As it flashed to life, the diaphanous whatever-it-was must have gotten the hint, because it let go and began to withdraw, receding into a black spot in the air which soon winked out of existence.

Not satisfied, Morrok leapt from her seat and scuttled across the ceiling. She leveled the razor-thin arc of her glowing blade at me. "You have been keeping secrets, human."

I sank into my seat as far as the gel would allow. My eyes were fixed on the plasma blade just inches from my chest, its heat a warning of what would come if she didn't like my answer. I held up my hands in a lame protest. "I tried to tell you."

Morrok studied me and kept the cutlass aimed at my chest. I backed away as her limbs began trembling. She shut the blade down and slid it back into its sheath, this time not without some noticeable fumbling. She let go and fell back into her—Bjorn's—chair.

I shook off the threat, grabbed my trauma bag, and rushed to her side. It pains me to admit I was thinking of the opportunity to get some hard data on this creature's anatomy more than attending to a patient.

"I think you might be in danger of shock." I snapped on a pair of exam gloves and took a temperature-regulating pack out of my bag, a smaller version of the kind Thubans used to keep their cold-blooded bodies functioning outside of their native environment. If Morrok was turning shocky I'd have to get her body temperature under control. I trusted the regulator could figure out her normal range on its own.

"Impossible," she argued as I set the device in place, but there was weakness in her voice. "You have no knowledge—"

"I'm a quick learner," I interrupted, feeling bold enough to take the chance. I retrieved the transducers from my bag. "These will let me scan you for any internal injuries. But first, it would help if you could tell me what you're feeling."

"I see no point, human. What is done, is done."

"You were about to take me on as your ship's physician, remember? You're going to have to trust me."

"Very well." She leaned her head against the gel and relaxed her neck. "I did not feel anything. It was as if my arm was no longer part of me."

I examined the adjacent arm for a baseline. It was my first time touching a Da'Farrii and I needed to see what "normal" felt like. I worked through her range of motion, which was considerable as she was double-jointed. I began feeling for a pulse and palpated the areas where veins might be.

I moved on to the affected limb, which looked and felt noticeably different. It had a distinctly blue-gray pallor which stood in stark contrast to her ruddy brown complexion. The skin was cold to the touch, and I could feel her arteries pulsating furiously to restore missing blood. It was as if the limb had become cyanotic. "No wonder. You've lost blood flow."

"It was more than that, human." She must have been feeling better, as she was returning to her overbearing self. "I have withstood many injuries, had limbs severed and regrown. This was not like that. It was as if a part of me had been removed from existence."

A thoughtful "huh" was all I could offer. I set the discs on opposite sides of her head and began working my way down, pressing firmly to get a deep scan of her innards. My visor filled up with vital sign traces and 3D images of her organs. Interestingly, her circulatory system was distributed. Instead of one heart, she had four, matching her external quadrilateral symmetry. I finished with each limb, getting a clear picture of their inner workings. Sure enough, the arm which had been immobilized returned some strange results.

It was as if her limb had been disassembled, and even that's not going far enough. Where the deep scan had presented traces of cell senescence—that is, normal aging—there were no such signs of it in the affected area. It was as if the tissue had been dissociated down to the atoms and remade, like the dead Chalawani we'd encountered.

I pressed a thumb against her forearm. "Can you feel that?"

"Barely."

I pinched at her skin. It was spongy and gave way easily. "How about this?"

"Yes."

"Would you say that felt normal? Any numbness in your arm?"

"It was devoid of feeling, if that is what you mean. Now it... tingles."

"That's a good sign. Blood's returning to the affected area. Would you say it's getting better?"

"I believe so."

"Do you feel cold at all?"

Morrok shifted uncomfortably. "Warm." She poked at the regulator pack. "Get this machine off of me, human."

I lifted the regulator off of what passed for her abdomen and rocked back on my knees. "I don't think you're in danger of shock anymore, but I want to keep an eye on you."

"Keep an eye?" She appeared uncertain until her translator caught up. "Ah. That will not be necessary, human." She pushed herself out of the seat, flexed all eight of her limbs, and pointed two of them at Deela's station. "Besides, there are more important things to 'keep an eye on.'"

I followed her gesture. In all the excitement, I hadn't noticed that we'd returned to normal space. "What do you mean?"

"We are being probed."

I took Morrok down to the med bay to rest while her arm healed. Much as I hated her, she was now just another patient.

"I trust you will not try to restrain me, human. It would not turn out well for you, I think."

I held up my hands. "Wouldn't dream of it, as long as you promise to not get combative." Not that I'd be able to do a damned thing about it if she did: Twice as many limbs, with an impressively dense musculature, not to mention the weapons.

"None of your Union medicines, either," she insisted as she climbed onto the exam bed.

"That's not even a consideration at this point, not until I know more about your metabolism." I didn't mention there were half a dozen different formulations in the med cabinet that were almost certain to kill her, given the right dosage.

It was tempting. I'd learned just enough from the preliminary scan to know what would do the trick. A long time ago, I'd had to treat some Indy gangbangers who'd thought it was a good idea to try and plant their colors out in farm country. They had learned better, the hard way. Those were just kids, really stupid kids. They hadn't been threatening me or trying to kidnap my friends.

I set those thoughts aside and pulled the scanning hoops into place on opposite ends of the exam table. "These will monitor your vital signs and alert me if anything gets out of range. They'll also build up a complete picture of your internal anatomy, so you'll need to keep still until they finish."

"And if I choose not to?"

I sighed and placed my hands on my hips. "Then you'll leave me guessing if you need any further treatment. You don't want that in an emergency."

I left the scanners to work on her and grabbed a small equipment pouch from the corner. Booger had made that his home while I was working, and it didn't seem like a good idea to leave those two in the same room together. A quick peek inside the pouch confirmed it—he was bristling, his iridescent fur sticking up in a way that made him look like a bottle brush. I gave him a quick pat on the head.

Headed back for the control room, I nearly fell over Kal on my way out. It was the first time I'd seen him outside of his nook in the logic center since he'd come aboard. My first thought was that something was wrong.

"Are you okay?"

"Hmm...no and yes," he said, silently moving along on his hundreds of feelers. He seemed wobbly, favoring one side. "Much to discuss, much indeed. You will join us?"

"Absolutely. Those black things we talked about? They're back."

"Hmm. Yes and yes. Encountered myself. Most disconcerting."

Kal wasn't the only one to feel 'disconcerted.' We soon learned Deela wasn't happy with her experience, either.

*There were fewer entities, but more... corporeal, if that makes sense.*

"It does," I said. "The one that materialized in here physically interacted with Morrok in a really strange way, like the tissue and bones were dissociated and reassembled. Like they'd become part of something else."

"Hmm," Kal rumbled as we entered the control room. "Yes and yes. I had a similar experience. Most unpleasant."

"One of those things got to you? Where?"

He flexed his feelers and pointed to the site, lower left quadrant. I grabbed a scanner. "Same thing I saw in Morrok, no traces of cell senescence in the affected area." I put the gear away and stood. "How did it feel?"

"Hmm. No pain, but very disagreeable. Could not see or move."

"That makes sense." I showed him the scan on my data crystal. "See here? It clipped your occipital lobe and cerebellum; those control your sense of sight and coordination. You looked like you were having some balance problems."

Deela interjected. *Then we got lucky, as you might say, if the entity did not contact his temporal lobe. That is where intellectual functions are located, are they not?*

"You're right. Kal's fortunate that it didn't scramble his brain."

Gideon was still a bit fuzzy from the sedative and had been listening with uncharacteristic patience until now. "Tell us what you saw, Mooney."

I crossed my arms. Where to start? Patient confidentiality wasn't at the top of my mind now, so I told them of everything I'd seen from Morrok's interaction with the black wisps. "Kal showed the same markers: No signs of cell senescence. It's like they were taken out of existence and regenerated, if not replaced entirely."

"Is that dangerous?" Gideon asked. "Any side effects he should be concerned about?" He notably left off any concerns about Morrok, not that I could blame him.

"We'd need a doctor to tell us that. All I can do is read the signs, assess the condition, treat whatever can be treated." It went without saying that miraculously youthful tissue replacement was not a condition I'd ever run across in the field.

*It is obvious now that we are dealing with conscious entities, though how they move freely through extradimensional space is a mystery. They can apparently change states at will. It is difficult to see how they could be biological.*

"My experience is limited to the biological," I said. "They're moving with purpose. Are you suggesting they're some kind of free-floating consciousness?"

*To your point, my own experiences are limited. I can only relate what I have sensed, threads of their thoughts. They are questioning. It is possible they feel threatened.*

"Morrok thinks they're probing us."

"Hmm," Kal quivered. "Yes and yes. The entities in the logic center appeared purposeful, quite interested in the processor cores. This I could tell from my interface."

"That's not good at all," Gideon said. "If they can penetrate the core..."

*Yes,* Deela agreed. *We have not seen this behavior during previous encounters.* Her black almond eyes fixed Gideon in a way that signaled there was much more to the story.

"What are you holding back, Gideon?" It was clear to me now that whatever we'd been encountering had not been a complete surprise to him.

He sighed. "Very well, then." Gideon closed his eyes and collapsed against his chair, deflating like a spent balloon. "Yes, I've seen these things before. It was during the shakedown flight, first time Deela and I were aboard. She'd suspected the experience would be disorienting and we needed to see for ourselves."

I was stunned. "You took an enormous risk. The jumps have been hard on your heart. What if—"

He waved at the air. "I'm well aware of all that, Mooney. Why do you think I was so insistent that you come along in the first place? But I had to find out for myself, otherwise there wasn't much point in going any further."

He wasn't entirely wrong, and I suppose deserved credit for going into harm's way to test his bleeding-edge technology. "To be honest, that seems out of character for you."

"Not as much as you'd think, Mooney. Did the same thing with our autopilots during the war. Stayed on the shop floor while they were being built, rode in the back of the planes to collect data myself." He chuckled at the memory. "That was probably more dangerous given the state of technology. About made my heart stop a couple of times."

"But you didn't have extradimensional beings interfering, either."

"Felt like it sometimes. We saw all manner of inexplicable glitches. The pilots called them 'gremlins.'" Another dark chuckle. "Maybe that's as good an explanation as any."

He was avoiding the subject again. "What did you see during that first jump?"

"Same thing you did. The whole universe swirled out of existence, leaving us in this tunnel of nothing. Hints of structure, but everything changed so fast we couldn't keep up. Deela was seriously disoriented and for a time it felt like we were going to be utterly lost. She had to keep reminding me we were already at the exit point, we just couldn't perceive it."

That sounded familiar, and it made me wonder if Deela had been saying that for her own benefit. "When did the 'gremlins' appear?"

Gideon closed his eyes and drew his lips tight. "Almost immediately. At first they were just part of the background, not that we knew what we were looking at in the first place. We started noticing ripples, almost as if the air had become like water. It was hard to tell what was real and what wasn't. Then the shadows came." He paused and took a deep breath. "My first thought was something was wrong with the ship, like maybe the gravity projectors were off kilter. That would've explained the ripple effect. Deela assured me they were just fine, of course. That's when I realized we were looking at something else entirely."

"Did you make contact with them?"

"No," he said stiffly. "Doubt I'd be here if that'd happened. Deela didn't even pick up on anything at first, though she had what I'd call 'tickles' in her mind. Hints of another consciousness, but nothing she could pin on any one apparition." He sighed. "That's been changing over time."

That fit with what we'd seen. With each jump, more of those "gremlins" appeared. And the longer they were moving among us, the less passive they appeared. They were becoming more purposeful. "What do you think they want with us?"

"It's not 'what,' it's 'whom.'" He patted his chest. "I think they're after me, Mooney."

# ⚕ 23 ⚕

I excused myself from the control room confab, reasoning that it was time to check in on my other patient. The scans would be done by now, and she'd no doubt be impatient to hear the results. It was as good an excuse as any, because I wasn't ready to face the thought that these dark beings might not only be intelligent, but actively malevolent.

When I came to the med bay, she was gone. The scanning hoops had stowed themselves on opposite ends of the exam bed, steadily strobing green. They'd completed mapping her body and the results were waiting for me to pull up on the wall projector.

After a cursory look at her internal anatomy, I decided to distract myself by taking inventory of our supplies. My mind wasn't yet ready to study a new species. Inventory was a task that was necessary and comfortably mind-numbing, the right kind of work to keep busy while I cleared my head. I set my crystal on top of the bay's small desk. "Clara, could you play some music?"

"What sounds good to you?"

"Something relaxing," I said. "Jazz piano?"

"That's a great choice. Give me a sec, I have to pull it together out of native memory. It'd be easier if we could link to the Union network."

"Yeah, that's not happening."

"That's okay, it'll give me a chance to be creative." Over the years, conversations with my little crystal assistant had taught it how to talk like a normal human. Sometimes it was almost enough to make me forget I was talking to a slab of smart glass.

It wasn't long before the med bay was filled with the soothing melodies of a piano trio. My musical tastes had evolved over the years, but this was the style I'd always relied on when I needed my nerves calmed and my mind uncluttered. "I don't recognize that. Who is it?"

"It's me. There wasn't much to pull from memory, so I improvised. Do you like it?"

"Love it." I looked down to my hip pouch and saw Booger peacefully swaying to the rhythm. "I think he likes it too. Just don't get into any of that weird experimental stuff. Keep it simple."

"Will do. Shout if you need me."

I went on to busy myself with opening cabinets and checking supplies against the tally scrolling past in my visor. No cumbersome checklists or bar code scanners, just focus on the item and let the visor do the work.

Even with that, I was tired, physically and emotionally. We'd run into roadblocks at every turn, yet still managed to keep going. What else was waiting out there for us to stumble into? Bjorn had already sacrificed his freedom to allow us to go on. In his own words, he was our hole card and it felt like we had no more hands left to play in our gamble with time and space. Was there some final, unknowable move from the universe that would eventually call our bets?

The stakes were now about as high as they could get, all or nothing. We were resigned to whatever fate awaited us, and I was just along for the ride.

Of course that wasn't quite right. Gideon had brought me on because he'd needed me, which told me he'd known this trip wouldn't be easy. He'd been holding back, that much was clear now. It was more than just failing health, he had known about the strange effects of transiting higher dimensions. A little warning would've been nice.

Would knowing that have stopped me? It was too much to consider right now, and I was tired, so tired. I laid down on the exam bed and dimmed the lighting, immersing myself in the gentle melodies emanating from the crystal.

I awoke to a flat, elongated head hovering over me. I sat up with a start, clutching my chest. I felt Booger stiffen too, and reached down to calm him.

Morrok's head pivoted atop her retractile neck. "Did I disturb you?" Not that she seemed to care.

"A little," I mumbled, and slid off the exam bed to collect myself. "What do you want?"

"I wish to understand your capabilities, human." She pivoted her head in a circle, studying the med bay. "Your equipment is impressive, though your supplies are decidedly inadequate."

"Inadequate? I suppose that depends on what you need. Most Med Corps gear is multipurpose, except for some species-specific attachments. Meds are also multispecies, with some exceptions."

"Yes. You seem to have brought very few 'exceptions.'"

"This isn't a medical transport," I reminded her. "It's a private vessel. Gideon had it loaded out for the individuals aboard."

"His own welfare being the primary concern, I gather." She awkwardly folded herself into a chair, and I make no excuses for taking pleasure in her discomfort. "No consideration for other species. Typical Union thoughtlessness."

"We didn't plan on taking aboard a Da'Farrii pirate."

She pushed at the gel with her four arms. "No matter. We will outfit this ship accordingly when the time comes."

"And when would that be?" I sniffed, not hiding my skepticism.

"We have made a deal, and I shall keep my word," she countered. "You Union types could learn something from the Sisterhood's code of honor."

I crossed my arms. "Some code you have. You raid border settlements, commandeer ships . . . how is that honorable?" I wasn't in an accommodating mood.

"I will overlook your insolence, human, for you are clearly out of your depth. Tell me, how long have you been in the Union?"

"Almost five years in human terms. I don't know how well that translates into yours."

"It translates well enough," she said, with a gurgle approximating a laugh. "You are an infant."

Didn't feel that way, but I was willing to allow it. "I'm sure it's not long by your reckoning."

"It is not." She flexed all four of her arms. "From what I know of your calendar, I am almost one hundred years old. Barely middle-aged. But my knowledge goes much deeper, centuries upon centuries of collective wisdom passed down through generations of Sisters. There is much you could learn from our kind."

"Learn what? Looting and pillaging? Thanks, I'll pass."

Morrok shook her broad head, imitating a human gesture. "As I said, you have much to learn. You no doubt believe the Union to be peaceable. My kind's perspective is somewhat different."

"I know the Union doesn't go around raiding other worlds."

"Perhaps not in the sense you seem to imagine. But once a new species is in their clutches, all their world's freedom is lost, subservient to Union ministers in their glorious Capital."

I have to admit that threw me off. "You've been to the ring?"

"Sisters before me have, and their knowledge is now part of mine. What occurred generations ago is as if I experienced it myself. There is more to us than you may care to believe, human."

"If your ancestors have been to the Capital, then they must have been invited."

"They were," she conceded. "Grand promises were made to them about the rewards of being part of a galaxy-spanning league of civilizations, how each race contributes to a greater whole. In the end, we could not submit."

"I may not know much, but it doesn't seem like submission to me. If anything, it looks like every race is given a free hand to govern themselves."

"Once again, that depends on your perspective. Who knows what each race had to give up? I can tell you that for mine, the terms were unacceptable."

"They expected you to behave yourselves."

"They expected us to forsake our code! Our way of life!" She rose, angrily jabbing at the air. "Tell me, what is the difference between our Sisterhood and your Thuban protectors? That they are willing to be cannon fodder on the Union's behalf? No, we look out for our own. For this, the Union ostracizes us. We are left to provide for our kind in the way we see fit."

"Looting and pillaging your way through life sounded like the better option, then?"

"Commerce takes on many forms. One culture's market is another's thievery. You know nothing of life in the rest of the galaxy, human. It is not so benign as you might imagine." She extended her neck, looking me up and down. "That you and your master were accorded membership says much. It will not be long before your world is approached by the Union." She said it with a distinct air of caution. "Tell me, what are you willing to give up to be under their protection? What can they provide that my Sisterhood cannot?"

"Maybe that they'll mostly leave us alone. I know they have pretty strict protocols to limit any culture shock."

"Oh, I assure you they do. They will draw you in slowly, bit by bit, until the day comes when your kind realizes they cannot survive apart from the Union."

"If I've learned anything, it's that the galaxy can be a dangerous place. Earth can be like that, too. Nations form alliances because other nations show they can't be trusted to mind their own business."

"If that is the way of your kind, if you do not value your freedom, then perhaps you will make perfect Union citizens."

"Then you and I have different definitions of freedom." Hers sounded a lot like anarchy.

She tipped her head. "Tell me, human, what drives you to return to your home if the Union treated you so well? I wish to learn about your world."

"So you can make us your next target?" I was already uncomfortable with the thought of her coming anywhere near our corner of the galactic neighborhood.

"We have no interest in primitives," she scoffed. "I doubt there is anything you could contribute to the Sisterhood."

I hesitated, remembering Bjorn's warning. "Gideon has unfinished business back on Earth, and so do I. It's a mutually beneficial arrangement." For my part, it was true enough. She didn't need to know anything else.

"Finally, something I can appreciate." She lowered her head, which I gathered was a sign of respect. "I believe we have reached an understanding, human. Thank you for enlightening me."

She skittered away, lowering her body to propel herself with all eight limbs. I let out my breath, relieved to have her out of my sight. She was trying to form a relationship, find a way to gain advantage, and I hoped I hadn't given up too much.

The thing about conversation is that it works in both directions. While she had learned something about me, I'd just learned a lot more about her.

✠ ✠ ✠

It was bad enough that we had shadowy gremlins moving through the ship at will every time we entered high space. The idea of them targeting one of us was chilling, especially when their target might have been my patient. It was time for a hard conversation with our pilot.

My first stop was the control room, which to my surprise was empty. I shouldn't have been, we were in a distant orbit around Sargas and there was no need for active piloting. Even a Gray couldn't stay on duty forever.

I found her in the galley, picking from a bowl of what looked like moss-green cabbage with a scent reminiscent of truffles. It was *suliquo*, a staple of the Reticulan diet. She ate delicately, her elongated fingers pulling thick leaves one bite at a time. The galley was empty but for the two of us, so I waited for its door to whisper shut behind me and pulled up a chair to face her. Her massive brow wrinkled; of course there was no surprising a telepath. She placed her *suliquo* leaf back into her bowl.

*You are troubled, Melanie.*

"You don't know the half of it." Okay, she probably did. In all my time in the Union, Deela was the lone Reticulan with whom I'd had trust issues. Maybe that had come from working so closely with them; it had turned out to be a big help when your partner could literally read your mind. It was different outside of a working relationship, or at least one where we weren't mutually dependent on each other.

*That is not entirely accurate. We are greatly dependent on each other.*

I flexed my hands in frustration. "See, that's the problem. You don't hide the fact that you know what I'm thinking before I say anything. The Grays I've worked with in the past at least maintained a polite show of privacy."

*It was likely more than polite, though it is an acquired skill similar to your ability to block your thoughts from us.*

"And here I thought I'd gotten the hang of that."

*I believe you have. That ability depends greatly on an individual's level of comfort, and you were not completely comfortable with me.*

"That's because you were spying on me before I even came aboard."

*Correct, to an extent. Understand that I held no ill intent. I was performing "due diligence," as Gideon explained it. Your medical skills were not in question, but we had to be confident in your ability to remain composed under uniquely trying circumstances.*

"Anything else?"

*After our test jump, it was obvious that the experience taxed Gideon's health. He would require someone who could attend to him, and you were an obvious choice. It became more obvious once I sensed your desire to return to Earth.*

"Exactly how deep into my head did you go?"

*Not deep at all. That quandary was almost always at the top of your mind.* She reached out to take my hand. Her skin was cool.

*While I do not presume to fully comprehend human psychology, it was evident that your inner conflict was becoming a distraction. This could have led to making mistakes, which in your profession can have most unfortunate consequences. You needed a change of focus. In my judgment, you made the correct choice in joining us.*

"We'll see about that." Though it pained me to admit she was probably right. "If we make it home without blowing ourselves up or getting stranded in another dimension, that is."

*I would not worry about the former.*

It didn't escape me that she'd said nothing about the latter. "Why didn't you warn us about those gremlin things before?"

Deela pushed her bowl aside and clasped her hands together. *Forgive my recalcitrance. I am not prone to offering explanations for phenomena I do not understand.*

"What about threats you don't understand? A warning would have been nice."

*Again, their nature was a mystery to us. They could just as easily have been an illusion, a visual artifact of our three-dimensional bodies experiencing six-dimensional space. I did not trust my own judgment in our earlier encounters. Consciousness was difficult to perceive.*

"And now you have."

*I have. These entities are difficult to read. I would say they are quite good at blocking their thoughts, but that could just as easily be from my own physical limitations.*

"That makes sense. The telepathic center of your brain is like any other sensory organ. Same reason your eyes can't see into other dimensions."

*Precisely. It is similar to how we perceive high space during jumps:*

*suggestions, reflections of the higher dimensions, not the space itself. I can sense the outlines of consciousness in these shadow beings, but cannot yet read them. I suspect they could project their thoughts if they chose to.*

If Deela was right, that wasn't a good sign. "I don't like the idea that they can read us, but not the other way around. That leaves each jump up to their good graces."

*Yes, I can see that now. Please understand that in the beginning, I did not have enough data to determine whether or not these entities posed a threat.*

I jerked a thumb over my shoulder toward the med bay, where Morrok had been recuperating. "I'd say we have plenty of data to go on now."

*Still, they may not be malevolent. Any harm brought to us from physical interaction may be unintentional, a side effect from our species evolving in different dimensions. I would compare it to the cavern slugs of Zeta Reticuli. They do not intend harm, though their secretions are highly toxic.*

"Comparing them to poisonous slugs doesn't help, you know." I rested my chin in one hand and drummed my fingers on the table. "Gideon says he was concerned about them right away, yet he still forged ahead. Any insights you're willing to offer?"

Deela's ogive head tipped stiffly, left to right, in the manner of Grays when they were having an internal debate. *Understand that I am under a strict confidentiality agreement. However, there is some latitude when discussing matters with his physician.*

Again, not a physician, but I'd allow it.

*I attributed his concern to a normal human fear of the unknown. Gideon is an educated man and quite clever, though he remains largely driven by instinct. His instinct told him the "gremlins" were not to be trusted or trifled with. At one point he even referred to them as malevolent creatures from your religious folklore.*

"Demons?"

*Yes, that was the term he used.*

It sounded nuts, but I could see how someone might think that. And if so, why would he risk everything to take such a dangerous path home when there were more conventional ways to get there?

Deela, of course, knew what I was thinking. *Remember, Gideon has the same need to avoid the complications of relative time as you. I had proposed using our Element 115 stockpile to outfit his yacht's gravity drive for the journey, but he was insistent. His remaining offspring are themselves of advanced age, and their offspring are in late middle age.*

Gideon did face a conundrum. If he'd taken the normal way home, his children would likely be dead before he got there, while his grandchildren would not be far behind. "He's not only looking for last rites, he's looking to pass down an inheritance." Somehow, Gideon thought he could make up for decades of lost time by showering his descendants with money. He was willing to risk everything for it and drag the rest of us along. It made me wonder about my own choices, if knowing that would've made a difference.

*The desire to protect one's legacy is a powerful motivator among most species. The question remains—would knowing what you do now have changed your mind?*

She had me there.

# ⚕ 24 ⚕

At my insistence, Gideon was secure in his bed for the next jump with discs fixed in place on opposite sides of his chest. They were feeding a steady stream of vitals into my visor while the holoscreen above his bed gave me a 3D view of his internal organs. In my hand was a syringe, the old-fashioned kind with a needle and plunger. Form follows function, though this device was shiny Med Corps tech and so absurdly light that I had to concentrate on holding the thing. It was loaded with Type II sedative, roughly equivalent to diazepam, good old Valium. We were going to start with a low dose, hopefully taking the edge off just enough for him to tolerate the psychological effects of extradimensional space. I had no idea if the absence of visual cues would help keep his cardiac rhythm from going haywire, but speaking for myself I was happy to not be facing that unreal gods-eye view of the universe again.

During my early days in the Union, I'd spent a lot of time studying Survey Ministry records from Earth. I had been curious about their take on human history, and it was by turns depressing and surprisingly optimistic. Being a new space traveler, I was also eager to sift through their archives of our space program. From my newfound perspective, the early assumptions of scientists as to how the body would adapt (or not) to outer space were hilarious. More than a few thought we weren't psychologically suited for it. Humans needed that firm grounding of gravity, where up is up and down is down, and it was believed that being exposed to the Big Nothing would drive astronauts mad.

Of course the first space travelers proved that humans could adapt remarkably well despite the occasional bouts of nausea. Ultimately they could adjust because they still existed in three-dimensional space.

If they'd only known how limited their thinking was. If those same eggheads had been able to experience what lurked behind the veneer of what they *thought* was the universe, they'd have crawled down a hole and pulled it in after them.

Infinity is not for the faint of heart, maybe not for humans at all. If there hadn't been a patient to look after, I'd have gladly pumped myself full of sedatives. They could wake me up when it was over.

It was a nice idea, at least.

Deela's thoughts intruded on mine. *We are ready up here. Please let me know when you are able to proceed.*

I wondered how much of my internal dialogue she'd been listening to. I'd become good at compartmentalizing around the Grays for privacy's sake, but the occasional intrusive thought had a way of escaping my mental lockbox.

"Stand by." I faced Gideon and held up the syringe. "I'm going to administer the sedative now, okay?"

"Just get on with it," he grumbled.

I wore a neutral mask of civility, but it was tempting to just shove in the needle and make it as uncomfortable as possible. I fancied his reaction to something truly unpleasant, maybe a course of rabies treatments, as I pressed my thumb on the plunger.

"All done. You should start feeling it right away." I imagined the comforting warmth that would be coursing through his veins right about then, and was a little jealous. I kept an eye on his vitals and let Deela know I'd give her the signal as soon as he was stable.

It didn't take long. Gideon was still awake but quickly slipping into la-la land. Cardiac rhythm and respiratory rates were on the low side of normal but holding steady, as was his BP. I was satisfied he wasn't going to crash on me, and let Deela know.

*Very well. Engaging drive now.*

We might have been spared the exterior visuals, but that only seemed to amplify the other weird effects. The second hand of my watch was doing its strange in-between-time dance again, which was oddly reassuring now that we couldn't see outside. As long as that was happening, I knew we weren't in normal space.

The walls, floor and ceiling seemed to ripple and stretch. I hadn't noticed this before, but then I'd been focused on the surreal vista outside. With nothing else to distract me, I was seeing the physical effects for the first time. I reached out to steady myself against Gideon's bed railing, but found my hands already there. I twisted one of the discs for higher resolution, but the images resolved on the holoscreen before I thought to do it. Everything was everywhere at once again.

I screwed my eyes shut and shook my head, risking taking my attention off Gideon to blank out everything else. In what seemed like hours later, I opened them to check his vitals. Everything was right around where they had been a few seconds (hours?) ago. He was still stable, which was a relief. He wasn't about to lose his life, and in turn I wasn't about to lose my ride.

I might have been white-knuckling it, but for Gideon the sedative was working. If I could hang on, we just might make it home. "How's it going up there?" I thought at Deela.

*Nominal, as far as we can tell. Kal-Nuala assures me we are within probabilistic limits.*

I supposed that was good. "How much longer?"

*Impossible to say. By one measure, we are already there.*

That's what I got for asking. For being instantaneous, these damned jumps seemed to last forever.

Around this time is when I started noticing more weirdness. The shadows I'd seen during our last jump had reappeared, emerging from the forward bulkhead to swirl through the cabin before disappearing through the other side. Some lingered, growing in size and seeming to fill the room like an ebony mist before dissolving.

What the hell were these things? And why was I seeing so many more of them? I'd heard of St. Elmo's fire, an odd discharge of static electricity that sometimes formed around the masts of ships and wings of airplanes. Was this something akin to that, a buildup of static energy that came from leaving 3D space? That had to be it. Gideon's imagination had been getting the better of him, and in turn I'd allowed him to get me spun up. Even Deela had to be imagining things. She was a biological being like the rest of us, which meant her senses could be fooled.

There was always a rational explanation. This had to be a natural effect of 3D beings interacting with 6D space. Gideon's rantings about demons were just that, fanciful imaginings of a physical effect. Like ball lightning or swamp gas. Had to be.

That was the thought I comforted myself with until another thin shadow appeared, diaphanous yet now strangely organized. It seemed to move with purpose, pausing to hover by Gideon's bedside and within my arm's reach. I let go of the bed rail and reached for it. My hand went through, feeling nothing. I halfway expected it to disperse, like steam off of a hot kettle, but it didn't react to my touch at all. Likewise, I felt nothing. Literally nothing. My hand went numb, as if it had left my physical self for something else entirely. I recoiled, pulling my arm to my chest and frantically rubbing my hand to make sure it was still there. Booger was on alert now, leaping out of my hip pouch up to my shoulders, his fur standing fully on end. He let out a low, menacing growl which I'd never heard from him before.

The shadow began to move like the others, but now was coming straight for me. I was frozen in my seat. It passed right through me, and for a split second my entire body had that same disconnected sensation. I felt physically unmoored from reality, as if for that brief moment I ceased to exist. Not dead, just not *there*. Everything turned to that unreal monochrome palette that I'd first seen through Deela's viewscreen, as if I was existing outside the confines of our ship.

The shadow passed, and I was back to reality. My visor lit up again with Gideon's vitals, which were suddenly elevated. His heart was racing at 140 beats per minute and he was drenched in sweat.

How long had that lasted? I checked my watch to see its second hand was moving normally again. We were back in 3D space.

Gideon was agitated but steady. ECG traces didn't show any signs of an impending event. He looked to me with wide, pleading eyes. I took his hand and urged him to breathe deeply. To calm down.

Physician, heal thyself. My own breathing was rapid and I could feel my pulse throbbing in my neck. I took a few deep breaths to bring my heart rate down.

I was about to ask Gideon if he'd experienced the same thing, but was distracted by a message that had just appeared in my visor. I pulled off the visor, thinking it was some kind of glitch, then saw it repeated on the holoscreen:

YOU DO NOT BELONG HERE.

"Mooney."

I was examining my visor in a vain attempt to determine what would make it throw out a warning like that. They worked in concert with our translator implants. If it were possible to fool myself into thinking I was hearing voices, why couldn't my eyes start seeing things as well? Of course, that left the small matter of the same message appearing on Gideon's monitor.

"Mooney!"

What? Oh yeah. Gideon . . .

"We finished the jump. Care to get these things off of me?"

"Right. Sorry. Had a glitch in my readouts for a second there." I set the visor aside and took the scanner discs off of him. I fumbled and dropped one to the floor. When I slipped it back into my bag, I found the counteragent was still there with a full vial. The sedative had worn off on its own. That would've taken at least two hours. Had I been sitting here in a stupor the whole time?

"Anything I need to be concerned about?"

I shook my head and scrolled through his telemetry. "No. You did fine, in fact."

He fixed his eyes on me. "You look a bit worse for wear, Mooney. Like you've seen a ghost."

I slumped into a chair. "You may be right."

"They came back, didn't they? The black demons."

There. He'd finally said it. "I liked it better when you called them gremlins."

"Touched you, did they?"

"I . . . I don't know. More like moved right through me."

"What did it feel like?"

"A warning." I still wasn't convinced there hadn't been some bio-technical hiccup. Or maybe I was convincing myself there had been. "Like we're messing with things we don't understand."

"Told you they were real."

I rubbed at my temples. "Then why keep doing this? Why don't we just use the gravity drive to get home and suck up the time lag?"

He drummed his fingertips on the head of his cane, wearing a faraway look. "Obligations, Mooney. The initial conditions haven't changed: I need to get back before the time lag makes it irrelevant, same as you. We keep going." He eased himself down from the bed. "And I'm going to be in the control room for the next jump. Next time maybe you should take the sedatives."

# 25

Matching Gideon's stubborn insistence on returning to the control room, I had just as stubbornly insisted on bringing all the gear we might need on hand if he took a turn for the worse. My makeshift ER ward, with its collection of meds, monitors, and lifesaving equipment, took up a good portion of the already limited space. This especially irritated Morrok. I won't lie, that didn't bother me a bit.

"Are all humans this weak in their old age?" she grumbled as she wormed her way into her seat. Gideon was about to protest just as I was administering his sedative, which fortunately worked quickly.

I'd been busy securing Gideon in his seat, which gave me a good excuse to keep my back to her. "Some more than others, but we all decline at some point." It was a blessing to still be young enough to not worry about that for myself. "Is that not a problem with your race?"

"Elders in the Sisterhood remove themselves from society before they become a burden to others."

It was a chilling thought, and I wondered what "removing" oneself involved. Did they simply go find some quiet place to die, or was it a Da'Farrii version of hara-kiri? My money was on the latter.

I looked over my shoulder. "Our kind sees it as an obligation to take care of its elders."

She made a gurgling noise, which I took as the Da'Farrii version of a skeptical grunt. "Wasteful, prolonging the lives of ones who are past their usefulness."

Interesting, considering her earlier pronouncements about

Da'Farrii impetuousness. Maybe having a few old pirates around would've tempered the younger hotheads. I didn't want to have this discussion, and apparently neither did Deela. She cut in just in time, keeping us on task.

*Projector arrays are at nominal output, on standby. Kal, have you completed your route analysis?*

The Mintakan replied over the intercom. "Hmm. Yes and yes. Vectors have been sent to your console."

I hurried to my seat, knowing that Deela wouldn't waste time.

*I see that, thank you. Vectors are set and matched. Stand by.*

She tapped at her holoscreen, and the hum of pent-up energy filled the cabin. The stars ahead appeared to converge into a single point as we accelerated, just as quickly exploding into a tight circle to envelope us before disappearing. Black sky turned white, with undulating shades of gray suggesting features of this previously invisible level of the universe. Even now, it was hard to comprehend that we were actually *seeing* gravity.

I felt lighter, that sensation of your stomach rising up through your throat like going over the top of a rollercoaster. I grabbed for the seat restraints, which I'd forgotten to snap in place. Right. Internal gravity was turned off, otherwise it would bend our path to the exit point. We were in freefall, careening through this narrow tunnel beneath our reality.

*On course, within tolerance.*

"What's our predicted error?" Gideon asked, slurring from the sedative.

*Zero point two,* Deela replied. *The best we have yet achieved.*

Gideon grunted with satisfaction and closed his eyes. The old guy was finally relaxed. Maybe this would convince him to stay in his suite next time.

Hard as it was to believe, we were finally adapting to the surreal experience of crossing extradimensional space. My watch was doing its moving-not-moving thing, which I'd come to ignore. Instead of propelling ourselves by bending space in a dimension where everything that could happen, had happened, coasting along between gravity wells had so far avoided causality loops.

It was even harder to believe I'd become passably conversant in this stuff. Maybe I needed to rethink my plan to study marine biology when we got home. Astrophysics, perhaps? I'd have a natural advantage, having experienced enough of the phenomena firsthand. There'd be a lot of difficult math, but—

What was that incessant beeping noise?

*Structural alarm. Outer hull breach, Z1 sector.*

That stirred Gideon right out of his pharmaceutical stupor. "What . . . say again?"

*Projection plates along the Z1 seam have been dislodged. Pressurized section has vented to space.*

Gideon cursed under his breath and pointed at me, then at his arm. I got the message and unstrapped to fly over to his side. I grabbed at his seat rails to steady myself. Meanwhile, Morrok was demanding answers.

"Tell me what has happened, Reticulan."

*I cannot say with any certainty beyond what I have already explained. Part of the field projector array has been damaged, and the associated neural relays have gone into fail-safe mode.*

"You said the pressurized section vented. Does that present any danger?"

Deela was about to answer her when Gideon interrupted. "No," he said with a sleepy voice. "There's . . . protective membrane . . ."

Deela finished for him. *The hull's individual relay centers are isolated from each other within the neural network. Each network sector is a separate pressure vessel.*

"I gather this neural network is rather important, then. It is undamaged, I take it?"

Kal had been listening over the intercom, and had his own problems. "Hmm. No and no. I detected incongruities in the logic cores at the same time."

"Incongruities?" Gideon slurred. "Be specific." He motioned for me and pointed at my go-bag. *Right.* I injected the counteragent.

"Hmm. Yes and yes," Kal continued. "The logic center is generating several probabilistic outcomes, all at odds with each other. It is as if the logic center is in conflict with itself."

Great. So the ship's brain had become schizophrenic?

With the sedative neutralized, Gideon returned to his irascible self in no time. "Deela, how's this affecting our trajectory?"

*Unaltered. The projector plates are in standby mode while we are in high space.*

"But having a whole sector offline is going to affect our projection field when it's time to come out."

*Correct. The adjacent sectors can compensate to a limited degree. We will not have full field integrity.*

Morrok watched their interplay silently. At least she was smart enough to know when to be quiet.

Gideon worked his jaw as he thought through the problem. "Kal, you heard all this. How's that affect your probabilities?"

"Hmm. If our trajectory is unchanged, we will hit our mark. But perturbations in the gravity field will alter our exit vector."

"How far off center?"

"Hmm. Known and unknown. Uncertainty is within standard deviation and without at any given moment. Will not have a solution until we arrive."

"So you can't give Deela a callout when it's time to make the exit jump?"

"Hmm. No and no. There is no single outcome the probability routines can settle on."

Gideon took a long breath. "Then we're flying by the seat of our pants."

*An apt analogy,* Deela replied. *I have a rudimentary backup.* She pulled up a new hologram, a simple graph of our track indexed against time. *I tracked the last two jumps against our perceived time, and used that data to create a prediction for this jump. It is imperfect, but may be close enough to identify our exit point.*

Gideon nodded appreciatively. "In my day, navigators called that 'dead reckoning.' They'd use it to check against where our autopilots were taking them."

*Another apt analogy. That is precisely what I am doing.*

Morrok fixed her bulbous eyes on Gideon. "This is not acceptable, human."

"It's the only play we've got." Gideon sank into his seat and met the pirate's angry stare. "We'll know when we get there. Or when we don't."

*Everyone please secure yourselves in your seats. The inertial dampers will remain deactivated until we achieve orbit.*

Grays are so steady-handed and efficient that it can be hard to tell when they're under stress, but Deela's terse command spoke volumes.

She wasn't entirely certain her back-of-the-napkin calculations were going to put us where we needed to be, and I didn't like thinking about what that would mean if we missed. With the projector plates off-kilter, we'd need the next star's gravity to help pull us out of high space. If we missed, they might not be able to generate an opening on their own, leaving us stranded.

Outside, the monochrome vista continued to swirl around us. I checked my watch out of nervous habit, and of course it was still frozen in place. It made me wonder how in the world Deela was tracking time if the chronometer was just as unreliable. Reticulan brains were larger and even more complex than a human's, with a third lobe whose function was something of a mystery beyond being their telepathic center. Did that give her the ability to compartmentalize, to mark off time and still manage the cognitive functions it took to pilot a spaceship? I imagined her counting off one Mississippi, two Mississippi...

*I cannot explain the physiological process, but you are in essence correct.*

Good grief. Even now, she was listening to us? "You need to pay attention to your piloting, not to me," I muttered.

*Multitasking, as you would say. It is part of our nature. Do not be concerned, I am still keeping time.*

"My apologies. It's a mistake to ever doubt you." Deela had the situation in hand, so the best thing for me was to stay calm. I closed my eyes, took a deep breath, and settled back into the inertia gel.

When I opened my eyes, it was time to get worried again.

A black cloud had appeared ahead of us, dead center. It grew steadily, relentlessly, becoming more defined as it drew closer until it nearly filled the holoscreen. "Deela...?"

*I cannot alter our trajectory. I suspect it would do no good regardless.*

The cloud was in the cabin, a formless, depthless apparition of black so deep that it made me dizzy. Everything began to grow dim, as if any light in the universe unlucky enough to fall into its grip was erased from existence.

A warning flashed in my visor: Gideon's heart rate had shot up. *Damn.* I should've known not to give him the sedative counteragent; he wouldn't be able to take another dose for at least an hour.

And he had good reason to be agitated. The apparition was hovering over him now, a mist that began to resolve into something not quite solid. It was a writhing knot of emptiness, black tendrils stabbing at the air, grasping.

The tendrils reached for Gideon. I moved to unstrap my harness when Deela shouted me down.

*No! Melanie, you must remain seated!*

When a Reticulan yells inside your head, you know it's important. I could only watch in horror as the smoky tendrils snaked down, curling around Gideon's legs. They moved up to his torso, then reached for his head. Gideon was ashen, his face a twisted mask of terror. His mouth hung open; if he was screaming I couldn't hear it.

The apparition disappeared as if someone had thrown a light switch. I looked ahead and saw we were back in normal space. The holoscreen displayed a comforting blanket of distant stars, but it was obvious we weren't home free yet. The one star we were supposed to be orbiting wasn't in view, and Deela was all asses and elbows at her station.

*Entry vector offset seventeen degrees, compensating. Everyone remain seated.*

We were right on the edge of our entry cone and barely within our target star's influence, but at least we were in normal space. The stars ahead wheeled about and we were pushed hard into our seats as Deela hit the brakes. Orbits are essentially a balance between velocity and gravity; if one force exceeds the other you'll either go skipping off into space or crash into whatever you're orbiting. Deela was decelerating hard, and the ship was howling in protest. After years of counting on extraterrestrial tech working perfectly, it was alarming to be in of a spaceship that felt like it was shaking itself apart.

The groans and vibrations finally subsided, ending with a gut-wrenching snap that reverberated from high above us.

Gideon swore under his breath. "That would be the Z1 panels." I shot a glance in his direction. He was wiping sweat from his brow with an embroidered handkerchief.

"Report. Reticulan, what is our status?" It was laughable that Morrok was still trying to assert her authority.

*We are in an elliptical orbit around Nunki, eccentricity zero point eight, period nine point four annums. We are sufficiently clear of any habitable planets. Internal gravity is restored, you may now leave your seats,* Deela replied to no one in particular, not ready to surrender authority to this pirate. Good girl.

I unsnapped my harness and pulled myself free of the inertia gel to move to Gideon's side. The scanners had become dislodged in all the excitement. He was trying to get free and I laid my hand on his chest. "Not yet." His shirt was drenched. "You're clammy."

Gideon tugged at his clothing. "I'm well aware of that." He was trying to project authority, but his shaky voice wasn't fooling me.

I moved the discs to opposite sides of his chest and pressed. Vital signs and 3D images of his chest cavity appeared in my visor. "Heart rate and BP are elevated, but heading back to normal. Nothing to worry about for now, probably no worse than mine, in fact. That was some ride," I offered with a reassuring smile. When in doubt, keep the patient calm while you figure things out.

His eyes darted around the cabin, big as saucers, before fixing them on me. "That . . . thing," he whispered. "It . . ." He trailed off.

I leaned in closer and lowered my voice. "I saw. How do you feel?"

Gideon pointed to his legs and kneaded at his abdomen, still speaking in a gravelly whisper. "Disconnected, like it pulled me apart and put me back together." He paused. "Violated."

There was a shuffling sound behind us. Morrok had extracted herself from the inertia gel and was down on all eight limbs, stretching the kinks out. "When the mongrel weaklings are sufficiently recovered," she announced with distaste, "we meet in the galley. I want the Mintakan there as well."

We watched her skitter away into the corridor. I turned back to Gideon and our eyes met, perhaps the first time human understanding had passed between us. Personality clashes aside, we shared a common goal and it felt like Gideon had finally realized that made us a team.

He punched at the restraints and held out a hand. "A little help?"

I pulled him free of the gel and got him to his feet. Even with the cane, he was unsteady and leaned on me for support. Helping Gideon bear his weight, for the first time I could feel how frail he was. The old coot knew how to project a strong image, but it was of course all a charade. "I can get you a hover chair."

"No," he protested, "I need to walk. Get my strength back."

"Galley's at the far side of the torus. Let's take it slow."

Gideon wrung out the tail of his shirt. Stale drops of perspiration fell to the deck. "My suite first. I need to change." He pointed his cane down the corridor with a devious grin. "And our 'guest' needs a reminder that we're not on her schedule."

# ⚕ 26 ⚕

It would've been better to take Gideon straight to the med bay, but his quarters would have to do. I held on to his arm and pushed some pillows aside on his divan. "Lie down."

"I really need a shower, Mooney."

"And I need to examine you before letting you go on your own. That is, unless you want me to bathe you too."

My threat had the desired effect. He settled onto the couch with a stubborn grunt.

"Good. Now, take off your shirt and pants."

He arched his brow warily.

"Oh come on. I'm your *medic*. I'm allowed to see you naked." Not that it was doing anything for me, mind you. In this job, one tends to become unimpressed by the nether regions of the human body in short order. That was especially the case for a 111-year-old man.

Gideon unbuttoned his drenched shirt and dropped it to the floor in a soggy lump. "Down to my skivvies and that's it."

"That's all I need. Just get comfortable." While he finished stripping out of his damp clothes, I pulled out a fresh pair of discs and a small holoprojector. I set the projector cube on a table by his feet and got to work.

Starting at his head, I moved the discs along opposite sides of his body. As the projection filled with vital signs, imagery began to compile layer by layer. Soon we had a 3D hologram of his insides floating in the air by Gideon's feet.

"That's actually rather remarkable," he said. "I suppose I hadn't paid enough attention before."

I slipped the discs into my pocket. "I've come to love these little things. I'd have given my right arm to have them at my old job." I swiped at the image to display his vitals. "Heart rate, BP, respiration are all back to normal. ECG shows no signs of abnormalities, same with EEG." I glanced at his pile of wet clothes on the floor. "How do you feel right now? Any headache?"

Gideon kneaded the back of his head and nodded. "Raging."

"You sweated off about four pounds. You're dehydrated. I'll have the nutrisynth whip up some electrolyte juice." His mouth turned down at the thought. "That is, unless you'd prefer IV saline."

"Ugh. You win, Mooney. I'll drink the damn juice."

I told the synth what to mix and swiped back to the full body scan, starting with his legs just above the knee, ending at his abdomen.

The affected regions showed no trace of cell senescence. It was the same as Morrok's injury, if you could call it that. It was hard to see how having your cells rebooted could be called an "injury" other than it being a generally terrifying experience. What the long-term effects might be were way beyond my skill set; I could only identify the markers. The rest would be for an MD to decide, preferably one specializing in research. I doubted Gideon would be willing to offer himself up to a research scientist on Earth. For that matter, what would he tell them?

"Makes sense," Gideon said after I explained this. "My legs feel better than ever now, at least in the thighs." He tapped a finger at his chest. "Too bad they missed up here."

"Be careful what you wish for," I cautioned him. "The heart is the only organ in the body that can't heal from an injury. The tissue can't repair itself, which also means cells can't start reproducing out of control. That's why there's no such thing as heart cancer."

"Point taken." He sat up. "Can't say it even hurt at the time, it was more like something was happening that shouldn't. Like part of me was missing."

"That's what Morrok said, too. I'm going to want to keep a close eye on you. Don't give up your cane just yet."

A rare smile crossed his face. "Doctor's orders?"

"Close enough." I packed away the cube. "We're done. I'll be waiting while you shower."

✠ ✠ ✠

I paced in his bedroom, never straying far from the bathroom door while Gideon cleaned up. It looked nothing like the rest of the ship. In fact, it was as if the room had been pulled from a 40's-era mansion and shoehorned into the torus. The walls were built of what I assumed was synthetic cherrywood paneling, with a four-poster bed dominating the room. Along the opposite wall was a six-drawer dresser. A thick leather binder sat atop it.

Still listening for him, I started flipping through it out of curiosity. I was surprised to see it was a photo album. The first couple of pages held a handful of old black-and-white photos, full of children and happy-looking adults. Judging by the background, they were all in the Southwest.

One caught my eye. It was a much younger Gideon, had to be, standing in front of what looked to be a World War II-era airplane and wearing a triumphant smile. He was holding up a small metal box covered in buttons and rotary dials. That must have been the autopilot he'd talked about.

The rest of the photos were color of varying quality. Some looked to be recent, or at least relatively so. The clothes and backgrounds were more modern, in fact some not too far removed from the Earth I'd left behind. Some looked like they'd been pulled from news feeds. I wondered if these were his offspring. It also made me wonder how he'd gotten hold of them. The man had connections throughout the Union, after all. It stood to reason he'd have been able to cull data from their observatories in our solar system. More so, it made sense that the Union might want to keep tabs on the family their visitor had left behind.

In the back of the album was a pressed five-petaled flower, pale blue and long since dried out. Beside it was a black-and-white photo of a woman holding a bouquet of the same. Her eyes were bright and her dark hair tumbled over her shoulders. On a hunch, I pulled out my crystal and held it over the page. "Clara, what type of flower is this?" I whispered. "Assume it's from Earth."

"Hang on … okay, the common name in your language is bellflower," she answered in an equally quiet voice. "This one is from the species *Campanula Americana*, found in—"

"Thanks, that's good enough." And now I knew something else about my patient.

I heard the bathroom door open. Gideon emerged in a fresh linen suit, leaning against his cane. Whatever the gremlin had done to him, the effects seemed to be wearing off. I hadn't seen that with Morrok, and made a mental note to look into it. Could be differences between species, could be due to his decades of gene editing to stave off old age.

I suddenly realized I'd been standing there like a fool, flipping through his private mementos. "Sorry. Didn't mean to pry."

"Don't concern yourself." Gideon idly turned through the last pages before pushing the album aside. He collapsed into a nearby chair, his face contorted in anguish. "I've not been a good man, Mooney."

Ever had one of those times when you'd stored up every withering comeback and cutting insult in your mind, ready to unleash a soul-melting tirade against some asshole who richly deserved it, only to find yourself unable to say a word when the opportunity finally arrived?

This was one of those times. No, he hadn't been a good man. A gifted industrialist, maybe, but that hadn't been enough. He'd bribed, grifted, and sometimes stolen his way to the top, and he'd brought that same burning desire for more to the Union. I so badly wanted to confront him with all of those flaws, but there was no sense piling on the old man anymore. He'd arrived there all on his own.

Still, there was one question that wouldn't leave me. I'd never understood what drove people like him. It couldn't be as simple as attributing it all to sociopathy. "Why? You'd already accumulated more wealth than most people could dream of. Why put all of that at risk?"

He looked away, stroking his chin. "That first taste of success is like an addict's first hit of heroin. The euphoria draws you in, consumes you, then leaves you wanting more. So you go on to the next venture, then the next. Success has a way of convincing the successful that they're above it all, that rules are for suckers. So you start making your own."

That was where our thinking diverged. Modern medicine works precisely because of the rules built around it over generations. Strictures like do no harm and informed consent led to licensing and certifications and protocols and . . . well, the list is interminable. Violate them and the penalties are severe, yet even that wasn't enough to stop some people who ought to know better from playing God. "That's what gives me trouble," I finally said. "I'm a rule follower, and maybe that comes with the territory. There's not much room in our business to color outside the lines. Personal hubris can get people killed."

Gideon pressed his lips together, a faraway look in his eyes. "So it can."

Without intending it, I'd still managed to throw his past in his face. "I didn't mean—"

He waved it away. "I know. Those are my burdens to carry, Mooney. Hubris and luck have brought me a long way. Now, at the end of the road, I seem to have run out of both." He stared into the virtual window at distant pillars of incandescent gas and the stars they were giving birth to. "They're chasing me down," he muttered. "Demons."

"Memories can be like that." I was trying to deflect. "They can torment us. It took me a long time to learn how to keep my own in perspective." It was a pitifully weak attempt at reassurance which felt foolish as soon as the words left my mouth. I'd watched my father die, had lost patients just as they'd seemed to be coming back from the brink, but not once had I caused anyone's death from pushing boundaries for my own gain. If Gideon's past was about to come crashing down around him, he'd need a different kind of medicine than anything I could provide.

He shook his head slowly. "That's not what I meant."

It took a minute to realize he was serious. "You're talking actual evil spirits."

"It's more complicated than that." He became disarmingly patient, as if about to instruct a thickheaded student. "Any doubts I might've harbored about a supreme being have been steadily chipped away over the years. Now, I'm left to confront eternity."

"We've had a taste of it in high space," I said, trying to be noncommittal. I'd never been sure how to handle conversations when they veered into this kind of territory. My dad had once joked that the reason people his age spent so much time in their Bibles was that they were cramming for finals.

"My first thought when I learned that the little green men were real was that it proved the universe was random. Seeing firsthand evidence of other intelligent species clinched the deal. I was safe from any notion of a higher power governing the universe. That freed me to pursue whatever ventures caught my fancy, in whatever way worked best. It was a license to steal.

"I've learned better since. The universe has order and symmetry, and the more I see of it the more I'm convinced it's part of some master plan beyond our understanding. Now that we've figured out how to poke a hole in its fabric, we're playing around with forces we can't comprehend.

"We've seen the deeper levels of the universe with our own eyes. If there is a supreme being and what I was taught as a child is even half right, then it seems to me those extra dimensions are where we'd find heaven and hell."

I didn't know how to process that. It sounded delusional, yet the notion gnawed at the back of my mind. "You're suggesting we're traveling through hell?"

He shrugged.

"If those are conscious entities we're seeing, then where are the good guys? If they're demons, then where are the angels?"

He sighed. "I don't know and I'm tired of trying to figure it out. Maybe it's purgatory. Either way, those things aren't happy with us being there."

When we finally made it down to the galley, the compartment had been turned into a makeshift troubleshooting center. A trio of holocubes had been placed strategically around the room, and the air was filled with intricate projections of the ship's innards, a rotating diagram of what appeared to be a nervous system which Kal fussed over, and a plot of our current location in the galaxy relative to Earth. The swirl of 3D images made my head swim, but it was enough to see that we still had a long way to go and there were a number of obstacles in our way.

Through the cloud of holograms, Morrok turned on us. She extended her neck, putting that ugly bug-eyed hammerhead right in front of us. Her breath was like stale fish. "You are late, mongrels." That was as clear a signal as any that she wasn't happy with us.

I shrugged and helped Gideon into a nearby chair. "Needs of the patient come first."

"Not when the integrity of my ship is at stake, human."

"That's not my priority." I could feel the anger welling up, and jabbed a finger at Gideon. "He is."

To his credit, Gideon reached for my arm to settle me down. "Not now, Mooney." He sipped from a squeeze bottle of freshly synthesized electrolyte juice. "She's not wrong. We're all in the same boat, literally." He looked around. "Where's Deela?"

"Returned to the control room, said she could not complete diagnostics from here." Morrok didn't sound entirely convinced.

Gideon nodded with satisfaction. "If a Reticulan says so, then that's all you need to know." When Morrok started to get her back up, he waved her down. "Enough posturing, damn it. We agreed this is your ship after we get to Earth, and I'm not welching on that deal. In the meantime, let's get to fixing it." He pointed at the indecipherable knot of the *Campanula*'s neural network. "Kal, what happened in there?"

"Hmm, yes." Kal pivoted on his feelers to face us. "It is as I feared. The ship's higher logic center has become disconnected from itself. The cores are at odds with each other, each generating conflicting probabilistic outcomes."

"What about essential systems? Life support, deflection fields?"

"Hmm. The network was designed to function like an organic nervous system. In the same way cognitive impairment does not stop one from breathing, yes and yes."

It could if the damage was bad enough, I thought. Late-stage dementia patients lost control of their bodily functions. Could the same thing happen to a damaged synthetic brain?

Gideon frowned, and I wondered if he'd had the same thought. "What would cause that?"

Kal's membrane quivered. "Hmm. This has been a concern, yes and yes. Any synthetic intelligence is at risk of the same disorders that can affect biological intelligence. Disorganized thinking, delusions, even hallucinations. Hmm. These symptoms can be mitigated by removing conflicting information streams. Decoupling the logic core from the master chronometer was one such mitigation."

"It apparently did not work," Morrok groused.

"Hmm. Yes and no, no and yes. Isolating the logic core worked precisely as expected. Outside interference was not expected."

I tapped my foot impatiently. It could take Kal an agonizingly long time to get to the point. "What do you mean by 'outside interference'? Did one of those things appear in the core?"

"Hmm. No and yes. More than one. First one, then several.

Appeared and disappeared, disappeared and appeared, probing the logic core and neural network. This I could sense. It led me to disconnect, partition myself from the core."

That was even more alarming. "They were trying to get into your head?"

"Hmm. Yes and no. If I am bonded with the logic core, it stands to reason I could suffer similar ill effects. It seemed best to sever that bond."

That felt like an understatement. "You said you could sense them probing the network. What about you—did you feel anything unusual?"

His feelers danced about, a clear sign of agitation. "Hmm. Yes, yes and yes. Quite disturbing."

I knelt beside him, studying the reaction from his ocular patches. They were shifting between shades of gray and white. "Can you be more specific?"

"Confusion, hmm, conflicting thoughts. Could no longer think clearly. All became one, yet one was separate from all. Great divides, yes and yes. Probabilities became certainties, all of them."

I probed around his outer membrane, searching for new signs of physical interaction with the apparitions. So far there were none. "So you disconnected yourself from the network as a precaution."

"Hmm, no and yes. There was more, very frightening to me, which I could not bear. There were voices, around and inside me." He tensed up once more before settling on his feelers like a deflating balloon. "It is called *valloleo* by our kind. Begins with disjointed thinking, hearing voices, ends with cognitive paralysis."

Though I'd never encountered a Mintakan that had become psychotic, I was aware of the malady. A race of giant brains was especially susceptible to mental illness.

Deela had been listening from the control room and was pragmatic as ever. *If I may offer an opinion? I would not presume to make a diagnosis of any kind, however Kal's symptoms may not be due to incipient psychosis.*

"What makes you say that?"

*I could hear them as well. At first they were unintelligible, not unlike voices lost in a crowd. I must admit it made me wonder if it was all in my mind as well. My translator struggled to discern vocabulary and syntax.*

"If that's the case, then what makes you think they were voices?"

*For my kind, the difference between the translation implants and our telepathic senses are obvious. They are learning our languages. The entity I heard was speaking directly to me.*

I was afraid to ask, especially having a good idea of the answer. "What did it say?"

*We are not welcome.*

When we returned to the control room, warnings lit up Deela's panel like a Christmas tree. Gideon shuffled up next to her. "Status?"

She pulled up a diagram of the ship and pointed to a cluster of hull plating where all of the panels had been highlighted in amber. I assumed that wasn't a good thing. *There appears to be damage to the field projectors in sector Y-1. The nature of the damage is unknown, but it is consistent with a drop in output.*

"Can it be repaired?"

*Unknown. Plate integrity appears intact, but they have been disconnected from the relays.* She zoomed in on an area underneath the plates. *You can see the junctions went into safe mode immediately.*

Gideon rubbed his chin as he studied the damage. "So we at least know the fail-safes worked. What did that do to our field projection, though?"

She pulled up a hologram of our current position. *The field distortion caused us to emerge in normal space at a tangent to our targeted entry angle. You can see that it was a rather close call.*

I might not know the particulars of interstellar navigation, much less when it involves extra dimensions, but I could read a graph well enough. Our optimum entry point was a narrow cone, and we'd hit the outer edge of it. If we'd gone off course enough to miss the star's gravity well, we'd have been stuck in 6D space until we eventually stumbled onto another star system at just the right angle. I didn't need Kal to tell me the probability of that happening was close to zero. "So what do we do now?"

Gideon turned on his cane. "Someone's going to have to go out there and fix it."

Deela stood. *I am prepared to do so, but I will need assistance. An extra set of hands, if you will.*

They were both looking at me now. "Wait a minute . . . I don't know the first thing about any of that stuff."

*You don't have to. I will be doing all the work, you need only assist. The relays are delicate and I will need someone to hold conduits in place while I work. Think of it as mending our ship's peripheral nervous system. You would be my surgical assistant.*

"That's not making it any easier, you know."

*I will carry all of the necessary instruments. You would carry the replacement parts.*

Morrok had been quietly listening in the corner. "You say you need extra hands, Reticulan?" She waved all four of her arms for emphasis. "That is something I am prepared to provide."

Gideon stiffened. "That won't be necessary."

"You misunderstand, human. This vessel belongs to me now, only by my good graces are you being allowed to complete your journey. I require that it be fully spaceworthy."

Gideon looked her up and down, defiantly working his jaw. "I understand your position," he said through clenched teeth, "but we seem to be short on eight-limbed spacesuits."

"There is a pressure suit in my trunk, with an atmosphere generator," she said. "No corsair of the Sisterhood travels without one."

For her part, Deela was resigned to it. *Very well. All the same, I would prefer to have Melanie accompany us.* She glanced at me. *I believe you will find the relay network to be more familiar than you might realize. Please bring a full field medical kit.*

# 27

You'd think that over time I'd have become more comfortable with spacewalks. You'd be wrong.

I won't deny the first time had been a little scary, but any fear of springing a leak or tumbling off into the void had been overtaken by sheer exhilaration. That's how it goes when you're a rookie—you don't know any better. It takes experience to learn just how many things have to go right in concert, and how much can go wrong in a hurry. Even with Union gear that was many generations improved over the kinds of suits human astronauts were still using, accidents happen. Visors crack, seals wear out, air regenerators become gummed up, directional units fail, any one of which could lead to death of the instant variety.

These thoughts swirled through my mind as we drifted out of the landing bay. My last "outside work" had been uncomfortably close to a black hole. Had some unknowable effect from that extreme environment weakened my suit in a way the built-in diagnostics missed? Was there some small kink that would make the intricately woven counterpressure fabric suddenly decide to unravel?

We'd barely made our way out of the bay, and my breath was already coming rapidly. A warning flashed in my visor, so I dialed down the O2 saturation before hyperventilating.

Morrok watched me fumbling with the suit controls on my wrist. "Nervous, human?"

I shook my head out of habit. Gestures like that were invisible beneath my helmet. "I'm fine," I groused. "Don't worry about me."

237

"That I will not do. Work outside of a vehicle demands mutual support. I trust you will let me know if I appear to be in danger, human?"

"Sure. Of course." Not that I was feeling it, but if she could be magnanimous then it fell on me to return the favor.

*Morrok is correct. We must watch out for each other,* Deela thought at me as she hooked each of us to safety lines at the lip of the bay, as if to illustrate the point.

"A decidedly antiquated solution," Morrok said. "You do not trust your own directional units?"

*Gravity projectors can confuse the orientation sensors. I will not take unnecessary chances.*

*Good girl.* I hoped Deela heard me.

We pushed off, headed for the cluster of damaged plates near the top of the ship. Being spherical, directional cues like that were kind of subjective. Oriented to our living quarters in the torus, that part was overhead so "top" it was. Deela jetted along gracefully, while Morrok used all eight of her limbs to scramble across the field of triangular gravity plating like a silvery spider.

I focused on the hull, having learned long ago that was the best way to keep from becoming hopelessly disoriented. We had no planet spinning below us, only more depthless void. The star we'd targeted was a dim light in the distance, barely distinguishable from the stellar background. Planets orbited it somewhere, far out of sight. We were in the ass-end of nowhere, galactically speaking, which made space feel even emptier than it already was. When you've become used to crossing such distances in a matter of days, being reminded of how immense those distances are is a shock to the system.

Deela came to a stop, and as I settled in next to her the damage was obvious. Where the hull plates had been joined seamlessly, here a good half-dozen of them had been dislodged. One in particular seemed to be hanging by a fistful of thin, gray cables.

She pulled another tether from a pouch by her waist and fastened it to a nearby plate with a magnetic trunnion. Morrok waited nearby, hanging on to a gap between plates with her legs.

Deela waved for me. *Melanie, if you please?* She pointed to the array of cables and shone a light down into the deeper structure. *I would like you to see what we will be working on.*

I followed the spotlight. The fine cabling attached to the plate reached down into the depths of the ship, where they connected to thicker bundles of fibers which in turn branched off from even denser bundles, each ending at the conduits that spiraled down into the ship's core. The deeper I looked, the more obvious it became. "You weren't kidding. It looks like a nervous system."

*That is in essence correct. The relay fibers function in the same manner. Each plate is not only a projector, but similar to a nerve receptor.*

"Where does all this end up? The logic core?"

*Again, correct. The logic core can be likened to the ship's brain stem.*

I turned my own light on the fibers beneath the plate for a closer look. "They're organic."

*They are. These fibers were cultivated using the same technology used to grow synthetic limbs and organs. At much larger scale, of course.*

"Why not just use whatever it is you build other ships with?"

*The jump drive required a more finely tuned feedback loop with the logic core. Organic nervous systems excel at that.*

Morrok did not seem as impressed as I was. "Reticulan, it sounds as if you are suggesting this ship is a living organism."

*I would not go that far. The relay network does require nutrients, otherwise the rest of the ship is traditionally mechanical.*

If the ship's nervous system needed to be fed, then it also needed oxygen. All of a sudden, I had a much greater appreciation of the problem. "They're exposed to vacuum. That ain't good."

Deela took a bundle of fibers in her hand. *It is not. We must work quickly.*

"What's first?"

*I believe you call it "triage." We must examine each plate to determine the extent of the damage.* She pried the plate free after disconnecting its nerve endings from their trunk, about arms-length into the ship, and handed it to Morrok.

Deela then pulled herself inside the opening. *Protective membranes appear intact. That is good.*

I poked my head inside. Each bundle was surrounded by a transparent sleeve. "This is for damage control, isn't it?"

*Quite. Every plate's relay bundles are individually isolated.*

I poked at the membrane. It was taut, giving way a little before springing back. "Also organic?"

*No, purely synthetic, though it mimics organic properties.* It was tight quarters, too tight for me, but Deela was able to turn about to inspect it with her light. *The other plates appear to still be attached to their membranes, we need only get them back into place.*

She pulled herself out and together we started edging plates back together. Once in place, their self-healing seams began to knit themselves into place. That left our single, gaping wound in the ship's skin. Deela pulled a sealed package from her equipment pouch.

*This is oxygenated neural fiber. We will replace the junction, then reattach the membrane to the plate's underside.* She pointed at the pouch on my waist. *I trust you still have vacuum tape and bioadhesive?*

"Never go anywhere without it."

*Very good. Let us get to work.*

I've done more than my share of invasive procedures in the field, but brain surgery on a sort-of living spaceship would go down as the weirdest experience yet.

While Morrok kept the plate in position, Deela reached down for the trunk and held it in place while I got to work with a plasma scalpel, cutting it free at the base of the nerve bundle. The tendrils rapidly turned ghostly white. She could read my alarm.

*That is to be expected. Now, if you will please make an incision three centimeters below the base, one centimeter deep.*

I calibrated the plasma blade to one centimeter and made a fresh cut into the nerve trunk while Deela opened the sealed package and pulled out a mass of pink tissue which she wrapped around the trunk. The tissue immediately began to spread and knit itself to the peripheral ganglia through the incision I'd made. Following Deela's instructions, I wrapped a length of vacuum tape around the fresh tissue and sealed it tight. Color began returning to the tendrils as the oxygen-rich patch did its work.

*Excellent. The tape appears to be holding, but we must hurry.* She motioned for Morrok. *Now, bring the panel back into position if you please.*

To my surprise, Morrok did as she was told. Deela projected such quiet calm, under such remarkable conditions, that it was easy to forget she wasn't a surgeon. Morrok held the triangular plate steady while Deela and I reached for opposite ends of the protective membrane. We stretched the elastic sleeve around the repaired nerve endings and set it against the back of the plate. After a quick pass with bioadhesive, the junction was sealed.

*I believe we have been successful. Now, both of you please move clear and I will set the projector back into place.*

As we hovered over the hull, Deela guided the panel into position and pressed it back into place. Self-healing seams began to seal themselves against the surrounding plates until they were barely discernable, as if the ship's skin was itself alive. I would have many questions for Deela about our newest patient when we were back inside.

*Yes,* she thought, reading my mind. She pivoted and reached down to release her tether from its trunnion on the hull. *I believe it is time we—*

Light surged from around the plate as the last seam knit itself into place. An electric hum rose and fell in my helmet speakers, as Deela's body stiffened and then became limp.

What the hell was that? "Deela! Can you hear me?"

There was no response; she floated still at the end of her tether. The counterpressure fabric of her suit had gone slack. I was reaching for her as a pair of vacuum-suited hands shot out to grab my arm.

"No touch!" Morrok barked. She drew one of her plasma cutlasses and poked at the panel. The blade glowed from a brief surge, then went dark. "As I thought. Stray current." She grabbed Deela, disconnected her tether, and began scrambling back toward the open landing bay. "Hurry, human. You have work to do."

I was counting off the seconds in my head as we hurried down the hull. The demonstrated upper limit of Reticulans to vacuum exposure was just shy of 120 seconds, but it was thought they could survive a full three minutes without permanent injuries.

By my count, we'd passed 144 seconds when the outer door finally slid shut and air began filling the landing bay. I opened the inner door to the torus and Morrok scurried ahead with Deela still in her arms.

We laid her on the exam bed. I peeled off my counterpressure suit and got to work. First order of business was to get Deela's helmet off and free her from her suit, an easy task now that the intricate weave of the carbon flex fabric had been compromised. The suit fell open lazily as I drew my finger down its seam.

Her gray skin was covered with petechiae, angry purple bruises from her blood trying to leach out of her body. Her black eyes were rimmed with red. I set up the scanner hoops to begin searching for vitals, but first leaned in close to her slit nostrils and mouth. She was exchanging air, weakly. I set a multispecies O2 mask over her face and waited for it to mold itself into place as the scanners moved down to her abdomen.

Vital traces indicated her heart had stopped, but had begun beating again on its own once she was back in a pressurized environment. Reticulan hearts were incredibly resilient compared to ours; if this had been a human I'd have been be doing CPR right then. That didn't mean Deela wasn't still in danger. The hoops moved up and down the length of her body, compiling a full picture. When they'd finished, I didn't like what they showed me..

"Barotrauma," I muttered, and tore open another supply drawer.

"That does not translate," Morrok said.

"Sudden expansion of gases in the blood and body cavities," Gideon interjected. "Commonly occurs after rapid decompression."

I turned at the sound of his voice. He'd been standing in the doorway, keeping his distance while I worked but watching carefully.

"How's she looking, Mooney?"

"You said it yourself. She had air in her lungs when her suit gave way, which ruptured the alveoli in her lower lobes. All of that gas leaked into her mediastinum."

"In English?"

I kept my back to him and my focus on Deela. "Space beneath the breastbone," I explained quickly. "Trapped air is compressing her lungs and heart. We have to relieve that pressure." I grabbed Morrok's hand and placed it on a scanner disc. She recoiled at first, but this wasn't the time for me to worry about interspecies dynamics. "Keep that disc right where it is. I need it to see where I'm going."

I pulled out an old-fashioned syringe and a long 18-gauge needle from the drawer. This was one of those instances where advanced Med Corps tech wouldn't do any good if I couldn't punch a hole in just the right place.

I placed the needle just below Deela's breastbone, aimed at her left shoulder. I'd done this once on a human patient in my previous life, but that was like comparing apples to orangutans. There were enough differences in our anatomy that the old training and muscle memory had to be forgotten. If I went in at the normal 45-degree angle, the needle would puncture her heart. I'd have to go in at a shallower angle.

I pulled out my data crystal, not taking any chances. "Clara, give me the procedure for pericardiocentesis. Adult Reticulan female."

A 3D diagram materialized in my visor. The image oriented itself over Deela's chest, following my eyes to match the exact location of her organs and pericardium. I now had my insertion point and approach angle, a shallow 30 degrees.

Working with a holographic road map sounds easy, but the devil's always in the details. An image can show me where to go, but it can't tell me anything about how it feels. Reticulan skin is tough, owing to their race evolving largely underground. This can make for tricky injections. I had to push with enough force to penetrate the skin, but not so much that the needle would keep going and puncture her lungs. Everything from this point relied on my sense of touch.

I pushed the needle in, feeling my way through Deela's rugged epidermis. As badly bruised as she was, it was that tough outer layer that probably saved her from even worse damage. It took steady force to push my way through, but soon enough I felt the needle break free into softer tissue. This was where the holoprojection helped. I could see the tip of the needle resting just above the pericardial sac. One more light push, and we were in. I pulled out the plunger to aspirate and kept the needle inserted. I grabbed a cannula with my free hand and fed it gently through the opening, replacing the needle with flexible tubing to release all of that trapped air. I finished the job with a quick squirt of bioadhesive around the site.

Deela's vital sign traces moved in response. With the pressure relieved, her cardiac rhythm and respiratory rates were headed back to normal range. I blew out a sigh; I'd been holding my breath the whole time. "Okay, that part's done." I took the transducer back from Morrok and grudgingly thanked her for the assist. She didn't look especially pleased, and I was expecting to get a lecture about being touched by "mongrel" races when Deela's thoughts intermingled with mine.

*That was rather uncomfortable.*

I took a step back. "How long have you been conscious?"

*Difficult to say with certainty. I was aware of you placing this mask over my face. Before that, I remember securing that loose panel. I do not recall the intervening period.*

"You gave us a real scare. Morrok said it was stray current. Your suit fabric just kind of came unglued."

*Ah. Yes, that can be a hazard. That is my fault. I must be more careful next time.*

"Let's hope there isn't a next time." I made another pass up and down her body with the scanners. "Your lungs were damaged from all that gas trying to escape, not to mention extensive subcutaneous hematomas. Your whole body is pretty much one big bruise."

*It certainly feels that way.*

I moved Deela onto her side and pulled the rest of her suit clear. "I think you know what comes next."

*Of course, but do not concern yourself. My kind is somewhat more comfortable with such treatments than yours.*

"That you are." Her spirits were up, a good sign. I opened another drawer to reveal a neatly arranged selection of shiny metallic cigar-shaped implements. I caught Morrok's revulsion out of the corner of my eye.

"Are those what they appear to be, human?"

I selected one of the glossy cigars. "Nanobot probes. Most are broad-spectrum, a few are species specific." The probe activated and linked to Deela's case in my data crystal, calibrating itself for the task ahead. "This one will mend damaged tissue. The probe dissolves and its nanobots disperse through the bloodstream immediately, but the repairs will take some time."

The labia around Morrok's mouth twisted into a grotesque frown. "I am familiar with Reticulan anal probes," she said with disgust. "They seem to have one for everything."

It took a lot for me to not laugh. "That they do." I hadn't been too keen on them at first either, but there was no denying they worked. "Deela, are you ready? Afraid I can't give you any sedatives until your lungs are restored."

*Sedatives won't be necessary in any case. Please proceed.*

Of course. The Grays had invented these things. No need to go into details here, other than I put the probe where it needed to go and let the nanobots get to work. At that point, all I could do was monitor Deela's condition as the microscopic machines did their thing. I paid particular attention to her lungs as they knitted ruptured alveoli back together. It was fascinating to watch them swarm over the damaged tissue, rebuilding her lungs one cell at a time.

*Is something wrong, Melanie?*

I must have been staring at the holoscreen for some time. "No. It's going very well, in fact. How are you feeling?"

*Better, but it feels like I must concentrate to breathe. And I am rather sore.*

I glanced up at the monitors. "Your lungs are exchanging air, but they're not going to be at full capacity for a while yet. Tell me about the pain—is it localized anywhere, or all over?"

*All over.*

"It's from all the brusing. Even when the bots are done repairing the damage, it'll take time for that to clear itself up. Corticosteroids can speed things along, but you're going to be tender for a while."

"How long until she's back on duty?" Gideon was back to his usual peevishness. I could see something different in his eyes, though. He was afraid for her.

I turned and shot him an angry look. "Not any time soon. She needs to heal."

"And we need to keep moving." He looked past me at Deela. "Right?"

I stepped between them. "Let's get something straight. She is no condition to do anything right now. All I've done here is keep her from getting worse. She's damned lucky the neck seal kept air in her helmet, or we'd be talking about brain damage right now."

"If she can think, she can work."

I was tempted to lay into him, but if he was reacting out of fear that would only make things worse. "She's been exposed to vacuum, for longer than anyone of her species on record. That's not something you just shake off. It'll take the nanobots a couple of days just to repair the damaged lung tissue."

Morrok had been watching from the corner, her four hands resting on what passed for her hips. "You still forget this is my vessel now, human. And since the Reticulan is its only pilot, I am bound by common sense to follow your physician's instruction. I have no intention to place ourselves in danger by entrusting that task to one who is not ready for duty."

For a pirate, she showed a lot of common sense. Maybe that came with the job when you made a career of skirting the law. Gideon looked between us, angrily worked his jaw, and hobbled back into the corridor.

I plopped onto the stool by Deela and wiped my brow. "Thanks for the assist," I said to Morrok.

"Do not thank me, human, nor think that I harbor any sympathies for this crew. I take whatever actions are necessary, and saving your pilot was necessary." She leaned in close, lowering her voice to a quiet burble. She wrapped two of her pads around my hand and squeezed hard. "And do not think you can touch me in the manner you did ever again."

"I'll keep that in mind." Meet the new boss, same as the old boss.

It took some time for Deela's system to flush the nanobots from her subcutaneous tissue. Repairing her lungs was more delicate work, and those bots would be at it for a while. Grays respond to extensive injuries by regressing into a near-dormant state, which can be a tricky thing to watch. Was she healing, or about to crash? It can be hard to tell the difference. Once I was satisfied she was stable, I set up some alert parameters on my crystal and left her to rest.

Though exhausted myself, I was far from resting. As Deela had slowed herself into torpor, anger had risen in me. By the time I reached Gideon's suite, it was threatening to boil over. I stood in front of his door, took a deep breath, and commanded it to open. A benefit of being his personal medic was having emergency override authority.

He was sitting in one of his wingback chairs, apparently lost in thought. His head snapped up when I stormed into the room.

"Sweet Mary!" he exclaimed. "What do you think you're doing, Mooney?"

I stood in front of him with my hands on my hips. "Looking for answers. I can't do my job if you're keeping secrets."

He laid back into the chair. "And what secrets might you think I'm keeping?"

"The one about using living tissue for a neural network. That's kind of an important detail."

Gideon rubbed at his chin. "Do you always make it a point to know precisely how every machine you use works?"

"To the extent I can understand it, yes." That was admittedly a heavy lift when it came to Union tech.

"Regardless, maintenance is not part of your job description."

"It is if the damned ship is alive!"

Gideon shook his head wearily. "It's not an organism, Mooney." He tapped his cane against the wall for emphasis. "That's standard Union composites. Internal structure is graphene and self-healing alloys. Outer hull is Moscovium."

"And the neural network is made of synthetic nerve fibers," I reminded him. Really big nerve fibers, but alive just the same. "I just assisted Deela in emergency neurosurgery. We grafted *living tissue*." It was tempting to launch into a lecture about how that was wildly outside of my scope of practice, but there was a lot about our current arrangement that was outside scope. I set my professional reflexes aside to focus on the practical. "She's going to be out of commission for a while, so you're going to have to rely on me if we have any more surprises."

He sighed. "How long?"

"Hard to tell. She's in torpor now while her body heals. I'm guessing a week."

Gideon rubbed at his forehead. "I'm going to ask if there's anything to speed that along, and you're going to tell me no."

"That's right. I don't have the equipment or skills to bring her out early. That requires an actual doctor to manage, and it's still risky. Grays heal at their own pace, the nanobots only kick-start the process."

"Then let's hope she's fast." He tapped at a nearby chair with his cane. "Have a seat, Mooney."

I perched on the edge of the chair, not wanting to let my guard down. Gideon sat still for several moments, rubbing his knuckles as he thought.

"The ship does function like a living organism, out of necessity. Navigating extradimensional space presents unique challenges, as you've seen for yourself. The projector array not only has to create a gravity field focused enough to open a portal, it has to sense perturbations and react immediately. Even neuromorphic quantum networks weren't sensitive enough. They couldn't precisely emulate the feedback loops of a Mintakan's nervous system."

I rocked back. "This whole ship is patterned after a Mintakan brain?"

"The logic and neural networks are." He broke into a wry grin. "Which is, of course, most of the superstructure. That shouldn't be so surprising when you think about it."

I settled into the chair and thought it through. No wonder our navigator was so comfortable with being jacked into the logic core. He was commiserating with one of his own. "Does Kal know this?"

"Haven't told him in so many words, but he's pretty smart. I imagine he figured it out right away."

"Is it conscious?"

"Limited," he said. "It can sense, react, reason. All within prescribed limits."

"Any chance it might try to break free of those limits?" I wasn't relishing the idea of being inside of a giant self-propelled brain that might decide whatever we were doing wasn't in its best interests.

"Self-awareness," he said. "That's always a risk with synthetic intelligence. The Union learned how to get a handle on that a long time ago. One of those 'civilizational thresholds' they talk about."

"Yeah," I muttered. "That was becoming a problem back home, around the time I left." I traced a finger across my lips as I thought about that. The Survey Ministry might be on the lookout for robot overlords enslaving the human race, but I was more concerned about other conscious beings. "Is it possible there's a connection with the gremlins?"

Gideon paused and pursed his lips. "Probably," he finally admitted. "My guess is they sensed a new consciousness in their midst, and they didn't like it."

The problem was they'd not only shown interest in the *Campanula*'s brain, they'd become more and more threatening to the squishy biological beings inside. The message that had appeared in my visor still haunted me. "What do you think they want from us?"

"I think they want us to get the hell off their lawn."

# ⚕ 28 ⚕

After almost a week in torpor, Deela looked completely at home seated behind her controls. I knew better, having helped her in earlier. Still tender from being exposed to vacuum, her gait had been uncertain. Grays are exceedingly precise in their movements, and seeing her even the slightest bit unsteady was an attention grabber. She'd managed to allay my concerns after settling in at her station, fully in her element. She'd wanted to hide her injuries to instill confidence for what she was about to propose.

*The projectors are functional, but field integrity is barely within tolerance. This will no doubt degrade over time. In my estimation, the drive is good for only one or two more jumps.*

The news hit like a gut punch. We were still a long way from home, six hundred light-years by my rough estimate.

Gideon, for his part, seemed nonplussed. "Then we'd better make it count."

*Precisely. I have calculated a trajectory which will bring us into your star system in a single jump. Kal-Nuala agrees it is feasible.*

"We can do that?" My elation would prove to be short lived.

*This plan is not without considerable risk, as we cannot travel in a straight line. We must rely on gravity assists, which until now we have avoided.* She pulled up a plot on the hologram. It bent around two different stars which stood between us and home. *The principle is similar to our entry and exit vectors, but in this case we will use their gravity to bend our trajectories onto the final vector.*

"A Hail Mary pass," Gideon muttered. "You're confident in this plan?"

*I would not present it otherwise. Kal-Nuala's modeling predicts a point-zero-four error probability.*

That didn't sound like much until you considered it was over six hundred light-years. "What about the logic center?" Gideon asked. "It's still full of bugs."

*We will remove the navigation routine. Logic will be strictly limited to critical functions.*

"Navigation's mighty damned critical," Gideon said, pointing at Deela's yellow brick road through space. "That's beyond dead reckoning, even for you." He paused, uncharacteristically hesitant. "No offense."

*None is taken. You are absolutely right. Kal-Nuala has offered himself for this task.*

Gideon turned to our navigator. "You sure you can handle that?"

Kal quivered excitedly. "Hmm, yes and yes! The challenge will be satisfying, most satisfying. Your ship's neural network is patterned after mine, is it not?" A half-dozen feelers reached for his implants. "Though I will need Melanie to refresh my connection, as it were."

Gideon eyed me. "Mooney?"

"Sure. I can do that." Hopefully that sounded more certain than it felt. What else was I going to say—I'm a medic, not an engineer, damn it? That line only worked in the movies. It was a lot different when your options had run out.

*There are other risks which we must consider. A jump of this distance will present greater exposure to the "gremlin" entities. We can limit this by accelerating to maximum relativistic velocity ahead of the jump.*

"Near light speed?" Gideon asked. "That'll complicate your gravity assists."

*Hadar and Spica are rather massive stars.*

So we had that going for us. She'd better not miss.

Morrok had been listening quietly until now. "A risky plan indeed, Reticulan. I have another proposal."

Gideon leaned on his cane. "I'm afraid to ask."

"We put an end to this foolhardy errand and return to the Sisterhood immediately. Perhaps the ship can be repaired, perhaps not. Either way, you shall continue to live."

All of a sudden, Deela's crazy plan sounded infinitely preferable. Fortunately, our pilot had come prepared. Before Gideon could protest, she swiped at the hologram to spin it about.

*We considered that, and I'm afraid the geometry makes it unfeasible. As you can see, there are considerably more star systems between here and Sisterhood space. We could make it no farther than the Vela Ridge before probabilities break down to an unacceptable degree. I am sure you can appreciate the . . . gravity . . . of the situation.*

Nice one, Deela.

Morrok extended her neck, twisting her head back and forth as she studied the plot. She pointed one of her arms at the pale yellow star in its center. "This is the human system?" After a few unhappy burbling noises, she retracted her neck. "So I see. From there, the path back to Sisterhood space is almost devoid of obstacles."

*Quite so. May I presume we have your approval?*

"Only grudgingly, Reticulan. Intentionally or not, you have maneuvered us into an untenable position. I see only one way forward which does not leave us stranded." She turned to Gideon. "Very well, human. Now, I believe you all have work to do."

Morrok remained in the control room while the rest of us dispersed. Kal scurried ahead for the logic center while I stayed by Gideon's side. He was noticeably slower.

"Almost home, but still a long way to go." He had a faraway look, like he was working through scenarios in his head.

"Not much you can do by worrying," I offered, "other than make yourself worse."

"Trust me, I'm not worrying about it. It'll work, or it won't. If it doesn't, we're screwed. If we don't try, we're screwed." He shook his head. "No, I'm thinking about what comes next." He slipped me a piece of paper, a 50's era postcard taken from his album. "If something happens to me, this is where I need to go. Dead or alive, make sure I get there."

The worn card bore the image of a desert chapel. I slipped it into my hip pocket. "Let's get you there alive, then." We stopped at the med bay. "I'm going to have to insist on you being secure in here this time."

"No argument from me. I'm too tired to fight you anyway."

"Great." I guided him by the elbow to the exam bed. "Because if this goes the way I think it might, restraints are in order. Won't do to have you bouncing around the room if Deela has to get creative."

He frowned. "Let's hope she doesn't. I suppose you'll want to sedate me too."

"For a jump this long? Absolutely. It'll be a low dose, just to take the edge off. You're in no condition for anything stronger. I'll be in here watching you the whole time."

He settled into the bed. "I know you'll try, but don't make promises you can't keep. Deela's trying to hide it, but I've known her long enough to tell she's not in great shape. And if anything happens to Kal, we're done for."

I pulled a pair of straps across him and locked them into place, hoping that his fears wouldn't be realized. The internal gravity fields would be turned off again, and I didn't relish the thought of flying around the torus in freefall if someone needed me.

Gideon's eyes fluttered as the sedative did its work. After watching his vitals for a few minutes, I was satisfied he was stable. I pulled the surgery bot from its cradle and rolled it into the corridor. It was time to hot-wire Kal into the *Campanula*'s nervous system.

It goes without saying that surgery is delicate work. Field surgery is particularly dicey. Brain surgery in the field is unheard of, yet here we were. I wouldn't be slicing and dicing Kal's considerable gray matter, but placing a single implant in just the right spot was no less stressful. This would be more complicated than the superficial leads I'd implanted before. He'd prepared what amounted to a wiring diagram, which I used to program the surgery bot for the dirty work.

I wore a pair of haptic-feedback gloves to run the bot, and had it start with an incision in the membrane above his longitudinal fissure, just below the occipital lobe. This was the dividing line between cerebral hemispheres, and would be our entry point. Wisps of smoke curled away as the bot's plasma scalpel cauterized the incision. The smell was like overdone fried chicken.

"I'm in. How do you feel?"

"Hmm. I feel fine, Yes and yes. Does all appear well to you?"

Not that I knew enough to tell, other than he wasn't bleeding all over the place and didn't show any obvious signs of brain damage yet. "The bot isn't throwing out any warnings. Afraid that's all I have to go on."

"Hmm, yes and yes, it is enough. I am ready to proceed if you are."

I took a relaxing breath and mounted the first implant in the bot's mechanical hand. "Here it comes." The bot's prehensile arm was more like a mechanical tentacle, not much thicker than a strand of yarn. It snaked the lead in through the incision and made its way down to Kal's cerebellum with more precision than I could've managed. By the time it was finished, he looked like a hashed-together science fair project, a living Jell-O mold trailing hair-thin cables. "How will you know it's working?"

"Hmm, yes. We shall learn soon enough."

Kal's photoreceptor patches faded to white as he fell into a trance. The processor columns came back to life, pulsating in rhythm with his EEG trace. I presumed that meant he was in control.

I focused my thoughts on Deela. "We're done. What can you see up there?"

*Logic functions and neural net appear to be restored. This is all coming from Kal-Nuala?*

"I think so. All the lights are synchronized with his brain activity."

*There is a status panel on the inner bulkhead, directly across from the entryway. Can you tell me what you see?*

It was blank rectangle embedded in the wall between two of the columns. "Nothing. The screen is dark."

*Remarkable. The processor unit is offline. He has successfully taken over the neural net. It has become an extension of his mind. We will be ready to jump as soon as you are secure.*

"On my way, then." I locked the surgical bot down within reach of Kal and hustled back to the med bay.

The jump was coming soon. After accelerating us to entry velocity, Deela turned off the artificial gravity which took the inertial dampers with it. I began to rise up against my restraints, and Gideon's arms hung limply in the air above him. He was dozing from the sedatives and his vitals were steady. I hoped they would stay that way.

A barely perceptible ripple moved through the med bay, distorting the air as it passed. A quick glance at my watch confirmed we'd left normal space for the last time. I'd turned off the external viewscreens on purpose. We'd be in 6D space for a long time—whatever that meant anymore—and didn't need it in my face for the whole ride. Blissfully free of distractions, and for once I could keep my attention focused on him and not the fact that we were trespassing in a place where we didn't belong and weren't welcome.

I can't say when the first gremlin appeared, maybe after our first slingshot around Hadar. I recall being pushed into the acceleration gel for what felt like a long time as it bent our path toward Spica, another two hundred light-years distant. With everything happening all at once, time and distance were as meaningless as ever. I kept reminding myself that we were already there and just didn't know it yet.

A coal-black pinprick materialized in the air ahead, growing to the size of a baseball. Its edges were misty, tendrils reaching out and curling back on themselves as it moved about the med bay like a sea anemone looking for purchase. It came to a stop in front of me and began to grow, to open. Dozens of ebony tentacles exploded from its center, flailing at me out of the emptiness. I pushed into my seat, deep into the gel, like a child burrowing under her bedcovers to keep the monsters away.

It stopped just inches away, hesitating as if something else had gotten its attention. It froze in midair, then disappeared.

I clutched my chest, willing myself to not hyperventilate. This one was gone for now, but it likely wouldn't be the last. I punched the intercom panel by my seat. "Deela, they're back."

*We have seen them as well. Two appeared in the center of the control room. Morrok successfully engaged one. The other disappeared on its own.*

"Same here. We had one in the med bay until it changed its mind." I took a breath. "I think it was after me this time."

In my head, Deela's voice was filled with concern. *Do not let them touch you, Melanie.* She was dead serious, more so than usual. *Fight them off any way you can.*

I was about to snap that it was a lot easier said than done, when I heard a commotion outside. "Where's Morrok now?"

*Chasing more gremlins. She was headed toward your location.*

An unearthly wail echoed down the corridor, a cry that penetrated into my bones. I tore off my harness and pushed free of the gel, aiming for the door. I grabbed the sill before flying out into the corridor.

Morrok was clinging to the sidewall with her legs, while both pairs of arms held white-hot cutlasses. A cloud of black dust dissipated into the air close by, and her labia quivered in a flatulent victory cry. The pirate was finally in her element.

Her head turned to me, and she skittered past along the ceiling.

"Watch and learn, human. These creatures are not so invincible as they would appear." She raised the plasma blades above her head and brought them down through another black gremlin as it began to materialize. It disintegrated into another cloud of black dust.

It was stunning to watch. Morrok wielded her weapons with grace, her limbs and swords moving with remarkable precision. That she didn't manage to lop off one of her arms in all the action was a testament to her skill. She spun about, dispatching another gremlin with barely a look in its direction.

"How?" I stammered.

Morrok scampered down the wall to stand before me. "We may only be able to see their shadows, but they are most certainly present." She held her swords at the ready, pivoting her head to search for more threats. "It only requires the proper tool for the job."

I nodded at one of her weapons. "Any chance I could—"

She reached out with a free arm to push me back into the med bay. "Stand clear!"

My first thought was that I'd insulted her, until I noticed the corridor had begun to dim. A swarm of gremlins had materialized, surrounding her. She leapt for the ceiling again, pirouetting in midair to take out two of them.

It wasn't enough. They came quickly, appearing from nowhere. Four of them attacked, each going for her legs. She twisted along her torso, slicing through more of the things until that was immobilized as well. More went for her arms, and she began to disappear into the growing black mist. One lone arm, cutlass still in hand, reached out from inside the assaulting darkness. It released its grip, and the blade tumbled through the air.

I stared in horror as the black wraiths consumed Morrok, shrinking into nothingness and taking her with them. All that was left was her cutlass, spinning idly in zero gravity. Had she meant to do that?

The blade eventually embedded itself in the deck and I grabbed its hilt, feeling a bit like Arthur pulling Excalibur from the stone. I could feel its energy through the handle, a barely perceptible vibration that warned of its danger. The proper tool for the job, she'd said.

I held the blade in front of me and pushed back into the med bay. I still had Gideon to worry about, and after what had just happened to Morrok I was determined to not attract attention to myself.

# ⚕ 29 ⚕

That last part was impossible, of course. Gremlins had filled the torus, and from what I could hear from Deela the damned things were all over the ship. They were in the control room, the logic center . . . there was no corner of the *Campanula* that didn't have some black phantom invading it.

"Deela, how are you doing up there?"

*We still have directional control, but I am struggling with the other systems.*

Alarms started howling as soon as she said that. PRESSURIZATION WARNING—LANDING BAY, the synthetic voice blared. I stuck the tip of the cutlass into the deck so it wouldn't go floating away and scrambled into my vacuum suit, leaving it halfway sealed so I could help Gideon with his. He was still listless from the sedative, and it was a workout getting the tight counterpressure garment in place and sealed.

I pulled on my hood and drew a finger across its seal, then did the same for Gideon. I hoped to God his ticker held up, because even the auto compressor would have a hard time working through the suit's fabric. The carbon-flex weave would absorb and distribute the force, which meant I'd have to dial up the output to dangerous levels. If he coded, he'd wind up with a fractured rib cage at minimum. The scanners were keeping a close eye on his cardiac rhythm and could send pulses like a pacemaker if needed. It would have to be enough. "We're almost home. Don't you die on me."

Gideon looked at me through his faceplate with pleading eyes. "Do your job, and I won't."

"You're gonna be a crusty old bastard until the end, aren't you?"

"It's gotten me this far." He laid his head back and closed his eyes. "Kal," he mumbled. "Have to protect. Everything depends on him."

With what? There was only of me, and that plasma cutlass was almost as terrifying as the gremlins. I couldn't be in two places at once . . .

"Clara! Activate the surgery bot!"

Her voice chirped from my hip pocket. "Are you sure? There should be a medic in attendance."

"No time for that! Restrict all movement within . . . ten centimeters of the patient, and remove the safeties. Now!" A plasma scalpel with no safeties becomes a small torch, and I had no intention of accidentally amputating any part of Kal's anatomy. But it would sure as hell slice through anything else.

"What's the objective? It has to know what it's looking for."

"Anything that moves."

I turned back to Gideon and laid my hand on his chest. "Kal will be safe," I said, hoping against hope. "Now, try to relax."

Another gremlin emerged from the forward wall and drifted toward us, as if to demonstrate the foolishness of my advice. It was like the damned thing heard me, which it probably had.

Gideon's eyes snapped open. "They're here, aren't they? I can sense them." He grabbed my hand. "Don't let them take me," he said firmly, "or this will all have been for nothing." He was serious, not panicked at all. If only I could've felt the same.

The shadow grew ever darker, collecting itself into a depthless black cloud that seemed to suck all light from the room. It moved with purpose, hovering over the array of life-preserving equipment. Tendrils formed like black smoke, reaching into the monitors, the infusion pumps, the scanners. It seemed to be studying, deciding what to do next. Soon the thing gathered itself into its full form, stretching from floor to ceiling, pulsating with dark menace.

A keening voice invaded my mind: *You do not belong.* It was beyond the Reticulan brand of telepathy; this corporeal nothingness had taken over my thoughts. If Gideon was convinced these things were demons, I was suddenly more inclined to believe him.

Its voice was everywhere. I could feel its consciousness coursing through mine, taking over, pulling me into the madness of infinity.

"Then leave us be." It sounded shaky even to my ears.

The shadow pulsed again, and my body shook with each syllable. *That is not possible.* More smoky tendrils reached out, this time for Gideon. Not knowing what else to do, I charged at the thing. It dissipated, dividing itself for me to run right through, then collected itself. A tendril shot out and threw me against the sidewall. If it weren't for the hood of my pressure suit, the impact would've knocked me out.

But now I knew more about them. I might only be able to see whatever bits my 3D eyes could perceive, but something physical was there. If they could hurt me, damn it, then I could hurt them back. Just like Morrok had done.

The gremlin apparently had no more use for me. It was hovering over the exam bed, its tendrils reaching into the machinery. Into Gideon. His mouth fell open in a silent scream as the tendrils probed deeper. His vitals began flatlining. No, not flatlining—disappearing, as if he was being removed from our reality. Like Morrok.

I clenched my jaw. Enough of this shit.

I pulled the cutlass from the deck and launched at the apparition from behind, hoping that it somehow couldn't see me coming. I squeezed the handle and swung away, its needle-thin white beam slicing through the air, the IV stand, and the bulkhead behind it.

More importantly, it sliced right through the black tendrils worming their way into Gideon's body. A dissonant wail filled the air, and the tendrils dissipated into nothing.

I swung again, this time at the thing's body, what looked to be the least amorphous part of the living cloud. I must have hit something solid, because the plasma beam stopped before cutting into the wall behind.

The wail became a roar. The creature reassembled itself and shot its black tendrils at me. They didn't grab so much as they entered me, taking me by the hands, then the feet, then my torso. My mouth opened to cry out, but there was no sound. It felt like everywhere this thing touched me became disconnected, down to the atoms, like bonds were being broken and remade in its image.

A mass of tendrils reached for my face. Depthless black, beyond space and time, overcame me.

The room, the ship, everything I knew disappeared. I was disembodied in six-dimensional space, at the mercy of this creature.

For the first time, I could see it in all of its unholy grotesqueness. It was a writhing, ropy knot of ethereal not-matter, a black consciousness without form other than what it needed in the moment. It was as much a part of this higher dimension as it was a creature of it, indistinguishable from 6D space itself.

And I was bound to it. Part of it. Somehow I knew that my essence—my soul—had been ripped from my physical body.

Its unfiltered voice boomed like thunder. "You do not belong here."

"No shit," I gargled. I wasn't in the mood for a philosophical discussion.

"See now." It spun me about, not letting go, but also leaving me free to bask in the unreality of where we were. Of where we should not be.

Where before I could only see reflections of the deeper universe, that strange photonegative effect, now I saw the full, terrifying scope of the infinite. Eternity was laid out before me as if it were something I could manipulate, in spectrums human eyes were not meant to see. Stars flared to life, burned bright, and winked out of existence, leaving ghostly traces in ultraviolet and infrared. The universe heaved as if moved by swells on the ocean. I was *seeing* gravity. Entire galaxies appeared in their full lifetime, along with every creature within them. It wasn't some unfolding display, a movie chronicling their beginning and end, it simply *was*. I could enter any place in the universe at any point in time, have my way with it, and move on. I was not only outside of time, I was above it. Beyond it. Utterly detached from it. Time was both meaningless and apocalyptic.

The being spun me back around, drawing me once more into its depths. "Now you see what you were not meant to see."

It was a struggle to speak. "Why?"

"That is for us to ask, not you. You do not belong."

You've made that pretty clear, dickhead. "Going...home," I rasped. "Let us go." We were almost there, damn it. Just leave us alone.

"That we cannot do."

"Why?" It was worth another try.

"You have shown your kind what they must not know," the thing rumbled. "You have shown them how to enter the deep reality."

Again, just trying to get home. Let us go on our way and we won't bother you again. Deela was ready to go back to using boring old gravity drives anyway. "Then let us finish."

More ropy tendrils entered me, the creature drawing me deeper into itself in an eternal mind-rape. "We cannot."

I gathered my strength. "Then kill us and be done with it."

Another rumble of thunder. The thing was laughing at me. "You cannot die here. You cannot live here. You exist, or you do not. There is no other."

Wasn't that the same thing as dying? Maybe Gideon had been right. If heaven and hell existed in six-dimensional space, then I had a feeling which side this guy was on. All I knew at that moment was I didn't want to spend eternity with this asshole.

"Let...me...go."

More tendrils bore through me. "That is not possible."

I was frozen, unable to move against its dark malevolence. It was consuming me, making me a part of it, pulling me into a timeless, depthless void. I didn't think it was possible to feel any more disconnected from reality, yet there I was. Separated from everything. My mind was screaming but my voice was gone. *No no no...*

There was a thunderclap and a flash of light. Was this it, then? Was this the final, mad descent into hell?

# ☤ 30 ☤

I was back in the med bay, crumpled on the floor. Gravity had returned. There were more thunderclaps, distant now, and shouts in a language I couldn't recognize. A pair of emerald-green feet were planted in front of me. There was another boom of thunder. The feet moved, and another dark green mass followed close behind, scraping the floor like a tail. A thick claw reached down for me. The creature's voice came in a hiss.

The room spun as the creature lifted me to my feet. "Mel!"

"Hmm?" My vision was fuzzy and I still wasn't sure what this thing was, but it was big and green with a splash of violet.

The creature gave me a mild shake. Another, longer hiss. "Melanie."

My eyes snapped fully open. At first I was startled by a mouthful of sharp teeth. I looked up into golden, catlike eyes under a heavy brow whose ridges met in a peak. Feathers dangled from the back of its head, like a Native American headdress. Or a mullet.

I was afraid to hope. The ridges of his lips curled back, approximating a smile. It was either happy or about to make me a tasty meal.

"Chonk?" I stammered. "It's you, for real?"

"Is me." He lifted me into his scaly arms and let me down onto the empty gel couch. "Safe now. But not finished."

I screwed my eyes shut, having to convince myself that this was good old 3D reality. The counterpressure suit was a firm reminder. "You're in danger," I said. "We had a pressurization alarm."

"Not worry. Was us," he said. "Had to force entry in landing bay. Doors sealed now."

"How did you—"

"Long story," Chonk said. He lifted a crumpled piece of paper from his tunic. "Got your note. Been looking for you since. Had help from friend."

He stuffed the note back into his pocket. That's when I noticed the dull silver weapon slung over his shoulder, unlike anything I'd seen before. It was long and tapered to a sharp point, like a lance, with a pair of pistol grips sized for Thuban claws. A single, thin cable connected it to a backpack he wore.

I pulled off my helmet. "What is that thing?"

The ridges of his lips curled to reveal a toothy grin as he unslung his new toy. "You like? Some call gravity lance, others call portal gun. Many years to develop, to counter Inters."

"Inters?"

"Dark beings."

"You mean 'interdimensional'?" It was as good a name as any. "What's the backpack for?"

"Power source. Zero point reactor. Need for projecting portals."

"Ah," I said nervously. So the Thubans had been making themselves comfortable with the technology too. I wasn't sure that was a good thing, but also wasn't about to argue if it got the job done. "What happens when you project a portal?"

He pointed at the ceiling. "Same as ship, just smaller. Send Inters back where they belong."

Thuban Ghostbusters. I chuckled and winced. It hurt my ribs.

He slung his weapon and laid a claw against my sternum. "You hurt."

Probably broken ribs, I was thinking, when an alarm began bleating at me. It came from Gideon's bedside monitor. My brain had been so scrambled that I'd forgotten about him. I flipped down my visor angrily. "Later," I barked. There'd been a glitch in his vital sign traces, but now it was obvious that Gideon was crashing.

I leapt out of the gel couch and hurried to open up Gideon's counterpressure suit. Chonk had to grab my arm to keep me from stumbling. My vestibular system wasn't all the way there yet. *Get it together, girl.*

I didn't have a full stream of vitals yet, but his pallor told me all I needed to know. I felt for his pulse. "Cardiac arrest!" I shouted.

*Shit.* What happened to the damned scanners? They should've automatically regulated his heart rhythm. One was still in place, but the other had been knocked free in the struggle. I found it against the bedside, flashing yellow to get my attention. Gideon's heart had stopped, and the rest of his vitals were bottoming out in turn.

I wiped the transducer clean and slapped it into place on the opposite side of his chest. There was a high-pitched hum as the discs charged. "Clear!"

Chonk took a step back. I tapped at the controls, commanding the miraculous little hockey pucks to do their thing. Gideon's body jerked from the blast of voltage, then went limp. His ECG trace didn't change.

On their own, the transducers built up another charge. "Clear!"

Another jolt. Nothing. *Come on, old man.* "Clear!"

His body spasmed, and finally the ECG began to come alive. *Come on, come on...*

I gave it a minute to see if his heart would keep beating on its own. "He's back in normal rhythm," I breathed in relief, and slumped to the floor.

Chonk knelt beside me. "You okay?"

I pulled my hair back and wiped the sweat from my brow. "For now. Thanks for the help."

"Is nothing." There were more thunderclaps from outside, farther down the corridor. He stood and unslung his weapon. His golden eyes narrowed. "You stay here. Still work to do."

"How many are with you?"

"Seven Thubans. Breaching team. Came with as medic. One more insisted."

"Insisted? I don't understand."

Chonk sniffed at the air. Something had gotten his attention. "He explain. Must go now." With that, Chonk shouldered his gun and charged down the corridor. There was another booming clap, this one too close for comfort, and I heard my warrior friend howling with glee. The hunt was on.

I was pulling myself up to check on Gideon when more movement caught my eye. Something had entered the room. Not black this time, but white. What had they come up with now? I slowly reached down into an open drawer for a plasma scalpel, flicked off its safety, and took a deep breath. They would not take me again. I would plunge this thing into my own head if it came to it.

I spun and whipped out the scalpel, ready to fire its beam into whatever this thing was.

"I would prefer you to not do that."

Before me was a tall, imposing figure, clad in pearly white robes with silver piping. In his hands was a weapon like the one Chonk had carried. Golden hair reached to his shoulders. He studied me with radiant green eyes.

"Bjorn?"

He smiled. "It is good to see you again, Melanie." He nodded at the scalpel. "Now, if you please . . ."

"Oh. Right." I flipped the safety on with shaky hands and put it back in my pocket. "Sorry."

"Quite understandable," he said, and slung the gravity lance over one shoulder.

I ran across the room and wrapped him up in a tight hug. "I didn't think I'd ever see you again."

"I promised that you would, if you recall."

"How did—"

"How did I escape? It was rather simple." He smiled and held up his biometric ring.

Of course. "Chonk's people tracked down your signal."

"Well, perhaps not quite that simple." He motioned for me to sit by Gideon while he took up position in the doorway. He looked awkward, miming the stance of a warrior on guard but missing the subtle efficiency of a seasoned pro like Chonk.

They weren't finished yet, a point driven home by the booming of more interdimensional portals being blasted open in the bowels of the ship. Bjorn stuck his head out into the corridor, checking both ways before coming back in. He kept his place there, not yet willing to relax.

"Da'Farrii are nothing if not impatient. Morrok's crew was not content to wait for her return. They demanded that I take them to Gideon's research site."

"You know where that is?"

"I had some idea, from information I'd pieced together in Science Ministry records." He frowned.

"You don't look too happy about it."

"I am not fond of secrets. Be that as it may, there was enough for me to deduce a location."

"And the pirates were willing to risk crossing Union space to get there? They *are* impatient."

He held up his ring again. "They were convinced my presence would mask their intentions. I did not seek to disabuse them of this notion."

That was a gem of Emissary understatement. "How long did it take to find you?"

He smiled. "A day, perhaps two. I waited until we had located Gideon's test article before activating my distress signal. The Da'Farrii were not pleased when a Thuban quick-reaction force arrived in orbit."

"I'll bet they weren't. What happened then?"

"They attempted to hold me hostage, but Thubans are not known for their negotiating skills."

I imagined a toothy seven-foot warrior lizard wouldn't be so inclined. "And . . . ?" I prodded.

"A pair of Thuban light patrol ships disabled the Da'Farrii frigate. We were soon boarded, and they dispatched the pirates with rather extreme prejudice." He wrinkled his nose. "Our Thuban friends do not take hostage situations lightly, particularly when Union officials are involved."

"I don't understand, though. How in the world are you even here right now?"

He leaned against the wall, relieving himself of some of the backpack's weight while keeping his lance at the ready. The contraption was sized for a Thuban, not someone even remotely humanoid. "As you can imagine, the Thuban patrols had many questions. I was able to impress upon them the danger you and your companions were in. They have been aware of the Interdimensionals for some time, and had been developing weapons to counter them."

I pointed at the lance in his hands. "That seems a little out of character for you."

He lifted the weapon. "Not my first preference, I must admit, but there are times when one must give in to necessity."

I nodded tiredly. "These 'Inters' aren't much for diplomacy."

"Quite." His ears perked up at the sound of another thunderclap, closer this time. They were no longer confined to the bowels of the ship, where the zero-point reactor and drive conduits were. He held out one hand, patting at the air. "Please stay where you are."

Bjorn closed his eyes. He was sensing their consciousness, anticipating where the next demon—yes, I said it—might appear. Sure enough, a shadow began to coalesce out of the med bay's aft bulkhead. "Cover your ears!" He aimed and squeezed the oversized handgrips.

The weapon itself barely made a sound, just a low electric hum. But when the portal opened, *BOOM*. It was like a lightning strike right there in the room. A point of light flashed in the shadow's center of mass, exploding outward to consume it before disappearing.

I stared, slack-jawed, with my hands still over my ears. Just like that it was gone, leaving only the smell of ionized air behind. "That thing packs a wallop."

Bjorn studied the lance appreciatively. "I have never been much for weaponry. This has given me a new appreciation."

"Same for me, first time I tried out Daddy's shotgun. Chonk said that thing projects a portal?"

"That is all I know. Aim, pull the trigger, and it sends the target somewhere else." There were more thunderclaps from the far end of the torus. Bjorn looked up and down the corridor, his lance at the ready. He pressed against his ear and let out a sigh. "The team leader says we are clear."

I staggered to my feet. "You never explained how you found us."

"I began pressing the Thubans as soon as they'd secured me aboard one of their cruisers. 'Spilled the beans,' as you might say. They were extremely interested in Gideon's experimental drive. I'd already led the Da'Farrii to his test article." Bjorn looked around our accommodations. "It is a considerably smaller vessel."

I smirked. "It had to feel a lot smaller with a half-dozen Thubans stuffed into it."

He arched an eyebrow. "Quite. I impressed upon them the precariousness of your situation. Our mutual friend made a rather convincing argument in your favor."

"This was Chonk's idea?"

He held a hand to his chest. "Oh no, I take full credit! It was he who convinced the Admiralty that we needed to intercept your vessel. This was complicated by it not having a transponder, but we could make some rather accurate projections given what we learned from Kal. By reconstructing a trajectory based on the gravitational anomalies each jump created, it was possible to predict when you would arrive at this point. I regret we were a bit late."

Another thunderclap sounded from farther down the torus. I gave Bjorn a hug and kissed his cheek. "I'd say you were just in time."

"My ears are ringing. What happened?"

Where to begin? I leaned over Gideon to check his pulse by hand, the old-fashioned way. "Things got a little exciting while you were out. Gremlins were swarming all over the ship." I took in a breath. "One of them got to you. I tried to stop it."

"I remember that much," he said wearily, and rubbed at his ears. "Whatever you did, it must have worked."

Worked for him, not for me. I decided to leave that part out. "We had some help." I stepped back.

Gideon's eyes flashed recognition at Bjorn, then went wide at the sight of Chonk. "Well then. Never met a Thuban in all my time here."

Chonk bowed slightly. "At service. Threats neutralized."

Gideon looked around the med bay. "Morrok?"

"Gone." Exactly where, I didn't want to think about.

Gideon grunted. He tried to sit up, and I eased him back down into the bed. "Take it easy. You went into cardiac arrest."

"Again?" He let out a long sigh of resignation. "I can't take much more of this, can I?"

"Not up to me. I'm just a medic, remember?"

"I get it, this calls for a real doctor." He grabbed my hand. "No offense, Mooney."

"None taken." I laid my free hand on his. "We'll see to that soon. We're almost home."

# ⚕ **31** ⚕

We'd reappeared in normal space deep inside our solar system, but it still felt like a long way from home. We'd emerged in orbit around Saturn, safely hidden from any Earthbound detection as the planet would be on the opposite side of the Sun for many more months.

It wasn't home, but we were in the neighborhood. Bjorn helped me lift Gideon into a hover chair. It floated on antigrav cushions, and I worried how we might explain this contraption when we finally arrived on Earth. Gideon was his usual cantankerous self, at that stage not giving a damn. "We'll worry about that when we get there," he'd groused. "We'll stop at a drugstore and buy a wheelchair if I need it."

Any Earthly concerns were pushed aside when we entered the control room. My jaw fell open, and even Gideon was speechless.

There was Saturn in all its glory, backlit by the distant Sun, its rings shining like a halo in the dark. I'd seen plenty of pictures, but never in person, not that I'd ever had the opportunity. I'd been to ringed planets before in my travels through Union space, but this . . .

I was reminded of childhood road trips to the beach, and of passing through the Appalachian foothills. Once we were on the back side of the Smokies, I knew we were almost home. Mom and Dad had a particular spot just across the Kentucky border where they'd stopped for pictures long before I'd come along, and they'd always made it a point to go there on every trip. They'd kept a photographic record of my growth over the years against that backdrop of hills fading into the summer haze. Much as I'd missed the welcome distraction of mountains after hours of driving, they were our final goalpost before crossing the Ohio river and returning to endless farmland. It might've been boring, but it was home.

This felt the same. Spectacular beyond words, the kind of raw beauty that could bring you to tears, made all the more eyewatering because at long last we were in *my* neighborhood again. Saturn felt like it belonged to me, like that last ridge to cross before the final leg home. I would never make it out here again, and I savored every minute of it.

Bjorn stood beside me, silently. "Deela says the saucer is ready. Shall we?"

I nodded and turned to Gideon. "Any parting words?"

The old man eased out of his hover chair and stood, stubbornly refusing his cane. "For the first time in my life, I don't quite know what to say. You have all gone to a great deal of trouble on my account." He turned to me. "On *our* account. And you have endured a great deal more trouble along the way. Any further compensation I might offer would seem like an insult now." He turned up a corner of his mouth. "But I'm going to try anyway. I've arranged for a considerable amount of Union kuulas to be deposited in your accounts upon your return." He turned to Kal. "Including financing of your research, in an amount I trust will be enough for many annums."

"I thought all of your wealth was tied up in this ship?"

Another lopsided grin. "A good businessman always keeps some in reserve, Mooney." He looked up at Chonk, still not sure what to make of his Thuban rescuer. "In all my years in the Union, I was never able to meet any of your kind. I regret ours was under such unpleasant circumstances."

Chonk lifted a claw to his chest, the Thuban salute. "Is no worry." He flashed his own toothy grin. "Thrive on unpleasant circumstances."

Gideon quirked a wizened, bushy eyebrow. "I suppose you do. In any case, well done. I trust the security of the *Campanula* to you."

With that, he settled back into the hover chair. "Now then. I believe it's time to go home."

The final leg of our journey took a few hours at a leisurely one-fifth of light speed. "Humans have made many advances into their Solar System in your absence," Bjorn explained. "I do not wish to attract undue attention."

I didn't care; now that we were almost here I wasn't in any particular hurry for my last hours with my friend to end. It had already been hard enough to say goodbye to Chonk, giving him a final bear hug and a peck on his scaly cheek.

The pale blue dot that had emerged as we curved around the far side of the Sun had been steadily growing as we drew closer. It was as I'd left it, a world of sapphire blue oceans, lush green forests, and stark yellow deserts.

Home. Everything and everyone I'd ever known before being whisked away into the deeper galaxy was there. My heart was filled with anticipation and loss. I was about to say goodbye to the life I'd made, returning to a life that held more questions than ever. There were vague plans for what might come next, but in the moment all of that evaporated. I wanted to feel its grass beneath my feet, watch thunderstorms build in the distance, chase fireflies around the yard.

Home, but not quite. I couldn't go back to Indiana any longer than would be necessary to get my affairs in order. For now that wasn't a concern, as our first stop would be nowhere near there. We were headed for a small chapel in northern New Mexico, at the feet of the Sangre de Cristo mountains.

I was skeptical. "How do you know it'll still be there?"

Gideon was firm. "It's over two hundred years old. It'll be there."

After double- and triple-checking that the saucer's cloaking field was working, Bjorn set us down in a dry riverbed on the outskirts of Taos. It was a short walk from there to the chapel, and Gideon insisted on leaving his high-tech conveyance behind.

That ended up lasting about three steps. The uneven, rock-strewn riverbed was too much for his uneven gait. Bjorn held him steady while I retrieved the hover chair from the cloaked saucer, and we made our way up a slight rise onto the chapel grounds.

The compound was cluttered with low-slung adobe buildings that looked as if they'd grown naturally out of the ground, reminiscent of the Thuban architecture I'd seen in their sector of the Union capital. The chapel itself stood in the center, only a couple of stories high. A white arch, adorned with a cross, rose between a pair of adobe towers.

"This is where it all started for me," Gideon explained as we approached a pair of ornately carved doors. He pointed to an open field nearby. "I left this place and wandered into the desert. Ready to end it all." He looked at Bjorn. "Then I met these guys. Standard Union survey team, an Emissary and a couple of Grays."

"And that was that?"

"Not quite so simple. They took some convincing."

"I imagine so," Bjorn said.

"A long story, and I don't have much time left to tell it." He pointed his cane at the doors. Bjorn pulled them open, I gave the hover chair a nudge, and Gideon floated through. I'd draped a blanket over his lap, which brushed the floor as he made his way inside. I hoped it was enough to disguise the alien tech, but it would turn out Gideon had other plans.

We were soon greeted by a priest, and from there it was best to let Gideon do the talking. I was almost as far out of my element as Bjorn. "My companions have gone to considerable trouble to bring me here," he explained, "so allow me to get right to the point. I am at the end of my life." He turned to me. "My personal medic has kept me alive in spite of my heart's best efforts otherwise."

The priest nodded his understanding. "You wish to receive last rites. Were you a member of this parish?"

"It's been a while. A long while."

"I see. When was your last confessional?"

Gideon turned to each of us, a rare twinkle in his eye. He was about to do something, and I had a feeling it was a bad idea. He turned back to the priest. "By your calendar, about a hundred years. It's been rather less by mine." And with that, he whipped the blanket away.

The priest was wide-eyed at the sight of the old man in his gravity-defying chair. "That's . . . that's amazing. I've never seen such a thing," he stammered. "I don't even know how it's possible. Where did you get it?"

"It will make a lot more sense after confession," Gideon assured him. He glanced back at me. "Relax, Mooney, it's as rock solid as attorney-client privilege. Maybe even more so. Right, padre?"

The priest's jaw was still hanging open like a hooked fish. "I . . . yes. Of course." He motioned toward the confessional booth.

Gideon handed the blanket to me and stepped down, determined to make the short walk on his own. "You two might as well get comfortable, this will take a while."

We sat in one of the pews as Gideon presumably laid out every shady deal and underhanded maneuver he'd made over the last century or so. I tapped my fingers impatiently on the railing while Bjorn sat with his hands clasped.

"Do Catholic confessionals normally take this long?"

"Wouldn't know. My family was Lutheran."

"Ah. I'm familiar with the history, just not the particulars. There is a certain degree of tension between the two."

"It used to be a lot worse." I rested my chin in my hands, imagining the tales Gideon was regaling that poor, unsuspecting priest with. He was getting his affairs in order, whereas mine had barely begun. "The old guy is not the same person we left with, is he?"

"He is not," Bjorn said, studying the carvings and stained glass surrounding us. "Perhaps there is more to this than we supposed."

"A higher power?"

He knitted his brow. "Perhaps. Certainly a higher plane of existence, as we have seen for ourselves. Though I have come to believe that, at the very least, the acknowledgment of such is beneficial. It is humbling."

We'd certainly been humbled over the course of our journey home. Near-death experiences will do that to you, especially when they come at the hands of beings you can't understand. Gideon's rantings about being chased down by demons had become a lot more believable after being in the grips of one myself, whatever it was.

"We weren't meant to leave," I finally said. "Our universe, that is."

"More properly, our level of the universe," Bjorn said. "Though I agree with your sentiment. I do not believe we will return to Union space by the same method. Nor do I wish to." He mischievously arched an eyebrow. "However, the *Campanula*'s drive promises considerable gravity warping potential. I suspect our trip back will be rather brief."

"In your time. Might be a good bit more back at the capital."

"I am almost three hundred years old by your reckoning. At that age, time becomes even more relative than you think."

The door to one of the confessional booths creaked open. Gideon stepped out, spry as a spring chicken. I could practically see the weight that had been lifted from him. He motioned for me to bring the hover chair. He collapsed into it, tired but happy.

I laid a hand on his shoulder. "Feeling okay?"

"Relieved," he said. "And drained. It was a lot."

As if to illustrate the point, the priest emerged, more wide-eyed than before. He looked past Gideon to me, then Bjorn. My friend stood calmly with his hands clasped, his Emissary regalia having taken on new meaning as he acknowledged the priest with a slight bow.

"I am happy to answer any questions you may have," Bjorn offered.

"No, that won't be necessary," the priest said with a shaky voice. Gideon must have warned the poor guy that a memory wipe might be part of that deal.

"May I trust that whatever was said between you will remain in the strictest confidence?"

"In confessional? Of course." The priest crossed his chest. "You have my word."

Bjorn nodded. "Thank you. I believe that will do."

The priest looked relieved. He collected himself. "Now, Mr. Stone, we may complete the sacraments."

They moved to a corner by the vestibule, where Gideon received communion. I excused myself and stepped outside, not wanting to be there when the priest administered last rites. It felt like an invasion of privacy, or maybe I just didn't want to hear a ritual that carried such finality. It's fair to say I'd begun this journey hating Gideon's guts, for a lot of what had felt like good reasons. He was abrasive, self-centered, and greedy. He was also ailing, vulnerable, and alone. Alone in a way that I was literally the only other human in the galaxy who could appreciate it. And in the end he was redeemed, at least according to the doctrine of his church.

What did that mean for me? Did I need redemption? I certainly didn't think so, but then again I'd had a taste of the bigger picture, and it was horrifying. There was still so much of the deeper universe that we didn't understand, and I include the big brains of the Union in that. The more we learn, the more we find left to learn. If there was any being in all of existence who actually did grasp the full picture, then maybe that being was worthy of being called God. Gideon certainly thought so.

We took Gideon back to the saucer, waving goodbye to the priest who remained safely in the chapel's entryway. As I watched Taos recede into the distance, I couldn't help but feel bad for the guy. He looked to be so full of questions which he didn't dare ask. What do you do when a real live space alien shows up on your doorstep?

I knew a thing or two about that, and we were finally on our way back to where it had all started.

# ⚕ 32 ⚕

Bjorn made a wide, sweeping turn over the farm. I was like a little girl on her first airplane ride, marveling at the view. The sky was that deep blue we only see in late fall around these parts. Handfuls of darkened leaves clung stubbornly to the trees, waiting until the next windstorm blew them free. The surrounding fields were mostly harvested by now, and I saw a trio of combines stirring up dust in the distance as their drivers rushed to finish off their work for the season.

The house was as I'd left it, its red metal roof shining brightly in the low afternoon sun. Its white paint was weathered and would need to be refreshed soon, but otherwise the property managers had done a good job keeping up the place. My knees were bouncing from anticipation as he set us down in the front yard, the same spot where we'd left from years before.

I stepped out of the saucer and took my shoes off, eager to feel natural grass beneath my feet again. I'd always been one to run around barefoot regardless of the season, which had sometimes driven Mom to distraction. I took in a deep breath, reveling in the scents of newly harvested fields and fresh air. I ran around to the back porch, joyfully kicking clumps of fallen leaves along the way. The key box was right where I'd hidden it.

The old wooden steps creaked beneath my feet. I nervously unlocked the back door, as if someone might be inside.

Sheets had been draped over the furniture, the management firm's handiwork, making it feel like a house full of ghosts. I methodically went through each room, uncovering the backdrop of my former life

279

one ghost at a time. Memories came like a flood with the lifting of each sheet. There was the antique hutch filled with knickknacks and yellowed family photographs. Dad's old rolltop desk, still cluttered with his notebooks. I'd not touched it since he died.

My room was the last stop. Grandma's quilt was neatly folded at the foot of my bed, just as I'd left it. My clothes still hung in the closet, all of them hopelessly out of date. A barrister bookcase filled nearly to bursting occupied a good chunk of one wall. It held nearly every single thing I'd read since elementary school, including a few choice titles that I'd neglected to return to the library. My old—really old—iPhone was still in a bedside drawer. The battery would've been long since drained, so I plugged it in just to see what would happen.

While the phone did its thing, I spent a long time staring out my bedroom window at the backyard and the fields beyond. After all I'd been through, the comforting normality of it all felt surreal. Zipping around the galaxy, treating patients from a dozen different species, witnessing indescribable sights along the way, then hazarding the unseen depths of our universe before culminating here in a century-old farmhouse.

Yeah, I cried a little.

Okay, a lot.

There was no other way to process the conflicting emotions that crashed over me like a tidal wave. It had taken a long time to admit it, but in the end I'd run away from life here. Granted, my life had been going to shit at the time, so grabbing hold of an unimaginable opportunity to escape it all felt like the right choice. And it had been, for a while. There aren't enough words in the dictionary to describe how amazing it was to live among so many other intelligent species, to experience their cultures. To learn once and for all that not only were we not alone, for the most part they were all really good people...or lizards, hexapods, insectoids, whatever. Even the Da'Farrii pirate had turned out okay in the end, even if her sense of honor had been a little twisted.

All good people, but not human.

Of everything that had come from this experience, perspective might be the most valuable. From now on I would look at the night sky with different eyes. In that moment I resolved that wherever I ended up, it would be a place where the stars weren't obscured by city lights.

Not that it was much of a problem in farm country, but being back here drove home the fact that I couldn't remain. Once again, I was the alien.

My phone buzzed, pulling me back into the here and now. It had glitched after the first dozen or so updates, but the home screen was still there. I now had a firm reference of the current time and date, which froze me in my tracks.

Eighteen years, but barely five for me. That my running tally of time dilation had only been off by a couple of months was of little consolation. *You knew this was coming,* I thought. *Put on your big girl pants.*

Right. Get on with life. The people I'd grown up with would now be pushing fifty, whereas I was starting over. I'd been given a gift, one of which was learning how relative time actually was. You'd better make the most of it, otherwise it absolutely will get away from you.

I bundled up the sheets and brought them downstairs, piling them on top of the kitchen table with the others. I wandered back into the living room, collapsed onto the old floral pattern sofa, and kicked my feet up on the coffee table. One more thing that used to drive Mom crazy. I drew in a deep breath and blew out a long sigh.

I was home, if only for a little while.

Bjorn had been keeping a respectful distance while I scurried about the house. He quietly took a seat beside me. "I trust everything is in order?"

I patted his hand. "Perfect. Thanks for finding someone to look after the place."

He studied me from the corner of his eye. "You will not be staying for long, I think."

"A few days. There are a lot of loose ends to tie up. And I still think you can read my mind, you just won't admit it."

"Not at all. I am just very good at my job, as you would say. But I am interested in your plans."

I was about to come up with an appropriately catty comeback when my stomach rumbled. "Supper, for now." I looked past him at the empty kitchen. "Can't trust anything left in the pantry," I said. "Eighteen years is a long time."

"Quite," he agreed. "I made certain the nutritional synthesizer aboard the saucer has a full stock of base protein and vegetable matter, anticipating we may need it."

"Base matter. Sounds delish," I muttered. My F-150 would need work to get back to running order, and we couldn't very well take the saucer out for Chinese. I stood and slapped my thighs. "Tomorrow we're going to do something about that."

It took the better part of the next day to bring the truck back to life, and fortunately the property managers had kept the utilities paid up. I was relieved to find the landline still worked, because we needed to have a lot of parts delivered. By lunchtime we had a new battery, four fresh tires, two gallons of motor oil, and a five-gallon can of gasoline sitting in the barn.

The kid driving the farm supply's delivery van couldn't stop looking at Bjorn. To be fair, his long blond hair and brilliant green eyes contrasted sharply with the flannel shirt and jeans I'd pulled out of Dad's closet.

The kid, head shaven and covered in tattoos, eyed Bjorn as if he was the weird-looking one. He then turned his attention to the truck. "Restoration project?" That was when I noticed the delivery van was electric. If the supply store had gone green, I wondered how many others had.

Bjorn nodded amicably. "It's my friend's. I'm just here to help."

He gave us one final odd look, shrugged his shoulders and left. I reached for a weathered ballcap hanging from a nearby hook, wiped off the dust and cobwebs, and handed it to Bjorn. "Here. You'll need to do something about that hair before we go out in public."

Bjorn slipped the hat on, bunched his hair up underneath, and we got to work. By early afternoon we were trailing a cloud of dust down the gravel driveway and headed back into my world. I hung my arm out of the open window and slapped the door, excited to be behind the wheel again and showing my friend around. I made it a point to take the back roads, elated by the falling leaves swirling around us. We came up on a sharp turn and I hit the brakes, too hard. We skidded to a stop.

"Is something wrong?"

"No," I stammered, staring into the woods. "It's just . . . this is it. This is the spot."

"Ah," he said with recognition. "So it is."

Five—no, *eighteen*—years ago, I had pulled up here in the middle of the night, sure that I'd seen an airplane crash deep in the woods. Of course it had been anything but an airplane, and life had taken a wild turn after that. There was still a faint hint of a trail leading to the crash site, where the treetops had been snapped off.

I must have been staring for several minutes, because it took Bjorn to prompt me out of my stupor. "Do you wish to visit the site?"

I shook my head. "That's okay. I just wasn't expecting it. Forgot where we were." I put the truck back in gear. "Maybe later."

The town had remained largely as it had been when I'd left, except for the addition of another stoplight. More shops were open than before, a hopeful sign. Fully half of the cars around town were electric, and some in pretty odd shapes. Working vehicles hadn't changed much, and I couldn't blame the farmers for stubbornly hanging on to their gasoline and diesel engines. There probably weren't many charging stations in the middle of thousand-acre fields.

Our first stop was a small electronics store, which thankfully was still in business. I'd never been one of those who simply had to have the newest device, but this time I made an exception. What I picked out was nothing like my now-ancient phone; if anything it was startlingly similar to my Union data crystal. It was a small rectangle of translucent glass that responded to my touch with holograms projected just above its surface. I laughed like a little kid and showed it to Bjorn.

He did his eyebrow-arch thing. "Interesting technology," he said, pretending to be the country bumpkin he was dressed as.

The young lady behind the counter looked confused. "You seriously haven't seen these before?"

"Heard about them, never seen them," I said, covering for us. "Our cellphones are pretty old."

"Cellphones?" Her head jerked and she stared at us incredulously. "I'm surprised they even work. I wouldn't even know where the nearest tower is anymore."

"There's still one on our property," I said. At least there'd been one when I'd left.

"Everything's connected by satellite now," she said, thankfully answering the question before I could ask it. "A lot cheaper, too."

I was in a hurry to end the conversation before saying something really stupid. I paid for the phone, activated a new plan with all the bells and whistles, and got us out of there. It was a short walk down the street to a clothing store, which Bjorn endured with supreme patience. He'd have made a good husband to someone.

Dressed in decade-appropriate attire and with a sparkling new satphone in my pocket, we climbed back in the truck and made our way home. I took another back way, this time along the river, hoping that my next destination would still be there.

We turned a bend and there it was, overlooking the river in all its ramshackle glory. The place didn't even have a sign outside, everybody just called it "Mac's," after the owner. We slid to a stop in the dirt parking lot and I bounded out of the cab. "You, my friend, are in for a treat."

My first bite of an actual human-made cheeseburger in years was a damned near religious experience.

Mac was still there, now well into his seventies but still running the place. He'd given me a curious glance when he brought our plates, but thank goodness he hadn't asked any questions. Out of the corner of my eye, I'd seen Bjorn slip a small black cube into his pocket while wearing a look that told me he might or might not have just Jedi-mind-tricked the old guy. We weren't the droids he was looking for.

"You look pleased," he said with amusement.

I rolled my eyes. "You have no idea." I took a pull from an ice-cold longneck and tipped it in Bjorn's direction. His plate was untouched. "Go ahead. Guarantee you it's better than anything from the nutri-synth."

He took a tentative bite and raised his eyebrows. "Quite." After savoring another, more confident bite, he followed with his first taste of fresh-cooked onion rings. "Yes, excellent."

"Can't make a diet of it," I said, and patted my stomach. "Not that I haven't tried. Guess I'm old enough now that I have to start paying more attention to that stuff." Union nutri-synths precisely calibrated bothersome measures like total calories for the individual's metabolism; no matter how much food was on your plate, you could rest easy knowing it wouldn't end up adding to your waistline. I would have to get used to watching that again.

"I'm afraid there is quite a lot you will have to pay close attention to," he said seriously.

I looked around the deck where we sat, at the woods around us, and to the river below. "We can't stay here much longer. I know that. Let me enjoy this while it lasts."

The next morning, over gloriously fresh coffee and real scrambled eggs, I set up my new phone and started to catch up on Earth's current goings-on. While the particulars might have changed, the general background noise of life hadn't: worries about the economy, crime, distant percolating wars, and mindless celebrity news, while politicians and talking heads angled for advantage against each other.

One thing that gave me hope was that social media didn't seem to have nearly the influence it had when I'd left. From what I could piece together, a cultural backlash against the endless dopamine hits of likes and forwards and trolling had finally reached critical mass years ago. I mentioned to Bjorn how it gave me hope that our species wasn't about to sink into an AI-driven abyss of stupidity.

"Do you remember my warning of civilizational thresholds?" Bjorn replied. "Synthetic intelligence is one of them. Will a civilization learn to harness such advances, or become slaves to them?"

I took a sip of black coffee. "It appears we passed the test."

"Indeed."

I stared at the little glass rectangle and the holograms hovering just above its surface. Before, I would've been captivated by it. Now, it was nothing more than a quaint approximation of technology I'd become used to. It held none of the addictive power it might've had over me just a few years ago. Still, there was one last thing I wanted to check.

I typed a name into the phone's search engine. The results were immediate. "Gideon's dead."

We had taken him to a hospice outside Indianapolis, close enough to where I could check in on him. Bjorn had secured all the arrangements through some clandestine and not entirely legal manipulation of their records system, the same way he'd conveniently removed my property from county tax rolls.

He leaned over to read the brief obituary. It was perfunctory, probably written by someone at the funeral home. "Are you surprised?"

"Not really. He was ready to go. You could see it in his eyes." If medicine had taught me anything, it was that the will to live is real.

When someone had had enough, they let go, while some patients who by all rights should've been dead managed to hang on. That reminded me of a particular accident scene I'd worked not long before leaving Earth, and of Gideon's final request.

I stood and set my plate in the sink. "I believe it's time for me to go."

We spent the rest of the day gathering my things and loading up the truck. I'd gone through every room of the house, picking out the items I didn't want to part with. Most of it was small stuff, trinkets that held outsized memories, along with a few pieces of heirloom furniture that barely fit in the truck bed. My books weren't all going to make it, so I'd had to make some difficult choices there. The property managers could ship the rest to me. I'm pretty sure Bjorn pretended not to notice my Med Corps trauma bag, and all of the alien tech within, sitting in the back seat. After the last box was loaded, he helped me pull a tonneau cover over the bed.

"Where will you go?"

"Indianapolis first." I held up a sealed envelope Gideon had entrusted to me which contained his final instructions along with his Union ID ring. His great-grandchildren were about to become fabulously wealthy, and in more ways than they could imagine. "It'll take a good lawyer to make all this happen. I have an idea of who to call."

"And after that?"

"West coast. UC San Diego is supposed to have an excellent marine biology program. Doubtful I'll run into anyone who knows me out there."

"A good plan." His green eyes twinkled mischievously. "Do you require any assistance with the application process?"

I smiled. "Probably. I've been out of the system for so long that getting back into the academic pipeline's going take some work. I might need some of your extraterrestrial hacker wizardry."

"The challenge will be in translating your experience with us into something human academics can understand...without giving anything away, of course." Bjorn pulled his crystal from an inside pocket of his robe and made some notes. He lifted his chin triumphantly. "Consider it done."

"Thanks, friend." I stood there like a dummy, not having the slightest clue what to say. Last time we'd said goodbye, I'd thought that was it. He'd been consigned to a future that almost certainly promised misery and death, but something deep inside had told me he'd be okay.

This felt different, even more final, in too many ways. Ours had been the first Union footprints on Earth since I'd left. Their closest outposts were scattered across the asteroid belt and were only occasionally visited by Survey Ministry teams. The chances of ever seeing my friend again were slim.

For that matter, this recent visit to the old farmhouse would likely be my last. I'd come home but couldn't stay, there was too much risk of running into people who hadn't seen me in almost twenty years. Spotting me around town would raise too many questions, and I couldn't be certain how many people Bjorn had surreptitiously mind-wiped during our last outing. For their sakes, my ties had to be cut completely.

There was one last thing which I had been putting off long enough. At the end of the back yard, by the edge of the woods, were two stone markers. Mom and Dad. The wind picked up as I walked toward them, swirling the leaves around my feet. It was like they knew I was coming.

I sat by their graves and laid a bundle of late-season wildflowers between their headstones. "Hi, Mom; hi, Dad. I'm home," I muttered. "Sorry it took me so long." What else was there to say? I knew it was stupid, I knew they couldn't hear me—though given my recent experience, who could say for certain? So I spilled my guts, told them everything about my life among extraterrestrials, about the Grays and the Emissaries, about doing field surgery on giant arthropods and rescuing insectoids from collapsed tunnels and how the Grays had a rectal probe for every malady known to the Union. "You'd have loved it, Dad." Mom I wasn't so sure about. She'd always been the more religious of our family, whereas Dad and I went along with it. I didn't know how any of this would've comported with her. I wasn't sure for myself, either.

I looked back to the house and stared at it for a long time. This was it. Once the papers were filed, it would feel as far from my reach as it had been when I was a thousand light-years away.

Tears stung my cheeks. I wiped at them with my sleeve. *Sorry, Mom and Dad. I hope you can forgive me.*

"I do believe they would understand."

I sniffed. "You really can read my mind, can't you?"

An impish grin. He pinched his fingers together. "Well, maybe a little." He held me by my shoulders. "Your parents loved you deeply and wanted the best for you, that much I could tell just from our time in your home."

"It feels like abandonment." Pretty sure I'd said the same thing the last time we left this place.

"It is anything but. Your parents would have wanted you to chart your own course, which you have. Which you still are. You have much left to do, work just as valuable as anything you did in the Union." He turned pensive. "Perhaps even more so."

"You said we'd survived one of those civilizational thresholds. Are we any closer to first contact?" Can't blame a girl for being hopeful.

One last time, I got to see those emerald eyes light up. "Trust me, you'll be the first to know."

# ☤ EPILOGUE ☤

I dipped my feet in the water, relaxing beneath the July sun. It had become a habit despite the Salish Sea's perpetually cool temperatures. Like the rest of coastal Washington, even in the middle of summer the waters off of the San Juan islands weren't conducive to swimming without a dry suit. They were perfect for gray whales, however.

A familiar pair had breached alongside my boat not long after I'd dropped anchor, a mother and her calf announcing their arrival with a playful heart-shaped blow of seawater that fell like rain across the stern. I covered my head to no avail.

"You don't have to make such a show of it." I grabbed a towel to wipe my sunglasses clear and wring the salt water out of my hair.

I was answered with the burbling baritone of whale song. My translator chips had been steadily compiling their language over the months I'd spent here trolling the waters and getting to know the locals.

"We had been below for a long time. We needed to clear our lungs. And your little friend seems to enjoy it."

She wasn't wrong. Booger was having the time of his life. He leapt up from the calf's back onto the deck beside me, wriggling in pure amphibian joy.

I finished my fruitless attempt to dry off and tossed the towel aside. "How deep this time?"

"Four hundred feet, I think?"

Almost to the bottom. "Getting your little one ready for migration, then?"

"Yes. In another month we will begin heading south. Will you be coming along?"

"Of course. I won't have anyone else to talk to once you're gone, Gertrude." That wasn't her actual name, but it was the closest translation I could manage from whale-speak. Like the many aliens I'd come to know in the Union, I'd taken to giving my newest friends more pronounceable nicknames. Her calf didn't have a name yet—in whale culture that was something accorded to them in adulthood. Until then, whale moms simply addressed their offspring as "child."

My boat was a forty-foot SeaRay cabin cruiser, good for short jaunts on the ocean. Normally a vessel of this size could accommodate up to ten people, but mine was more than a little outside the norm. Among other things, I'd outfitted it with radar, sonar, underwater cameras, and a translator I'd jury-rigged from a spare transducer disc out of my old Med Corps gear. It was my private oceanic research vessel, with just enough living space for me and maybe a couple more if they didn't mind tight quarters. It would be enough for me to follow Gertrude and her clan all the way down to Baja California for the winter.

I'd be doing it alone, of course. It was ironic that for as much as I'd needed to be back among humankind, I'd chosen a life that necessarily kept me isolated. No matter how useful it would've been to bring others along, it wasn't yet time to reveal my unique methods of communicating with certain marine mammals. The friends I'd made at the university's oceanographic institute were puzzled enough that the local whale population was so remarkably attracted to my boat, and you'd better believe I kept a tight lid on things in port. I practically lived aboard ship, and when I wasn't there, private security kept any curious onlookers at a respectful distance. Truth be told, that probably attracted more attention than if I'd just left the thing alone, but I couldn't afford to take any chances.

If you're wondering how a simple medic managed to pay for all this stuff, it's a great lesson in the power of compounding interest. It's amazing how much your investments can accumulate over a couple of decades if you just leave them alone, but it was the value of farmland that really went into orbit while I was gone. Throw in a house that had been meticulously cared for and was ready for immediate occupancy, and the potential buyers had been falling all over each other to throw money at me.

So yeah, I'm a multimillionaire now. They say money can't buy happiness, but it'll for sure buy you a boat big enough to sail right up next to it. Besides the tricked-out cabin cruiser, the proceeds had paid for my PhD in marine biology.

I realize all that may sound cold, but remember, I couldn't just move back into the farmhouse and pick up where I'd left off. There would've been too many questions: Where had I been for the last eighteen years, and why did I still look barely a day over thirty?

While that might sound like first-world problems, there was too much at stake. I was sitting on a gold mine of alien technology, not to mention the accumulated knowledge of years living in the Union. Bjorn had stuck his neck out for me, even if he'd justified the risk by wanting to have someone reliable among the human race if the GU decided to make first contact in my lifetime. Much as I'd wanted to return to a normal human life, there were always going to be some aspects of it which would have to remain out of reach.

Of course, there'd still been the complication of selling the farm while keeping a low profile. It helped having a good lawyer, especially one who felt like he owed his life to me. I remembered his name, Andrew Larsen, from my last run as an Earthbound medic. I'd kept him alive and mostly in one piece as we extracted him from a grisly accident on US 40.

He, of course, didn't recognize me when I called on him at his office back in Indy. It wasn't personal, as he'd barely been conscious when we first met. For my part, I'd been delighted to see he'd shifted his focus from vehicle accidents to real estate law, which was just what I'd needed at the time. He had one of those classic lawyer faces, all sharp-nosed and clefted-chin and sporting a perfect coif of wavy blond hair. Or so it had been before his car had ended up crushed beneath a tractor-trailer. The scar across his forehead brought his otherwise perfect visage down to Earth, along with his prosthetic legs. I hadn't known him before the accident, but I could tell the experience had left him humbled.

Being a good lawyer, Andrew didn't ask what I'd been doing during the intervening years, though he did have a few probing questions about selling the farm. He was more concerned that I was doing it for the right reasons, which my evasiveness surely hadn't helped. He'd mentioned once helping a family sell some property which they'd ultimately regretted parting with, and he'd vowed to never risk doing that again.

I mean, what could I possibly say? Yeah, I was sort-of abducted by aliens and spent almost twenty years working as galaxy-spanning medic, but it was only five for me thanks to relativity. And to prove it, I still have a bag full of super-high-tech gear along with these neat little universal translation implants in my head, along with a magic ID ring that lets the aliens keep tabs on me.

That had been a tough call to make, but I appreciated his concern. Selling the house and farmland wasn't an easy decision, and I eventually convinced him it was necessary for me to make that hard break. I hadn't been lying.

The sun was going down and my visitors were needing to move on. Whales had to eat regularly, after all. They couldn't just float around gabbing with me, though that was often what happened. When word had gotten out among their kind that a human had gained the ability to talk to them, I'd become the most popular sailor on the West Coast.

Gertrude and her calf were the only ones here today. She'd already heard my whole story, but with the interesting twist of having had her own interactions with Union survey teams many years ago.

She moaned in whale-speak, and I waited for the translation. "Do you believe they will return?" Of the many things we'd talked about, she had never broached that question before.

"Eventually, yes. In our lifetimes? I don't know. It would be nice to be here to see it. I imagine you and I would become awfully popular if that happened."

Another keening burble from below. "I'm not sure we want that. In fact, I've wondered if the Emissaries would prefer we establish more of an interspecies bond before they initiate contact."

Gertrude could be a particularly insightful whale. "Good point. How would your kind feel about me letting more people in on our little secret?"

"My kind would welcome it, though I'm not sure about the Orcas."

"They can be a little testy, can't they?"

"They're hunters. It comes with the territory, as you might say."

*As you might say.* Hadn't heard that qualifier in a while. "For a minute there, you sounded like an Emissary."

Gertrude let out a high-pitched moan, a lively tone in whale-speak.

"We were always delighted to interact with them. I've had many conversations myself. Their belief in your kind's potential confirmed our own. We've desired communication with humans for a long time, but overcoming that gap was always beyond our reach."

"Same here. Too bad it took a little alien tech to cross that bridge. I like to think we could've figured it out for ourselves."

"Many of your kind have tried. A few have come close. We had hoped there could be something other than a technological solution." She rolled over and spread her flippers for emphasis. "We cannot do much on our own."

I'd considered bringing a few select people in on my secret, but the ramifications of it getting out into the open were too severe. Though there was one person who I'd learned to trust implicitly, and as if on cue, my phone buzzed with an incoming message.

Another gurgle from Gertrude. "Is that your boyfriend?"

"He's not my boyfriend, he's my lawyer. And we're just friends."

A skeptical whale groan. "What does he want?"

"He wants to know how long I'm going to be here in the islands."

There was a long, deep gurgling this time. Whale laughter. "Ah. That is how it starts among your kind, isn't it?"

"It's strictly professional," I protested. "Okay, *friendly* professional. He's the only other human who knows my story." While I couldn't risk letting my coworkers in on my secret, attorney-client privilege was a powerful incentive for Drew to keep it to himself. "I still need actual people to talk to, you know. Do things with. That is, unless you think you can climb out of the ocean and go to a concert with me."

"I'm afraid our kind is at least another half-million years from that ability." Gertrude rolled over and dove for the depths, she and her calf waving their flukes goodbye. "See you tomorrow, Melanie."

I locked up my translation gear below decks and took a quick shower—all showers at sea are quick—changed into a clean T-shirt and shorts, and opened a bottle of cabernet. I went forward and made myself comfortable on the prow, watching the moon come up over the sound.

It didn't seem so far away anymore. For that matter, neither did the stars beyond. After settling in the San Juan islands, I'd invested in a high-quality telescope and made it a point to learn the constellations.

I could now pick out the star systems where I knew other civilizations had prospered, see places where I'd been.

Where others wondered, where some hoped, I *knew*. We weren't alone, not even on our own planet. There were others out there, waiting until we were ready to receive them. And behind it all, even more that couldn't be seen. That part still gave me chills. I hoped, even prayed, that they would stay on their side of the veil that separated us.

Such was the way of exploration, of setting new boundaries. For every opportunity, there were threats. How would my fellow humans react to knowing, once and for all, that we weren't the only intelligent beings in the Universe? And for that matter, knowing that a race of highly evolved dinosaurs were patrolling our neighborhood in some seriously kick-ass space battleships, all so we could remain secure in our current ignorance?

I'll tell you what, it sure humbled me. My conversation with Gertrude had stuck with me. In my heart I hoped that Bjorn and my other friends would return to Earth, this time with formal greetings. First Contact. Opening the door for the human race to a wider reality our kind had only dreamed of.

It was getting late. I stretched, took one last look at the night sky, and headed below. My bunk was tucked away in the lower cabin, and I secured everything for the night. I'd learned that lesson during my first night on the water, when a half-dozen books had fallen on my head in my sleep after a big swell.

I reached down to lock the drawer by my bunk and noticed its edges glowed with a pulsing white light. Had I put my phone in there?

No, it was secured on the shelf over my head. But there was one other thing, the last remaining piece of Union technology I'd brought with me. The one Bjorn had actually insisted I keep close.

My heart pounded as I pulled the drawer open.

There sat my old data crystal. What had been a dormant slate of translucent golden glass was now changed. It was strobing slowly, commanding my attention. My eyes were drawn to its center, where a summons from long ago had reappeared.

The outline of a single handprint pulsed in the dark, waiting for my response.